ANTON WAS PERCHED ON THE EDGE OF THE BACKSEAT, FLICKING THE SAFETY OF THE BIG AUTOMATIC ON AND OFF. CAGE KNEW WHAT HE HAD TO DO . . .

As he crested the top of Topanga Canyon, Cage abruptly picked up speed. The oncoming traffic was heavy, but Cage's lane was relatively clear. He began juking the Camaro back and forth, coming dangerously close to the cars on the left and the guardrail on the right, which was all that separated them from a sheer drop of hundreds of feet.

"Goddamn it, slow this thing down!" Anton shouted into his ear.

Cage said, "You got two choices. Pull the trigger and send us into a head-on collision or over the cliff, or drop the gun over the seat. Otherwise I make the choice myself."

"You crazy son of a bitch, I'll kill you!"

"Go ahead, but you're coming with me." Cage swung the wheel hard to the right, straight at the guardrail, and let out a Rambo yell that was echoed by Anton screaming. *"Here!"* He dropped the automatic over the seat, where it bounced once before coming to rest against Cage's leg.

Cage yanked the wheel left and braked, scraping the tail of the Camaro against the metal rail until it stopped. Anton was pressed into the far corner of the backseat, eyes closed and arms spread wide for support. His face had an ashen tint and he didn't appear to be breathing.

"Next time you decide to take somebody for a ride, use the front seat. Now give me a name. Who put you up to this?"

Books by Edward R. Jones

Alarm
Cage
Hacksaw

Published by POCKET BOOKS

ALARM

EDWARD R. JONES

POCKET BOOKS

New York   London   Toronto   Sydney   Tokyo   Singapore

An *Original* Publication of POCKET BOOKS

POCKET BOOKS, a division of Simon & Schuster Inc.
1230 Avenue of the Americas, New York, NY 10020

ISBN: 0-671-68837-5

First Pocket Books printing December 1990

10 9 8 7 6 5 4 3 2 1

POCKET and colophon are registered trademarks of
Simon & Schuster Inc.

Printed in the U.S.A.

For Angela . . .
for all the right reasons

Chapter
—1—

It wasn't that Bobby Lee Gettis had made a conscious decision to kill someone; not really. The thought had certainly not occurred to him on the three-hour bus ride from Walla Walla to Seattle, Washington, while he sat at the very rear of the big Greyhound, sipping openly from a pint of Jim Beam, while alternating his gaze between the other passengers and the world outside the thick tinted window. It flashed by at seventy miles per hour, bathed in a uniform shade of pale green that diffused the bright August sun and made him feel like he was looking through a giant pair of Cool-Ray Polaroids.

No, it wasn't a conscious decision at all, even though he knew—just knew—that he was going to do just that. As though the decision had already been made for him; dictated by some secret portion of his brain that he couldn't get to or control. And so he accepted it, the way he accepted breathing, because it was the natural order of things and he refused to waste time and energy on something as irrelevant as rationalization. Bobby Lee was a taker, and the only rationalizing he ever worked at was deciding how to gain the maximum reward with a minimum of risk and effort.

Yes, he was definitely going to kill someone. Because if you took something you wanted and the owner objected, it considerably reduced the risk of getting caught if you didn't leave him around to identify you later. And it required very little effort to pull a trigger. This was a philosophy Bobby Lee had lived by for the last eleven years, and it had worked just fine.

Until four years ago, he thought, when he'd lost it on that little bitch Amy Bartlett, who had been trying to take advantage of his good nature.

Bobby Lee took a long drink from the bottle, leaned his head back against the cushion and closed his eyes. That could have really been bad news, he thought, could have put him down for the count. But Amy Bartlett had finally gotten to him with her constant whining and sniveling and threatening to go to the police if he didn't give up his dealing. Three grand a week he was taking in pushing good Mexican brown and pure crank, and she wanted him to just walk away from it. Sure. Fucking brain surgeons didn't make that kind of money.

And then the corker, him coming home from a really great Seahawks game one Sunday to find little Amy sitting at the kitchen table in her white shorts and red halter, swinging her leg and tapping her fingers, waiting for him. She had a pained expression on her freckled face and half a kilo of crystal meth in an open mason jar in front of her. The mason jar had been at the very back of the top shelf in the pantry, buried behind his tool box, but the little snoop had found it. Nothing was out of her reach or imagination when it came to sniffing out his stash. "What's this?" she'd asked, really smart-mouthed. "Looks like Epson salt. Is that what it is, Bobby Lee? Epson salt? Or maybe it's granulated soap for when you get your hands dirty from all that manual labor you do. Is it soap, Bobby Lee?" And as he'd stood there in the doorway wondering whether to hit her or baby her, she had leaped to her feet, grabbed the mason jar and spun around to the sink. "Let's just see which one it is, Bobby Lee," she'd said. "Let's see if it foams or dissolves." And before he could get to her, she had the jar in the sink and the hot water running full blast right into it, and there went about eight thousand dollars right down the goddamn drain.

And Bobby Lee had gone completely nuts. He'd grabbed her by her red ponytail and slammed her speckled face repeatedly against the porcelain sink, knocking out most of her teeth and shattering her jaw and left cheekbone. A table fork had jarred loose from the drainage board and worked its way to the edge of the counter. He had snatched it up and, still holding the semiconscious girl by her ponytail, began stabbing her in the head, neck, back, shoulders—anyplace he could hit with a downward plunge, until the prongs bent and refused to penetrate. But even then he wasn't through—shit, he hadn't even started—but Amy Bartlett was blessedly beyond the point of feeling anything as he threw her to the floor and continued the assault with his pointed two-hundred-dollar lizardskin cowboy boots. His enraged kicks dislocated her collarbone, snapped her right wrist, and fractured four ribs, one of which penetrated her right lung, and the only reason he had finally called it quits was because he had just plain wore himself out and ended up falling exhausted onto a kitchen chair, puffing and cursing the broken figure lying in a bloody heap on the linoleum. It was a full five minutes before he had recovered sufficiently to pack his two suitcases, hop into his new Thunderbird, and head for a motel.

Remarkably, Amy Bartlett survived. She had regained consciousness sometime later, and with dogged determination managed to pull herself up to the wall phone. She dialed 911, hung on just long enough to give her name, then collapsed again, leaving the phone swinging from its cord. Which was a good thing, because the operator had been able to trace the call, and within ten minutes two police officers were kicking in the door of the small four-room wood-frame house in Lake City.

Three months in the hospital and four surgeries restored Amy Bartlett to a semblance of her former self, but she was never quite the same. Her shrill voice had been reduced to a timid whisper, and the judge constantly (but kindly) had to remind her to speak up as she told her story from the witness stand six months later. Bobby Lee had almost felt sorry for her himself as he listened to her tearfully explain to the jury how she had taken him into her home out of love and the prospect of marriage, only to learn later that he had only wanted a safe base of operations from which to run his drug empire. Bobby Lee had blinked at that and wished with all his heart that he could get to her again and finish the job. Drug empire? Who did she think he was, Carlos Lehder?

The jury must have thought so, because it took them exactly fifty minutes to reach a verdict: guilty as charged, assault with intent to commit grave bodily harm. The judge had given him five years on the spot, and fumed because he couldn't give him more. Bobby Lee had maxed out the sentence without benefit of parole by serving the required two thirds.

And Amy Bartlett had promptly left the Seattle area for parts unknown.

"You're not suppose to be doing that."

Bobby Lee let his eyes drift open and settle on a small round face peering at him from over the seatback in front of him. It was a little boy about eight, lots of curly brown hair spilling out from beneath a cream-colored cowboy hat with the drawstring pulled snug under his chubby chin. His look was direct and disapproving.

"I'm not suppose to be doing what?" Bobby Lee's drawl was pure South Florida, having been born and raised in and around Opa Locka, and his lips barely moved when he spoke.

"Drinking that whiskey." The boy's eyes dipped to the pint bottle of Jim Beam clutched between Bobby Lee's thighs. "It's against the law."

Bobby Lee grinned. "Are you a lawman?"

"Special sheriff." The boy raised himself a little higher and proudly thumbed the star pinned to his pinto vest.

"Hey now, that's something," Bobby Lee said, and glanced at the boy's companion. Only her head was visible, resting on a small pillow jammed into the space between seat and window. Frizzy brown hair tied with a red kerchief. She was sound asleep. "And who's that, your deputy?"

"Aunt Gladys," the boy said. "We're going to Seattle to see my dad. He's a real policeman, and if he saw you drinking that whiskey, he'd put you in jail. You're not suppose to do that on a bus."

Bobby Lee raised the bottle deliberately to his lips, took a deep pull and let out an exaggerated sigh. "Mighty good, Sheriff," he said, and held out the bottle. "Sure you don't want a hit?"

"That did it," the boy said, and stuck a very realistic long-barrel revolver over the seatback, pointed in the general direction of Bobby Lee's nose. "You're under arrest."

"You'll never take me alive, Sheri—"

BAM!

Bobby Lee went sprawling across the seat with both arms wrapped around his head, ears ringing and eyes squeezed shut, the forgotten whiskey bottle now somewhere on the floor. He held that position for several seconds, mentally checking himself for damage, then said, "Jesus Christ in a box car!" And scrambled out of the seat and into the aisle.

Aunt Gladys was wide awake now, trying to wrestle the smoking cap pistol away from the little sheriff, who was squalling and putting up a good fight.

Bobby Lee, enraged, said, "You little son of a bitch," and gave the kid an open-handed slap across the back of his head that would have sent the cowboy hat sailing if it hadn't been anchored by the drawstring. The kid let out a fresh wail and buried himself into Aunt Gladys's lap, who was looking up at Bobby Lee with a horrified expression.

"How dare you," she said, and wrapped her arms protectively around the sobbing boy. "He's just a child!"

"Child's ass, lady," Bobby Lee said. "The little prick could've put my eyes out with that thing. I ought to sue you."

"That gives you no right to attack him!"

"It gives me a right to defend myself. Shit, my heart ain't right yet."

Bobby Lee looked around, calming himself, noticing that the bus was now moving slowly through downtown traffic, heading for the terminal. Several passengers were half out of their seats, craning their necks to see what was going on back here. He drew a shaky breath and eased back into his seat, retrieved the pint bottle of Jim Beam from the floor and gulped down the inch or so that hadn't leaked out.

Aunt Gladys was struggling out of her seat, trying to manage the still sobbing boy with one arm and a canvas tote bag with the other. She threw Bobby Lee a withering look, said, "Animal!" and went swaying up the aisle.

"Fuck you, cow," he muttered, and turned his attention back to the window. He was thinking that the kid's old man must be a holy terror when it came to arresting suspects.

When the bus pulled into the terminal, Bobby Lee waited until the other passengers had collected their belongings and filed off. Then he stuffed the empty Jim Beam bottle between the seats and trudged up the aisle. The driver, a thick black man with wraparound shades and a bandit mustache, was turned sideways in his seat, chewing a match stick and waiting for him. Bobby Lee ignored him and headed for the door— which suddenly closed with a pneumatic hiss.

"Just a minute, my man," the driver said, "I'd like a word with you."

Bobby Lee turned and touched his chest. "You talkin' to me?"

"You see anybody else on this bus? Yeah, I'm talkin' to you. What's this shit you was pulling back there? Lady says you slapped her boy. You get off beatin' kids?"

"First of all," Bobby Lee said, "that kid pointed a pistol bigger'n Clint Eastwood's about a foot from my nose and pulled the trigger. You hear the sound that sucker made? Sounded like a fuckin' cherry bomb goin' off. My heart ain't right yet. And second, I didn't hit him that hard. And third," he said, putting his hands on his narrow hips, "what business is it of yours?"

The driver tilted his cap back and spat out the match stick. "Everything happens on this bus is my business, at least when I'm drivin' it. And take some of that base out of your voice, save that shit for somebody be impressed." He had been giving Bobby Lee a close inspection, taking in the cheap brown shoes, polyester pants, and stiff white shirt with the sleeves rolled up to the elbows, which was a size too large for his five-foot-eight frame. He grinned at Bobby Lee and said, "You just got out the joint, didn't you?"

"That's none of your business either, now open the door."

The driver chuckled and looked off through the windshield. "Yeah, I thought so. Had a friend did some time there once. He come out wearin' the same shit you got on. Same attitude too. Tough guy, playin' the role. Had that swagger when he walked, like he was wadin' through water. Grand theft auto. What they snatch you up for, stealin' old ladies' pocketbooks?"

"Are you gonna open the fuckin' door?"

The man turned back to him with a puzzled expression and shifted his wide body to a more comfortable position. "Open the door? No, I don't think I'm gonna do that right now. Not till the lady gets back with the biggest cop she can find. You know what, my man? You just might set a record for the shortest time on the street—"

Bobby Lee kicked him under the chin, a knee-jerk snap kick he'd learned from his Hawaiian cellmate,

Ronnie Oweia, and it landed clean and solid. There was a sharp *click* as the man's teeth collided and the shades leaped forward onto the tip of his nose to show wide, astonished eyes that slowly rolled upward as he slumped sideways against an armrest, semiconscious.

Bobby Lee reached for the lever and swung the door half open, keeping his eyes on the limp driver. It would take a couple of minutes before the man would be able to function again.

"I bet next time somebody asks, you'll open that door . . . my man," Bobby Lee said. He pushed the driver's shades up over his closed eyes and stepped off the bus.

Most of the passengers were milling around outside, waiting for someone to open the bus luggage compartment. Which didn't affect Bobby Lee, since all he'd walked out of Walla Walla with were the bargain-basement clothes on his back, a Timex wristwatch, fifty dollars gate money, and a newspaper clipping in his hip pocket. Not much to face the world with, but he'd done it with less. He stood there a moment watching the side entrance to the terminal building, alert for any sign of a cop or Aunt Gladys and her midget version of Dirty Harry, but didn't see either. Not out five hours yet, he thought, and dodging The Man already, jeopardizing the big plans he'd been rehearsing in his mind for the past five months, the easiest score of his whole life. He hoped this wasn't an omen.

Bobby Lee walked away, moving quickly now, passing two other buses waiting in the staging area with their engines idling, the scent of diesel fuel tickling his nostrils, out to Stewart Street and into the first yellow cab parked at the taxi stand in front of the terminal.

The driver, an old man with gray whiskers and stained teeth, hooked an elbow over the seat and looked back at him. "Where to, young fella?"

"Zayre's Discount Store," Bobby Lee told him.

The idea that he was now actually free and once again back in the real world started sinking in as Bobby Lee wandered the aisles of the big Zayre's store and felt his senses being assaulted from all sides. It hit him like a rush of speed, and he was overdosing on it, his breath quickening and his heart moving into passing gear. It had happened once before, right after he'd walked out of Lake Butler, Florida, after doing twenty-eight months for burglarizing a Rexall Drug Store in Clearwater, so he was expecting it. Hell, he was *welcoming* it. So he rode with the experience, knowing the high would soon fade.

He stopped at the cosmetics counter and sniffed from a sample bottle of Carrera perfume, holding the sprayer directly beneath his nose and slowly inhaling while a saleslady changing her register tape looked on in amusement. He strolled over to the record department and ogled a pair of teenage girls in tight shorts who were giggling their way through a rack of Van Halen albums. He meandered into the lingerie section and dipped his hand sensuously into a bin of discounted panties, reviving ancient memories as he fingered the silky crotch linings. . . .

He came back to earth and jerked his hand away as if he'd been burned. Enough of *that*. Diane would take care of those needs when he got to L.A. But now he had to take care of business, and that meant getting his hands on a gun and some operating money, instead of panties.

He went back to the cosmetics counter and asked

the saleslady for a bottle of clear fingernail polish. Bobby Lee didn't like the way her mouth maintained a knowing smile as she bagged up the polish and took his money, obviously recognizing him as the perfume sniffer and probably taking him for some kind of closet queen. He snatched the bag from her hand, gave her his most intimidating jailhouse look, and went searching for the men's room.

It was at the rear of the store, next to the garden supplies. He went in, found an empty stall, and sat down on the commode. He took out the polish, gave the bottle a few good shakes, and began painting the clear liquid onto his fingertips and palms. He sat there awhile after he finished, humming softly and waving at the air while he contemplated the names and catchy shithouse one liners etched into the cubicle walls. When the polish had hardened into a thin glaze, he put the bottle back into the bag, tucked it behind the commode, and went back into the store. His fingertips and palms felt smooth and tight, but he certainly wouldn't be leaving any identifiable prints on anything for a while.

His next stop was in sporting goods, where he bought a box of standard twelve-gauge .00 shotgun shells. He made another trip to the men's room, thought for a moment, then took out three of the shells and stuck them in his pocket. He dropped the rest into the metal waste bin and went back—all the way through the store and out the front entrance, where he stood squinting in the harsh sunlight.

There was a phone booth next to a coin-operated popcorn machine near the entrance. Bobby Lee stepped inside and began flipping through the phone directory that was chained to the frame, wondering what made phone books so fucking valuable that anybody would want to steal one. He found GUNS in the yellow pages and let his fingers do the walking until he found what he was looking for. He put a quarter in the slot and dialed.

A man's voice said, "Clifton's Guns and Sporting Goods, may I help you?"

"Yes," Bobby Lee said, "my name's Pope—John Pope? I was in your place a few weeks ago, you know, just lookin', and I saw this real honey of a shotgun. It was a Remington, the commemorative edition. You know, the one with the heavy scroll inlay on the stock and the pump action?" Bobby Lee knew what he was talking about because he was reading from the display ad—"Ask about Our Special Low Price on Remington's 12-Gauge Commemorative Edition!" There was a picture of the shotgun in all its decorative splendor beneath the caption.

"Yes sir," the voice said, "she's a beauty all right."

"You betcha," Bobby Lee said. "Anyway, the reason I'm callin', tomorrow's my dad's birthday and I just found out from Mom that he really loves that gun, so I want to get it for him. Trouble is," he said, still reading from the ad, "I don't get off work till four-thirty, and if I recall correctly, I believe you close up at six, is that right?"

"Yes sir, nine a-yem till six p-yem."

"Damn! And I'm clear on the other side of town. I can maybe get away a little early, but . . . Look here, do you leave right at six?"

"Close to it as I can, Mr. Pope. But normally it's about six-twenty before we get out of here."

"Well, what if it's a little after six when I get there?" Bobby Lee asked, sounding concerned. "Could you still take care of me?"

"Just a minute."

There was a pause, and Bobby Lee could tell the man had covered the mouthpiece, could hear muffled voices in conversation. He wondered how many employees the place had. Judging from the size of the ad, he figured no more than three or four.

"Mr. Pope? That's a big ten-four. If we're still around when you get here, we'll fix you up."

Bobby Lee sighed into the phone. "Hey, that's great. Who should I ask for?"

"My name's Weldon, but either me or Mr. Clifton can help you out."

Two. Perfect.

"Okay, Weldon, thanks. I'll make it as close to six as possible. Don't go gettin' rid of all those Remingtons now."

"No way, Mr. Pope. I got one right here with your name on it. Drive carefully."

Bobby Lee hung up and glanced at his watch. Three thirty-five. Two and a half hours, give or take a few minutes. Time enough to take care of transportation and do a little reconnaissance work before making his move. Should be a piece of cake if he timed it right.

Bobby Lee stepped out of the phone booth, stretched, and surveyed the parking area, considering. Then he smiled and patted the round lumps formed by the shotgun shells in his pocket.

Wrong, Weldon, he thought. I've got one with your name on it.

Parked across the street from Ace Hardware, Bobby Lee had a pretty good view of Clifton's Gun and Sporting Goods three doors down. The place looked more like a neighborhood bar than a gun shop: one-story concrete with no windows, and a heavy glass-paneled door with a sign above it spelling out the name in Old English script. Bobby Lee thought the place was probably built like a bunker to make certain that no potential accident occurring inside took out a plate-glass window and maybe a few pedestrians to boot.

Considering the circumstances, Bobby Lee thought that was a real good idea.

He was scrunched down behind the wheel of a very common five-year-old Ford Fairlane that could have passed for an unmarked police car, except for the whitewall tires. He had taken it from Zayre's, then driven out to the airport and switched plates with an identical make and model he'd found in long-term parking, only it had been tan instead of blue. The owner was going to be in for a big shock when he or she got back from Muncie, Indiana, or wherever, and got arrested for stealing their own car.

Now he was here, watching the entrance to Clifton's and counting the customers. Since his arrival twenty minutes ago, three had gone inside and five had come out, all men. But he was missing one—a guy in an orange cap and white T-shirt. He'd gone in at five-forty and hadn't come out yet, and here it was five till six. Any time now.

Bobby Lee leaned to the side and pulled the newspaper clipping from his hip pocket. It was crinkled and frayed at the edges, and he unfolded it carefully. A man and a woman smiled up at him, a waist-high closeup showing them with their arms around each other, tuxedoed and gowned in high-society fashion, toasting the camera with glasses of champagne. The woman was middle-aged, wore too much makeup, and had a jeweled necklace around her skinny neck whose value Bobby Lee didn't even want to guess at.

But it was the man who held his attention: about

forty-five, smooth features set in a square face, dark curly hair and thick sideburns. Really having a gay old time. The caption beneath the photo read: "Horance Griswald, L.A.'s up-and-coming designer of fashionable jewelry, displays one of his original creations on the elegant neck of Frances Maljean during her annual fund-raising bash for the National Wildlife Federation."

Horance Griswald. Eleven years ago, when Bobby Lee was a twenty-two-year-old first offender doing three to five in Lake Butler, the guy's name had been Harry Grisom. And *he'd* been doing a nickle in the same joint for ripping off his insurance company by staging a fake robbery of his own jewelry store in Fort Lauderdale.

And now old Harry was an up-and-comer with the Beverly Hills crowd, and how the fuck did he pull *that* off? Bobby Lee didn't know, but he sure as hell was going to find out. He had a hunch old Harry boy would pay a nice piece of change to keep his covers from being pulled. A *real* nice piece.

Bobby Lee put the clipping away and looked up just in time to see the man in the orange cap and white T-shirt coming out of the gun shop. "All *right,*" he said out loud. The guy had a large package under one arm. He turned left and walked a half-block in the opposite direction, got in a green pickup truck parked at the curb and drove away.

Bobby Lee looked at his watch and saw it was five after six. He gave it a couple more minutes, drumming his glazed fingers against the steering wheel, then got out and trotted across the street.

The door was locked, as he expected. He shaded his eyes, peered through one of the glass panels and rapped sharply with his knuckles. A large man with a stubby cigar in his mouth came into view and peered back at him. He looked about fifty, with a frizzy patch of gray hair circling his otherwise bald head.

Bobby Lee raised his voice and said, "Hi there. I'm John Pope. Remember? I called earlier. Did I make it in time?"

The man nodded, turned the inside bolt and opened the door.

Bobby Lee stepped into a cloud of cigar smoke and resisted the urge to wave his hand. "Thanks a lot," he said. "Man, that traffic's murder this time a day."

"Heat don't help any either, I imagine," the man said. He bolted the door, turned and stuck out his hand. "Dan Clifton. You wanted the Remington Commemorative Model, right?"

"Right. Pardon me if I don't shake, but I got a bit of a sprained wrist here, and you look like a firm grip man to me."

"Sorry to hear it."

Dan Clifton led the way to a long glass display counter at the front of the shop that held a wide variety of handguns, everything from a matched pair of pearl-handle flintlock dueling pistols to a wicked-looking Smith & Wesson .44 Magnum. A young well-built guy in a short-sleeve yellow shirt with the National Rifle Association logo on the back was cashing out the register. He gave Bobby Lee a friendly smile and nodded.

"That's Weldon, my nephew," Dan Clifton said. He went behind the counter, moved to a wall rack lined with shotguns, and took one down. Handling it reverently, he passed it across the counter to Bobby Lee. "There she is. Isn't she a beaut?"

"Sure is," Bobby Lee said. He hefted its weight and admired the intricate art work on the stock and pump, the polished blue steel barrel that glistened under the fluorescent lighting above the display counter.

"That's real cherrywood there," Dan Clifton told him. "Hand finished and seven coats of varnish. And that steel's the best tungsten money can buy, made right here in the good old U.S. of A."

"Oh yeah?" Bobby Lee pumped the action and turned, bringing the gun to his shoulder. He sighted along the barrel and traced a slow line between the aisles of backpacks, camping goods, camouflage outfits, and fishing rods. He elevated his aim, steadied on the mounted head of a nine-point buck on the back wall, and pulled the trigger. There was a satisfying *click,* and in Bobby Lee's mind the head exploded into a thousand bits and pieces.

"Feels good, don't it?" Dan Clifton was leaning over the counter, chewing on the cigar that had now gone out.

Bobby Lee lowered the weapon and turned back, bouncing it in his hands. "Bet this thing really packs a wallop, huh?"

"Well, that depends on the load you're using. With your bird shot now, you're gonna get about a five-foot scatter pattern at say fifty yards. Then you move all the way up to your double-O buck, and you're gonna leave a nice compact hole you could throw a curve ball through. I take it you're not a shotgun man."

"Naw, that's my dad's game. I'm more into pistols."

"We got a pretty fair selection of those too."

"So I noticed." Bobby Lee turned the shotgun so the bottom was facing up. "This where you load it?"

"That's right. Just push the shells into the feeder there, pump one into the chamber, and you're in business. Holds seven."

"Okay." Bobby Lee had one hand in his pants

pocket now. He came out with the three shells, shoved them quickly into the feeder and jacked the pump. "Like that?"

Dan Clifton stiffened and said, "Hey, what the hell are you doing?"

"Just seein' if I know how to make it work. And if you was payin' attention, you might've noticed that those were double-O buck I stuck in there."

Weldon was standing at the register, looking at Bobby Lee in amazement.

Dan Clifton removed the dead cigar from his mouth and threw it to the floor in disgust. "Is this some kind a joke? That fucking Bryant over at Shooter's Emporium put you up to this? Give me that goddamn thing!" He made a move to come around the counter, then stopped as Bobby Lee leveled the shotgun at the center of his chest, something in his eyes telling Dan Clifton that this was no joke at all.

"That's right, Dan. Think about it."

The man looked around, confused, then said, "What do you want, the money? That it? Weldon, give him the money."

Weldon, moving cautiously, stuffed several stacks of bills into a Bank of America money pouch, brought it over and laid it on the counter.

"There you are," Dan Clifton said. "Take it and go. Evidently you need it more than I do."

"Don't be in such a hurry. Open up that case, I think I'll take that .357 Colt Python too. Throw in a box of shells while you're at it."

Dan opened up the sliding door, took out the chrome-plated .357 and placed it next to the money pouch. Then he turned to a row of shelves behind him that were stacked with boxes of cartridges, selected one and set it beside the magnum.

"Now will you leave?"

"In a minute," Bobby Lee said. He walked around the counter and motioned with the shotgun. "Facedown on the floor, both of you."

The two men looked at each other, then slowly lowered themselves to the floor and stretched out on their stomachs.

"I said facedown, Dan, not turned to the side. I don't like you cuttin' your eyes up at me, makes me nervous."

Dan Clifton turned his face down and stared at the beige tile.

Bobby Lee broke open the box of cartridges, loaded the magnum and tucked the box into the money pouch. He leaned the shotgun against the counter, assumed a wide stance above the two men with their foreheads pressed to the floor, and extended the magnum, centering on a spot just above the nape of Dan Clifton's large neck.

"I'm leavin' now," he said softly.

"Great," Dan said. "Go, get the hell out of—"

The magnum roared and Dan Clifton's head seemed to swell and burst from the impact of the 160-grain slug. Bobby Lee immediately shifted the weapon to Weldon and another explosion shook the room, sending a hollow point into the nephew's right temple that abruptly ended the scream that was leaving his throat, sent blood and skull fragments flying, and bulged his right eye completely out of its socket.

Bobby Lee held his pose, ears ringing and the odor of cordite heavy in the air, and waited until the bodies stopped twitching. Then he lowered his arm and looked away, a somewhat dazed expression on his face. He hadn't been prepared for the eye coming out—Christ, just hanging there on the guy's cheek like a button on a string. It had fascinated him in a morbid way, like he supposed some people felt when they witnessed a particularly gory car crash. He had killed two other guys in the last eleven years, both in drug rip-offs, but those had been body shots with small-bore automatics that had left nothing more dramatic than puckered holes and puzzled expressions.

Nothing like *this*.

Still shaken, Bobby Lee jammed the magnum into the money pouch, zipped it closed, and hurried to the door. He slipped outside, crossed the street, and made his way to the stolen Fairlane with a casualness that was a far cry from what was really going through him. He got in and slumped behind the wheel, composing himself and letting the adrenaline ebb. It was stuffy inside the car, and he was conscious of the overpowering scent of warm vinyl. He felt like he was hyperventilating, and frantically rolled down the window, gulping at the humid air outside which wasn't much better, except it didn't smell like vinyl.

He turned his thoughts to Harry Grisom, aka Horance Griswald, L.A.'s up-and-coming designer of fashionable jewelry, and gradually began to perk up. After another minute or so he reached for the dangling ignition wires beneath the dash and brought the engine to life. He could handle it now, no big deal. Big holes, little holes, what the hell was the difference as long as the ticket got punched?

When Bobby Lee finally drove away, he was humming and fooling with the air-conditioner, trying to get rid of that irritating vinyl scent.

Chapter
—2—

Caprita Arciaga rose from the dressing table, gave her image a final side-to-side inspection in the oval mirror, and smoothed the white uniform across her hips. Satisfied, she crossed to the bathroom door and knocked.

Raising her voice against the sound of the running shower, she said, "Allen, are you almost finished in there? I'm going to be late and I want to talk to you before I go."

"Come on in if you want," Allen Cage said, "it's unlocked." Caprita entered, leaving the door open to disperse some of the steam. She could see his fuzzy outline through the opaque glass of the shower stall, could smell the pleasing fragrance of Aramis soap as he lathered.

"I'll be out in a minute," Cage said. "Unless you want to talk now."

"I'll wait. I'm not going to compete with the shower." She moved to the fogged mirror, pulled a Kleenex from the box on the marble counter and wiped at the glass until it was clear. She began fiddling with her shoulder-length brown hair, enjoying the domestic coziness of the bathroom scene. It was warm and comfortable, and she felt a tranquil sense of security.

Quite a contrast from eight months earlier, when she and Allen were making a mad dash up the coast from Poneloya, Nicaragua, to Ensenada, Mexico, aboard a thirty-six-foot Sport Fisherman, accompanied by a six-foot-seven-inch, red-haired murderer who had no intention of letting them off the boat alive. Caprita shivered thinking about it now. She had met Allen in a hotel lounge in Managua while she was doing volunteer work at a local hospital—her own personal protest of what she believed was America's immoral funding of the contra war, which had taken the lives of thousands of innocent people. He'd been sitting alone at the bar, pale and drawn, methodically working his way into complete inebriation (she later discovered that he didn't even drink). Her heart had immediately gone out to him, and she had shocked herself by striking up a conversation, coming on to this strange man in a bar when all she'd wanted was a drink after a hectic day of tending to maimed and incomplete bodies.

Later she had learned the unbelievable reason for Allen's presence in Nicaragua. Namely, that the FBI had taken him from a maximum-security federal prison in Illinois and arranged to have him arrested and placed in the notorious Tipitapa prison north of Managua. He was supposed to escape—if possible— with a monster of a man who had hijacked and hidden a shipment of deadly nerve gas in the United States and who had subsequently fallen into Sandinista hands. Had she known this before falling hopelessly in love with this tall, pale man with the southern accent, she would have fled in terror. Her life hadn't been ready for that kind of complication. By the time she found out, it was too late. She was inextricably committed. And she had been ever since.

She heard the shower stop and turned around to lean against the counter, watching the refracted shadow inside the stall as he brushed water from his body.

"What time is your interview?" she asked.

"About ten. She's supposed to be bringing a photographer."

"Is she pretty?"

"How do I know? I've never seen her before. Larry and Paul set this deal up with her editor, all I did was talk to her on the phone. Why don't you stick around and judge for yourself?"

"You know I can't."

Allen didn't like her filling in for her friend Leslie the last few days, getting up six-thirty in the morning to be at Wilshire Memorial by eight, then pulling her regular four-to-midnight shift on top of that. They had hardly seen each other since Monday, except to fall into bed and get up together, Caprita too exhausted even to make love. And he refused to go to sleep until she got home, which was usually around one at the earliest. Thank God Leslie would be back tomorrow; Allen would love that, Caprita thought. But she had the feeling that his elation was going to be short-lived, and she wanted to get it over with.

Impatient, she said, "Are you coming out of there?"

"Yes, *ma'am.*"

Cage stepped from the stall and Caprita handed him a fluffy blue bath towel from the rack. She watched in silence for a moment as he dried, enjoying the sight of him and thinking how much better he looked now the prison pallor had been replaced by a light tan. Lean and solid, with good shoulders and a firm butt, not too much chest hair. She was reminded again that they hadn't made love in three days—or was it four now?

Cage said, "Well, here I am. What did you want to talk about?"

Caprita reluctantly changed her thoughts. "I thought you'd be pleased to know that Leslie's coming back tomorrow, so now you can stop grumbling about my hours."

"That's the best news I've had all week," Cage said. "About time."

"There's just *one* little teenie thing," she added, and cringed inwardly when he stopped his drying and asked what. She took a breath and blurted, "I have to work graveyard next week while Bev Cripen goes on vacation."

Cage resumed his toweling without comment.

Caprita looked away and sighed. "Well, go ahead and say it."

"Nothing to say."

"You're pissed, aren't you?"

"I haven't been too thrilled about the four to twelve, how do you think I'm taking this graveyard stuff?"

She grinned at him and said, "Yes, but there's good news too, dear. I saved the best for last."

"Caprita, there's nothing you can tell me that's gonna make me feel better about this. This is L.A., remember? Street-gang capital of the world and a magnet for every two-bit hustler in the country who's looking for action. And they're all just getting warmed up by midnight."

He wrapped the towel around his waist, edged by her and went into the bedroom. Caprita followed, mimicking his walk and puffing out her cheeks, then peeled off and headed for her dressing table and purse.

"So you don't want to hear my news then?" she asked.

Cage was flipping through the closet, trying to decide what to wear. "Sure, go ahead. I know. You're gonna tell me you're giving up cigarettes."

Caprita let the pack of Marlboros and the battleship Zippo fall back into her purse. "No," she said meekly.

"Well, you ought to. I mean just till this lung-cancer scare blows over. Then you—"

"*Allen.*"

"All right, I'm listening."

"I'm trying to tell you that after next week I go on day shift. There, satisfied?"

Cage turned and looked at her. "No shit?"

"No shit. I talked to Dr. Landis yesterday and told him what a bear you've been about me working nights. I said if he didn't put me on days, I'd probably end up leaving you, and he said okay, if I'd just help out with Bev Cripen next week. So there. Feel better?"

He thought about it, then said, "Only if I can drive you and pick you up."

"Oh *brother,*" she said, and decided to have a cigarette anyway.

"What's the problem with that?" he asked. "I'll be home when you leave anyway, and I'll be home when you get off. Come on, humor me."

"All right, all right, you can drive me in and pick me up, and while you're at it, you can tuck me in and tell me bedtime stories."

"I already do that," he said, grinning.

"Jeez, you're worse than my father."

Caprita took two impatient puffs and jabbed the cigarette out in a glass ashtray with Las Vegas Hilton stamped in the bottom. Cage came up behind her and wrapped his arms around her slender waist, snuggling against her spoon-fashion.

"Oh, sure," she said. "Get your way and you're all lovey-dovey again."

"I just don't like taking unnecessary chances," he said, and nuzzled her ear.

"I'm a big girl, in case you haven't noticed."

"Believe me, I noticed. But if big boys get shot on the freeway in broad daylight, then it's always a possibility that something can happen to big girls in the middle of the night. I've only had you eight months."

"And already acting like we're married."

"Uh-huh."

"Getting all bossy."

"I know."

"What are you doing?"

"Who, me?"

"No, I'm talking to the bedpost. Come to think of it, that's what it feels like."

"That's just your overworked imagination," he told her, pressing closer.

"Oh, really? Well let's just . . . *see.*"

She spun around, jerked the towel from his waist and backed away, an impish grin on her face.

"Wow!" she said. "I must have a very vivid imagination."

Cage, embarrassed, turned his back and tried to assume a nonchalant pose, searching the ceiling in mock innocence. Caprita twirled the towel in her hand and snapped it whiplike at his exposed buttocks. Cage yelped and made a dash for the bathroom with Caprita and her flicking towel in hot pursuit. He barely made it, slammed the door, and immediately began calling for a truce.

"Say you're a devil," she demanded.

"I'm a devil."

"Okay, truce. Open the door."

He opened the door slowly and stuck his head out. "You ought to drive mules for a living, woman."

She handed him the towel, gave him a kiss on the cheek, then rubbed the lipstick off with her thumb. "After living with you," she said, "I'd probably be good at it. Now I gotta run. Good luck on your interview."

They sat at either end of the living room sofa, with the glass coffee table beside them. Cage was drinking a 7-Up from the can and feeling a little self-conscious in the presence of his first reporter. Margot Finley Sheffer, the lady from the *L.A. Times,* held a yellow legal pad on her lap and occasionally sipped from a hot cup of tea Cage had fixed for her.

The photographer had come and gone, explaining that he had three other assignments to cover before calling it a day, saying a staff photographer's work was never done. A hippie-looking guy in blue jeans and a denim vest, he had pulled the easy chair over beside the aquarium, arranged Cage in it, and took about twenty rapid-fire shots with his Nikon. Then, whistling softly to himself, he shouldered his camera bag and left. The whole thing had taken less than fifteen minutes.

Now, Margot Finley Sheffer was saying, "So, I understand you've gained a little notoriety for yourself."

Cage thought Caprita would be pleased to know that the lady reporter was in her mid-fifties, portly, and bore a mild resemblance to Margaret Thatcher.

"What I did," he said, "was gain myself a lot of

unnecessary years behind bars. And to tell you the truth, I don't think many people are gonna find this stuff all that interesting."

"Quite the contrary, Mr. Cage. I'm sure a great many people will find escaping from seven prisons very interesting indeed. Especially when the person who did it is now legally free and working for a security firm. Equally amazing is why you were sent to prison in the first place. An ounce of marijuana, wasn't it?"

"I think it was less than that. Had it in my glove compartment coming back across the San Ysidro border. The U.S. Attorney in San Diego had just started this get-tough-on-drugs policy called Zero Tolerance, and would you believe I was the first one they got? Guess they wanted to set an example for the public, so they gave me two years."

The lady was scribbling on her legal pad. She looked up and said, "And you had no previous criminal record?"

"Two traffic tickets, and I paid 'em both."

"You owned a carnival, didn't you?"

"Yes, ma'am, a small one. Had to sell it to get money for a lawyer."

She pursed her lips, studying him. "So you go to prison, an average tax-paying citizen with no criminal intent, and now you're in with the hard cases. Did the experience change you any, do you think?"

"Prison changes everybody, if you spend any time there to speak of. The first thing you learn after the gate closes is that you have to discard all the little niceties and social graces of civilized society. Prison is not a very civilized environment, and the rules are different. Totally opposite to what you were raised to believe in."

"For example?"

He searched for the right words, feeling an urgency to make her understand even if it didn't make it into print, which it probably wouldn't.

"The biggest difference," he said, "is perspective. It changes, and always for the worse. In prison—and I don't mean those so-called Club Fed joints, but *real* prison—the law of survival of the fittest is alive and well. Your values and humanity have to be put on hold, and if you're lucky or work at it real hard, maybe you won't lose them completely and you can pick 'em back up on your way out. But it takes a little time, and it can be difficult. A lot of guys never make the transition at all. They've become so perfectly adapted to life on the inside that they're no longer capable of functioning in society. It's like putting a double-A fuel dragster on the freeway at rush hour. They just can't seem to get on the right track."

"What you're giving me are generalities," she said. "Give me an *example,* something I can relate to."

She still wasn't getting it. He drew a deep breath and gave it another shot. "Okay, example. In society, if someone threatens to harm you or yours, or steal your property, you call the police and let them handle it for you. In prison it doesn't work that way. You're expected to take care of those things yourself, usually with a knife or iron pipe. Otherwise you're going to become a perpetual victim, because the amount of respect you receive is gonna be measured by how well you stand up for yourself and your friends. Cons believe that the only earth the meek will inherit is an early plot in a cemetery. Outside, kindness and gentleness are virtues to be praised. Inside, they're weaknesses to be exploited. After a few years this new code of conduct becomes second nature, and it's like nothing else ever existed. But then, when the gates suddenly open and you step back into civilization, you have to reeducate yourself to doing things society's way; it isn't that easy, and it doesn't happen overnight. For a lot of guys it doesn't happen at all. They just can't last long enough to make the transition complete. And that, Miz Sheffer, is one of the major causes of recidivism. Is that specific enough for you? Can you relate to that?"

The reporter recrossed her legs and adjusted her skirt before answering. "Yes, I think I get your meaning."

"Then why aren't you writing it down?"

"Because it really isn't germane to the story. I was only trying to satisfy my own curiosity."

It may not be germane, Cage thought, but to his mind it was the most important thing he'd said in the entire interview.

The reporter flipped through her yellow pad, found the page she wanted, and her voice took on added enthusiasm. "Now then. You get to prison and right away decide to escape. Actually, the first of many escapes. That was from the federal prison at Bastrop, Texas, I believe. Then from Talladega, Alabama. Next came Memphis, Tennessee, then Terre Haute, Indiana; Lewisberg, Pennsylvania; Lompoc, California; and last but certainly not least, Atlanta, Georgia. Quite an impressive list."

Cage drained his 7-Up and set the can on the coffee table. "Nothing I'd want to put in a résumé," he said, "but I see you've done your homework."

"But why did you do it? You only had a two-year sentence, and you probably would have been out in half that time."

Cage had lost count of the times he'd been asked

that question. He wondered if anyone had ever understood the answer.

"Because I didn't belong there," he said. "I was doing the same kind of time as guys who were in for rape, murder, and armed robbery, only I was hurtin' a hell of a lot more. I couldn't see any logic in that, so I decided not to accept it. Because if I did accept it, then it would be like *admitting* I belonged there. Know what I'm trying to say?"

She didn't look very convinced. "I think so. But escape is also a crime, and you committed seven deliberate acts. Didn't you think the law applied to you the same as other prisoners? I'm sure you weren't the only one who thought that he didn't belong there."

No, she didn't understand at all.

"Miz Sheffer, I didn't put myself above the law. I did what I had to do so I could live with myself, not to mention the fact that I happen to take confinement very hard. It doesn't bother career criminals that much because prison's a calculated risk with them. An occasional jolt comes with the territory. They just kick back, get high, and plan their next score. But I felt every damn day of it, and I don't apologize for anything I did. Who would I apologize to?"

The lady was writing again, her pen moving swiftly across the page, leaving a trail of what appeared to be hopelessly illegible script. She paused and took a different tack. "You were paroled in December, weren't you?"

Cage said, "That's right," and thought, Here it comes.

"Only eighteen months after your last escape from Atlanta. Why did they let you out so soon?"

He was tempted to tell her the truth and shock that prosecutorial attitude right out of her. He'd been languishing in the federal government's top-security prison at Marion, Illinois, when the FBI had suddenly whisked him away to Raleigh, North Carolina, on a fabricated bank robbery charge. Larry Twiford had been special agent in charge of the Raleigh field office, and Larry had turned out to be the best friend and ally he'd ever had. Larry had also been firmly opposed to the FBI's plan for Cage, what he considered a desperation ploy dreamed up by the executive assistant to an associate director in Washington, D.C. They wanted to send Cage to Nicaragua, railroad him into Tipitapa prison and have him escape with a guy who had twenty-eight canisters of hijacked nerve gas stashed somewhere. They had wanted the canisters and the guy who stole them in the worst way—bad enough to offer Cage a pardon if he could just deliver the guy outside the prison walls. Cage had delivered him, all right, but it hadn't been easy. And the promised pardon had been downgraded to an unconditional parole, a twist that still didn't sit right with him. But at least he was free.

He could have told her this, but he didn't. Aside from the obvious sensation such a revelation would cause, it might also land him right back in federal prison for ten years. The same executive assistant from Washington had him sign an agreement not to disclose any aspect of the deal pursuant to the Official Secrets Act. It was questionable whether or not it could actually be enforced, but he wasn't about to run any tests to find out.

So Cage gave her his prepared "sanitized" version of the truth, a combination of fact and fiction that shouldn't invite further digging. He told her the federal prison system had been bursting at the seams and the Parole Commission was being pressured to set early parole dates for as many nonviolent offenders as possible. Also, the new sentencing guidelines enacted by a commission established by Congress had been about to take effect, and prison officials were expecting a large influx of new boarders. He told her about Larry Twiford, who had personally arrested him after his last flight from Atlanta. Twiford thought that Cage had gotten a bum deal by being sent to prison in the first place. So Larry had made a personal appeal to the U.S. Parole Commission and offered to accept full responsibility for Cage if they agreed to parole him. The commission, impressed by the unique experience of having a senior agent of the Federal Bureau of Investigation plead for a con's *release,* agreed, and he was let out a week before Christmas.

"Some Christmas present," the reporter said. "He sounds like quite a guy."

"They don't come any better," Cage agreed. "I literally owe my life to him. Three weeks after I was paroled, he resigned from the FBI, moved out here, and opened up a private security firm with his brother-in-law, Paul Banes. And he offered me a job." Cage grinned. "I remember him saying, 'Since I'm responsible for you, I guess putting you to work for me is the best way to keep an eye on you.' What he was really doing, though, was easing me back into the real world. Larry's like that."

"Did you have any special experience that qualified you for security work?"

Cage said no, but he had gotten a crash course from two of the best in the business. At first they had left him to run the small office on Santa Monica Boulevard, utilizing the business skills he'd acquired as owner of a traveling carnival. He had arranged the limited space for maximum accommodation, set up an easy-reference filing system, designed their own letterheads and report forms, answered the phone, and served as janitor at the end of the day. A regular Man Friday, that's what he was. But he watched, listened and learned, and he'd been a straight-A student. Larry Twiford had shared the knowledge gained from nearly twenty years of being part of the best investigative agency in the world, small secrets and little known techniques that had amazed him and would have sent many street hoods rushing out to buy lunch boxes, had they known.

And there was Paul Banes, the habitual gum chewer and very rotund electronic genius who had on occasion been mistaken for the actor William Conrad. Paul would let him watch in fascination as he created microchip and minicircuit wizardry in the cramped utility room he had converted into a workshop. For twelve years Paul Banes had been the number-one troubleshooter for Vindicator Security Systems, Inc., of Sunnyvale, California, racking up frequent-flyer mileage as he crisscrossed the country lecturing company reps on the proper installation and maintenance of such sensitive perimeter devices as the MD2100 Map Display, VC Sonic Alarm, and the Laser Optic Intruder Scan. But Paul had grown weary working for others, and turned his talents to his own benefit. Besides, he had said, "I can beat 'em all anyway." Paul Banes was the backbone of Banes and Twiford, and if he couldn't burglar-proof your building, then it couldn't be done.

Margot Finley Sheffer listened, nodding occasionally, and speed-wrote across two pages of legal pad. Then she stopped, took another sip of tea, and said, "Well, they sound like a fascinating pair. You're a great P.R. man."

"I'm not trying to extol the virtues of Banes and Twiford, Miz Sheffer. What I'm trying to do is get my record out in the open, and you know why."

"Of course," she said. "Because of the editorial we ran last Sunday."

"You betcha," he said, feeling the back of his neck grow warm as he thought about it.

The editorial had been a four-column spread questioning the wisdom of a security firm hiring an ex-con parolee, effectively placing him in a position to gain inside information on any given alarm system. What would prevent that ex-con parolee from using this knowledge to gain entry into homes or businesses employing those alarm systems, or from selling this information to "prison confederates"? The editorial had been aimed directly at Banes and Twiford, "the newest kid on the block in a town already inundated with security-oriented enterprises," and it had identified Cage by name as "an ex-felon with eight convictions, recently paroled from the nation's toughest prison, the United States penitentiary at Marion, Illinois."

The reporter said, "Actually, Mr. Cage, the editorial—though it had nothing to do with my department—wasn't meant as a condemnation of either you or the firm you work for. If you recall, the main thrust of that piece was a call for licensing *all* individuals who work with such systems, and—"

"And to deny a license to any ex-felon," Cage said. "Yeah, I know. And I got no problem with putting it that way. Hell, stick it on a referendum or something and let the people vote on it. But that was no editorial, it was an *exposé,* and it caused Larry and Paul some grief. They lost three jobs over that thing. Where'd the guy get his information from, a competitor?"

"I would imagine the usual reliable source. I do know the U.S. Bureau of Prisons was contacted, which confirmed your . . . stay with them. The convictions came from your FBI rap sheet."

"Well, I don't particularly care one way or another how people take me," Cage said. "But those are good guys, and I don't want my actions reflecting on them. So we want to clear the air, and I hope you'll be fair about it. Except for the marijuana thing, every one of those convictions was for escape, and without force or violence, at that. But for all your readers know, I could be that guy running the Bates Motel."

"And that's why you're getting equal time, Mr. Cage. In fact *more* than equal. How's that for fair?"

Cage nodded and stretched his legs. He asked if she would like some more tea, and she said no. He told her that he thought he'd have another 7-Up, and excused himself to go into the kitchen. When he came back she was still writing, pausing a few seconds to gaze openly around the living room, then recording her observations on her pad. He hoped she wasn't going to ask for a tour of the apartment, or maybe want to look through photograph albums. He didn't have much of anything that was more than eight months old.

He sat down, and she said, "Just a few personal questions, if you don't mind, Mr. Cage, and I think we can call it a wrap. Has prison changed you in any way, do you think? Given you a bitter or cynical outlook on life, for instance?"

He mulled that one over before answering. "I don't think enough about the past to be bitter about it. Maybe I've gotten a little cynical about a few things."

"Such as?"

"Oh . . . religion, for one. I spent so much time in

solitary, I ended up reading the Bible twice from cover to cover. And anyone who insists that's the word of God hasn't really read it. Because if you believe it, take it literally, then God is the worst child abuser in the history of the world."

"And where do you get that?" The lady seemed genuinely taken aback by this revelation.

"Second Kings, chapter two, verse twenty-three," he said. "In clear and precise language it says that God sent a she-bear out of the woods to rip forty-two kids to pieces for teasing the prophet Elisha about his bald head. Now that's discipline." Cage grinned. "Look it up."

"I intend to," she said, and scribbled on her pad. "And how about you? What do you believe in?"

"Me? I'm just a plain old agnostic, I guess. And I believe if we ever do learn the secrets of the universe, we really will be dangerous."

Margot Finley Sheffer asked him a few more questions, then tucked pen and pad into her leather satchel, shouldered her purse, and let him escort her to the door.

"Well, it's been nice," she said, and held out her hand. "We'll run it Sunday, the magazine section. Still mad at us?"

"No, we're square," he said, accepting her hand and relieved that it was finally over. "I just don't want anyone having the wrong impression. Not everybody who comes out of prison is a monster. They're just usually the only ones you hear about."

After the reporter left, Cage cleared the coffee table, went into the kitchen, and fixed himself a bowl of Raisin Bran. Caprita's tiger-striped tabby cat, large and furry, came ambling in from wherever he'd been hiding. He gave Cage a superior look, did a lazy stretch, and sashayed over to his dish. Caprita had named him Grits, because according to her, he meowed with a southern accent, a long drawn out "yaaalll" that Cage thought sounded more like a rusty iron door opening. When they had decided to move in together, it had been a love-me-love-my-cat deal. "Besides," Caprita reasoned, "you're both obviously southerners, so you should get along just fine." Grits, however, had accepted the strange male with wary tolerance and simply ignored him whenever possible.

Cage ate his Raisin Bran and reflected on his interview. He wished now he hadn't made that comment about the Bible, and wondered if the paper would print it. Not that it wasn't true, but he was beginning to imagine the phone ringing off the hook at Banes and Twiford, people saying what a blasphemous heathen he was, saying if God sent that she-bear to rip apart forty-two kids, he must have had a good reason for it.

Cage liked to refer to his inner voice of reason as his own personal dinosaur, because every now and then, whenever he screwed up or was about to, it would roar at him from the tar pits of his mind.

And it was doing that now. *You dumb shit, you just had to run off at the mouth, didn't you? What, you never heard the old cardinal rule about politics and religion? People can get serious about their Bible.*

Cage spooned up the last of his cereal and thought it was probably just as well that churches didn't have much use for private security firms.

Chapter

Sunday morning, just about the time most early risers were collecting their fat editions of the *Los Angeles Times* from front lawns and doorsteps, a tired Bobby Lee Gettis was taking the Sunset Boulevard exit off the Hollywood Freeway. He'd driven straight through with only four stops; twice for gas and burgers, once to grab three hours sleep at a rest stop outside Eureka, and again about an hour ago to let Diane Acres know he was here and to get directions. Only he'd gotten her answering machine instead, her little Southern Belle voice telling him she couldn't come to the phone right now but to *please* leave a message because she'd *love* to talk to whoever it was. Shit, he could've been the Green River Killer who'd been raising hell with all those Seattle prostitutes for all she knew, calling to tell her he was expanding his territory. He *hated* answering machines.

Bobby Lee turned left on Sunset, cruised all the way down to Western, then hung another left over to Hollywood and cruised back. Playing tourist at ten after eight on a Sunday morning, the famous boulevards he'd heard so much about but never seen looking like they were under air-raid alert.

He gave up, found a Chevron station that was open, and pulled in for gas. He asked the old rummy-looking geezer running the place where Hawthorne was, 2100 block, an apartment building named Sundial Hollywood.

"Straight on down Hollywood," the old man told him. "Second street past the Chinese Theater. Only goes one direction though, so turn left at the old Roosevelt Hotel. Right across from the high school ball field. Can't miss it."

Bobby Lee thanked him and tipped the old man a five-dollar bill, feeling generous with over two hundred dollars in his pocket, and another six hundred stuffed between the seats.

And a lot more on the way.

Bobby Lee found the apartment building with no trouble, a gray stucco monster that took up the whole block. He circled it once, came back and parked on the opposite side of the street. There were a few serious joggers on the big track that bordered the Hollywood High School Athletic Field, and some kids were running pass patterns on the thirty-yard line.

He got out and crossed to the glass-fronted lobby entrance, went inside and checked the directory above the triple row of mailboxes. There she was: Acres, D. #309.

He took the elevator to three, followed a burnt-orange carpet that was beginning to go bald down to #309 and rang the door bell. He didn't hear anything inside, so he knocked. He was about to rap again when he heard the deadbolt turn and the door swung open.

A little girl about five, wearing pink pajamas decorated with Disney characters, was hanging on the doorknob and looking up at him through solemn eyes.

"Well, hi there, cutie," Bobby Lee said, "how you doin'?"

"Fine."

"You must be Lori."

She nodded shyly. "Do you want to see my mommy?"

"I sure do, sweetie pie. My name's Bobby Lee, and I've sure enough heard a awful lot about you. You're just as pretty as your mama said you were."

"She's still sleeping."

"Well, then I'll just come in and give her a nice big surprise. How's that?"

He pushed past the little girl without waiting for an answer and closed the door, leaving Lori standing there in confusion, plucking at her pajama top. Bobby Lee pulled out his roll and peeled off another five.

"Here, honey, that's for your piggy bank. Now where's Mommy's bedroom?"

Lori took the bill, examined it a moment, then pointed to a closed door at the end of a short hallway.

"Thanks, honey. Now why don't you go watch cartoons or somethin' while I say hello to your mama."

"There aren't any cartoons, just church."

"What, you ain't got cable? Watch church then, it's good for you. Watch Jimmy Swaggart. Just don't get too close to the TV."

Bobby Lee moved to the end of the hallway and slipped quietly into the bedroom. A woman with stringy blond hair in bad need of a root job was sprawled across the bed, curled on her stomach in a jumble of maroon colored sheets. She was in white panties and bra, and a trail of black high-heel pumps, blue miniskirt, and white pullover sweater led from the bathroom to the bed. A pair of panty hose dangled from a half-open drawer in the nightstand, and the room reeked of cheap perfume.

He eased over to the bed and looked at her, feeling really horny now at the sight of the first undressed real-life female he'd seen in three and a half years.

So little Diane Acres was blond now, huh? Not a real one, he knew that for a fact. And she'd picked up a few pounds, judging from the way the waistband of her panties got lost in the soft fold of flesh above her hip. But she still had that nice rounded ass he remembered so well.

Bobby Lee took off his clothes and slid into bed beside her, charged up and fully erect. He ran his hand lightly over the curve of her hip, traced a path down the outside of her leg, then back up along the inside of her thigh, pausing to make little circular motions at the crevice beneath her buttocks.

Diane Acres moved, shifted position, made a weak swipe at his hand. When it persisted, her eyes fluttered open, then widened as she came fully awake and bolted upright in bed, gawking at him.

"Holy shit!" she said, immediately recognizing him even after all these years. "Bobby Lee, how the hell did you get in here?"

"Surprised to see me, Boots?" Using the nickname he'd given her back in Florida.

"I wasn't exactly expecting this." She lowered her eyes to his naked middle, then raised them back to his grinning face. "You're just making yourself right at home, huh? Just like nothing never happened."

"Aw, that's no way to treat an old friend, Boots. Ain't you glad to see me?"

"I haven't made up my mind yet. And I don't wear boots no more, so don't call me that. Sounds like some kind of hick."

Bobby Lee thought, Shit, she *is* a hick, and watched her trying to comb her stringy hair with her fingers. Used to be a foxy hick, but now she'd started to let herself go. He could see her breasts sagging, straining the thin bra, and she still had on last night's makeup. The maroon pillowcase was smudged with dark mascara.

But still . . .

Bobby Lee reached for her and she pulled away, her heart-shaped mouth forming a pout. He tried again, and this time she didn't move, just said, "Bobby Lee . . ." sounding tired.

"I really missed you, Boots . . ."

"*Diane.* And I know what you missed. Anything female would look good to you right now."

Bobby Lee was pushing her down on the bed, saying, "That's not true, hon, not as good as you. At night, when I was in that place? I kept seeing you and me back together again, tellin' myself, 'Bobby Lee, you was a goddamn fool ever lettin' that girl go, and you know it.'" He had his thumb in the waistband of her panties now, not getting much resistance, pulling them over her fleshy hips. "See, now I know what I had, and I'm gonna make it up to you, hon, just watch. It's gonna be better'n ever."

Diane said, "My daughter—"

"She's watchin' TV. Besides, this won't take long."

Diane sighed. "At least let me get something to use first, okay?"

"That's all right," he said, sliding the panties over her feet and tossing them to the floor. "I trust you, Boots—I mean, Diane."

Six years earlier, before Bobby Lee Gettis left Florida for good, he and Diane Acres had been a pretty hot item. She had been waitressing in the lounge at the Newport Resort Hotel in Miami Beach, and he had been parking cars at the Americana, occasionally doing a little lightweight dealing on the side. He had discovered her while bar hopping one night, liked her saucy ass, perky tits, and trademark boots and was immediately hooked. He asked her out, she accepted, and the rest, as they say, was history.

For about three months they had been practically inseparable; beachcombing the oceanfront behind the expensive hotels on Collins Avenue, discoing in the popular night spots along Route A1A, and generally not taking life too seriously.

And then Bobby Lee heard that a middle-row pusher named Danny Silvo was making a major run to New York to unload a shipment of coke. The word was that Danny would be leaving on a Monday morning. Bobby Lee decided that he was hearing opportunity knocking, so when Danny Silvo got into his new Seville parked in the subterranean garage of his West Miami condo, Bobby Lee had been waiting for him with a .38 Smith & Wesson. He forced the pusher to drive to an old deserted restaurant off A1A, where Bobby Lee had stashed his '72 Dodge Duster. He had cuffed the pusher to the steering wheel, checked the trunk, and found eight kilos of high-grade coke and $32,000 in a green duffel bag.

That was good enough for Bobby Lee. He transferred the duffel bag to his Duster, shot Danny Silvo three times through the heart, then headed west. He ultimately decided on Seattle, mainly because he was a big Seahawks fan and had always wanted to see the Space Needle. He never said one word to Diane Acres, just up and went. A year later he met Amy Bartlett, moved in, and began a downhill slide that landed him in Walla Walla for forty-four months.

Diane Acres, devastated at finding herself tossed out like a used condom, rebounded by marrying a vacationing body-and-fender-shop owner from Pasadena, who ended up carting her back to California instead of the Blue Marlin he'd been fishing for.

It took Diane fifteen months to finally recognize she'd made a mistake. She had tried, but the magic wasn't there, and life in the shadow of the Rose Bowl was no bed of roses for her. So one day while hubby was pounding out dents at the repair shop, Diane withdrew $5000 from their checking account, packed her bags, and took a taxi into L.A. What Bobby Lee could do to her, she could do one better. She took her old name back, dyed her hair, and went back to waitressing. But she had made her move three weeks too late to prevent the seed that was to become Lori from being planted.

Then one day, during one of her infrequent phone calls to her mom back in Dania, Florida, Diane learned that Bobby Lee had been sent to prison in Washington State for nearly beating a woman to death. Diane's mom had heard this, she said, after running into Bobby Lee's aunt while grocery shopping at IGA. "She said that boy's done gone plumb crazy, or sumpthin'," Diane's mom told her. "I swear, honey, you was sure lucky gettin' shed a him when you did. I always did think he was trouble."

But the truth was that Bobby Lee had always been in the back of her mind. He had been her first love, the only man who had ever touched that special place inside that made her *tingle.* And she had driven herself half crazy trying to figure out what had made him pick up and leave her without even so much as saying good-bye. She *still* wanted to know the answer to that one.

So she had written him a letter—not asking The Question at first, only saying that she had heard he was in trouble and was there anything she could do for him.

A week later Bobby Lee wrote back saying, "Yeah. How about finding out everything you can about a jeweler named Horance Griswald."

Sitting at the breakfast table over scrambled eggs and bacon, Diane Acres asked Bobby Lee, "How come you won't tell me about this Horance Griswald? I mean I do all the private detective stuff for you, find out where he lives and all, and you just sit there saying 'we got private business to discuss." What's the deal?"

Bobby Lee, wearing only his pants, was thinking that Diane sure hadn't changed in the nosy department. She always wanted to know *everything,* couldn't let a man have his secrets. One quick fuck and it was off to the races—where had he been besides prison? What had he been doing? Why did he almost kill that poor girl? Why did he take off six years ago without even so much as a by-your-leave? "You could at least tell me *that,"* she'd whined, standing at the stove with a spatula in her hand and her blue-veined breasts falling out of her robe. He had told her it was just one of those things men do sometimes that couldn't be explained, and watched her cheeks puff out the way he remembered when she didn't get her way. The hell with her.

Now he scratched his hairless chest and looked at Lori stretched out on the floor surrounded by crayons, working on a clown in her coloring book.

"The man owes me money," he said. "Okay? I knew him a long time ago, before I met you even, and we did some business together he forgot to pay me for. Back in Florida."

Diane held her coffee cup in both hands and blew on it. "Well, he sure ought to be able to pay you now," she said. "He's got a nice big house out there in Brentwood and some absolutely *gorgeous* jewelry in that store window of his. It's not real big—I mean the store—but boy, it sure looks expensive. He runs it by himself and you have to have an appointment. How'd you know he was here anyway?"

Bobby Lee licked bacon grease from his fingers and dug into his hip pocket. He came out with the worn clipping and tossed it on the table. "Some guys up there in Walla Walla use to get the L.A. paper. That was in one of 'em."

She picked it up and studied it. "Yep, that's him. Boy, some people got it all, don't they?" She sighed, put the clipping down and gave Bobby Lee a serious look. "What are you gonna do after you get your money? Did you mean what you said in the bedroom, or was that just pecker talk?"

He covered her hand with his. "I meant every word of it, sugar. I want to give it another go, make up for the shitty way I treated you. We'll scoot on outta here and start over somewheres else, me, you, and the button. How 'bout that?"

"You really mean it?"

"I mean it."

She squeezed his hand and looked at Lori coloring her clown. "What if he don't pay you?"

"Oh, he'll pay me. But even if he didn't, I'd stay right here with you, get me a job."

Diane said, "Oh, shit!" And got quickly to her feet.

Looking at the wall clock, which read nine-fifteen. "I only got forty-five minutes to get to work."

"You work on Sunday?"

"Uh-huh. Ten to six, my regular shift. I got Wednesdays and Thursdays off. Last night we had a private banquet, that's why I was so out of it this morning." She reached down for Lori. "Come on, baby, we gotta get you ready and down to Miss Bidwell's."

"Who's she?" Bobby Lee asked.

"A lady lives down the hall. She keeps Lori for me. You finish your breakfast, I won't be long."

Bobby Lee poured another cup of coffee and stood at the sink looking out the kitchen window. His view was of a concrete courtyard with a picnic table and two barbecue grills.

He thought about Horance Griswald, with his exclusive jewelry store in Century City and his fancy house in Brentwood, and debated with himself about how much the guy would be good for.

He thought about chubby Diane Acres, who was in there getting dressed with visions of a happy threesome dancing around inside her bottle-blond head, and wondered how she'd take getting dumped again.

He thought about a hot Ford Fairlane parked downstairs with six hundred dollars stuffed between the cushions and a .357 magnum under the seat, and wondered if the plates were in the computer yet. He'd have to wipe it and dump it somewhere.

He wondered how much sweet-talk it would take to get Diane's car for a couple of days while she waited on tables.

Chapter

—4—

Cage couldn't believe it.

He had just parked his '78 Camaro in the lot across the street from Banes and Twiford, and was standing outside the attendant's shack staring incredulously at the opposite sidewalk. The kid with the punk haircut and silver earring who ran the lot was sitting on his stool inside the open door, staring in the same direction with a silly grin on his face.

The kid said, "Just what you need first thing Monday morning, huh? Man, what the fuck did you *do?*"

He was referring to the small group of people who were parading to and fro in front of the office, every one of them carrying a picket sign. Some of the catchy slogans were: Put Cage Back in His Cage! We Don't Need Ex-Cons Telling Us Our Bible! Banes and Twiford—Watchdogs for Satan! There were men, women, and a few children, and their leader appeared to be a large bearded man in a black suit and string tie whose sign read: God Is My Security—Not Banes and Twiford!

Cage shook his head and bounced his car keys in his hand as he watched. "How long have they been there?" he asked.

"About a half hour," the kid said. "They drove up in one of those little yellow school buses and started right in marching. You burgle a church or something?"

"It's a long story, Chopper. I'll tell you about it later. Paul or Larry see this yet?" He'd noticed Paul's blue Chevy Caprice and Larry's green and white Mercury Cougar in the lot. So was Brenda Alworth's brown Datsun. Brenda had been hired three months ago, when Cage had finally been let out of the office to do fieldwork.

"Brenda got here before the action started," Chopper said. "But Paul and Larry had to wade right through 'em. Man, I thought Paul was gonna choke on his gum."

"Lovely," Cage said. "Just lovely." He sighed and tossed Chopper his keys. "Might as well get this over with. Keep those handy, I might be back real soon."

No way was Cage going through that mob. He walked to the end of the block, crossed against the light, and turned into the service alley.

Brenda Alworth was waiting for him with the rear door open. She was tall and thin, with large dark eyes, and wore her black hair in twin braids. The three men affectionately addressed her as Olive Oyl, but she had the sexiest phone voice any of them had ever heard, and more than one male client had fallen in love sight unseen.

"Coward," she said, smiling. "Get in here."

Cage went in and waited until Brenda bolted the door before saying, "I guess they're a little upset, huh?"

"Let's say I've seen Paul in a better mood and let it go at that," she said cheerfully. "But Larry thinks it's kind of humorous. You want some coffee?"

"No thanks," he said. "How about calls? You getting your ears burned with many of those?"

"A few. You really stirred things up, buster. Do you have to work at these things, or does it come natural?"

"Pure talent, Olive Oyl. Pure talent."

They went through Paul's cluttered workshop, past the tiny kitchenette, and through the curtained doorway into the office. Paul Banes was reared back in his swivel chair with his size-fourteen crepe soles on the desk, picking thoughtfully at his fingernails. Larry Twiford was straddling a chair across from him, peeking through the blinds that covered the big picture windows facing Santa Monica Boulevard.

Brenda said, "Ta-daaa!" and made a sweeping gesture toward Cage before continuing on to her desk, where the phone had just started to ring.

"There he is," Paul said. "The anti-Christ. You trying to run us out of business?" His voice was mild, but there was concern written in the lines of his face as he watched Cage take a seat at his desk.

"I guess I misspoke myself," Cage said. "But I didn't expect this kind of reaction."

"Of course not. You only told every Christian in the country their prayer book is a piece of garbage, that's all. Did you have to go and cut up the Bible? Were you smoking or something?"

"All I said was you shouldn't take it literally, like you shouldn't take a lot of things you read literally. And it wasn't like I told a lie. Whatever happened to free speech?"

"I know you didn't lie," Paul said. "I looked it up myself, and that's what it says all right. But we're in the public service business here, and you can't go around saying things that insult a good chunk of the public."

Larry Twiford let the blinds fall back into place and turned away from the window. "Yeah, but he's got a right to his opinion, Paul. Shit, I've heard you say things in public that made me mad."

"Not to a reporter, you haven't. They get off on crap like this. We could be in the news for a fucking week, maybe even end up like one of those abortion clinics they've been blockading, for Christ's sake." This was apparently a new thought for Paul and he leaned over and took a quick peek through the blinds himself.

Cage was getting tired of being on the defensive, having Paul, who was normally like a good-natured bear, take him on this guilt trip. It was Cage's belief that you should speak the way you felt and not worry about crab-walking around people's sensitivities. At least that made your position clear, if not right, and those who didn't agree could choose their own course.

"So what do you want me to do, Paul?" he said. "Crawl out there on hands and knees and beg for forgiveness? Or how about I print a retraction, tell all the good people I'm sorry I had the nerve to read the Old Testament instead of the new and improved version that censored out all the original stuff the theologians figured they couldn't explain. Or maybe I should just quit."

Paul sighed and pinched the bridge of his nose. "Don't get so testy. Hell, it's as much my fault as it is yours. I'm the one who came up with this brainstorm, and I never put a muzzle on you. Couple days and it'll be forgotten, I hope."

"I just want to do the right thing," Cage said in a softer tone.

"There's nothing to make right," Larry told him. "So don't let me hear anything else about quitting or I'll pull your parole—I still have a few connections."

Cage looked at Brenda, who was still on the phone. "Brenda said something about calls. What's she been getting, bomb threats?"

"Fanatics, mostly," Larry said. "You know—God's-gonna-get-you stuff. A few preachers who want to save your soul before it's too late, which might not be a bad idea. But most of 'em saying, what can you expect from a marijuana-smoking ex-con."

Cage's jaw muscles bunched at that and Larry grinned.

"But a few thought it was great, saying it's refreshing to see somebody tell it like it is for a change."

"And two desperate women who think you're cute and want your body," Brenda said, off the phone now. "I took their names and numbers in case Caprita decides to raise her standards."

"Well, she never accused me of being a role model."

"And . . ." Brenda waved a yellow message slip at him, "you got a call from Mr. Michael Grady, no less."

"Who's Michael Grady?"

Brenda was shocked. "My God, Allen, where have you *been?* He's only the hottest director in Hollywood right now. Did you see *Angel Wars?* He won an Academy Award for that one. Best Picture."

"I didn't see it but I've heard of it," Cage said. "Some nonsense about a band of angels attempting to overthrow God, or something like that. Didn't like the way he was running things down here. Caught a lot of heat from the church."

"I remember that," Larry said. "The guy said he couldn't understand what all the bitching was about, since God won and decided nothing was gonna change. What did he want with Cage?"

"Wants him to come out and talk about a security system," Brenda answered. "How about that?"

Paul perked up a little and raised his bushy eyebrows. "Why Cage? He must've read that article."

"He did. Said Allen was a man after his own heart. He wants him to come out sometime this morning, if possible."

"Well now," Paul said. "Things might be looking up after all. You think he really wants to discuss business, or just compare notes with our local celebrity here?"

"Probably both. But he said he's not satisfied with the system he has and wants to see what we have to offer."

Paul thought a moment, then swung his feet off the desk. "All right," he told Cage. "Go check it out. But if this guy only wants to reminisce, make your excuses and get out of there."

"I'm supposed to be at Tower Records at ten-thirty," Cage said. "Remember? Perry Sanderman wants a demonstration of the remote lock, and I think we can sell him on it. And they have a lot of outlets."

"Larry can handle that—if I can get him to stop sticking his nose in that window. The guy asked for you and he's gonna get you. Maybe we can salvage something out of this."

Brenda got up and handed Cage the message slip. "Lucky dog," she said. "It's a beach house in Malibu, so maybe you should take your swim trunks."

Cage tucked the paper in his shirt pocket. "All right, I'll take a run out there and see what's up. But I'm leaving the same way I came in. I don't think I'm ready for that crowd outside."

"I ought to push you right out the freakin' door," Paul said, beginning to sound like his old self again.

"And I would too, if I wasn't afraid they might stone you to death."

"You'd probably do it anyway," Cage said. "If it wouldn't be bad for business."

The house was red brick, Spanish tile, and lots of glass, with a redwood sun deck that ended right at the cliff's edge overlooking Pacific Coast Highway and the endless ocean beyond.

Some beach house, Cage thought as he parked behind a white Mercedes in the circular driveway. Nothing to worry about except mud slides and brush fires, which seemed to be minor inconveniences to these modern cliff dwellers. As soon as one went slipping down the face of the slope, up would go another in its place, bigger and glassier than ever. Cage didn't think the view was worth the risk.

He rang the bell and stood back admiring the ornate double doors until one opened to show a middle-aged Oriental lady in a dark silk kimono.

"Morning, ma'am," he said. "My name's Allen Cage, and I believe Mr. Grady's expecting me."

She smiled and bowed slightly. "Please come in, Mr. Cage."

The foyer was parquet, with a gleaming suit of armor standing guard in one corner and a potted orange tree in the other. Cage followed the Oriental lady through a sunken den dominated by a fully equipped wet bar, through the open patio doors and out onto the sun deck.

A tall wiry man in a green bathing suit was sitting at an umbrella table reading from a bound volume. He couldn't have been more than forty, but his fashionably long hair was almost completely gray and contrasted nicely with his deep tan.

The Oriental lady said, "Mr. Al-Lan Cage to see you," then backed away and disappeared into the house.

The man stood and held out his hand. "Well, now. This is a real pleasure," he said. "How you doing there, guy? Sit down, take a load off. Want something to drink?"

"No thanks, Mr. Grady," Cage said. He pulled out a chair and angled it so he faced the ocean. "No pool?"

"Don't need one," Michael Grady said, and waved his hand in the direction of the blue Pacific. "Got the biggest pool in the world right out there. And call me Mike."

"Nice place."

"Yeah, it'll do. Beats the shit out of Beverly Hills, that's for sure."

"I wouldn't know."

"Take my word for it. You can *breathe* up here, got a little elbow room. And the view ain't bad either."

"No chance of being blocked out by a condo, I don't guess."

"You got it. Well, not for a while anyway. The way things are expanding nowadays, you can't really be sure." He tapped the bound volume lying closed on the table and made a face. "But they keep sending me garbage scripts like this and it won't make any difference, 'cause I won't be able to stay here anyway."

"Making a new movie, are you?" Cage asked.

"Not with this piece of shit, you can believe that. You see *Angel Wars?*"

Cage shook his head and hoped the guy wasn't going to remake the film for his benefit. "But I heard about it. Won an Academy Award, didn't it?"

"Yeah, Best Picture. Luckiest break of my life. I'm just glad I did the thing for points instead of salary.

That was a piece of shit too, but it was different and controversial and I guess I did put in a lot of my own personal beliefs and skepticism about this God who's supposed to be so interested in everybody down here. Touched a lot of raw nerves. People either hated it or loved it. There was no in between. But it was successful, and you know why?"

Cage thought a moment, then said, "I believe you already answered that. It touched nerves on both sides."

Michael Grady slapped the table and said, "Exactly! Hell, you ought to be a producer. Now they want a sequel . . . *Angel Wars, the Second Battle.* Only there's not a goddam original scene in the whole script, and it'll bomb bigger'n the one they dropped on Hiroshima if I can't juice it up."

Cage nodded politely and watched the director light a Camel with a gold Dunhill lighter. He was beginning to like Michael Grady, thinking at least the man wasn't coming on like some hotshot genius with talent to burn. But he wished he'd get to business.

"Anyway," Grady said, "that's another story. Now you're probably thinking I got you up here just to shoot the shit 'cause I read that article and was curious."

Cage smiled. "Now that you mention it, the subject did come up."

"Then you were partly right. You've got a colorful background, speak your mind, and I love that crack about old Elisha and the she-bear. And you know what? I predict you're gonna get a lot of attention behind that comment, just like *Angel Wars.*"

Tell me about it, Cage thought.

"And that kind of publicity studios spend millions in P.R. to get. But I've been worried about my security setup here too, and I been thinking about maybe upgrading it."

"You've already got ADT," Cage said. He'd noticed the lock box set into the doorframe while he was waiting to be let in. "That's a good system."

"And I know three people with the same system, or something similar, who've been ripped off in the last ten months. Same routine every time. They'd be out partying, getting their pictures in the paper, come home about dawn and find out they'd had a visitor. Two homes in Beverly Hills, and then, would you believe they got a friend of mine right down the road. Now that's getting too fuckin' close for me. If me and the wife decide to make a night of it somewhere, I want to make damn sure nobody gets in here undetected. Miko, the Japanese woman who brought you out here, only comes around three times a week to keep things in shape. My wife don't get around too good. So if you can guarantee me that at a reasonable price, you got yourself a customer."

"We can guarantee that," Cage said, feeling more comfortable now that he was on familiar ground.

Michael Grady dropped his cigarette in a copper cuspidor beside him and pushed back his chair. "Then let's go inside and have something cool and see if you can convince me."

They were at the wet bar, perched on high-backed stools of chrome and beige leather. Michael Grady had found a ginger ale for Cage, saying that he didn't have any 7-Up, and had fixed a Bloody Mary for himself. Miko had reappeared on silent feet with a bowl of macadamia nuts and just as silently withdrew.

"So tell me about this system," Grady said. "How does it differ from what I already have?"

"The only problem with ADT and others like it," Cage said, "is the external wiring. It's easy to get to, and all a guy has to do is look for the activating box, or even a decal, and he knows what you've got. Or if he's not sure, he can always check your power lines and identify everything coming out of the house. Then he simply feeds back the identical voltage through a loop running from a voltage meter, cuts the wires, and does anything he wants without interrupting the current. It would take a pro about fifteen minutes."

"Jesus, you make it sound like a piece of cake."

"For the right person, it is. I'm giving you a simplified version of how it's done, but I think you get the picture."

"And you've got something better?"

"We think so. At least for your purposes. We've sold several to people who had the same concerns as you. It's a specially modified ultrasonic vibration unit that's installed in the ceiling. Works on oscillators that generate compression waves capable of picking up any vibration above the frequency of thirty cycles per second. This allows small pets to move around without tripping the alarm, but makes it impossible for a burglar to do the same. It comes with a relay-signal intensifier and a small receiver similar to a beeper that you carry on your belt or in your pocket."

"Motion detector, huh? Nothing new about that."

"It's not the concept but the application that makes ours different," Cage explained. "No external wires to give it away, and it lets you monitor the system yourself instead of being plugged into a private firm. That's what really costs you. See, the relay-signal intensifier is mounted on the roof and looks just like a standard TV antenna. The oscillator sends a signal to it, which is intensified by twenty-eight hundred and transmitted out on a present frequency to the receiver. Just like you were being paged. From that point on it's up to you. You can either dial 911 or call him through your answering machine and ask him to kindly vacate the premises. I recommend 911."

"How far does the signal carry?"

"A minimum of forty-five miles, depending on height and terrain. It has a max of about seventy, but if you plan on being farther away than the minimum, I suggest you leave the receiver with a friend."

"And the cost?"

"Twelve hundred per unit, installed and calibrated, plus nine fifty for the relay. I figure a place this size will take two units upstairs and two down. We take measurements to make sure. So we're talking in the neighborhood of fifty-eight fifty, plus tax. No charge for the receiver."

Grady got up, went behind the bar and began building another Bloody Mary. He worked in silence, and when he was finished he leaned over the bar and gazed out through the patio doors with a thoughtful expression. Cage tossed a couple of macadamia nuts into his mouth and washed them down with ginger ale while he let the director consider.

"You say these units will cover the whole house?" Grady asked.

"Every inch of it," Cage said. "And no one will know they're here. We don't use decals, we don't advertise our products, and every client we have is kept strictly confidential."

Grady took a long pull from his glass, then nodded. "Okay, my friend, you got a deal. How soon can you get it installed?"

"Tomorrow. Only takes a few hours."

"Give me a call first so I can have Miko take my

wife to the beauty salon or someplace. Marilee caught polio as a kid and has to get around on crutches. She's a little shy with strangers. After we were married she had a series of operations and all kinds of therapy and finally regained the use of her legs. Now the disease is coming back. Post-polio sequela, the doctors call it, and not a damn thing they can do about it." He lifted his glass again and turned his attention back to some distant point beyond the patio doors.

"Sorry to hear it," Cage said, meaning it.

"I know you are, and I appreciate it. But she's a good woman, and I'm a better man because of her. Got the calmest spirit I ever saw."

The director seemed to shake himself, as though with a sudden chill, and came back from wherever his mind had taken him. He walked around the bar, cocked a hip onto the stool and shook out another Camel. He lit it and blew a cloud of smoke at the high-beamed ceiling.

"You know what I like best about this?" Grady said. "The idea that some clown might be in here not knowing that *I* know he's here. Thinking he's safe, got all the time in the world. I picture me being close enough to haul ass back here with that thirty-O-six I keep in the trunk and dropping the bastard in his tracks."

"I'd strongly suggest you not do that," Cage said. "Not that I have any particular qualms about it, but it could backfire. Guys on that level aren't amateurs, and chances are they'll be armed. Let the cops handle it. That's what they're paid for."

"Anger demands its own satisfaction, Allen. My dad used to say that."

"Did he also say that the only difference between anger and danger is one small letter?"

Grady lowered his eyes to Cage. "Let me tell you something," he said. "I got a little money. I live well, buy nice things, and if I never made another movie, I'd still be set for life. But it wasn't always that way. You wouldn't believe the years I spent scrounging bit parts in B movies, not knowing if I was gonna have enough to eat tomorrow. I lost count of the times I sweated through jungle scenes and war flicks, fighting mosquitos and poisonous snakes and eating quinine tablets like M&M's to ward off malaria. Christ, I developed ulcers when I was thirty-two from dealing with prima donna actors, pissy scripts, and thumbnail budgets. And now it's started paying off, well it bites my ass that some sonofabitch might think he can just waltz in here whenever he wants and help himself to what I went through hell to get. No sir, if that should happen and I get the chance, I'm holding court right here, right fuckin' here."

Grady got up and moved to a section of wall covered with framed photographs. He removed an eight-by-ten glossy, came back and handed it to Cage. It showed two couples in evening dress sitting in a plush horseshoe booth. One was Michael Grady and a pleasant-looking brunette with a sweet smile. The other was a small man with thinning hair and horned-rim glasses and a thin lady with short, silver hair. They appeared to be somewhere in their mid-fifties.

"That's James and Frances Maljean," Grady said. "The friends of mine who got hit last Friday night. This was taken in Vegas a couple months ago. See that necklace she's wearing?"

Cage could hardly miss it. Hanging around the lady's thin neck, it was as conspicuous as a horse collar.

"Quite a piece," Cage said.

"You bet it is. Eighty grand worth of Russian diamonds, fire rubies, and Burmese jade. Jim had it made special for her their last anniversary, their twenty-fifth. I had an emerald choker and matching earrings made for Marilee at the same time. See? She's wearing them here, if you look past all the hair. Anyway, they got Frances's necklace and three or four other pieces. Altogether about a quarter-million dollars worth. And the poor bastard didn't even have it insured. And you know why? Because he trusted his security system."

Cage handed the picture back. "That's a hell of a loss."

"Damn right it is. And they're good people—which is another reason I don't intend to involve the police if the right situation ever presents itself. Whoever it is, they can read him his rights in the morgue."

"Then let's hope it never presents itself, Mike," Cage said. He sat the half-finished can of ginger ale on the bar and glanced at his watch. "Well, I guess I better be going."

Grady thought of something and snapped his fingers. "Hang on a minute," he said, and went behind the bar again. He removed a House of Windsor cigar box from beneath the counter, opened it, and took out a transparent Ziploc packet containing a small amount of marijuana.

"Little something for you," he said, and winked. "All buds, the best Humboldt County has to offer." He dropped it on the bar. "Enjoy."

"I appreciate the thought," Cage said with a grin. "But I'd better pass." Then he thought about the pickets marching back and forth in front of Banes and

Twiford and said, "On the other hand, it has been a while," and tucked the little bag in his jacket pocket. "Thanks."

"My pleasure. Now let me ask you something, just between you and me. Did you really escape from all those prisons, or did you invent two or three?"

"Still curious, huh?"

"More like intrigued."

"No," Cage told him, "I didn't invent any. I guess I'm just lucky I didn't get killed. Wardens have a tendency to take these things personally."

"I bet they do. You know, that might make a good film itself. Ever think about that?"

Cage thought about the pickets again. "I don't think so," he said. "Right now I've had about all the exposure I can stand."

Chapter

Naturally, Brenda Alworth just had to call Caprita and tell her all about the pickets marching up and down in front of Banes and Twiford—and why. Couldn't *wait* to call her. So after dinner that evening Caprita wanted to hear the details. He could fill her in while he helped her put up a new shelf in the bathroom, she said, one of those little prefab imitation-wood things with sliding doors she'd bought from Builders Emporium. She already had the area measured and marked off, deciding that right above the towel rack would be a good place.

So he told her all about it while they worked, trying to gloss over the incident and make light of it and not let on how intimidating it was to see people carrying protest signs with his name on them. Caprita thought it was kind of amusing, standing there supervising while he hammered in the screw anchors, making certain he had them centered exactly on the chalk marks. But then she knew all about that kind of stuff, having carried her share of Get Out of Central America banners. None with her name on them, though.

"What did they say?" she asked. "The signs."

"I don't know, really. I didn't pay that much attention."

"Didn't one of them say, 'Put Cage back in his cage'?"

He looked at her. "What did Brenda do, write 'em all down? Where's your list?"

"Oh, don't be so sensitive. She just told me about that particular one because she thought it was really cruel. Don't let it bother you. It's just somebody trying to be cute."

"Who says it's bothering me?"

"You do—or at least your attitude does. You've been moping around all evening totally preoccupied and not even asking me what the shelf's for. And you haven't made one bitchy comment about me starting graveyard tonight, and that is *definitely* not you."

"Think you know me, huh?"

"Like a book, sweetie," she said, and smacked him on the butt. "Now cheer up, they'll probably be gone tomorrow . . . and move that one up just a tad, it's leaning toward Magic Mountain."

Cage had to grin. That was one of the things he loved about her, the way she could zero in on whatever was gnawing at him when he wasn't even sure himself, and help him deal with it. Yeah, she knew him. In some ways better than he knew himself.

"But I knew you were going to get in trouble," she said, "as soon as I read the story. Didn't I tell you?"

Only sometimes she didn't know when to quit.

"Caprita, I got nothing against the Bible, you know that. I was only making a point. People have a right to believe in whatever they want. But so do I. Anyway, from now on I'll keep my mouth shut. Now can we change the subject?"

"Sure," she said, and handed him a support bracket. "I want to know about Michael Grady anyway. What's he like?"

Cage said, "Is there anything Olive Oyl doesn't tell you?"

Caprita shook her head, emphatic. "Nope. Including the two desperate women who left their phone numbers—which, incidentally, have now gone by way of the shredder, so forget it."

"Damn, and I was saving those for emergencies." He paused, then said, "You know who Michael Grady is?"

"Of course, he directed *Angel Wars*. It won an Academy Award for Best Picture. Everybody knows that."

He let that one go, then said, "Well, how about this—does everybody know he's getting ready to make a sequel?" Sounding a little smug about it. *"Angel Wars, The Second Battle."*

"Certainly, it was on *Entertainment Tonight* about three weeks ago. I don't think he likes the script though. Why?"

"Just testing," he said. Shit, where had he been?

"So tell me about him. He really asked to see you?"

"Yeah. Wanted a backup intruder system. He's a little paranoid 'cause a friend of his got hit last week for a bundle in jewelry. One necklace alone worth eighty grand—Jesus. Paul and I are putting in some oscillator units for him tomorrow."

"Is he nice, or is he one of those snooty Hollywood types you hear about?"

"Seems like a regular guy. I like him. His wife's got polio and he dotes on her. I figure a guy does that deserves a lot of respect, especially a big-time movie mogul."

"How awful. Did you see her?"

"No. I think she's a little self-conscious, stays out of the way mostly. Saw a picture of her though, from the waist up. Kind of nice looking in a subtle way. Lots of hair, about thirty something. The quiet type."

"Poor thing. Good for Mr. Grady. My opinion just went up another notch. Here."

She handed him the other support bracket and he screwed it in place. Then he set the shelf snugly into the brackets and Caprita backed off, her head tilted.

"Perfect," she said. "Sometimes you're really nice to have around."

"Okay, now what's it for?"

She wrinkled her nose at him. "About time you asked. You're almost normal again. Come on."

She led him by the hand back into the kitchen, sat him at the table, then hurried out again, leaving him staring at Grits the cat, sniffing suspiciously at his food dish. In less than a minute she was back, carrying a shoe box. She placed it on the table and began taking out small glass beakers she'd apparently pilfered from the hospital lab. There were seven of them, all corked and labeled and containing greenish-brown flaky stuff that looked like something from her spice rack. Or something else.

"What's that?"

"Herbs," she said.

"You don't mean *grass,* do you?"

"No, dummy. Medicinal herbs. Some of us girls have been doing a lot of research, you know, reading through old medical journals and stuff like that?" She sat down and hunched over the table, brushing her hair back from her forehead, really getting into it. "Anyway—now we've been doing this for weeks you understand—and we found out that certain mixtures of certain herbs have great medicinal properties. And it's all totally organic, no chemical pollutants at all."

Cage gave her a dubious look. "What kind of herbs?"

"Well, don't ask me for exact ratios or blends, because Alice Wilmont took care of all that in the lab. But basically what we have are carefully measured portions of water violet, willow, jude weed, gorse, rock rose, and of course, clematis."

"Oh, of course."

"Don't be flippant, Allen, this is for real. And it certainly can't hurt you. Ancient Tibetans used it for centuries to treat everything from headaches to colds to constipation. Great cleansing agent. Try some. Just for a while, to see what happens."

"Caprita, you got to be kidding. I'm not taking any of that stuff."

"One teaspoon in a glass of water," she said, "That's all it takes. You should do it about once a month anyway, according to the old recipe. Keeps the system running smoothly."

Cage said, "Is this part of your back-to-nature kick or something? 'Cause if it is, you're on your own. I'll stick to Excedrin and Di-Gel."

Caprita stood and began replacing the beakers in the shoe box. "Suit yourself," she said, a bit miffed. "But I'm going to try it. Thirty million monks can't be wrong. Now if you'll excuse me, I'm going to put these on my shelf and take a bath." She started away, then turned back. "Incidentally, since you insist on being my chauffeur this week, I hope you don't mind getting me in about an hour early tonight. I'm charge nurse and I have to be briefed on procedure."

Cage checked the wall clock. "It's not even nine yet," he said. But she'd already gone, leaving an after-image of beige cutoffs, white sneakers, and tan legs. He grunted, thinking she was taking this herb business pretty seriously. Lately she'd been getting a little uptight. Being abrupt with him; taking it personally whenever he showed disinterest in or disagreement with things that could get her inspired. It might be a good idea to patch things up before their relationship took on any added strain.

He wandered into the bedroom and found Caprita at her dressing table, pinning up her hair. He sat on the edge of the bed and waited for her to say something, but she ignored him and continued pulling bobby pins from her mouth, jabbing them into the loose tendrils at the nape of her neck with enough force to cause him concern.

Cage said, "You're gonna hurt yourself, you keep doing that."

"Do I tell you how to shave?" she said around the mouthful of pins.

"*Now* what did I do? Just because I don't want to take any of your herbs?"

"It's not just that, Allen. And don't act all innocent, like you're being persecuted."

"My complaints about your hours?"

"That too. Among other things."

He searched his memory, then said, "What other things?"

"I really don't want to discuss it. And if I have to tell you, then you're more insensitive than I thought."

"All I'm asking you to do is tell me what other things. And I'm not insensitive, that's why I came in here."

Caprita slammed home the last of the bobby pins and twisted around to face him. "All right, I'll tell you what else. You have this infuriating way of making me feel like I'm being patronized sometimes. As if I were a child to be humored. I don't care if you take any of my herbs or not, but I do expect you to be supportive instead of painfully tolerant. And as for my hours, I happen to be a professional nurse. That's a twenty-four-hour-a-day job, Allen, and a certain amount of inconvenience is to be expected."

Cage spread his hands and said, "We've already covered those, and I'll admit you've made a case. I'll work on it. But what *else?* Let's get it all out while we're talking."

"Okay," she said, "how about when I wanted to visit my parents last month, who I haven't seen since we were there for Christmas. No, you said, you didn't feel like spending a weekend in Portland listening to my mother hinting about marriage and grandchildren."

"She's about as subtle as a train wreck."

"See what I mean? You shrug off the issue instead of confronting it. Grandchildren are important to my parents, especially my mother. It's only fair to let them know where we stand instead of keeping them guessing."

Cage watched her rise and walk to the closet, her movements quick and impatient. So that was it. Now they were getting down to what was really on her mind. He leaned back on his elbows and drew a breath. "What you mean is *you* want to know where *I* stand. I thought we'd already agreed on that."

Caprita whirled to face him, holding a peach-colored bathrobe. "*We* didn't agree on anything," she said. "It was your idea *and* decision to give it two years before committing ourselves in that direction. Since it generally requires mutual cooperation to manufacture a baby, I didn't have too much choice in the matter. Unless I wanted to be sneaky and go off the pill."

"I just want to make sure we're ready," he said. "It's a big step."

Caprita breezed by him again, sat down at the dressing table and began removing her sneakers. "You know what I think? I think you're just terrified at the prospect of being a father."

"Not terrified," he said. "Just hesitant. Remember, I spent almost seven years in federal prisons, not counting escape time, and I want to be sure I'm mentally prepared. I've only been out eight months, and I'm still trying to get used to that."

"Oh, come off it, Allen. That's a copout and you know it."

"*Now* who's being insensitive? Don't downplay this readjustment factor, babe, it's a valid concern. I've seen enough guys who thought they had it whipped, but didn't, to know what I'm talking about. It's the ex-felon's version of shell shock, only it's called culture shock. It might be a state of mind to you, but to me it's a way of life."

Caprita, softening, said, "I won't deny it might be a problem for a lot of people, Allen. But you're one of the most well-adjusted individuals I know." Then she added, "Most of the time."

"And on those occasions when you think I'm not, you're quick to let me know about it."

Caprita reached behind her and unsnapped her halter. She peeled it off with an unselfconscious motion and let it fall to the floor next to her sneakers. Her breasts sprang free, swaying as she moved, capturing Cage's attention and momentarily disrupting his thoughts. His concentration was drawn to the small strawberry birthmark above her right nipple that vaguely resembled the outline of Texas. Every time he saw it he was reminded of that country-and-western song, "My First Taste of Texas," and he smiled at the thought. He would sometimes sing a few bars in between teasing licks, which always made her giggle, both of them getting worked up until the giggles gradually turned into moans of pleasure.

"Do you really think I criticize you too much?" Caprita asked. She was looking at him now, waiting for his reaction. Apparently the thought had never occurred to her.

Cage said, "You've had a tendency to get on my case now and then, yeah. You want details?"

"No, we'll only get into a bigger argument. Just look at it as my contribution to your continuing readjustment."

She stood and slipped into the robe, then turned her back to him while she wriggled out of the cutoffs and panties. The sight of them falling around her ankles was highly erotic to Cage, who was fast losing interest in the conversation. She stepped out of them and turned around, belting her robe.

"Tell you what I'm going to do," she said, "since I seem to be getting on your case so much. From now on I'm just going to keep my mouth shut, regardless of whether I think you're wrong or not. But in return, come the first of the year, we're going to have a heart-to-heart baby talk. If you're not adjusted enough by then, you never will be. Deal?"

"Deal," Cage agreed.

"Good. Then that's settled."

She made for the bathroom, but Cage caught her wrist as she passed and tugged her onto the bed. Her small squeal of protest was cut short when he brought his mouth down hard against hers. His hand went to the robe, parted it, and creeped inside to find the small separation between her thighs, fingertips encountering soft pubic hair, then warm dampness as he found her cleft. Caprita moaned and arched her back, circling her arms about his neck. She strained against him as he fumbled with his belt and zipper, not wanting to lose contact with her even long enough to disrobe. They were both ready, and when he entered her she gasped and locked her legs around his waist with a strength designed to capture and hold as she matched him thrust for thrust. Cage pulled away, wanting to observe her passion, but she pulled him back and buried her face in his neck, muffling her pleasure sounds as they settled into their own rhythm. It didn't take long, not this time, both needing release for their own reasons. Caprita came first, stifling a scream by clamping her teeth on his shoulder in a way that would have had him flinching in pain under normal circumstances. Now it caused him to lunge like a spurred horse, galloping toward his own finish until at last he shuddered, trying to push himself through her while he spent, and then falling limp against her while she slipped her hands under his shirt and whispered comforting words as she stroked his back. He wanted to say something, let her know how he felt at that moment when he was most defenseless. But he knew it wasn't necessary. She was already aware of that. So he contented himself with a great sigh and lowered his head to her breast, nuzzling the robe aside until he came to the outline of Texas.

And Texas never tasted so sweet.

Chapter
—6—

Bobby Lee had decided to make his play on the jeweler sometime after nine o'clock Tuesday night, figuring that was the best time to catch him at home. It was now nine-thirty, and he was tooling west on Wilshire in Diane's '82 Gremlin, going over in his mind how he would greet L.A.'s rising star in the world of fashionable jewelry.

Earlier he had finally gotten around to doing something about that hot Fairlane. It was making him nervous, parked right out there on the street with the ignition wires dangling, six hundred bucks and .357 stuffed in and under the seat. A tenth grader's dream come true. So he'd moved everything to Diane's car, wiped the Fairlane clean and dumped it at a Safeway parking lot on Sunset. After that he'd made a quick trip to a men's clothing shop on Hollywood, where he bought a pair of dark blue dress slacks, a burgundy shirt, and a vinyl jacket, telling the salesgirl to keep his old clothes, maybe give them to her boyfriend or something. She had given him a pained smile and said she'd be happy to burn them for him.

Then he'd driven over to Century City to check out the jeweler's shop in the lobby of the Century Plaza Hotel. Designs by Griswald, sandwiched between

Gucci's and Century furs. He'd paused outside the show window admiring the display pieces of brilliant stones and intricate mountings against a backdrop of black velvet, and wondered again how the guy had managed to swing it. He must have had private financing from somewhere, a silent partner, maybe: It took a bundle to get this kind of operation off the ground. The inventory alone was probably worth four or five mil at least. It would've been nice to approach the man right there—just select a few choice pieces, say a hundred grand worth, tell the man his lips were sealed, and make his exit, mission accomplished. But if Horance decided he wasn't going for any blackmail scam and hit the panic button . . . well, there was enough hotel security lurking around to guarantee he'd never make it through the lobby.

So it had to be at the man's house. When Bobby Lee picked Diane up from her waitressing job at the Captain's Table on La Cienega a little after six, he told her it was time to pay his old buddy a visit and that he'd need her car tonight. "I have to go to the grocery store first," she told him. Bobby Lee said fine, he'd go with her and they would practice being domestic. Diane had liked that and scooted close to him, the tight waitress skirt hiking up to reveal her chunky nylon-clad thighs. Bobby Lee had patted one and said, "Anyplace but Safeway. Okay?"

The house was on Altwater Drive, a two-story colonial set back from the street and barely visible through the tall, neatly trimmed hedgerow that enclosed the grounds. A pair of iron lamp posts lighted the blacktop driveway entrance.

Bobby Lee slowed as he drove past, did a U-turn at the end of the block, came back and eased to the curb at a shadowed spot out of reach of the nearest streetlight. He took the magnum from under the seat, tucked it in his waistband behind his back, and got out of the car. He adjusted his jacket as he looked around, feeling the warm night air that carried the faint smell of flowers and freshly watered lawns. Yes sir, the man had done real well for himself.

As Bobby Lee walked up the driveway, his eyes were drawn to the three-car garage at the end of the house. Moonlight reflected off chrome and glass of what looked to be some sporty model, like maybe a Corvette, and a dark van. Shit, what if the guy was having company or something? He hadn't really considered that. Well, he would just have to play it by ear.

There were lights showing from behind drawn curtains at one end of the house and a night light burning next to the door. Bobby Lee rang the bell and immediately heard the shrill yipping of a small dog from inside the house. A voice said, "Quiet, Corky. Go to the kitchen . . . go!" And a moment later the door opened.

It was Harry Grisom, all right. Bobby Lee would have recognized him anywhere, only last time the guy had been wearing khakis instead of fawn-colored slacks and a soft yellow pullover. His wavy hair was gray at the temples now, starting to recede, and there was a haughty, irritated expression on his face.

"Mr., uh, Griswald?" Bobby Lee had to force the name out.

"That's right. What can I do for you?"

"I was wondering if I could maybe, you know, have a few minutes of your time."

"Am I supposed to know you?"

"Well, you should, but I doubt if you remember me. Which I don't guess is too surprisin', considerin' I was just a peon and you were the richest con in Lake Butler . . . Harry."

Bobby Lee was disappointed. He'd been anticipating this moment, really looking forward to the man's reaction when he hit him with this blast from the past. He'd been expecting slack-jawed amazement at the least, maybe even a slight buckling of the knees, but all he got was a narrowing of the eyes and an unflinching stare.

"Well," Bobby Lee asked, "ain't you gonna say somethin'?"

"I already did. I asked what can I do for you."

Bobby Lee shook his head in admiration and looked away. "I gotta hand it to you, Harry. You always were the cool one. Guy pops up at your door, lays this trip on you about knowing you in the joint eleven years ago, knowin' your real name and all, and you don't even blink." He looked back at him and said, "Man, don't you *get* it? Don't that tell you somethin'?"

The jeweler gave Bobby Lee a slow, appraising look. "First of all," he said, "my name is Horance Griswald, not Harry. Now who are you?"

"Robert E. Lee Gettis. Call me Bobby Lee."

"And you think I'm someone you know from someplace called—where? Lake Butler?"

"Man, I *know* you are." Who was this motherfucker trying to kid anyway? Acting all innocent. "You're Harry Grisom, and eleven years ago you were doin' a nickle there for stagin' a robbery of a jewelry store you owned in Lauderdale, so cut the shit."

The man just stood there looking at him.

Bobby Lee turned away. "Have it your way then. As they say on the six o'clock news—film at eleven."

"Just a minute."

Bobby Lee turned back, thinking now they were getting somewhere.

"Come on in and we'll discuss it."

"Thank you—Mr. Griswald."

The jeweler led him into a large study dimly lit by a single table lamp in front of a curtained window. A slide projector had been set up on one end of a desk, casting a blank beam of light onto a screen off to the side. One entire wall was lined with paintings, as though on display in an art gallery, with a cleared space in the middle where a grandfather clock stood.

Horance Griswald motioned to a leather wing chair and took a seat behind the desk. "Now then," he said. "Why don't you start with how you found me."

Bobby Lee made himself comfortable and stretched out his legs, liking the feel and smell of the soft leather chair. "First of all," he said, "let me tell you where I been, so you can get a better understandin' of my position. Know where Walla Walla is?"

"The Washington State prison."

"Right. Well, I just finished doin' forty-four months there, and let me tell you, it ain't Lake Butler. Assault with intent. Anyway, you know how it is in the joint. Guys like to keep up with what's goin' on outside, see what all they been missin'. Guys who never read a paper in their life, 'cept maybe the funnies, suddenly take a big interest in community activities and world events."

Horance Griswald waited, sitting motionless in his banker's chair like a patient spider. The only other sound in the room was the faint ticking of the grandfather clock.

"So I was goin' through the *L.A. Times* one day, figurin' I'd bone up on a little culture, when lo and behold what do I run across but a picture of my old Lake Butler buddy Harry Grisom. Only now he's callin' hisself Horance Griswald and hobnobbin' with L.A. socialites."

He reached into his inside jacket pocket, took out the clipping and unfolded it. He held it up, waving it slightly to capture the jeweler's attention, then shrugged and put it away when the man continued to look at him without expression.

"So I says to myself, 'Bobby Lee, you got to pay your old friend a visit when you get outta here. He'll be tickled to see you.' See, I figured we could kick it around and come up with a good plan to make sure all those high society customers of yours don't happen to find out who Horance Griswald really is. Don't that sound like a good idea?"

Horance Griswald began rearranging the slides and sketch sheets of mountings scattered across the desk. "So now we come to it," he said. "A neat little blackmail scheme."

"Blackmail?" Bobby Lee looked offended. "You got me all wrong, buddy. I just want to make sure your little secret don't get out and spoil this great setup you got goin'. And I think I got just the plan."

"Really? What would that be?"

"You pay me—oh, let's say a hundred grand. That's a nice round number. And I make sure Harry Grisom stays buried forever." Bobby Lee made a floating motion with his hand. "Otherwise, he'll arise just like Lazarus. How's that?"

The guy kept acting contrary to Bobby Lee's expectations. He'd been prepared for shock, outrage, even hostility. But the guy just continued to sit there with a neutral expression on his face, stacking those little square slides like they were chips and not even looking at him. Mr. Cool. Still walking C Unit at Lake Butler in his starched khakis with that haughty air that was supposed to set him apart from the riffraff. Like he was tolerating everybody and wanted you to know it. Shit, if he'd been doing his bit at Raiford instead of a pussy joint like Lake Butler, some buck nigger would've been pimping him off for commissary.

"I don't hear anything, Horance," Bobby Lee said.

"I'm thinking, Mr. Gettis."

"I told you to call me Bobby Lee. My daddy was Mr. Gettis. What's to think about? You want to keep Harry buried, or what?"

"Yes, Bobby Lee. I want to keep him buried. But I see a couple of problems here."

"What kind of problems?"

Horance swiveled his chair around and gazed at the blank screen, showing Bobby Lee his profile. "To begin with, I just don't have that kind of money lying around. Not many people do. And then again, supposing I did have and was of a mind to give it to you. How do I know that would be the end of it? People who engage in this sort of thing usually come back for more, once the initial windfall has been depleted."

Bobby Lee said, "Cut the bullshit, H.G. You don't mind if I call you that, do you? Covers all four names. It's up to you which two you end up havin' to live with. Now I don't see any problems. First, I took a look at that little shop of yours in that swank hotel, and there's enough shit in the window alone to cover fifty times what I'm askin'."

"Synthetics, Bobby Lee. All for show. Surely you don't believe I'd keep that kind of merchandise in a display window. Even at Century Plaza."

The hell he didn't. But it made sense, now that the man had pointed it out.

"What about inside?" Bobby Lee said. "I know you got some good stuff there. Little wax-paper packets with loose stones in 'em? I'll take two or three of those and call it even."

Horance was shaking his head, fingers steepled beneath his chin, still contemplating the slide screen. "I don't work that way. All my designs are originals, one of a kind creations that are drawn to scale and converted into color slides. That's my strong suit, Bobby Lee, my designs, my *creations*. I do with jewelry what Van Gogh did with paint."

Bobby Lee looked at him through squinty eyes and thought, Jesus, this guy is really sold on himself. He said, "What about the stones? Can't make your Van Goghs without them."

"I order them—after the customer tells me what he wants and pays his twenty-percent deposit. When the piece is ready, he pays me the balance and I pay for the stones. The only items of gem quality I keep on hand are a few ten pointers I use for bordering. You can have those if you want. As for cash, I have exactly eighty-two hundred dollars in the bank and about sixty in my pocket."

Horance Griswald swiveled around and faced Bobby Lee, who was sitting motionless in the wing chair with his ankle on his knee and nothing to say for the moment.

"You didn't do your homework, Bobby Lee. Success in the blackmail business depends on knowing how much your victim can pay."

Bobby Lee scratched his cheek and looked around, taking in the rich furnishings and framed painting, the

Certified Gemologist certificate on the wall behind the man's head. "I thought I did," he said. "But let me ask you a question. How the hell can you live like this if you're so fuckin' broke?"

"By making payments, like everybody else. Plus I have a couple investments that pay monthly dividends, and a few good customers I carry on installments." The jeweler shrugged. "I manage."

The grandfather clock began chiming, ten soft bongs that gave Bobby Lee time to consider this turn of events that threatened to send his visions of instant wealth right down the drain like his mason jar of crank. If nothing else, he could take the man's van, which he was pretty sure was a custom job worth twenty-five or thirty grand. Just leave Diane's Gremlin right where it was and head south, along with whatever else of value he could salvage. Check the names on those paintings, see if any were by this guy Van Gogh—put 'em in the van and go to Florida, find out how much they'd bring in Miami.

He said, "So what you're tellin' me, H.G., is you're a millionaire on paper and that's about all."

"Not even that."

"Barely gettin' by, huh?"

"Life's a constant struggle, Bobby Lee."

"Got any stamp or coin collections? Don't lie to me now."

"I haven't got time for them."

"Personal jewelry? Little pinky ring? Maybe a Rolex?"

Horance stripped off his wristwatch and dropped it on the desk. "Fourteen carat Omega," he said, "worth about twelve hundred. No rings."

"Those paintings real?"

"Reproductions. You can have them."

Bobby Lee was feeling this thing slipping away from him. He said, "Got a safe in the house, H.G.?"

"No."

Bingo. Bobby Lee could hear the lie in the man's voice, the quick way he said the single word as he eased the watch a little farther across the desk, concentrating on it.

"Why don't I believe you, H.G.?" Bobby Lee was back in control again, sure of himself. "Why do I get this feelin' you're bein' untruthful with me?"

"Because you want to," Horance said. "You don't want to accept the fact that this goose doesn't lay golden eggs."

"Where is it, H.G.?"

"I told you there isn't any. I don't know what else I can do."

Bobby Lee sighed and leaned forward, reaching behind him to pull out the magnum. He rested it on his lap and said, "Come around here, H.G."

Horance looked at the gun, then at Bobby Lee. "Are you crazy?"

"As a blind squirrel stuck in a drain pipe," Bobby Lee said. "At least that's what I been told. Remember that time in Lake Butler they locked the joint down for three days 'cause some fool in a hood robbed the pharmacist at knife point?"

"That was you?"

"In the flesh. Now is that crazy, or what?" When Horance didn't answer, Bobby Lee said, "Now come on around here. Don't make me ask you again."

Horance got up and walked slowly around the desk, casting a large shadow on the screen as he passed in front of the slide projector.

Bobby Lee said, "Hike yourself up on the edge of the desk there."

"Why?"

"Cause I'm gonna shoot you in the knee, that's why, just to show you how serious I am. You'll pass out, but I'll bring you around. Then I'll ask you again, and if I get the same negative answer, I'm gonna shoot you in the other one. If I get the same answer after I bring you around the second time, then I'll know you're tellin' the truth, at which time I'll apologize and leave. But see, I have to be sure. Now hike up on that desk."

Horance stood there looking at him for a moment, his face a mask, then turned without a word and went back behind the desk. Bobby Lee jumped to his feet and followed, the magnum cocked and extended, saying, "Where you goin'?"

Horance said, "You wanted to see the safe, didn't you? Okay, you're gonna see it. I don't want my kneecaps shot off, and I believe you're just insane enough to do it."

While Bobby Lee watched, Horance knelt down and rolled his banker's chair out of the way, slid the plastic carpet protector to one side and lifted up a foot-square section of the cream-colored carpet. Underneath was a circular safe embedded in concrete, the dial and face plate recessed to fit flush with the floor. Horance worked the dial and swung the lid open, started to reach inside.

Bobby Lee said, "Get your hand outta there."

"I'm getting your money. One hundred thousand dollars, that's what you asked for."

"I'll do that. You just go sit in your chair."

Horance moved to the chair. Bobby Lee squatted beside the hole, the magnum pointed at the jeweler's chest, and reached cautiously into the cylinder. He began pulling out crisp stacks of bills wrapped with rubber bands—tightly bound packets of twenties, fifties, and hundreds. Thirty-five packets in all, each with a slip of paper tucked under the rubber band bearing the amount.

"Jesus Christ in a boxcar," Bobby Lee said, awed. "How much you got here?"

"Four hundred and twenty thousand dollars," Horance said. "Take five stacks of those hundreds and you're paid in full."

"Man, I never saw so much fuckin' money in my life. Buddy, Harry Grisom is now officially *dead.*"

"One hundred thousand, Bobby Lee. That was the asking price." A thin bead of perspiration had formed on the jeweler's forehead.

"Yeah, but that was when it was blackmail," Bobby Lee said. "Now we're talkin' armed robbery, somethin' I know a little bit about."

"I thought you were an honorable person, Bobby Lee. That's all the money I have in the world."

"Don't talk to me about honorable. You're the one tried to fuck me, sayin' you didn't have a safe."

Bobby Lee stood and faced the jeweler, who looked up at him in calm resignation. The sweat beads on his forehead had grown heavy and were now trickling a wet path toward his bushy eyebrows.

"Turn your chair around, H.G."

Horance hesitated, trying to swallow, then slowly swiveled around and faced the opposite wall. He picked out a genuine Vega seascape, focused on it and said, "Just make it quick, will you?"

Bobby Lee raised the magnum, admiring the man's courage—then paused as he suddenly thought about Diane, who knew all about Horance Griswald. Wait a minute, he thought. Take out the jeweler and he had to take her out too, 'cause she was *really* gonna be pissed when he split this time. And if she went, the kid went with her. He could live with that, but why bring all the heat? What was Harry boy gonna do, go to the police and tell 'em some guy he'd done time with hit him for four hundred and twenty thousand untaxed dollars?

For the first time in eleven years Bobby Lee ignored his philosophy, stepped forward and smacked Horance Griswald a roundhouse blow just above the right ear with the heavy magnum, then hit him again when the jeweler, more surprised than injured, screamed and tried to roll out of the chair. Bobby Lee came after him in a frenzy pumped with rage, said, "You fuck!" and hit him three more times before Horance finally slumped motionless to the floor.

Bobby Lee stood over him, breathing heavy, and nudged him with his foot. Satisfied the man was out, he tucked the magnum in his waistband, smoothed his hair into place, and looked around for something to put the money in. There was an open briefcase next to the telephone on a mahogany table across the room. Bobby Lee went to it, dumped paper, slides, an appointment book and a set of keys onto the floor, came back and loaded the money. He closed the briefcase, stood up again and looked at Horance Griswald sprawled on his face by the banker's chair.

Then he got out of there, hopped into Diane's Gremlin and left a trail of black rubber ten feet long as he peeled away, the magnum on the seat and the briefcase on his lap, refusing to part with his treasure even for a second.

Four hundred and twenty thousand dollars, almost half a fucking millionaire. Bobby Lee could hardly believe it, and he kept a death grip on the briefcase as he drove with one hand, thinking first thing he was gonna do was get the fuck away from that cow Diane, with her water-balloon tits and Jell-O ass, wasn't even going *back* there. Let's see, what could he do? The airport was out. He'd heard about that Pan Am plane got blown out of the sky over Scotland. Scratch that. And forget about a bus, shit, he'd never be able to close his eyes. And he didn't know about trains, having never been in a station before in his life but figuring they were at least as bad as bus terminals— fags and rip-off artists lurking in the johns, cruising the lobbies. And it was too late to buy a car.

Bobby Lee went into a mild panic, wondering how the hell it could be so hard getting out of a town the size of L.A. with a briefcase full of money when nobody was looking for you. Unless he just kept going in Diane's Gremlin, and he didn't want to do that— then he remembered, hell, he didn't even have a driver's license yet, why did he keep taking all these chances driving cars? Being half a millionaire was fucking his mind up. It was amazing how wealth could change your perspective on life.

By the time he reached Westwood he had it all worked out. He'd spend the night in some middle-class motel, one that advertised X-rated movies and beds that took quarters. Dump the Gremlin a couple blocks away. In the morning call one of those limo companies and hire a long Lincoln to take him to Vegas. Buy him a wardrobe, hit a few crap tables, rent a couple of chorus girls who weighed less than he did. Then charter one of those Lear jets to take him to Hawaii, put it on like he was a major winner. Buy a condo on one of the smaller islands, shack up with a hula dancer and go to luaus.

Yeah, that would work. Just thinking about it got

him all excited again, picturing himself lying under a coconut tree in a wide hat sipping drinks with umbrellas in them. He was not even aware the speedometer needle was creeping up on fifty and that he was now in a thirty-five-mile zone on west Wilshire. He needed to look at the money one more time, reassure himself it was actually there and he hadn't lost his mind from wishful thinking. He fumbled with the briefcase latches, realized he had it upside down, pulled it up to his chest so he could flip it over—

And then everything went crazy.

Sixty-seven-year-old Bernice Wilkens saw the whole thing while she was trying to figure out a way to get into the Goodwill Industries collection box on the corner of Wilshire and Vaughn. Bernice needed a good heavy sweater, something she didn't have in her rusty Big Star shopping cart, to fight off the chilly nights that would be arriving in another month or two. She wanted to start her search now while it was still hot enough for sweaters to be high on the discard list.

Bernice was a bag lady, and five years ago had become famous for exactly two days when she was savagely beaten by a gang of teenage boys who had nothing better to do. The incident had been played up by the local media and generated a storm of protest and outrage from the citizens of Los Angeles and surrounding areas, who flooded her with checks and get-well cards and deliveries from FTD. The hospital and doctors treated her free of charge, and a local dentist had removed the few decaying teeth that hadn't been knocked out, and replaced them with a first-rate set of dentures, also free of charge. Bernice had given most of the nearly three thousand dollars in donations she had received to her married son in

Alhambra and went back to the streets, and within two weeks her name had been forgotten.

During the intervening five years Bernice had been beaten up, kicked around, spat on, sideswiped by a city bus, robbed of seven shopping carts, and had her dentures stolen. But she continued trudging the streets and alleys of L.A. behind her shopping cart, never crying or complaining, accepting such fare as part of the hazards that went with life in the big city . . . and she got to see such interesting things. . . .

Like tonight, standing there at eleven-thirty minding her own business, except for scheming on how to get into the Goodwill collection box—here comes this sky-blue funny-looking little car heading east on Wilshire, going *much* too fast for that particular stretch. The traffic light was just winking from yellow to red, and if the idiot driver was looking, he just had to see it. But he sure did miss it somehow, kept right on coming just as a Domino Pizza van waiting for the green pulled into the intersection. The blue car clipped the front end of the van a good one, skewed sideways, reared up on two wheels and skidded all the way across the westbound lanes before it rolled twice, landed right-side up on the sidewalk not fifty feet from where Bernice was standing, and slammed sideways right through the plate-glass window of the Baskin-Robbins ice cream parlor, which, thank the good Lord, was closed. Bernice stood there for a full minute or so, working her gums and watching people jump out of vehicles and run to where the little funny-looking blue car was now resting half in, half out of Baskin-Robbins.

Bernice figured she never would get into the Goodwill box now, if she could have in the first place, so she eased her cart to the edge of the curb, wanting to cross to the other side of Wilshire and away from all the commotion. She leaned out and looked up the street, making sure some other maniac wasn't set on running a body over, and her trained eye fell on something lying in the gutter only a few feet away. She shuffled over, bent down and picked it up. It was a gun, a big one. She held it up with both hands and looked into the barrel, then at the cylinders with the round hunks of lead looking back at her, and she knew it was ready to take care of business. She shuffled back to her cart and stuck it under her old army blanket, thinking the next meanie who decided to have a little fun with her was due for a rude awakening. Bernice Wilkens looked around one more time, making sure she didn't miss anything, and there, lying against the back side of the Goodwill Industries collection box, she saw a briefcase.

Chapter
—7—

The reflection in the bathroom mirror showed minimal damage. A little swelling and discoloration around the right temple was the only visible evidence of last night's attack, and that could be covered easily enough with a small amount of pancake. Most of his pain was from the wounds hidden beneath his tight curly hair—two lumps the size of fried egg yolks, one with a gash deep enough to probably require stitches and which had taken forever to stop bleeding.

But nothing compared to the pain inside, knowing he'd been hit for four hundred thousand dollars. And by a swamp runner at that, and not a goddamn thing he could do about it, because he knew the crazy bastard would have blown his kneecaps right off without even giving it a second thought.

Horance Griswald stared at his mirrored eyes and wondered why Bobby Lee didn't kill him. He had thought he was dead, looking into the muzzle of that .357 in a near hypnotic state, the way he had turned his chair around without even being aware of it. He had literally *felt* his body systems going into shutdown mode, controlled by some internal doomsday computer inside the brain that probably kicked in when it was absolutely certain the end had come. But Bobby

Lee didn't kill him, and Horance could see only one reason for that. The son of a bitch would be back for more. Horance remembered him now, thinking back to Lake Butler, and recalled a skinny speed freak who would come back from the visiting room about twice a month with a condom filled with methamphetamine stuck up his ass, him and his little loudmouth buddies running around wired to the gills. Four hundred and twenty grand wouldn't last that guy six months. Then he'd make another trip to the money pit.

Horance took a bottle of Motrin from the medicine cabinet, washed down three tablets with tap water, and went into the kitchen. A blond cocker spaniel was lying in front of the door leading to the backyard. He jumped up whining, wagging his stump tail, and Horance let him out. Then he filled the Mr. Coffee machine and wandered into the den, deep in thought. He settled himself on the couch and used the remote to click the TV on. Jane Pauley was interviewing Dan Quayle, asking how he thought his selection as George Bush's running mate would help George capture the White House.

About as much as it would help him get back his four hundred and twenty grand, Horance thought, and checked his watch. Seven-fifteen. That would make it ten-fifteen in New York. He could probably catch Maury Bingham about now. Horance winced, not in pain, but dreading the idea of having to call Maury for a favor and leaving himself vulnerable. But there was no getting around it now. Not with eighty-two hundred bucks in the bank.

Horance drew a deep breath and reached for the cordless phone on the end table. He dialed the number while he watched Willard Scott wishing Anna Marie somebody a happy one hundredth birthday.

Maury came on the line and Horance said, "Maury? How's it going?"

Maury said, "I got one question to ask you. You just get up, or just going to bed?"

"I haven't decided yet."

"Yeah, California'll do that to you. There's something unnatural about a state that lets you choose between snow skiing and suntanning in the same day. No wonder you're confused. What can I do for you to help straighten you out?"

"I got a problem, Maury."

"Not knowing if you're getting up or going to bed, I agree with you."

"I'm serious. I got hit."

"Hit? What do you mean, hit?"

"I mean hit, ripped off—robbed, Maury, I got robbed. Last night. Some hophead came busting in waving a gun, threatened to shoot me if I didn't show him a safe, and I fucking believed him."

Silence. Then Maury said, "How much he get?"

"Everything I had," Horance said. "Four hundred and twenty miles of railroad."

"Holy shit. Goddamn it, Horance, can't you use a bank? They only got about five thousand of 'em out there."

"You know why not, Maury, I'm surprised you even asked."

"I meant safety deposit boxes."

"Same principal. Too easy to seize."

Another silence.

Maury said, "Think this has anything to do with our recent transaction?"

"No. Like I said, he was some weirded-out junkie with a habit to supply and got lucky. A one-in-a-million shot, Maury, something you never expect."

Horance couldn't tell him the real story. Not if he wanted to stay in business. And he had to stay in business now more than ever.

Maury said, "The fucking guy faked you out, Horance. I can't believe you did that, just handed out that many miles 'cause a guy *asks* you if you got a safe. Shit, tell him no and throw him your wallet. Guy ain't gonna shoot you 'cause you don't have a *safe.*"

Horance closed his eyes and gripped the phone, trying to be patient and ignore his head, which was throbbing again.

"Maury, you weren't here, okay? The guy told me to sit on my desk and stretch out my leg, so he could get a good bead on my knee. Like he was making conversation. Said after he shot the first one off he was going to bring me around and do the other one, if I still didn't show him a safe. And Maury, he *meant* it, the goddamn guy was crazy. And I'll tell you something else. You'd have done the same thing. Jesus Christ, you think I *enjoyed* instant bankruptcy?"

Maury said, "All right, shit, I believe you. But you got to admit this is bizarre. What the fuck you gonna do now?"

Horance took another breath and said, "I need a little advance, Maury. On account. I got some major bills need to be paid the next week or so and barely enough to cover them." He paused, then added, "Ten would do it."

Another silence, Horance listening to faint static coming through the receiver.

Maury said, "On account, huh? How long?"

"Four to six weeks, that's all."

"A lot can happen in four to six weeks, Horance."

"You know I'm good for it."

" 'Course you are, no question. I'm just saying a lot

can happen. This speculation carries a certain amount of risk."

"Well how long would you suggest?"

"Ten days—tops."

Horance said, "Ten *days?* Maury, we just did a deal last week. Ten days is too soon. Talk about risk. Somebody's going to start putting things together."

Maury said, "Look, buddy, I like you, and we've made some money together. And we're gonna make more. But business is business, and I can't afford to keep principal on the street that long without something coming back. I mean, I got obligations too, people who need their shit quick or they go somewhere else." He said, "Now I'm willing to make an exception for you, Horance, because, like I said, I like you. And I don't do this for nobody else. But I got to have a return in ten days, that's my limit. It's up to you."

Horance sat there a moment, rubbed his forehead, gazed at a Tide commercial on the TV, then said, "All right, Maury. Ten days."

"You got something special in mind?"

"Yeah. My end should go twenty-five or thirty miles easy."

"Then you get the difference right away and you're back on your feet again."

Horance said, "When can I get the ten?"

"Same as usual. I'll express it to you this afternoon, you'll have it tomorrow."

"All right, Maury, thanks. I'll be calling you."

"I'll be waiting—oh, and Horance?"

"Yeah?"

"Forget the safe, huh?"

Horance hung up, leaned his head gingerly against the sofa back, then got up and went into the kitchen.

The coffee was ready. He poured a cup and stood beside the big chopping-block counter in the middle of the floor, sipping and thinking.

Ten days. That was really pushing it. Maury was getting greedier than a pawn-shop owner, and Horance wouldn't even consider less than three months between jobs under normal circumstances. He was already stretching things to begin with, seven jobs in the last twenty-three months, and sooner or later some bright cop with imagination was going to sit up and say, *Wait* a minute here . . .

And then along comes Bobby Lee Gettis, a bad dream with a big gun, a fragment of a past Horance had all but forgotten, and suddenly everything goes haywire. Two, maybe three more moves, and he was going to hang it up with Maury Bingham, play it straight the rest of the way. He was good enough to go right to the top—hell, he was the best and already starting to get a name. Maybe he could still do it, if he chose his targets carefully, he could get by with less than four hundred and—

God*damn* that motherfucker!

He took his coffee into the den, sat back on the couch and stared at the TV. The five-minute local news break was on, the smooth male commentator saying something about several crack houses being raided overnight in the Silver Lake area. There was a shot of two black guys without shirts lying facedown on the sidewalk, getting cuffed by what appeared to be about a dozen cops in dark jackets with LAPD stenciled in orange across the back.

He was forty-three years old—too old for this extracurricular activity that pickled the stomach lining and turned the nervous system to jelly. It had been fine when he was younger, even fun, and it had got him his start in the jewelry business. But with age comes caution, and that line of work required a certain youthful recklessness to cope with the stress. His hands still had it though, the artist on his mother's side coming out in him. He could compromise any alarm system on the market, including the lasers, and he had a thirty-thousand-dollar digital sequence counter that could give him the combination of the average safe within six minutes on a standard dial. That little baby was so sensitive it could detect the most silent of tumblers.

But it was time to get out, concentrate his talents solely on what had been his one true passion for eighteen years—working with the stones, clothing them in designer patterns that would make them twinkle and wink in silent appreciation.

The TV was showing a scene of an automobile accident now, a blue Gremlin sitting sideways in the window of a Baskin-Robbins, glass all over the place. Two medics were wheeling somebody to a waiting ambulance while a crowd stood around rubbernecking, tiptoeing to get better views, the commentator's voice-over saying that the owner of the vehicle had identified the driver as—

"Bobby Lee Gettis, a native of Florida . . ."

Horance leaned forward, glaring at the picture.

". . . who suffered a broken back and undisclosed head injuries in the accident. He was taken to Wilshire Memorial Hospital, where doctors list his condition as stable. The driver of the pizza van was treated at the scene and released. Police say that the driver of the car will be cited for careless and reckless—"

Horance clicked the TV off and eased back on the couch. He toyed with the remote, eyes fixed on the fading pinpoint of light in the middle of the screen. Seeing his own picture now: Bobby Lee tearing up Wilshire Boulevard, trying to count the money and ending up in the window of a Thirty-One Flavors. He bet anything that's how it happened. The bastard had taken his briefcase—Jesus Christ, with his goddamn initials and fingerprints on it!

He sat up and groaned, then held his head in his hands and wondered what Bobby Lee would say when the police came to his hospital room with a briefcase that had H.G. on it and over four hundred grand inside. "Excuse us, Mr. Gettis, we were just curious what a guy fresh out of Walla Walla was doing with this. And the initials don't seem to match either. Think you could clear that up for us?"

What would Gettis tell them?

Chapter

—8—

Cage was at his desk talking on the phone to Michael Grady, who was telling him how tickled he was with his new security system.

"I'm actually having fun with this little number," Grady was saying. "Hell, I wish I'd called sooner."

Cage said, "Always a pleasure to hear from a satisfied client."

"Yeah, it's great. I've made some money on it."

"How'd you do that?"

Grady chuckled. "You gotta hear this, you'll love it. Last night we had a few friends over, right? One of 'em is David Freemont, who did the screenplay on *Angel Wars*. Now David's a real mysticism freak. Thinks spirits are everywhere, always trying to commune with us. So I give Marilee a wink and say, 'Hey, David, did I tell you I got my own personal spirit right here in the house?' He looks at me real serious through his moon glasses that make him look like an owl and says, 'No, Michael, I don't believe you did.' I say, 'Yeah, he sends me telepathic messages the minute anybody comes in the house and I'm not here."

Cage grinned at the phone, having a pretty good idea what was coming.

"So David studies a minute, then says, 'Michael,

that doesn't sound like an endeavor a true spirit would engage in. I believe you're pulling my leg here.' So I say, 'Okay, I'll prove it to you. I'll run everybody outside, drive up the road a ways and park, and then you pick a time to go in. I'll know the exact minute you do.'"

Cage said, "And of course he didn't know 'bout the oscillators."

"Hell no! Anyway, to make a long story short, I told him to put twenty bucks on it just to make it interesting. Then we synchronized watches, I hopped in the car and drove up to that water treatment plant at the top of the hill, and sat there smiling at my beeper. He had me going for a while though, 'cause the bastard kept me waiting eighteen minutes."

"So it worked all right, huh?"

"Like a charm. David spent the rest of the night sneaking around the house, peeking under beds and shit, like he was expecting something to jump out at him. Guy's a little weird, but he's a hell of a screenwriter. Marilee kept giggling into her hand, and anything that makes her laugh always makes me feel good. Spending your life on braces and crutches isn't any laughing matter, I'll tell you that."

"No," Cage said, "I'm sure it isn't." He watched Paul come in from his workshop and go to his desk, folding a stick of Juicy Fruit in his mouth and dropping the wrapping on Olive Oyl's head as he passed. She shook it off without missing a beat on her computer and made a rude sound at his retreating back. Cage said, "How's she doing otherwise?"

"Not bad. Thanks for asking. Anyway, the main reason I called, do I have to charge the batteries or anything? I don't recall you or your boss saying anything about it."

"No. They're wired into your electrical system and stay charged automatically. The only time they come into play anyway is if the power goes out. Then they trip and activate the signal."

Grady said, "Good enough, I was just checking. You guys did a good job, by the way."

Cage said, "Thanks. Maybe you can pass the word. I'm sure Paul would appreciate it."

Paul steepled his hands and lifted his eyes to the ceiling, mouthing a silent please.

"I'll do that," Grady said. "Hell, I might even tell David, before he starts wanting to come over and hold séances. Meanwhile, keep in mind what I said about film rights to your story. I see real possibilities there."

"I'll let you know," Cage said. "Give my best to your wife."

"Will do. Let's keep in touch. Itchy-gay."

Cage said, "Excuse me?"

"I said, itchy-gay. Oh, that's right, you're one of those uncultured gnomes who didn't see *Angel Wars,* aren't you? Lel, the archangel of soul death who led the heavenly revolt, would use that phrase before going into battle. Loosely translated it means, 'Now I must be about my work.' I drive Marilee nuts, I use it so often. In other words, good-bye."

Cage smiled, said "Itchy-gay," and hung up.

Brenda stopped typing and looked over at Paul. "Is it my imagination," she said, "or have you noticed there's been an awful lot of sucking up going on around here lately to a certain award-winning director?"

Paul said, "Very perceptive, Olive Oyl. I was noticing the same thing. Some people'll do anything to get in the movies."

"You guys are just jealous you don't have what it takes," Cage said. "The man's an expert, he recognizes potential when he sees it. He'll probably ask me to star in his sequel."

"Yeah," Paul said, "as the devil. You're perfect for the part. All anybody has to do is take a look outside to see that." He eased his chair close to the window and peered through the blind. He said, "There's Larry. Shit, what's he doing?"

Cage and Brenda come over for a look. Larry was on the sidewalk talking quietly to the large, bearded leader of the protest group still pacing to and fro in front of the office. Larry even had an arm around the guy's shoulders, standing apart from the rest of the group, speaking earnestly into his ear.

Paul said, "I don't believe it. I told him to ignore them, leave 'em alone. Here he is, out there acting like he's happy to see 'em."

"Maybe he's offering Allen as a sacrifice," Brenda said.

"That's a thought," Paul said. "We're about to find out, here he comes."

When Larry came in they were all sitting down, gazing at him expectantly. He said, "Hi, gang," and kept right on going through the curtained doorway into the little kitchenette. In a moment he was back, popping the tab on a Diet Coke. He stopped, took a deep gulp, and then looked at them watching him in silence. He spread his arms and said, "What?"

Paul said, "That's my question. What were you doing out there hugging Moses? You two guys going bowling tonight?"

Larry went to his desk and sat down. He sighed and said, "Did it ever occur to you people there was something a little odd about that protest group out there?"

Cage said, "I never paid that close attention, you want to know the truth."

"What do you mean?" Paul asked.

"I mean," Larry said, "this is the third day they've been here now, and it's always been the same people. Two men, four women, and two kids. Eight altogether. What legitimate organization only sends out eight pickets, and two of them children? And remember, they show up here each morning in a minibus, so it *is* organized."

Cage said, "You mean somebody's paying them?"

"Yep."

Paul unwrapped another Juicy Fruit. "Who?" he asked.

"Howie Wallmeyer," Larry said.

Paul froze with the gum halfway to his mouth. "You sure?"

"Absolutely. When the bus picked them up here yesterday, I followed it. First it went to the Spring Street Mission downtown. Everybody got out except the big guy with the beard, and he went on to an apartment building on Medford, number 47. Name's Rudy Hicks, and he used to work for Howie up till about a year ago, when he retired for health reasons. Had open heart surgery and never bounced back all the way."

Paul said, "So he walks up and down carrying a sign all day and that's good for his heart?"

"It was only gonna be for about a week anyway. Howie was hoping the media would get interested and put it on the news, and I guess we're lucky there. Not a big enough crowd."

Cage said, "How'd you find this out?"

"I had his M.U.D. units pulled at the phone company," Larry said, and grinned. "Being an ex-Bureau agent is sort of like that American Express commercial—membership has its privileges. Old Rudy, the first thing he did when he got home the last two days was call Howie Wallmeyer."

Paul, working on his gum, said, "That sonofabitch. Larry, you sure that's what he was calling about? I mean, it couldn't have been just to pass the time a day with an old coworker or something?"

"Of course I am," Larry said, "I asked him."

"You *asked* him?"

"Yeah. Just now, outside. In a roundabout way, not that there was any doubt about it to begin with. I just walked up to him and said, 'Hey, Rudy? Howie just called me at home a little while ago and we've reached an understanding. He said to tell you to take the people back to the mission and call him when you get home, he'll explain it to you.'"

"What did he say to that?" Paul asked.

"Wanted to know if he could use our phone to call the bus."

"Sonofa*bitch*!" Paul said again, pushed his 260-pound bulk out of his chair, and nearly ripped the cord off the blinds jerking them open. He swung his head left and right, but the demonstrators were gone. "Where'd they go?"

"Will you relax?" Larry said. "I told him not to push his luck, use the phone down the street."

Paul stood there a moment, hitching at his trousers, then turned and stalked toward the back of the room. "The hell with it," he said, "I got things to do. I'll have a little talk with Howie later."

Brenda watched him disappear through the curtain before saying, "Would somebody please tell me who Howie Wallmeyer is?"

Larry dropped his empty can in his wastebasket and took out a handkerchief, began wiping his hands. He said, "Howie owns a middle-brow security firm called First Alert, deals mostly in the Hollywood and Valley areas. Just before you came here, Paul underbid him on installing a microwave system in Sergeant's Army and Navy Supply Center over on Western. It was a good contract, and Howie hated to lose it. He called a couple days later, after he'd had time to stew a bit, and got Cage here. You remember that?"

Cage said, "I remember. Started screaming about how we were going way below industry standards, undermining established costs. Hell, I wasn't even sure what they were. He kept on, not letting me get a word in edgewise. I finally told him to get lost and hung up."

"What he told Paul you said," Larry reminded him, "was to go sit on a fire hydrant and sink slowly to the ground."

Brenda let out a phony gasp and touched her throat. "Allen Cage, you *didn't*."

"You bet I did, but only after he called me a—well, it doesn't matter now." He looked at Larry. "You think he's the one who called the newspaper?"

"Wouldn't be surprised. But it backfired on him. Look at all these consultation requests. We haven't had this many calls in the last two weeks." He glanced at his watch and said, "Which reminds me, we have an appointment in Culver City. Come on, you can use the front door for a change."

Cage followed Larry to the door, then turned and came back to Brenda's desk. He said, "Do me a favor, will you, Olive Oyl? When you call Caprita to give her your report, tell her I didn't get in trouble after all. I mean, I wouldn't want to break precedent and tell her myself."

Brenda, typing again, said, "Anything else?"

"Yeah. Tell her I'll be a little late."

The man in the light gray suit parked his black Thunderbird on the second level of the LaBrea Towers garage and got out. He was careful to make certain the doors were locked and the alarm on, wanting to protect his expensive Pioneer quadriphonic stereo and tape deck, then took the elevator to the lobby. He said hi to the middle-aged doorman at his stand next to the double-wide, glass-fronted lobby doors and continued on across the gold shag carpeting, turning left into an adjoining alcove where a bank of mailboxes took up one complete section of wall. He opened the one numbered 1402 and removed a small stack of letters, then went to the far side of the lobby and pushed the elevator call button. He shuffled through his mail, mostly bills and credit card statements, while he waited. When the elevator arrived, he stepped inside and pushed 14—then frowned as a figure slipped in between the doors just as they were closing.

Cage said, "Mind if I ride up with you, Howie?"

Howie Wallmeyer said, "You know somebody lives in this building, Cage? 'Cause if you don't, I suggest you get the fuck out, this is a class joint."

"Recognize me, huh, Howie? Must have been reading the paper. Since you know so much about me, I thought it was time we got acquainted."

"If you came here to irritate me, you picked the wrong day. I'm not in the mood."

Cage looked at him, standing there with his arms folded and head tilted back, watching the floor numbers light up and trying to act cool-tough. The top three buttons of his herringbone cotton shirt were open, showing a single gold chain around his neck and an overabundance of curly, black chest hair.

"Heard from your man yet, Howie? What's his name—Rudy Hicks?"

"Yeah, I heard from him. He's as big an idiot as you are, maybe bigger. So don't try to impress me how slick you are."

"Oh, I'm not slick. Your man's just real talkative, that's all." Then Cage decided to try a shot in the dark, figuring what the hell, it worked for Larry. "Your little tip to the press didn't pan out the way you thought either. Business has really picked up, so I guess I should thank you."

Howie shrugged, watching the ninth floor light up. "People got a right to know who you are."

Cage sighed. "Yeah, I thought so," he said, and pulled the emergency stop knob. The car came to a halt with a small shudder.

Howie said, "Hey, what the fuck do you think you're doing?" He made a move for the control panel, but Cage blocked his path.

"This won't take long, Howie. I just think we need a little privacy."

"Privacy for what? What are you gonna do, threaten me? Don't even try it, pal, don't even think about it. I'll have your ass back in the joint so fast you won't even have time to make a call."

"I'm not gonna threaten you, Howie. I'm just gonna give you a choice."

"What kind a choice?"

"Either you call Paul Banes first thing in the morning and apologize for all the grief you caused him and promise you'll never do it again, or we settle our differences here and now. Either way, it'll only take a minute."

Howie gave a short laugh. "If you think I'm saying sorry to Paul Banes for *any*thing, you're crazy. And as for settling our differences, let me remind you you're on parole."

"Unconditional parole. I can't be violated unless I engage in any unlawful conduct."

"What do you call assault?"

"Who's gonna say I assaulted anyone?"

"Man, *I* am, you pull some shit like that."

Cage was shaking his head. "Won't work, Howie. See, you've already destroyed your credibility— calling the newspaper about me, hiring the homeless to conduct demonstrations outside our office, pretending they're an offended religious group. It would take a lawyer about five minutes to convince a jury you're out to get me. Meanwhile I'm sitting there with a who-me expression on my face and denying the whole thing."

Howie was looking more serious now, tapping his letters against his leg while he played the scene in his mind, knowing Cage was right but still not willing to back down.

"You can do what you want," he said, "but I'm not apologizing to Paul Banes or anybody else. And before you step off into something we both might regret later, I better warn you I got a black belt in—"

Cage hit him, a straight shot that traveled about two feet and landed just below Howie's third open button and sent the remaining air in his lungs exploding past his lips with a soft whoosh. Howie dropped his letters and pressed both hands to his solar plexus, face drained and mouth shaped in a small o, and sank slowly to his knees.

"In karate," Cage said. "Yeah, I know." He moved in behind Howie, lifting him beneath the armpits until he was nearly standing again, then let go and delivered a hard blow to Howie's right kidney. Howie twisted as he went down this time, holding himself front and back and still struggling for breath, and finally drew himself into a ball in one corner, his face pushed against the walnut paneling.

"That's what the Bureau of Prisons teaches their rookie guards at Glynco, Georgia, Howie," Cage said. "Only they use clubs. Doesn't leave anything a con can show in court when he alleges his constitutional rights were violated. A lot quicker to learn than karate."

Cage knelt and picked up the scattered letters, stuck them in Howie's jacket pocket, then helped the man to his feet. All the fight had gone out of Howie, and he sagged against the elevator wall, gasping and trying not to throw up.

Cage said, "Far as I'm concerned, we're square now. But I'm asking you not to play any more games, okay? Pretend you never heard of Banes and Twiford. Fair enough?"

Howie managed to get hold of the brass handrail and pulled himself to his feet. "You bastard."

"You're entitled to your opinion," Cage said. "Just as long as you keep it out of the paper."

Cage reset the emergency stop, and they rode the rest of the way to fourteen in silence. When the doors opened, Howie got off, moving slow, bent over and listing to starboard. He turned and looked at Cage.

"You'll pay for that, mister," he said. "Just wait. You caught me when I wasn't ready."

Cage lifted his hands in a shrug. "It was the only way I could do it, Howie. What the hell, you know karate."

Then the doors closed and Cage didn't have to look at him anymore.

Chapter
—9—

He was floating again, creeping in and out of weird dreams, and Bobby Lee knew the Demerol was starting to take control. Demerol did that to him, almost made him feel like he was having one of those out-of-body experiences some people claimed to have when they were near death or exceptionally stoned— hovering above the hospital bed looking down at his shell encased in a body cast, an IV dripping in one arm and a catheter running from his dick to the catch bottle on the floor. He could even see the old man on the other side of the curtain, lying there on his back with his mouth open, tripping out on a higher dope cloud than even Bobby Lee because of the liver cancer that was eating him up.

Then suddenly he'd be back inside his body again, aware of the cast and the numbness in his legs and pelvic region, but not really giving a shit. He could see the events of the day flashing against the back of his eyelids like strobe lights—Diane visiting him, sitting beside the bed honking into a fistful of Kleenex, then tugging them to shreds while she wailed about the possibility of him never walking again and her not having any insurance on her fucking car all in the same breath. He could still hear her telling him, "*What* briefcase, Bobby Lee? *What* gun? God, I didn't know you had a *gun*. You're not making any sense. You need a shot or something? Want me to get the nurse?"

And he knew she'd been telling the truth, that she didn't know the first thing about any briefcase with four hundred and twenty thousand goddamn dollars in it, and didn't have a clue about a .357 Colt Python whose serial numbers could be traced directly to a gun shop in Seattle and two dead bodies with slugs that would match it perfectly.

That was the part that kept dunking him in those weird dreams—that missing gun. Diane had told him she'd gone all over the car now junked in the yard at Dunbar Towing Service, but she was probably more concerned about her Gremlin than she was with him. And she hadn't found anything except six hundred dollars jammed between the seats, which she thought must be the money he'd collected from Mr. Griswald. Bobby Lee was having realistic hallucinations that his bed was surrounded by stony-faced cops who wanted to know about the magnum, holding it out to him in a plastic evidence bag and telling him this was it, this time he'd bought the big one, murder one. He could feel the cuffs being snapped around his wrists, securing him to the bed rail, making certain he didn't go anywhere even if he did have a broken back and a damaged spinal cord that might keep him in a wheelchair the rest of his life. Bobby Lee felt a touch of panic, it was so real, and he tried to free himself but couldn't. The cops had their faces right next to his now, still throwing questions at him, not letting up one bit.

"Where's my money, Bobby Lee?"

See? Too fucking real! When this shot wore off he for sure wasn't taking another one, that was it for the Demerol.

"You awake, Bobby Lee? Hey, wake up."

This voice was soft, insistent, demanding. And it was more than just a product of his drugged imagination.

Bobby Lee opened his eyes and saw a shadow bending over him, the figure outlined in the faint light coming through the partly open bathroom door. At first he thought it was that cute nurse with the funny name come to give him another shot. But no, this was a man, he could tell. Wearing some kind of long coat and a duckbill cap, of all things.

The man said, "I see your eyes open. I asked you where my money was."

Bobby Lee said, "Horance? That you?" Shit, he had to be hallucinating. He tried to reach out and touch him, reassure himself this wasn't real, but he couldn't move his arm—couldn't move *either* arm.

"No use, Bobby Lee. I tied your wrists to the side rails."

This was real all right, and Bobby Lee felt the panic coming back. He said, "What the fuck did you—" and tasted rubber as a surgical gloved hand clamped over his mouth.

"Not so loud," Horance said. "We wouldn't want to disturb anybody, would we? Now I'm going to take my hand away, and you're going to answer my questions quietly. Where's my money?"

The hand came away, and Bobby Lee moistened his lips with a tongue that was nearly dry from fear. He said, "I don't know, I don't have it."

"Who does, the police?"

"I don't know, honest to God."

"Have they talked to you yet?"

"The police? Fuck no, but I been expectin' 'em. I don't know where that gun is either, and believe me I'd sure like to. If the cops have it, I'm dead."

Horance was silent, letting that one sink in, and Bobby Lee seized the moment to plead for understanding. He had a bad feeling about his hands being tied to the bed like this.

"Look, Horance," he said, "about what happened—"

"You took my money, Bobby Lee."

"I know, Horance, and I'm real sorry about that—"

"You pistol-whipped me, split my head open."

Bobby Lee said, "Man, I could have killed you, but I didn't, did I? I just saw an opportunity to get me a stake after more'n three years in the joint, and you know how that is. Wasn't nothin' personal. In fact, I really hated to do it, I swear I did, 'cause I remember you was a solid guy in Lake Butler and all right with me. I had to think long and hard about it, Horance, I really did, but you know how your head can get all fucked up when you first come out, your thinkin' all warped and twisted—"

"Bobby Lee, just shut up."

"Okay, man, I'm shuttin' up, didn't mean to make you mad."

"It's a little late to worry about that, isn't it?"

Bobby Lee forced a laugh. "Yeah, you got a point there." But the man's calm tone was what really worried him, the way he was moving his hand around inside that coat pocket, and Bobby Lee tried a different tack. He said, "But hey, you know what? That nurse is due in here any time now to give me another shot, and we'll both catch hell if she catches you here like this."

"You had a shot twenty minutes ago, Bobby Lee, at 3:05. You don't get another one for four hours."

"How you know that?"

"It's marked on the chart hanging on the foot of your bed."

"Oh . . . yeah, but they got an old guy on the other side of that curtain they're always checking on 'cause he's got bad cancer and subject to die any time."

"He's on a monitor, Bobby Lee. Now close your mouth."

"What's that in your hand?" Bobby Lee's voice was rising again.

"Relax, it's only a piece of tape. I can't have you screaming your head off before I can get out of the hospital."

That made sense. Bobby Lee said, "Sure, Horance, go ahead. Put it on good and tight, I want you to feel comfortable."

Horance placed a two-inch-wide strip of duct tape across Bobby Lee's mouth, smoothing it down nice and firm, then took a small vial from his coat pocket. He said, "This is cocaine, which I'm sure you're familiar with. It's amazing how easy it is to get this stuff. Now I want you to take a couple of good snorts."

Bobby Lee was shaking his head, eyes wide, thinking he'd made a mistake not trying to yell when he had half a chance. But Horance grabbed him by the hair, jerked his head back and shook a good amount into each nostril. Then he pressed the vial against the fingers of Bobby Lee's right hand and placed the glass container on the nightstand.

"That's all right, Bobby Lee," Horance said.

"Didn't that much get in, so it's not going to kill you."
He reached into his pocket again and came out with a
loaded syringe. "This is what's going to kill you," he
said, removing the protective cap from the needle.
"One and a quarter grams of the same stuff, Bobby
Lee, real good quality, I'm told. You're about to go out
with a bang."

Bobby Lee's eyes were like Ping-Pong balls now, his
terror in total control. He thrashed his head from side
to side, strained in desperation to free his hands, and
made strange teakettle noises through his nose. His
Demerol brain told him that if he could only get up,
he could dash out of there faster than he'd ever moved
in his entire life, regardless of his condition.

But he couldn't get up, couldn't dash anywhere—
and suddenly discovered he couldn't do *any*thing
except stare with a horrible fixation as Horance
inverted the needle into the IV feeder and pressed the
plunger.

"Come to my house, take my goddamn money."

Bobby Lee felt the beginning rush, the cocaine
neutralizing the Demerol, putting him on a plane he'd
never experienced before.

"Pistol-whip me, tell me you're going to shoot my
kneecaps off."

The rush was building now, coming on strong, his
heart pumping like a piston. He no longer felt fear,
only an overpowering euphoria that supercharged his
body and made his hair feel like it was standing on
end.

"Take away, ruin everything it took years for me to
build up. A little loudmouth magpie wanting to fly like
an eagle. Well, you'll never tell anybody about it."

The coke hit him with a vengeance then, his throat
filled with the bitter taste of it, his heart switching to

afterburner, sending him soaring to heights he'd never known—oh, Jesus, what a fucking *rush* . . .

Horance said, "Roast in hell, Robert E. Lee Gettis," just as the corded muscles in Bobby Lee's left arm snapped the unbreakable plastic police restraint and his heart ruptured in an explosion of blood that flooded his chest cavity and killed him instantly.

Chapter

—10—

Cage arrived at Wilshire Memorial at seven-fifty and bought a cup of coffee to go in the cafeteria before taking the elevator up to Three West. Leslie Oglevie, the nurse who'd had the nose job, was at the chart station reading medication orders. Cage wasn't quite sure just what it was she had done to it, but he thought she should try again. It was short and narrow and didn't seem to go with her angular face.

She looked up and smiled as he approached, saying, "Hi there. Caprita's doing an Incident Report. I don't know how long she'll be, I just got here myself."

Cage could see Caprita hunched over a typewriter inside the glass-enclosed office, her hair tied back with a green scarf and an intense expression on her face.

He said, "What kind of an Incident Report?" It sounded like something they wrote in the Federal Prison System when a con violated some rule.

Leslie leaned over the counter, anxious to share secrets. "She had a patient expire during the night, and it looks like a cocaine overdose. Landis is fit to be tied."

"Why? Unless that's a prescribed medication, it can't be the hospital's fault."

"I know," she said. "But he was dead almost two hours before it was discovered."

Cage said, "Oh," and looked in again at Caprita frowning at the typewriter. "Okay if I go in for a minute?"

"I guess it's all right. Don't stay too long though, the doctors will be showing up soon to make rounds."

He went into the office and walked over to Caprita. He said, "Hi, babe. Rough night?"

Without looking up, Caprita said, "You heard, huh?"

"Yeah. Leslie said one of your patients *expired* from a cocaine O.D. I don't know why anybody uses that word when they talk about dying. Makes people sound like parking meters."

"Allen, you shouldn't be in here, I'm in enough trouble already. I'll only be another ten or fifteen minutes, why don't you wait for me downstairs in the cafeteria."

He gave her shoulder a gentle squeeze and said, "Are you all right?"

"I'm fine. Just a little tired."

A young woman about twenty-one came in carrying an armful of clothes with a pair of men's shoes on top. She gave Cage a timid smile, then looked at Caprita. "Here are all his things," she said. "I'll have to inventory them."

The young woman placed the bundle on the end of the desk and stood there wringing her hands. "Would you like for me to do it?" she asked. "I don't mind."

"That's okay, Dee," Caprita said. "Go home and get some rest, it's been a long night."

"Well, if you're sure."

"I'm sure. Thank you."

The young woman, looking awkward, flashed another brief smile at Cage and left.

Cage said, "Student, right?"

"Yes. She was with me last night."

Caprita removed the completed Incident Report, set it aside, took an inventory form from the bottom drawer and rolled it into the typewriter. Then she pulled the bundle of clothing toward her and began going through them—setting the shoes on the floor, checking the pants and jacket pockets.

Cage said, "Well, I can see you're in no mood for conversation, so I'll just get downstairs."

"I'm sorry, Allen, I'm really preoccupied here. I won't be long."

"Don't hurry on my account. Do what you have to do."

Cage glanced casually at the newspaper clipping Caprita was unfolding; it had come from one of the jacket pockets. He did a double-take, his attention caught by the woman in the photo, her features somewhat distorted by the crease in the paper. But there was no distorting the necklace she was wearing.

He said, "Can I see that a minute?"

"Why?"

"I've seen that necklace before. The woman too, I think. In a picture Michael Grady has hanging on his wall. It was stolen."

"The picture?"

"No, the necklace. That's the reason he wanted a backup system. Remember? I told you about it."

He took the clipping from her, smoothed the creases, and examined it more closely. "Yeah, it's the same woman," he said. "See here? Frances Maljean."

"So what's that mean?"

"I don't know, really. Just seems a little strange this guy would have a clipping of a necklace that was stolen less than a week ago."

Leslie stuck her head in the door and said, "Allen, Dr. Landis is coming, you'd better leave now."

"Go," Caprita said, and gave him a little push. "I'll be down soon."

Cage said, "Can I take this with me?"

"Why not?" she said. "He won't be looking at it anymore."

The cafeteria was quiet and uncrowded at this hour; a few hospital workers in green or white garb, lingering over coffee and pastry and personality changes—gearing up for or winding down from another episode of dealing with the dying and those who thought they were.

Cage sat at a table near the door, stirring his black coffee and contemplating the well-worn newspaper clipping. Frances Maljean kept looking back at him, overshadowed by the magnificent necklace that seemed almost out of place around such a thin neck. And beside her, poised and confident in his penguin tux, was one Horance Griswald, proclaimed by the caption to be L.A.'s most popular and flamboyant designer of fashionable jewelry and creator of the necklace. The guy knew how to mug for the camera too; head erect and mouth set in an open half smile, as if he were saying hi to the photographer. Cage made a mental bet that he could look at another dozen photographs of Horance Griswald and see that exact expression. Like a mugshot with class.

Maybe he was making too big a deal over the clipping, seeing things that weren't there. So it showed a lady wearing a necklace that would later end up stolen, and the clip turns up in the pocket of some guy who overdosed on coke. What did that prove? Maybe the guy knew Frances Maljean, or maybe this Horance Griswald, or both. Hell, he could know one or more of the people milling around in the background, could even be one of them for that matter. In fact, for all he knew, the dead guy could even be Horance Griswald himself.

Cage gave up and put the clipping in his shirt pocket. He would ask Caprita about it and go from there, quit trying to act like Dick Tracy.

It was another twenty minutes before she got there, and Cage knew something was wrong as soon as she walked through the door, carrying her shoulder purse by the straps as though it were too heavy for her. She saw him, came over and sat down, fatigued and defeated, and slumped in the chair.

"Well," she said, "so much for that."

"So much for what?"

"Dr. Landis hauled me on the carpet, which I had a hunch was coming. He said it was unconscionable that a patient could die for any reason at Wilshire Memorial and not be discovered for two hours, or close to it. He said that might be tolerated at L.A. General, but not here."

"Really chewed you out, huh?"

"He did more than that," she said. "He suspended me."

"*Suspended* you?"

"Yep. Pending further investigation. I may even have to go before the board, and if that happens, I can kiss nursing good-bye in this town."

"What happened up there, Caprita? How come you're getting saddled with this?"

Caprita sighed and dug her Marlboros and battleship Zippo from her purse. She lit one and sat back hugging her arms. "It was my fault," she said. "We're supposed to make a bed check on monitored and IV patients every hour, make sure everything is functioning properly. This particular patient—his name was Bobby Lee Gettis—was admitted some time Tuesday night, back fracture and spinal damage. He was on IV and catheter and four-hour pain medication. Anyway, I gave him an injection about three A.M., checked his IV drip and catch bottle, and everything was fine. At four I sent Dee around on the bed check—I mean it's no major thing, and I was in the middle of charting a respiratory problem we'd just had with an emphysema patient. Dee came back, said there were no problems, and I charted that."

Cage watched her take a final drag from her cigarette and put it out in the ashtray, quick, forceful stabs that revealed a controlled anger. Not a good time to badger her about smoking.

"So how does this fall on you? I don't see it being your fault at all."

"Allen, *I* charted the entries, put *my* signature to a statement that all functions were normal on a patient who was *dead*. Think about that for a minute."

Cage did. Then said, "How do they know he was dead then? We're only talking about an hour difference, right? How can they pinpoint it that close?"

"Body temperature, Allen, the rate of cooling. The sooner a body is discovered, the easier it is to determine the exact time of death. Mr. Gettis died within five minutes either way of three-thirty A.M. And Dee admitted afterward she didn't really look at the patient that closely—probably didn't bother to look at him at all. Besides, I should have made the checks myself, not left it to a student. So it was my responsibility."

"Who found him?"

"I did, at five-twelve. God, he must have been pouring the stuff in him. Massive coronary."

"Any idea where he got it?"

"A visitor, I suppose, though I can't imagine anyone being that stupid."

Caprita wiped a few stray hairs from her forehead and looked away. She sniffed, rubbed a finger in the corner of one eye and fell silent. Cage wanted to reach across the table and touch her, but she was too far away and had her arms folded again. The nail on her left little finger looked as if she'd been gnawing on it, a habit she had whenever she was especially upset.

He said, "You feel like having a little breakfast? Might make you feel better."

She laughed without mirth. "If I did, I'd vomit."

Cage said, "Look, babe, you've got to get off this guilt trip. You didn't kill the guy, and finding him an hour earlier wouldn't have brought him back."

"It's not that," she said. "I was charge nurse and I made a mistake, that's what really bothers me. Suppose he'd only been comatose? That *could* have cost him his life, Allen, because I let a student do *my* job. And for that, I most certainly am to blame. So don't try to find any loopholes for me, because there aren't any. What I'd really like you to do right now is take me home. I need a long, hot bath."

When they arrived back at the apartment, Caprita made straight for the bathroom and started the water running in the tub. She added a liberal amount of Milk Bath, a few caps of Et Tu Bath Oil, then turned to her herb shelf and removed beaker number two (Tranquility Aid—1¼ tbl. spn). Cage, appearing in the open doorway, watched her ignore the dosage instructions and dump a generous proportion directly from the beaker into a Dixie cup. She added water, swirled the mixture around a little, then downed it in three quick gulps.

Cage said, "If you're not careful you're gonna O.D. on herbs."

"I'm making up for yesterday," she said, and dropped the Dixie cup into the waste basket. "Would you be a doll and fix me a cup of hot chocolate, please? I think there are a few packets left in the cupboard."

When he came back she was in the tub, stretched out with her eyes closed and buried to her chin in bubbles. He sat the hot chocolate on the ledge, said, "There you are my lady," and was about to leave when she said, "Allen?"

"Uh-huh?"

"What are we going to do if I get fired?"

He looked at her and saw her gazing at her unpainted toes poking up through the bubbles. She wiggled them absently, and he had an urge to play with them until she broke into helpless giggles, get her out of this funk she'd fallen into. Only he knew it wouldn't work.

He said, "Caprita, they're not gonna fire you. You're damn good at what you do, and they know it. Are you telling me that's the first time a student nurse ever made a bed check by herself?"

"No, but it's the first time anything's happened. And don't be so sure about Dr. Landis, it all depends on how hard he wants to push it. Nursing's all I know, all I've ever done or really wanted to do, and if he takes me up in front of the board—"

"Babe, you're building a worst-case scenario here. You told me yourself they've been short this month because of vacations and whatnot, and that alone makes last night even more understandable. Let 'em have their little investigation, it'll show you acted reasonable. Look at it as an unexpected holiday."

"Sure, without pay. You know we couldn't keep this apartment, don't you? No way, not on your salary alone. And I'd hate to give it up."

"Salary *and* commission," he said, "don't forget that. And lately things have been picking up." He thought a moment. "That reminds me, I got to make a phone call. I'll be back in a few minutes, you just relax, drink your chocolate. Give that herb time to work."

Cage went into the kitchen and used the wall phone to call Michael Grady. The Japanese housekeeper answered and said that Mr. Grady was just finishing his shower, if he would like to hold a moment. Cage said fine, and got in a staring contest with Grits, perched in the kitchen window with Caprita's potted cactus while he waited, the fool cat knowing he wasn't supposed to be up there but daring Cage to correct him.

Michael Grady came on the line and said, "Allen? How you doing?"

"Good. Hope I didn't disturb you."

"You didn't. I start waking up around seven and usually finish about this time. What's up?"

"I was wondering if you knew a man named Bobby Lee Gettis. That name ring a bell to you?"

"Not really. Is it supposed to?"

"I don't know. The guy was a patient at Wilshire Memorial and died last night from a cocaine overdose. My fiancée's a nurse there, and she found him. He had a newspaper clipping of Frances Maljean and a jeweler named Horance Griswald in his coat pocket. It was taken at some fund-raising party she was giving, looks like it's several months old."

Grady said, "I know who Griswald is. He's the guy I had make that choker for Marilee, same one who made Frances's necklace. You know, the one in the picture I showed you that got stolen."

"Yeah," Cage said, "that's why I asked if you knew this Bobby Lee Gettis. Frances Maljean was wearing it in the clipping. Can you think of any reason why someone would be interested enough in the particular clipping to carry it around?"

"Not right off, but I guess there could be one. Frances always kicks up quite a stir when she throws her National Wildlife Federation shindig. She's a big animal lover, and a lot of these animal rights activists are always at her to speak out against lab experimentation. Usually she does too."

"Think she might know him?"

"I'll ask her. You say the name's Bobby Lee Gettis?"

"Right. I just thought it was a little strange and decided to run it by you."

"Frances will appreciate the concern. Probably just a coincidence though."

"Probably."

Grady said, "Hey, you sound like you're in a real ditch this morning. What's the matter, those protesters getting to you? I heard about 'em."

"No," Cage said, "they're gone now. Caprita, my fiancée, got in a little trouble over this guy dying last night. It shows, huh?"

"I'm a director, remember? I'm supposed to be able to read people, tell when they're not coming across. Nothing serious, I hope."

"She was suspended pending an investigation, and she's pretty upset about it."

"Oh, shit, that's a shame. Think she'll come out all right?"

"Unless they're looking for a scapegoat," Cage said. "But I think it's mostly overreaction because of the drug angle. Wilshire Memorial doesn't like that kind of publicity. Once they calm down I believe they'll come to their senses."

"Sure, hell, they got a nursing shortage anyway." Then Grady said, "I got an idea. I'm having another little get-together Friday night, about ten or twelve people. I try to do it once or twice a week, keep Marilee from getting too stir crazy. And it's easier than us going to somebody else's place. Why don't you bring your girl? She'll see and hear enough to keep her laughing a week. Who knows, you might even pick up another client."

Cage said, "Thanks, Michael, I might just do that."

"Anytime around seven or so. And come hungry, I'm barbecuing."

"We'll see you then. Itchy-gay."

"You got it."

Cage hung up and stood grinning at the phone thinking Michael Grady was one hell of a guy. Then he lifted the receiver again and called the office.

Brenda answered, and he said, "It's me, Olive Oyl. I'll be a little late, okay?"

"Where are you?" she asked and he marveled again at how such a plain woman could make a telephone practically drip with sex.

"At home," he said. "Caprita got suspended this morning."

"*What?*"

He told her, keeping it brief and to the point.

"That's terrible," Brenda said. "How's she taking it?"

"A little hard right now. That's why I'm still here, but I'll be in soon. Look, why don't you wait about forty-five minutes or an hour and give her a call, see if you can perk her up some. Right now she's taking a bath."

"You better believe I will. Don't let her go to sleep."

"Count on it," he said. "See you in a little bit."

Caprita had her eyes closed again when she heard Cage come into the bathroom. Without opening them she said, "Who'd you call?"

"Michael Grady, the office."

"I suppose you told them."

"I mentioned it. Michael Grady invited us to a barbecue Friday night, and Olive Oyl's gonna be calling in about an hour."

"Huuummm," she said, sounding totally relaxed now. She said, "I don't know if it's the herbs, the bath, or the hot chocolate, or maybe all of them, but I do believe I'll survive after all."

"Glad to hear it," he said. "Now how about moving your legs."

Caprita opened her eyes and looked up at Cage standing there completely nude.

He shrugged and said, "I told Olive Oyl I'd keep you awake, so I figured I'd wash your back. Is that okay?"

Caprita looked him up and down and smiled. "Don't knock over the hot chocolate," she said.

Chapter

—11—

Michael Grady had set flaming torches in cast-iron stanchions spaced evenly along the railing surrounding the sun deck, and Polynesian music came from twin speakers flanking the open patio door leading to the den that was open to provide ready access to the bar just inside. He had a fifty-five-gallon-drum barbecue grill with the lid closed to keep the shishkabob, corn on the cob, and baked potatoes warm, and he circulated among the guests lounging around the sun deck, wearing a Hawaiian shirt and tall chef's hat that read: COOKS DO IT BETTER! Most of the time he had a scotch in one hand and a set of tongs in the other, carrying both out of force of habit.

Cage and Caprita were at an umbrella table with Marilee Grady, who wore a pale yellow pantsuit that concealed most of her braces. Her aluminum crutches with the forearm supports were on the deck beside her chair. Cage, seeing her in person for the first time, upgraded her age by five or six years because of the fine spiderwebs at the corners of her mouth, which hadn't been noticeable in the photograph Michael Grady had shown him. But she was still a good-looking woman, he thought, calm and soft-spoken.

Sort of an Elizabeth Dole, with more hair and minus the accent.

Caprita was saying, "This is really a beautiful place you have here, Marilee, thank you again for having us."

"You're more than welcome," Marilee said. "Michael likes to pretend he holds these little gatherings for me, but in reality he enjoys them as much as I do, maybe more. Gives him a chance to show off his alleged culinary skills, which everyone is just too polite to criticize."

Caprita said, "Oh, I think it's very good," and forked a small piece of charred beef and bell pepper into her mouth to emphasize the point.

"Please," Marilee said lightly, "don't tell him that, you'll only encourage him."

Caprita said, "Allen can't even fry an egg without breaking the yolk."

Cage said, "I resent that."

Caprita ignored him. "We have this little hibachi on our patio, and about twice a month he'll do steaks or something and use about half a can of starter fluid before he's convinced the coals are going good. The food comes out tasting like my Zippo."

"Trash me, why don't you?"

"Michael used to do that," Marilee said. "He'd stand back three feet, toss in a match and create a fireball. I finally had to make him start buying the self-starting kind to make certain he didn't blow himself up."

Cage said, "Maybe that's what I ought to—"

"Did the meat sometimes end up looking like an overtoasted marshmallow?" Caprita asked.

"Yes," Marilee said. "And on the inside it looked like it was still alive. See that silly-looking hat he's wearing? He had another one just like it about a year ago, one of those paper things they give away at some char-your-own restaurant in North Hollywood. One time he squirted fuel onto some coals he thought were dead, and a tongue of flame leaped out and set it on fire. You should have seen him clodhopping on it, trying to put it out."

Caprita said, "Oh no!" and touched Marilee's arm, laughing with her.

Cage was glad to see Michael Grady peel away from a small group at the condiments table and head their way, snapping the tongs and looking pleased with the world.

Grady said, "Allen, you look like a man wiring dynamite during an electrical storm. These girls beating up on you, or just man-bashing in general?"

"Caprita won't let me get in a word edgewise. I'm beginning to think I should've left her at home."

"Caprita and I were simply discussing male pigosity and open-grill cooking," Marilee said, "and I'm afraid Allen found himself outnumbered."

Grady said, "Yeah? Well I'm here to even it up." He gave Marilee a quick peck on the cheek and sat down. "Pigosity," he said. "Now there's a word for you, Allen. Only a woman could come up with a word like that. Sometimes I think they got their own secret dictionary of anti-male jargon that would make us blush if we knew what it meant."

"Look who's talking," Marilee said "old itchy-gay himself. Caprita, doesn't that sound like something you'd say to a baby while tickling it?"

Caprita smiled, and Grady said, "See how much respect I get around here?" Then he had an inspiration and said, "Hey, see that bald-headed guy in the plaid walking shorts holding court over there by the rail? The short stocky one waving his hands around, spilling half his drink on my redwood deck?"

"I noticed him," Cage said. "He's got everybody cracking up."

"Right. Gus Silverstein. He writes gags for some of the best comics in the business. I want you to hear some of his Rodney Dangerfield stuff, the guy's a real trip . . . hey, Gus! Gus! Come over here a minute."

The man made his way to their table in a rapid, slightly bow-legged gait that had them all smiling before he even got there.

Grady said, "Gus, want you to meet a couple friends of mine, Allen Cage and Caprita Arciaga. How about giving them a little Rodney Dangerfield, see how it goes over with normal people."

Gus fingered a make-believe tie and stretched his neck. "I tell you I don't get no respect. The other day I got a postcard from my wife with a satellite picture of earth on the back. It said, 'Having a wonderful time, wish you were here!'"

Caprita laughed, delighted, and said, "My God, you even sound like him!"

"Yeah, my wife must really miss me. I just bought a used car and found one of her dresses in the backseat."

More laughter, Caprita and Cage applauding.

"My wife really thinks I'm ugly, though. She's got a lot of nerve. On the way over here she stuck her head out the window to ask a cop for directions. He arrested her, thought she was mooning him."

Cage nearly sprayed a mouthful of 7-Up on that one. People were starting to wander over, carrying drinks and plastic plates.

"Yeah, that's why I don't have sex with my wife anymore. Now whenever I get horny, I eat. She got so disgusted, she took down the mirror over our bed and hung it over the kitchen table."

Caprita was nearly in tears, holding both hands over her mouth.

"My wife wanted me to lose weight, so I went to a doctor. He said run five miles every day and call me in two weeks. I called him two weeks later and said, Doc, when can I stop runnin? I'm seventy miles away from home."

Gus kept up his routine for another five minutes or so before announcing he was out of material and Jack Daniels. He bowed to his appreciative audience and headed for the den as fast as his short legs would carry him without running, leaving Caprita with a stomach-ache from laughing so hard.

Grady said, "I told you he was a trip. If there wasn't a Rodney Dangerfield already, Gus would be a superstar. But he does all right." He rubbed the back of Marilee's neck. "Hon, you want anything? How about another drink?"

"Oh, I suppose I could be talked into another screwdriver. Easy on the driver."

Caprita said, "Please, let me get it. After all that, I could use the walk."

Grady watched her smile and weave her way through the guests on the way to the bar. "You got yourself a good lady there, Allen," he said. "Easy to get to know."

"The word is refreshing," Marilee said. "And that's a rarity in this town."

Cage said, "Thanks, I'll tell her you said that."

"So what happened with the suspension deal?" Grady asked. "She seems to be in a pretty good mood tonight."

"She got a call from the chief of staff this morning,"

Cage said. "They're not gonna fire her, but she's out for two weeks. She doesn't think it's fair, and neither do I, but I guess it's better than losing her job."

"Speaking of that," Grady said, "I asked Frances about this Bobby Lee Gettis, and she never heard of him. But if you think he might've had something to do with stealing her necklace, I kinda doubt it. Why keep a picture of something he's had almost a week?"

"I asked myself the same question, only I wonder why he had it for five months. That clipping came from the Sunday, March seventeenth edition, and there had to be some reason for him to hang on to it that long."

Marilee said, "Have you considered asking Horance Griswald? Perhaps the man knew him."

"I thought about it, but I wanted to hear from Mrs. Maljean first. And just to satisfy myself, I'm gonna ask Larry to run this guy through the National Crime Information Center Monday, see if he's got a record. If he comes back dirty, then we'll go from there."

"Go where?" Grady asked.

"Wherever he's been," Cage said.

"You can do that?"

"No," Cage said, "but Larry Twiford can."

Later, as they were driving home, Caprita curled up close to Cage and fiddled with the radio dial, searching for mood music. She found Whitney Houston doing "One Moment in Time," her favorite song, and started singing along with the chorus. Cage told her she was destroying what was otherwise a perfectly good song and that she ought to let Whitney do it, which only made Caprita lean toward his ear and sing louder. Since that didn't work, he tried to get her talking, asking what she thought about Michael Grady and his wife. That did the trick.

"They're terrific," she said, "not what I expected at all. I especially like Marilee."

"Yeah, you two seemed to hit it right off."

"I think she just enjoyed talking to someone closer to her own age. She doesn't get out all that much, you know."

"What do you mean, closer to her own age? She's a good forty, and you're what, twenty-nine now, I believe."

"Well thanks a lot for remembering. And she's forty-one, if you really must know. And if that's antiquated, then may I point out that you're only what, four years behind, I believe."

"I didn't mean she was over the hill, I was only disputing the difference in age."

Caprita said, "Did you notice the people there tonight? The average age was close to fifty, and all the women were either discussing gardening, bridge clubs, or plastic surgeons. One even asked my opinion about Retin-A, wanting to know if it really worked. Somehow I don't quite see Marilee engaging in those conversations."

"The lady's got a lot of class," Cage said, "that's for sure. I can understand why Michael Grady was attracted to her, even with her handicap. I guess it just goes to show it's all in how you carry yourself."

"I admire her," Caprita said, "but I wish she'd get out and do things, go to movies, plays, even ball games. She loves baseball."

"Too self-conscious, probably."

"No, it's not that. Not completely. I think mostly she's just a very solitary person, and that air of aloofness is her defense. She doesn't want to show how really vulnerable she is, how much she depends on Michael."

"I thought you were an R.N., not a psychologist."

"You don't have to be a psychologist to see that, Allen. I don't think she took her eyes off Michael for five minutes all evening." She made a sound of dismay and began turning the radio dial again. "Now look what you've made me do. I missed my song."

Cage grinned. "Psychology, babe. Me and Whitney had to have a break one way or another."

Chapter

—12—

Horance Griswald was sitting behind the wheel of his black customized Econoline van in the parking lot of Gladstone's for Fish, watching a steady stream of customers come and go from the popular seafood restaurant, feeling extremely nervous and uncomfortable. He wasn't satisfied with this deal at all, not even a little bit, and was tempted to call the whole thing off. Just go home and watch TV or something and save this business for another night, when it wouldn't draw so much heat.

And he would have, if he hadn't already committed himself to Maury Bingham for a lousy ten grand. Now he had to make a move, knowing it was much too soon after the Maljean job, because Maury had insisted on getting a return within ten days.

Greedy bastard.

Horance sipped at the thermos cup of black coffee and looked out at the heavy traffic moving through the intersection of Pacific Coast Highway and Sunset. He had a good view, and couldn't miss the man's distinctive car, a white '88 Mercedes. Michael Grady always took his wife to dinner at Chasen's on Saturday night, one of the few times the woman ever went anywhere with him in public. Coming from Malibu, they would have to drive south on Pacific Coast Highway and turn left onto Sunset, passing within fifty feet of where he was parked.

He was wishing now that he'd never called Maury Bingham, but at the same time he knew he had no choice. Not if he wanted to keep one jump ahead of the credit bureaus. And in his line of work, good credit was the cornerstone of solvency and respectability. You couldn't do business with some of the wealthiest and most influential people in the country when your mailbox was stuffed with past-due notices. It wouldn't take long for the word to spread, and that would be the kiss of death. He might just as well go back to peddling synthetic rubies and counterfeit Rolexes at local flea markets.

And right now Maury Bingham was his only source for quality stones. Because of his ex-felon status, Horance couldn't obtain the necessary line of credit from legitimate wholesalers to purchase top-notch stones. And he couldn't afford to pay cash. So he had to keep Maury Bingham happy.

And Maury knew it.

Horance leaned closer to the open side window and squinted at the southbound traffic on Pacific Coast Highway. Two cars were slowing, signal lights flashing, easing into the left-turn lane where the arrow was still green. A station wagon with wood panels, and a white Mercedes. Horance followed with his eyes as the Mercedes passed and made the turn onto Sunset, the two occupants clearly visible in the brightly lit intersection.

Michael Grady and his crippled wife, no doubt about it.

Horance drained his cup and screwed it back onto

the thermos, then checked his watch. Eight-twenty. They wouldn't be returning for a good two hours at the earliest. He'd have plenty of time to locate the safe. If they had one. It would be a welcome bonus if the Gradys were the type who placed all their faith in burglar alarms.

He fired up the engine and took mental inventory of his equipment. In the back were his portable voltage meter and dual twelve-volt battery pack, each in its own carrying case. In the deep left-hand zippered pocket of his three-quarter-length leather coat was his thirty-thousand-dollar sequence counter, the super-sensitive suction cups already attached. The right-hand pocket held a .380 automatic with a full fifteen-shot clip. A set of flexible steel lock picks was in his breast pocket, and on the rear of the van was a magnetized quick-change license plate that had come from a totaled Ford Econoline that was lying in a flattened heap in a Monterey Park wrecking yard.

He was all set.

But he still couldn't shake that nagging feeling that something just wasn't right.

"I'm telling you, honey, it's a mess, a goddamn mess," Michael Grady was saying. "The whole screenplay's nothing but a rehash of the original script, except for the dialogue and a few shifts in location. Other than that . . . listen to this, David's got *two* scenes in the sequel that are almost identical to scenes in part one. How about that? The guy's slipping, been staying up too many nights looking for spirits or whatever."

Marilee, sitting primly in the passenger seat, listened with amusement to her husband's tirade and waited for him to wind down. Occasionally she would brace herself against the door as, a little too fast, he took one of the curves that dominated lower Sunset. But she didn't complain; eighteen years of marriage had taught her the various methods Michael used to vent a hyperactive nervous system, knowing that when they reached Chasen's, he would be all smiles, waving and slapping backs as the maitre d' led them to their usual table where a vase of fresh yellow and white gardenias would be waiting for her. It was the one night of the week she really looked forward to, and none of Michael's blustering could dampen her mood. Quite the contrary, she found it very humorous, and she would sometimes turn her head to the window and smile at the passing night. Actually Michael was rather pleased with the way *Angel Wars II* was shaping up, though one would never guess to hear him carry on the way he did.

Like now, hearing him say, "And we really don't have a good strong heavy to replace Lel. Too bad I killed him."

Trying to keep a straight face, Marilee said, "You mean we won't get to hear someone yell 'itchy-gay' just before going into fierce battle?"

"No," he said absently, "and a lot of fans are gonna miss that."

"Too bad he doesn't have a son to carry on the family tradition," she said.

Grady snapped his fingers and nearly swerved the Mercedes into the path of an oncoming Federal Express delivery truck.

"That's it!" he said. "Son of Lel, archangel of soul death! Now why the hell didn't I think of that? I mean it's simple, so fucking obvious." He was getting excited now, inspired by the prospect. "He could pick up the old man's battle cry, maybe use it as a rallying call to gather his forces in a final attack! Marilee, you're a genius. Shit, I got to call David, get him working on this angle right now. There's a 7-Eleven just up the road, I'll call him from there."

"Michael!" Marilee said, giving him a sharp look. "Can't you at least wait until we get to Chasen's? My God, Justin will *bring* you a phone."

But Michael had that resolute expression on his face that told her from experience that he was no longer open to reason.

"I can't talk in that place," he said. "Too many cocked ears. Next thing you know, it'll be in *Variety*. This won't take long."

What it took was nearly twenty-five minutes, Marilee doing a slow boil as she sat rigid in the Mercedes that was aligned nose first next to the 7-Eleven entrance, staring a hole through Grady's back as he stood hip-cocked at the outside phone kiosk talking earnestly to David Freemont.

When he finally finished and got back in the car, he gave her a sheepish grin. "Guess I was a little long, huh?"

In a chilly voice she said, "That's an understatement," and looked off, tapping one of her metal crutches against the floorboard.

"Aw, honey, don't be—"

A sharp beeping sound coming from his inside jacket pocket startled him for a moment, bringing a confused look to his face as Marilee jerked her head around toward him in alarm. Then the confusion vanished as Grady pulled out the beeper, regarded it in silence for a few seconds, then pressed the deactivate button.

"Son of a bitch!" he said, and started the car, his face now a mask of anger. "Somebody's in the fucking house. His ass is mine!"

It was beginning to look like Horance had been worrying for nothing. In fact, this might turn out to be his easiest job yet, if he didn't count the unnecessary labor. He'd lugged his two cases of equipment nearly a hundred yards from where he'd left the van snuggled close to a clump of juniper bushes at the top of the hill, only to discover that Grady hadn't even bothered to set his alarm. The red light on the recessed panel next to the front door was dead and the key slot turned to the off position. Horance had to lug the cases back up the hill, put them back in the van, then return to the house a second time, feeling winded already and thinking he was definitely getting too old for this kind of work. The Corbin dead-bolt lock gave easily to his rake pick and tension lever, and within two minutes he was standing in the foyer next to the suit of armor that stood as a silent but impotent sentry.

He paused beneath the rheostat-controlled chandelier that was set on low and took his bearings, alert for sounds of human presence.

Nothing but an eerie silence so deep that he could hear the faint squeak of his latex gloves as he unconsciously clenched his fists.

Satisfied, Horance began his search, using a narrow-beam flashlight. He started downstairs first, in the den, slowly checking the carpeted area around the desk for signs of a floor safe. They were popular and easily concealed, but Grady didn't have one. He looked behind the wall pictures and an oval mirror, then went over the area behind the bar, where he found the man's marijuana stash in a cigar box. He left it alone and moved on to an ornate bookcase with glass doors, where he meticulously thumped each of the exposed leather-bound backs with his finger, listening for a hollow sound, then examined the electrical outlets in the walls to see if Grady had one of those tricky phony receptacles.

Nothing.

He went to the kitchen next, straight to the big double-door refrigerator, and carefully unwrapped three aluminum-foil packets he found in the freezer section—another sneaky move some people liked to make when hiding valuable jewelry. Two held Cornish game hens and the third contained two thick sirloin steaks. He put them back and went into the dining room and spent five minutes searching the hutch, the china cabinet, and peeking behind wall ornaments, until at last he was convinced that the ground floor was clean. He hadn't really expected to find any jewelry down here anyway, but he had the time and liked to be thorough. It was also a matter of anticipation; a gradual increase of excitement as he went through the obligatory motions while saving the best for last, knowing what he would eventually find. Like foreplay.

Moving silently on black Nikes, Horance headed for the staircase leading to the upstairs bedrooms.

Michael Grady drove like a man possessed, hunched over the steering wheel with a near maniacal expression on his face and paying absolutely no attention whatsoever to Marilee's pleading.

"Michael, *please* stop the car and call the police. This is insane."

They were back on Pacific Coast Highway now, the

Mercedes zipping in and out of traffic like a downhill skier on a slalom course.

Grady said, "I'm handling this myself. Whoever this bastard is, he's picked the wrong house."

"You're not thinking . . . Michael, will you *listen* to me? He could have a gun. Or there could be more than one. I'm begging you, don't do this."

"I've got a gun too, right back there in the trunk. And a whole fucking box of thirty-ought-sixes." Grady hit the horn and swung around a semi that was doing at least seventy. "I'm gonna put a stop to this shit, watch what I tell you. Somebody just *waiting* for us to leave, watching and scheming like a fucking buzzard. Well I got a right to protect what's mine, and by God I'm gonna do it."

Marilee was braced against the door, crutches between her knees. She stared anxiously at the road ahead and struggled to find words that would get through to him. She had a premonition of disaster that chilled her and caused her breathing to become ragged, certain that Michael was rushing them into some terrible danger with horrifying consequences. She felt like hitting him with a crutch, or snatching the keys from the ignition and tossing them out the window, anything to stop this madness. But the speedometer needle was passing eighty and still climbing, and she didn't want to kill them both. Where was the Highway Patrol? She took a quick look through the rear window, praying for a glimpse of red and blue flashing lights, but saw only diminishing headlights as the Mercedes pulled steadily away.

Marilee gathered herself for one final attempt, wanting to shake him out of his single-minded purpose. "If you go through with this, Michael," she said calmly, "I'll leave you."

Grady's jaw muscles bunched, but he didn't look at her and he didn't slow down.

"I mean it, Michael," she said, though knowing she didn't.

"We'll talk," he said tonelessly. "Later."

Marilee, with no words left to say, fell silent and closed her eyes.

She didn't open them again until after he had taken the turnoff to Malibu Canyon and was speeding up the narrow winding road leading to their house. Grady cut the lights when he was twenty yards from their driveway, eased the Mercedes to the side of the road and killed the engine.

"Stay here," he told her. "Lock the doors and don't get out regardless of what you hear. I'll be back soon."

"Michael—"

But he was already out of the car, closing the door quietly behind him. Marilee turned and watched him hurry to the trunk, open it, and take out his hunting rifle and a box of cartridges. He closed the trunk lid softly, rocking the car as he leaned his weight on it, then began to load the rifle, dropping several shells on the ground in his haste. Then he stuffed the cartridge box into his jacket pocket and headed for the house in a crouching half trot. In a matter of moments he had disappeared into the darkness, leaving Marilee staring after him with a sense of dread that she could almost taste.

For Horance Griswald the foreplay was over and he had achieved total penetration. He was kneeling in front of the five-hundred-pound safe he'd found hidden behind a rack of full-length evening gowns in the master closet, the most obvious place in the whole house. Five felt boxes were lined up in an orderly row on the carpet, their snap lids raised, the thin flashlight beam lighting a fire as it slowly moved from one to the next: a cluster cocktail ring with a canary diamond centerstone that would go at least four carats; a ruby and sapphire bracelet set in heavy eighteen-carat gold; a ladies' gold Tiffany Tesoro wristwatch with diamond bezels; a man's gold Rolex Presidential that appeared to be brand new. And finally, his baby, a platinum-threaded choker necklace with twenty-four perfectly joined and cloudless one-carat emeralds, flanked by matching earrings. He held the box up and played the light over them, admiring the green sunbursts created by the reflection.

Yes, he did damn good work. Too good to have to resort to this shit.

He put the box down and did some quick calculations. He placed the total value of the lot at around sixty thousand wholesale. Not as much as he'd hoped, but enough to get him out of the hole with Maury and give him a little breathing room.

He turned the light back to the safe and rummaged through the rest of the contents. No cash and nothing else of interest to him, only some banded personal documents and CD's in the name of Michael J. Grady.

Horance disconnected his digital sequence counter, snapped the lids on the jewelry boxes, and began tucking everything away in his coat pockets. He had to remove the automatic and jam it into his waistband to make room. All things considered, he thought, not a bad night's work.

Suddenly the bedroom was flooded with light and a voice behind him said, "Right there, you bucket of piss!"

For several seconds Horance was unable to move.

Then he slowly turned his head to see Michael Grady standing in the doorway, holding a rifle at hip level that was pointed straight at him. Grady's outrage turned to disbelief as he recognized the figure kneeling beside his open safe.

"Well I'll be go to hell," Grady said. "Horance Griswald. If I didn't see it, I wouldn't believe it. You making a house call to see if I need anything?"

There wasn't a lot Horance could say under the circumstances, so he kept quiet and stared at the man with the rifle, who was starting to get worked up again.

Grady said, "You son of a bitch, did you hit the Maljean place Friday before last? You did, didn't you?"

Horance didn't like the way Grady's hand kept opening and closing around the rifle grip as he stood there with his legs spread and his eyes narrowed.

"I asked you a question, mister. I expect an answer before I blow your fucking head off. And you know I can do it without anybody even blinking an eye. Now talk to me."

Horance said, "Take it easy, will you?" He was having difficulty swallowing, but his mind was racing, searching for a way out. "I didn't hit anybody Friday before last. And there's a good reason for me being here."

"This ought to be good," Grady said. "Let's hear it."

Horance said, "The necklace I made for your wife. I couldn't tell you at the time, but the stones were imitations. I'm a little embarrassed to admit it, but I was in a financial bind. Now I have the genuine articles and I just wanted to make a switch before you found out about it."

Horance knew the man wasn't buying any of it, and

he didn't expect him to. But he needed to buy some time, wanting to get that rifle pointing away from him, even for just a second.

Grady said, "Is that a fact? So where's the genuine article, huh? And how about the rest of that stuff in your pockets? You taking them back to see if they're fakes too?"

Horance had to do something now, and he tried the only thing he could think of. He made a show of shifting his gaze past Grady's left shoulder and giving a quick nod, as if signaling an unseen accomplice in the hallway.

Grady didn't fall for it completely, but he did react, as he almost had to. He took a fast look over his shoulder, causing the rifle muzzle to swing slightly away, then turned back when he saw there was no danger.

But the small distraction gave Horance his chance, and he ducked behind the open safe door, clawing for the automatic in his waistband. Grady fired just a hair too late, and the bullet slammed into the back wall of the closet, missing Horance by less than two inches. Grady worked the bolt on the thirty-ought-six and fired again, the slug ricocheting harmlessly off the four-inch-thick steel door that Horance was huddling behind, trying to keep his head and body parts from showing while he finally managed to get the automatic free. Grady, dropping to one knee, jacked in another shell and fired again, and another slug pinged off the steel door. "You cocksucker!" Grady screamed, and worked the bolt yet again, just as Horance, in desperation, stuck the automatic around the side of the door and without looking began pulling the trigger as fast as he could make his finger move. He didn't stop pulling it until he'd sent all fifteen bullets heading in the general direction of Michael Grady.

Horance stayed right where he was for what seemed to be the longest minute of his life after the shooting stopped, waiting for his ears to quit ringing and expecting any second to see Michael Grady leap into view with that rifle leveled at him, grinning hugely as he slowly squeezed the trigger.

But Grady didn't appear, and Horance gradually worked up enough nerve to peer cautiously around the safe door to see what was happening.

Grady wasn't there. But the rifle was, lying on the carpet just inside the doorway where the man had been standing.

Horance stood up and moved across the room, stooped and picked it up. The breech was open, a cartridge jammed at an angle between the magazine and chamber. And there was blood on the stock. Horance could also see blood on the silver-gray carpeting.

A sound came from the hallway, a low-pitched moan that sounded like someone gargling.

Horance edged sideways through the door and saw Michael Grady kneeling at the top of the stairs, hanging onto the handrail. His head was lowered and he was still making that strange sound, but Horance knew what it was now. Grady had been lung shot and was in the process of dying.

But he wasn't dead yet, and he could still identify his attacker.

Horance stuck the empty automatic back in his waistband, reversed the rifle so that he was holding it by the barrel, then stepped forward and smashed the heavy stock against the back of Grady's head with all his strength. Grady grunted, pitched forward and tumbled end over end down the stairs, landing facedown on the parquet floor. Horance came down after him, breathing heavily, and when he reached the bottom of the stairs, he could still hear that gargling sound coming from the man's throat, only not so loud now. Horance swung the rifle like a logger chopping wood, then again and again, until the stock splintered on what was left of Grady's head and he could no longer hear that fucking raspy gargle.

Then he dropped the rifle and ran.

Marilee gasped and held her fist to her mouth as she heard the first muffled gunshots come from the house, then screamed and covered her ears when they were followed by a series of sharper explosions that she instinctively knew could not be from Michael's hunting rifle.

She had no idea how long she had been frozen in this position, hunched over with her hands pressed against her ears, her mind a jumble of nightmare images that flitted across her tightly shut eyelids. But when she finally lifted her head and looked off at the darkened driveway that was barely visible under a weak moon, she was positive that her premonition of disaster had come true. The feeling brought a numbness to her brain and body, suspending conscious thought and setting her into blind motion.

Somehow she found herself outside the car, hip-shuffling her way on her arm crutches along the side of the road toward the house. She was vaguely aware that the Delgados, their closest neighbor, had turned on their garage light, and she dimly heard their dog barking. Then she heard another sound, a fast-approaching vehicle, and saw moonlight reflecting off chrome and metal as a dark van came out of the night with headlights off. It roared past close enough to cause her to stumble and nearly fall, and she gazed after it as it sped down the hill and disappeared around the curve with only a brief flash of brake lights.

She moved on, turned into the driveway and struggled toward the open front door. The dimly lit chandelier spilled a soft cone of light over a figure sprawled in the foyer at the bottom of the stairway. She hurried now, fueled by willpower only, unaware that she was whimpering, and when she pushed her way through the door to where he lay, she sank to the floor beside him and just sat there, gently rocking back and forth as she gazed unblinkingly at the bloody mass of broken skull bone and matted hair. "No," she said softly, and shook her head. "No . . . no." Unmindful of the pool of blood that was still spreading, she gently lowered herself across his body and rested her cheek against his back. "No."

She was still there ten minutes later when two highway patrol cars pulled into the driveway in response to an urgent call from the Delgados.

It took two very large men to remove Marilee Grady from her husband's body.

Chapter
—13—

Cage had told Caprita he wasn't going to the funeral. He hadn't been to one since he was eleven years old, he said, after his parents were killed by an out-of-control pickup that slammed into their car while they were gassing up at a Union 76 station in Greensboro, North Carolina. He vowed then he'd never go to another one, because he'd never been able to put that ritual of death out of his mind—the final vision of watching someone you loved or cared for being lowered into the ground and covered with dirt. He said he'd rather remember Michael Grady as he'd last seen him—full of life, warmth, and energy, carrying a set of tongs and a tall drink and wearing a silly chef's hat. He didn't want that image replaced by a cold coffin containing an empty husk that had been cut and stitched and drained and plugged. That wasn't Michael Grady. Cage said he thought Michael would understand. He hoped Marilee would.

Now he was waiting for it to be over and Caprita to get home, tilted back in the recliner with the living room curtains drawn and the only light coming from the aquarium and TV. He was saying good-bye to Michael Grady in his own way—watching a rented video of *Angel Wars* and smoking his first joint in five months, which he'd rolled from the small Ziploc packet Grady had given him . . . the day he'd sold him the backup security system that had gotten him killed.

Cage took a deep drag, held it, then sighed, watching the smoke swirl lazily in the back light from the TV. He was having a hard time concentrating on the movie, because he kept slipping deep inside himself to hold philosophical conversations with his private dinosaur.

What does it take anymore, Cage was thinking, for a man to secure his home and family from violent intrusion by the human predators of the world?

That's easy, my friend. When dealing with predators of your own species, you must be a territorial tyrant. Like the tiger who marks the boundaries of his hunting domain with the scent of his urine as a warning to other cats. Potential invaders must then be made aware that you, like the tiger, possess the will and fierceness to attack at the first hint of intrusion. The tiger does not need alarms, or even barriers, to safeguard his kingdom. The scent of his spray is enough.

Great, Cage thought. So we all just piss on our doors and snarl at anyone who comes too close, is that it?

That would do it.

That's insane.

So are violent intruders. And they only fear those who are equally insane. That's a universal rule, as unbreakable as the wind.

And what do you do if the piss shield evaporates and a predator crushes the head of someone you consider to be a friend?

Do you have to ask?

Not really. But you're supposed to be my voice of reason.

I am. But there is no reasoning with violent intruders.

Cage was still in the recliner when Caprita came home. She paused inside the door to pull off her black high heels, sniffed, then padded into the living room and slid a hip onto the arm of the chair.

"You've been smoking," she said, and stroked his hair.

"Just one. You have your herbs, I have mine. How'd it go?"

"About the way you'd expect. Cars were lined up halfway around Forest Lawn, and the press were everywhere. They stayed mostly in the background and tried to be respectful, but there was no escaping their cameras. I got to sit with Marilee and the Maljeans, which surprised me, but that's the way she wanted it."

"She held up all right?"

"A lot better than I ever could. She just sat there looking straight ahead during the entire service; her eyes never once left that casket. And the only time she came close to crying was when they were lowering it into the ground. I thought she might lose it then, but she reached over and squeezed my hand so hard my fingers went numb."

"Yeah," Cage said. "I know the feeling."

"She certainly is strong. In more ways than one." Caprita ran a finger along his cheek, leaned down and kissed it. "You need a shave. Are you all right?"

"I'm fine."

"Then why are you sitting in the dark staring at snow on the television?"

"The video ran out."

"Angel Wars? Did you watch it?"

"I watched it, but I didn't see much of it. And I guess I'm not doing so good in the conversation department either, am I?"

"You're just a little laid back, that's all."

"Wigged-out is a better phrase," he said. "I don't have a lot of friends, Caprita. I don't like losing one. Not that way."

"Boy, you really are down, aren't you? Want to talk about it?"

He didn't. But his private dinosaur, fueled by THC, was straining to speak out in profound and philosophical terms about friendships and not being too trusting.

Cage said, "Have you ever noticed how different we are in how we look at people?"

"I always thought we had the same criteria."

"We do, more or less. But we don't reach our conclusions the same way. You see the good in people, accept the face they show you as genuine. You like to believe that what you see is what you get until they prove otherwise. Me, I'm just the opposite. I'm on the lookout for the dark side of human nature, because I believe we all have one. I meet somebody, I automatically skip the smile and canned pleasantries and search for hidden motives. If I don't find any, I go from there. Michael Grady passed that test with flying colors. Everything he said or did was right up front, you knew exactly where he was coming from. He opened his home to me, shared his time and concern with you, and made us laugh in time of trouble even while watching his own wife's health deteriorate. I don't know about anybody else, but I call that a friend. And he deserves equal consideration."

"I don't mean to be cynical," Caprita said, "but there isn't a whole lot you can do for him now. I could come up with all sorts of clichés about letting go and life being for the living, but you know them all as well as I do. Right now you're angry and hurt and a little high, but you'll get over it. Everyone does. Now why don't you let me fix you something to eat. That will help."

"Later maybe," he said, and fell silent, the reflective mood broken. Now he was feeling only fatigue, and his eyes were smarting from staring at the flickering television. Caprita was right, he knew. In a few days the sharp pain of loss would subside to a dull ache, and soon after even that would fade. Before long Michael Grady would become a vague memory, no more pleasurable to recall than . . . well, one of his movies. That was also the way of the world. Everyone gets over it.

Only Cage didn't want to. Not yet.

Caprita got up, turned off the TV, and opened the curtains to let in the late afternoon sunlight. Cage followed her with his eyes, taking in the knee-length skirt and matching jacket with the flared waist, her hair windblown and out of place. What a shame, he thought, how good she looked in black.

She settled into the easy chair, tucked a leg beneath her and regarded him with concern. "Now I have to talk to you about something, but I'm a little reluctant to do it."

"Go ahead."

"Well, Marilee's housekeeper quit. Apparently she was terrified out of her mind over what happened."

"That's understandable. She was a little on the timid side anyway. Who's helping her now?"

"No one. Not on a regular basis. Frances Maljean, a few others, drop in and give her a hand with things.

But she really needs someone full-time, especially now, and she is not up to dealing with strangers."

"Caprita, if you're saying you'd like to help her out a few days, it's okay with me."

"I did kind of make the offer today. She politely refused at first, saying she could manage, but then I kind of insisted. I told her I still have nine days left on my suspension and absolutely nothing else to do. She was relieved, Allen. I could tell. But she said only on the condition that I discuss it with you first. Isn't that something? After all she's been through, she still has the dignity to be that considerate of other people's feelings."

"Like I told you," Cage said, "the lady's got a lot of class."

"Then you really wouldn't mind? Not even if I stayed over?"

Cage said, "Well, I might mind that, but I wouldn't object. Stay as long as you think is necessary."

"Good. I knew you'd understand. But I'm still concerned about leaving you alone right now."

"You don't have to worry about that," he said. "I'm gonna be busy anyway."

"Doing what?"

"Trying to find out who killed him."

Later, Cage carried her suitcase out through the enclosed patio to the carport and put it in the trunk of her Mazda, then leaned against the fender with his arms folded and waited for her. Pawing the asphalt and thinking. It was hot and sticky, and he could hear sounds of laughter and splashing coming from the swimming pool on the other side of the small single-story complex. Caprita's friend was out there, Kristina Urton, a dental assistant who lived three doors down with a Burmese cat even more stuck up than Grits, and Caprita was saying good-bye to her.

Finally she came hurrying through the side gate, checking her purse. Cage held the car door open for her and handed the keys through the window after she was inside.

Caprita said, "I'll call you tonight, okay? Now don't sit there and brood, it isn't healthy."

Cage said, "I'll probably stop by sometime tomorrow, if I have a chance. Tell Marilee if there's anything I can do for her . . . you know."

"I know," she said. "Now give me a kiss, I gotta go."

Cage leaned in and kissed her, then stepped away as she backed out, waved, and sped off down the driveway.

What a fucked-up day.

He went back inside and called the office. There was no answer, so he tried Larry's number in Glendale and got him on the second ring.

Cage said, "You closed shop early today. What's up?"

"We shut down at noon out of respect for Grady," Larry said. "We didn't think it was appropriate to attend the funeral since we really didn't know him. But Paul thought a token gesture was called for anyway. Did you change your mind and go?"

"No. But Caprita did. She sat with Marilee. The housekeeper quit, so Caprita's gonna be spending a few days over there till she can find a replacement."

"That was nice of her."

Cage said, "Well, the reason I called is to ask you a favor."

"What kind of favor?"

"I'd like you to run a check through NCIC on this guy Bobby Lee Gettis, the guy who I told you O.D.'d In Wilshire Memorial last week."

"What for?"

"It's possible he might've been involved in hitting Michael's friends' house," Cage said. "The Maljeans. You remember, the lady who lost that big necklace?"

Larry was quiet for a moment, then said, "Cage, the guy's *dead*. Whoever did the Maljeans almost certainly did Michael Grady too. That kind of lets your guy out, doesn't it?"

Cage said, "But he could've been working with somebody. If he's got a rap sheet, another name might pop up, a known associate. He had to have some reason for having that fucking clipping, Larry."

Larry, sounding tired, said, "All right, guy, I'll have him scanned. I'll need at least his full name and D.O.B."

"They'll have it on his admission form at Wilshire," Cage said. "Can you get it?"

"I can get it. I'll take care of it in the morning."

"Thanks, Larry, I appreciate it."

Larry said, "Let me stick my nose in here a minute and give you a friend's advice. Don't take this too personal, all right? I know you liked the guy, and it's a goddamn shame what happened to him, no argument there. But don't go on an emotional witch hunt for suspects. Number one, you're too close to it to be making objective observations, and number two, it's a police matter. Now I'll run this guy. But if we come up with anything promising, it goes to the proper people. Agreed?"

Cage said, "Larry, I can't stop you from doing

whatever you want with whatever information you get. I'm just asking you to get it."

"And you stay out of it, right?"

"Let's put it this way," Cage said, "which is about as clear as I can make it. I won't butt in any place where I'm not asked. How's that?"

Larry sighed and said, "Well, I guess it'll have to do."

Chapter
—14—

Cage decided to pay Marilee a visit the next morning to explain why he hadn't attended Michael's funeral. He wanted to do it in person, not over the phone, hiding behind miles of impersonal cable that carried your words but not your expression. She had that much coming. He also didn't want to be hanging around the office all morning like an expectant father, waiting for Larry to get the scoop on Bobby Lee Gettis.

It was quarter to ten when he got there. Caprita answered the door, wearing jeans and a tank top and her hair pulled back in a ponytail.

Cage said, "Hi, babe. How's she doing?"

"Right now she's about half smashed," Caprita said. "She's been downing Bloody Marys since eight-thirty. She won't take any calls and she won't eat any breakfast, and I'm getting a little worried about her. Come on in."

Marilee was in the den, reclining on the couch with her feet propped on an ottoman, rubbing a glass thoughtfully against her cheek. She had on a blue robe that was parted at her knees, and for the first time he was able to see her legs, thin and fragile inside their support braces. The stereo was on low, playing light jazz.

Cage said, "How are you, Marilee?"

"Jus' fine." She held her glass up to him, took a lengthy swallow, then set it on the end table. "Sit down, Allen, make yourself at home. Would you like a drink? I hate to drink alone, and Caprita won't join me."

Cage sat down at the opposite end of the couch, feeling stiff and awkward. "I'm not much of a drinker, Marilee, but I'll take some coffee, if you have any."

"I'll get it," Caprita said, and left the room.

Cage cleared his throat. "Marilee, about yesterday . . ."

"That's all right, Allen. Caprita already explained how you feel about—about funerals. Believe me, I understand. If it weren't expected, I might've done the same. I would've felt much closer to him sitting right here, where he would watch one of his films being shown on TV and curse a blue streak because they always cut the best parts."

She took another swallow of her drink, ice cubes clinking, and held the glass to her cheek again. "He used to hate that, having his films edited for television. Said they closed their eyes and used hedge clippers till they had it the right length."

Caprita came back with a mug of black coffee, placed it on the coffee table in front of Cage, then went over to the bar and hiked herself onto a stool.

Marilee continued reminiscing, her eyes focused on nothing. "Michael was impatient with everything. Except me. He treated me like a china doll, always hovering, overprotective, so afraid I was gonna fall or something. When the polio started coming back, he wanted to install a chair lift till I convinced him that using the stairs on my own was far better for me."

Cage said, "The man loved you, all right. That was pretty obvious."

"Yes he did, Allen, that he did. And it never ceased to amaze me in the eighteen years we were married. He could've had almost any woman he wanted. A whole woman, not some cripple who couldn't even make love properly."

"Marilee, that isn't fair and you know it," Caprita said. "You *are* a whole woman, more than a hell of a lot of others I've known, and I won't sit here and listen to you refer to yourself as a cripple."

Marilee smiled. "See why I like her, Allen? Won't let me get away with anything. Won't even fix me another drink, will you, 'Prita?"

"No," Caprita said firmly. "At least not until you eat something."

"But she's wrong, Allen, I am a cripple. Only with Michael I could almost pretend I wasn't. That's how good he made me feel. I was a twenty-three-year-old virgin when we met, a teller at Bank of America. One day Michael came in to cash a check and asked me out. I thanked him but said no. He could only see me from the waist up. After that he was in almost every day, laughing and teasing, telling me how much I was missing not letting him take me dancing, or to the beach. Even wanted to teach me how to play tennis. Then one day he showed up just as I was coming back from lunch, and for the first time saw me in all my radiant glory."

Marilee paused and peered into her now-empty glass, jiggling the cubes. She held that pose, like she was reading tea leaves, and continued.

"Well, after that he was all apologies, saying he didn't know and generally falling all over himself with embarrassment. But he still asked me out, and I finally went to dinner with him just to ease his conscience. The next thing I knew he was telling me how much he loved me, that he had from the first time he saw me, and that nothing had changed. And he made me believe it. Three months later we were married, and my life has been heaven ever since."

With a strength that surprised Cage, Marilee drew back and sent the glass flying across the room to shatter on the wood-paneled wall.

"Until some sonofabitch came along and turned it into a living hell!" she said, her voice cracking.

Cage and Caprita looked at each other in shock, then at Marilee, who just as suddenly regained her composure.

"Sorry 'bout that," she said mildly. "Wasn't that silly? 'Prita, I think maybe I'll eat a little something after all."

Caprita said, "Good! And then if you want, we'll both throw glasses. How about you, Allen?"

"No thanks," Cage said, "I have to get back. But I would like to ask you something, Marilee, if it's not a bad time."

"All right."

"Can you remember anything else about that night you haven't already told the police? I don't want to press you, but every little detail's important."

Marilee shook her head. "The only thing I saw was a dark van without lights. It almost ran me over. That's it."

"Okay, that's fine. Now just one more thing."

"Allen," Caprita said, giving him a sharp look.

"Just a second, babe. Marilee, would it be all right with you if I tried to find out who did this on my own?"

"By all means."

"Then you want me to?"

"Of course I want you to, you didn't have to ask me that."

"I know," Cage said. "I just wanted you to ask me."

Cage skipped lunch and worked steadily through the afternoon on the thick stack of paperwork that had accumulated in his tray, wondering where the hell Larry was. He'd been neglecting things the last few days, his mind too full of Michael Grady thoughts to be effective in business matters, and Paul Banes had started to show signs of impatience. Cage hadn't been making his call-backs, hadn't followed up on consultation requests, and had even missed an appointment with the owner of a large wholesale clothing outlet in Van Nuys who was interested in Paul's high-resonance microwave unit. Fortunately, Paul had salvaged the deal by going out and making the presentation himself. After that one Paul had cut his eyes at him, stated in a flat tone that his grace period was over and suggested it might be time to get his head out of the sand and get back to work.

It was after three when Larry finally showed up. Cage was on him before he even got to his desk.

"Well, what'd you find out?"

"Will you take it easy?" Larry said, settling into his swivel chair and reaching for the phone. "You're really starting to get pushy, you know it? Somebody had to pick up the slack around here, so give me a break."

Cage said, "All right, I got the message. I'm about all caught up now, so you and Paul can stop beating me over the head."

Larry, dialing, said, "Life does go on, my friend."

"Yeah, right. Who you calling?"

"The local field office, now will you be quiet for two minutes? . . . Yes, Jerry Culpepper, please. Larry Twiford." After a moment he said, "Jerry, how you doing? I was wondering if you got anything on that name I fed you. Yeah, I can wait." To Cage he said, "Where's Paul and Olive Oyl?"

"Paul's in back and Brenda's in the bathroom."

"Would you mind getting me a Diet Coke? I need something to cut this smog."

Cage went into the kitchenette, got a Diet Coke out of the refrigerator, and brought it back to Larry, who was writing on a message pad while he listened.

"Uh-huh. When was that? Anything the Bureau would be interested in? How about his data sheet, or do you have one? Okay, good enough. Thanks Jerry, I appreciate it."

Larry hung up the phone and said, "Well, he's in the computer. He's never been a major player, but he stayed active."

Brenda came in and went to her desk, saying, "Who's in the computer?"

"The guy who O.D.'d at Wilshire Memorial and got Caprita suspended," Larry said. "Cage wants to play detective. Gettis had four arrests and two convictions reported. He got three to five in June of 'seventy-eight for burglary, that was in Florida, another nickle in April of 'eighty-five for assault with intent. That was in Seattle."

Cage said, "April 'eighty-five, huh? Counting jail

time, and assuming he didn't make parole, he probably hadn't been out long. He just might've been the one who hit the Maljean place."

Paul Banes pushed through the curtained doorway and headed for the water cooler. A magnifying lens was pushed up on his forehead and a rubber skullcap covered his hair. He said, "The person who hit the Maljeans is the same one who hit Grady."

"That's what I told him," Larry said.

Cage said, "How can you be so sure? I know both places are in the same area, but that could just be coincidence."

"Nothing coincidental about the way they were done," Larry said. "The guy knows how to circumvent alarms and he knows how to open safes without peeling, burning, or drilling them."

"How do you know the Maljeans had a safe?" Cage asked him. "And that it wasn't peeled, burned or drilled?"

"It's my business to know these things," Paul said. "It's how I make my living. I've got a file on every professional hit reported in the L.A. area in the last five years, and these last two jobs were definitely professional. The odds of two pros hitting two houses that close together in the exact same way are astronomical. Plus, the guy's obviously got a sequence counter, and those babies are expensive and hard to get."

Cage said, "What the hell is a sequence counter?"

"A little electronic box with sensors that attach above and below the dial. As sensitive as a seismograph, picks up the sounds of the tumblers and displays the proper sequence when they're aligned. Safe manufacturers don't even like to admit they exist, for obvious reasons. But this guy has one, you can bet on it. And that puts him in very exclusive company."

Cage thought about it, not ready to give up his theory just yet, then said, "Well maybe Gettis was working with somebody. Does he have any known associates, Larry?"

"The Bureau doesn't have a data sheet on him," Larry said. "He's never done anything federal, not that they know of. All NCIC has is information reported by local agencies."

Paul crumpled his Dixie cup and tossed it into the wastebasket. He said, "Cage, what are you doing? We all feel bad about Grady, but you're getting carried away. The man was a client, you knew him less than a week."

"Six days," Cage said. "Larry and I became friends in two. Sometimes it happens that way. I knew I loved Caprita in three days. He wasn't just a client to me. And I sold him the system that ended up getting him killed."

"That system did what it was supposed to do," Larry said. "Grady got himself killed and you know it."

"I still say we should assume a little responsibility."

"And do what?" Larry asked.

"Find out more about Bobby Lee Gettis, for one thing. He fits in this picture somewhere, unless you think he carried that clipping around for five months because he had a crush on Frances Maljean. Let's talk to his girlfriend, the one who owned the car he was driving and visited him at Wilshire. We can get her address from the accident report."

Paul made a sound of disgust and stalked back to

his workshop, folding a stick of Juicy Fruit into his mouth.

Larry said, "You told me you weren't gonna butt into this. Didn't you tell me that?"

"I said unless I was asked, and I was, this morning. By Marilee Grady."

"Yeah, well I can imagine how that came about. You're not getting any more help from me, buddy."

"Suit yourself. I can get the address on my own."

"I'm telling you right now, Cage, don't do anything that's gonna reflect on this firm in a bad way. And remember, you're technically on parole."

"Whatever I do," Cage said, "will be on my own time and on my own conscience."

"And what if you did just happen to stumble up and find out who killed Michael Grady?" Larry asked. "What *would* you do?"

Cage was silent for several moments before answering. "I don't know, Larry," he said. "I really don't know."

Cage pushed the door bell of apartment 309, didn't hear it ringing inside, then knocked. He was ready to knock again, thinking he was being drowned out by the loud TV in there, when the door opened on its chain lock.

Diane Acres looked out at the tall man in the tweed sport coat and striped tie and thought, Oh my God, here we go again.

Cage said, "Diane Acres?"

Diane said, "I've already told you people everything I know. I have to get my little girl ready for bed."

"This won't take long," Cage said. "It concerns a homicide investigation."

"Homicide?"

"Yes, ma'am. May I come in? Or would you rather talk someplace else?"

Diane sighed. "Like downtown, I suppose, huh?" She closed the door to take off the chain, then opened it wide and turned away, resigned. "Let's do it here then and get it over with," she said. "I'm not goin' anywhere this time of night."

Cage followed her into the living room, noting that Diane Acres refused to acknowledge that she could no longer fit comfortably into her burgundy Bermuda shorts and white crop top. Parts of her were rippling outward like the man on the Michelin tire sign. She scooped up a little girl sprawled on the floor in front of the TV watching *Taxi* and lowered the volume.

"I'll only be a minute," she said. "Just sit anywhere." She headed for a bedroom with the little girl draped over her shoulder. Cage winked at the retreating face and was rewarded with a shy smile.

When Diane came back, Cage was sitting on the sofa pretending to be reading from a spiral notebook. She sat sideways next to him, and Cage put the notebook away.

"Now what's this about a homicide?" she said. "I don't know nothin' about any homicide."

Cage said, "Miss Acres, we can get through this a whole lot quicker if you let me ask the questions and you answer them." Larry had taught him all about the psych game that went with interrogation; always take the initiative, act like you knew a lot more than you did, and give the impression that the subject was right on the verge of being in deep shit.

"Fine," she said, and threw up her hands. "Ask away."

"When did Bobby Lee get out of the joint in Washington?"

"Oh, you know about that do you?"

"When, Miss Acres?"

"Okay, let me think. Let's see, he showed up here Sunday a week ago, straight from Walla Walla. He said it took him two days by bus. So that would make it, what? About Friday, I guess."

The same day the Maljeans got hit, Cage thought. Another coincidence? But if Diane was right, then he couldn't have done the Maljean job either.

"How long did you know him?" Cage asked.

"Oh, gee, a long time. A little over seven years. We met in Miami Beach in 1982, I forget the month. We kinda split up about six or eight months later. That's when he went up to Seattle and beat up that girl and got sent to Walla Walla." Diane looked a little wistful.

"Did you have any contact with him while he was there?"

"Some. We wrote to each other. That's after I— after I moved out here." She wasn't about to tell him anything about that jerk in Pasadena.

"So you decided to get back together, is that it?"

"Somethin' like that." Diane began picking at the sofa threads. "We talked about it. People split up all the time, you know, and they realize they made a mistake and want to try it again." She took a deep breath, her breasts straining the crop top to the limit, then let it out. "And then he had to go and pull that dumb shit in the hospital and kill himself. I couldn't believe it."

Cage said, "Where'd he get the coke, Diane? You bring it to him?"

"Oh no you don't," she said, and folded her arms

under her breasts, giving him a withering look. "That's the same thing that other cop asked me, sittin' right where you're sittin' now. He actually *accused* me of doin' it. I've never done coke, and I wouldn't begin to know where to get it if I did. I don't even drink, except maybe a beer once in a while."

Cage believed her. Diane Acres was not a good enough actress to fake that kind of righteous indignation. Diane Acres would have trouble faking anything, including overwhelming grief. Cage didn't believe she'd been that sure of Bobby Lee Gettis to begin with.

"Then where'd he get it, Diane?"

"I've wondered the same thing," she said. "I really have. I know he didn't have any here. And I sure don't see how he could've got any past the doctors in the emergency room after havin' his clothes cut off and him not bein' able to move. And that other cop said I was his only visitor. I might not be the smartest person in the world, but I can't for the life of me figure out where it came from. Can you?"

She had a point there. He filed the thought away for future reference and removed the worn newspaper clipping from his coat pocket. He unfolded it and held it out to her.

"Have you ever seen this?"

Diane barely glanced at it before saying, "Sure, Bobby Lee showed it to me."

"Why?"

"He was tellin' me about that man, Horance Griswald."

Cage, suddenly alert, said, "What was he telling you?"

"Just that this Griswald owed him some money for

somethin' they did back in Florida a long time ago . . . he owed *Bobby Lee* money, not the other way around. He was on the way back from seein' him the night he ended up in that Baskin-Robbins window."

Diane hesitated, a faraway look in her eyes, then said, "Wait a minute. This man Griswald, he isn't dead is he? Bobby Lee didn't kill him, did he? Jeez, I haven't been followin' the news or anything since all this happened."

"Why would you think that?"

She started plucking at the sofa again and said, "No reason. It's just that you said this was a homicide investigation and all . . . you know."

No. Not a very good actress at all.

Cage said, "Diane, you've done real good up until now. Don't blow it and make yourself an accessory after the fact by covering up for him. Bobby Lee can't be hurt anymore, but you can."

"Okay, I get the message," she said, and did her breathing routine again. "When I went to visit him in the hospital he kept talkin' about a gun and a briefcase, wantin' me to go out and check the car. I told him I'd already checked the car and there wasn't any gun or briefcase in it. He was all upset and looked really scared. I thought he was out of his head. And that's all I know about *that!*"

Cage sat there looking at her, watching her fidget while he tried to put all this unexpected information he was getting into context.

Diane was hoping he didn't know anything about the six hundred dollars she'd found stuffed between the car seats, most of which she'd already spent.

Cage said, "Diane, did you tell the other officer you talked to about this?"

"He never asked. He said he was from narcotics, and the only thing he was interested in was trying to get me to admit I brought Bobby Lee cocaine."

"Yeah," Cage said. "Those guys can get a little hard-nosed sometimes."

"Tell me somethin' I don't know! You're not too bad though, I don't mind talkin' to you. But can we end this now? I swear I've told you everything I know, and I have to iron my skirt for work tomorrow."

"I think that just about covers it. You've been very helpful, Miss Acres, I appreciate it."

"Am I gonna be bothered anymore by you people? I just want to mind my own business and be left alone."

"I'll tell you what," Cage said. "Just forget this conversation ever took place, and I'll guarantee no visits from the police because of it. Deal?"

Chapter
—15—

When Brenda Alworth arrived at 7:45 the next morning and found Cage already at his desk with his head bowed over an open file folder, she wrinkled her forehead in surprise.

"Well, what are you doing here so early?" she said. "Did you spend the night?"

Without looking up, Cage said, "I feel like it. Didn't sleep worth a shit. Coffee's already made."

"This is a day to remember," she said, and went into the kitchenette. She came back and went to her desk, turned on the IBM and looked at Cage, who was still engrossed in his reading. "Whatcha got there?"

"Paul's burglary file. He's got everything in here except the names of who did them."

"Paul says he could probably even get those if he had a computerized listing of all known professionals and detailed M.O.'s. He said that all pros with that kind of ability leave an identifiable signature somewhere on their work, just as if they'd left a business card behind."

"Eighteen jobs over a five-year period," Cage said. "Doesn't sound like a lot for the area he's including. But I guess these guys don't need to work very often, considering the size of the takes. Here's one right here for better than five million. Jewels and coins. Auction gallery in Anaheim. Jesus Christ, they had the laser optiscan *and* a pressure-plate system. This guy's good."

"Kind of disillusions you about how effective modern technology really is, doesn't it? Paul says that's why the best alarm system in the world is—"

"The one nobody knows is there," Cage said. "I know. Depends on how you look at it, I guess." He flipped a page, studied it a moment. "The police made arrests in three of these, huh?" he said. "This guy Kevin Dotson, they tagged him with two of 'em."

"And Paul's certain he's responsible for two others. Read the appendix."

Cage skipped down to the bottom of the page, where Paul had noted the reasoning behind his conclusion: One small but unique common denominator that police investigators had overlooked in each of the four burglaries was that the wire loops used to feed the corresponding voltage into the system while the primary lines were cut measured exactly seventeen and a quarter inches in length, signifying that they had all been prepared at the same time by a very finicky thief. Nobody had thought to measure them until Paul, quietly putting together his master file, asked Larry to make the suggestion. The information by itself wasn't enough to convict, but it allowed the police to focus their investigation on one suspect, Dotson, and to scare the shit out of him by making him wonder how they'd gotten on to him. Most alarm bandits simply cut their loops at random lengths, but Dotson had been too meticulous for his own good. They would probably end up charging him with all four burglaries and then plea bargain for a reduced sentence just to clear their books, since he was definitely going up on the two they had him on anyway.

Which brought Cage back to the issue at hand, and he turned to another page.

"Paul has asterisks next to seven cases," he said. "He summarizes them by saying they're definitely the work of one individual because of two distinguishing factors. One, they show evidence of a digital sequence counter to open the safes, and two, frozen foods in the freezers had been unwrapped. Even the police probably put that together."

"Make that eight cases," Brenda said quietly. "I'm working on Michael Grady's now." She turned back to her computer.

"Yeah," Cage said. "We can't forget him, can we?"

He closed the folder and returned it to the file cabinet, then thought for a minute. He said, "Isn't Paul leaving for Denver today?"

"Yes. The convention starts Monday, and he'll be gone all next week. He's demonstrating his remote lock at the products display."

"Where's Larry?"

"He has two appointments this morning. I don't expect him until this afternoon sometime." She checked her desk calendar and said, "Speaking of appointments . . ."

"I know. I have one at nine o'clock. Do me a favor. If Larry calls in before noon—and he probably will just to check on me—ask him to meet me at Pink's for lunch between twelve-thirty and one. And tell him it's important."

"Sounds serious," Brenda said, scribbling on a message pad.

"It is," Cage said. "You might have another common denominator to add to those seven cases we were just talking about . . . or I should say eight cases."

Cage was in his Camaro parked at the curb in front of Pink's Famous Chilidogs on Pico Boulevard, trying to eat one of the famous dogs without dripping the thick chili all over his charcoal-gray slacks, sipping occasionally from an Orange Julius perched on the dashboard.

He'd spent two hours at the small mom-and-pop jewelry repair shop on Melrose, patiently going through the Banes and Twiford product catalogue with the little sixty-three-year-old lady with the strawberry-red hair straight out of Lady Clairol.

She was fed up with the break-ins, she said, young whippersnappers cutting through the wire screen over the back window, crawling in and making off with anything they could get their hands on real quick. The accordion gate across the front was no big help either, she told him, they'd just break the lock with a crowbar or whatever, right there in front of God and everybody, and smash the fucking window—those were her exact words, just smash the fucking window—then grab whatever little trinkets she had in the case and run like hell. Her name was Velma Dykeston and she wanted something that made noise—a *lot* of fucking noise—the instant one of those little bastards so much as laid a finger on her accordion gate or the alley window, and she wanted it now. She just hoped the fuck he wasn't as expensive as some of those others she'd talked to, who obviously didn't give a good fuck for the God-fearing elderly and wanted to drain their life's blood right out of their bodies for a simple little alarm. Cage had finally sold her a pressure Klaxon that was guaranteed to shake her right out of her upstairs apartment bed whenever six pounds per square inch of pressure was exerted on the security gate or window screen. He told her he'd be back the next day to install it, and then got out of there, feeling like he'd just got off the granddaddy of all roller coasters and thinking that the ultimate sign that the world was on the brink of moral anarchy was when grandmothers started saying fuck.

Cage heard a horn and looked through the rearview mirror to see Larry's green and white Mercury Cougar pulling in behind him. Larry got out, held up a finger to signal just a minute, and went over to the serving window. He bought an Orange Julius, then came over and slid into the front seat beside Cage.

The first thing Larry said was, "You make your appointment this morning?"

"Yes, Larry, I made my appointment. I even sold a Klaxon, how about that?"

"Good man, you just made eighty-seven dollars commission. Now what's on your mind that's so important?"

Cage said, "Don't you like these chili dogs? You used to eat 'em all the time."

"I love those chili dogs," Larry said, "but they make me fart for two days after, and Doris doesn't like that. Anyway, I'm on a diet. Now what's up?"

"Slow down, will you? I'm trying to judge your mood 'cause I'm gonna ask you to do something for me."

"My mood's immaterial. I told you yesterday I wasn't helping you on this anymore."

"At least listen to what I have to say."

"I'm listening," Larry said, and sucked his Orange Julius through the straw.

Cage said, "First of all I went to see this woman Diane Acres last night, the one who owns the car Bobby Lee Gettis wrecked."

"So you found her, congratulations. Top-notch detective work."

"You might think that for real when you hear what she told me."

Cage detailed his conversation with Diane Acres between gooey bites of chili dog and quick swigs of his Orange Julius. Larry listened, half-heartedly at first, but then with growing interest when Cage told him about the briefcase and gun and that Bobby Lee Gettis's attention had all been directed at Horance Griswald and not Frances Maljean's necklace.

When Cage finished he crushed the paper wrapping, pushed the waste into the carryout bag, and said, "Well, what do you think?"

"I think it confirms that Bobby Lee Gettis didn't have anything to do with the Maljean burglary," Larry said.

"Not that. I mean what do you think Gettis was so interested in Horance Griswald for? And don't tell me you're buying that shit about him wanting to collect some money the guy owed him for doing some work for him back in Florida. You don't go collecting honest debts with a gun."

Larry gazed out at a small group of young Latinos coming down the sidewalk, rapping and tapping to the sound of salsa blaring from the ghetto blaster one of them carried on his shoulder. "I don't know, Cage. Sounds like he might've went there to rob him."

"Sounded that way to me, at first," Cage said. "Only Gettis lost a briefcase in the wreck, which signals that he might've got what he went after, and yet Horance Griswald never reported any robbery.

Did you hear anything about him reporting any robbery?"

Larry said, "Nope," and sucked his drink noisily, obviously irritated that Cage had scored a major point.

Cage said, "So what does that leave?"

"The only thing left—blackmail."

"There you go, I knew you FBI guys were sharp." Cage ignored Larry's nasty look and said, "But what could a man like Horance Griswald have done to leave himself open for blackmail? Remember, Gettis planned this for months, at least as far back as March when that picture came out in the paper. So that means he recognized him, right?"

"You seem to have all the answers," Larry said. "You tell me."

"I probably could, Larry. If I had access to NCIC and could run a make on the guy."

"Oh no you don't." Larry shook his head, emphatic. "I'm not running anybody, that shit's dead. I had a hunch you were leading up to something like that."

"Your attitude's really on tilt today, you know that? You know damn good and well something's wrong here with Griswald."

"If you believe Diane Acres."

"I do believe her," Cage said. "And I believe her when she says she didn't bring Gettis any cocaine. She wasn't frightened about that allegation at all, she was angry. It was the only topic she really felt comfortable talking about."

Larry reached over and took the crumpled bag from Cage's hand and added his empty cup to it. "It's not my business, and it's not yours either," he said, and opened the door. "I'm out of it."

Cage, exasperated, said, "Then just do one thing,

okay? Call those seven people Paul has listed in his burglary file that he thinks were all hit by the same guy. Ask 'em one question." He thought a moment, then said, "Actually you only need to call six, forget about Frances Maljean."

"Ask 'em what?"

"Ask if any jewelry they had stolen was bought from Horance Griswald. I know Michael and the Maljeans did. If all the others did too, would that be enough to make you run a check on the guy?"

Larry got out, closed the door and leaned in through the open window. "You think that's a possibility, huh?"

"The last two did. That's bucking the odds right there."

Larry drummed his fingers against the window frame, nodding to himself. "All right," he said. "I'll call 'em. But that's all I'm promising."

"Thanks, Larry. Talk to you later."

Cage started the Camaro and pulled away, heading for Malibu. Larry didn't have to make any other promises. If he learned that all six of the other burglary victims had bought jewelry from Horance Griswald, he was going to run him all right, and run him quick. After that . . .

Cage felt the excitement creeping up his spine, his palms on the steering wheel turning moist. "You moved too soon, Griswald," he said out loud. "Way too soon. And you picked the wrong house."

It was almost two o'clock when he pulled in behind Caprita's Mazda parked in the Gradys' driveway. She answered the door, gave him a quick kiss and let him in, saying he tasted like chili.

Cage said, "Is she still on the bottle?"

"No," Caprita said, "she hasn't had a drop since

yesterday morning. I guess she just had to get it out of her system."

"She was entitled. Where is she?"

"On the sun deck, sitting there gazing out at the ocean. She still won't take any calls or see any visitors. This is going to take a little time, Allen."

"I want to talk to her."

"Go ahead. I have to finish cleaning up the kitchen. At least she's eating."

Cage went through the den and out onto the sun deck. Marilee was lounging on a cushioned deck chair by the front railing, her face turned to the ocean. She wore white pants today, with a light blue sweater draped around her shoulders and buttoned at the neck to shield her from the stiff breeze that had her long hair whipping.

Cage walked around her and leaned against the railing so he could see her face, which was partially covered by a pair of large oval sunglasses. "How you doing, Marilee?"

"Fine, Allen," she said mechanically. "The sea has a calming effect, don't you think? The womb of all life. Do you think we have a subconscious desire to return to it, Allen? It has a hypnotic pull—like walking into the shallows while a wave is going out beneath your feet and you feel like you aren't moving at all. You look down and get dizzy, experience vertigo. Do you know what I mean?"

Cage thought, Oh boy, have to be careful here. "Yeah, I know what you mean. Is that how you're feeling right now?"

"Yes. Like walking in sand with an outgoing wave. I used to be able to do that, you know. After the operation and the therapy and the constant support from Michael. It was like a miracle, something I thought would never happen. And then about a year ago it started coming back. Post-polio sequela, the doctors call it, and it's striking a lot of us who thought we'd beaten this thing. They wanted to put me in a wheelchair at first, but I refused. I thought that would be the ultimate defeat, that as long as I could remain upright I had a chance. Talk about suffering from delusions."

Cage said, "I think you've done pretty good, Marilee," and immediately wished he'd kept his mouth shut. Marilee Grady was not a woman to be patronized.

She turned her head to him and said, "Do you really? Well I agree. I didn't know how well I was doing. Michael was my guy wire, and I wasn't afraid of falling no matter how fast the wave moved or how dizzy I got. He was my courage." She looked away again. "But now I don't feel so brave anymore, Allen. I'm even frightened to try those stairs now. Caprita has to help me."

"You're still the same person, Marilee. Nothing's changed there. What you're going through in your head right now is normal, but you'll come out of it. Do whatever it takes to get out your grief, only do it hard and quick and be done with it. And then when you're empty, fill yourself up again with all the best visions you ever had of Michael Grady. Then you'll have your guy wire back."

Marilee said, "Are you speaking from experience, or do you only deal in abstractions?"

"I'm talking about survival," Cage said, "and there's nothing abstract about that. A realist doesn't waste a whole lot of time on self-pity."

This time Marilee removed her glasses before looking at him, the lines around her eyes deepening as she frowned into the sun. "You believe in being blunt, don't you?"

"Especially with people I like." Cage cleared his throat and shifted position against the railing. "I also have something to tell you, and I want to make sure you're paying attention. We might've already lucked out and got a lead on who did this. Nothing definite, but it looks promising."

Marilee waited.

"I think it might be Horance Griswald."

"The jeweler? Why would you think that?"

Cage told her, leaving nothing out. Halfway through the story Caprita appeared and eased into a chair beside Marilee, listening with growing fascination until he'd finished.

"So now we're gonna see if these other people Paul thinks were all hit by the same guy bought any jewelry from Horance Griswald. If they did, then we got our man."

Caprita said, "Then what?"

"Then we go after the proof. And we'll nail him."

"Why do you keep saying *we?*" Caprita asked. "You mean the police, don't you." Making it a statement.

Cage shrugged. "Whoever."

Marilee had her sunglasses back on and was looking out over Pacific Coast Highway at the ocean again. Cage had been watching her, looking for a reaction, but she wasn't showing any. He was jumping the gun telling her this soon, and he shouldn't have done it. But he wanted to give her something else to think about besides Michael Grady.

Speaking softly, Marilee said, "If that's true, how much more proof would anyone need?"

"I'd be ninety-nine percent sure," Cage said. "But I'd want to go for that other one percent."

Caprita said, "Otherwise it would all just be circumstantial evidence, wouldn't it? A jury could still find a reasonable doubt."

"They could," Cage said. "But we're speculating right now. It could turn out none of the others even heard of Horance Griswald."

Marilee said, "But you don't think so, do you?"

"No, I don't. Because nothing else works."

Marilee looked at him. "Then if that's the case," she said, "find that other one percent, Allen. I don't want this man to walk, as they say."

Caprita started to say something, then changed her mind and looked away, worried.

Cage said, "You got it."

The door bell was ringing when Cage came out of the bathroom with a towel wrapped around his waist. He glanced at the clock radio as he passed by the bed on the way to the living room, and wondered who would be paying him a visit at ten-thirty at night.

He looked through the peephole, then opened the door and let Larry Twiford in, who brushed past him saying, "You got any beer in this place?"

"Well, come on in, Larry," Cage said to his back, and followed him into the kitchen, where Larry was already checking out the refrigerator.

"No beer," Larry said. "Shit, don't you drink anything besides 7-Up?"

"Have some of that Burgundy, Caprita says it's good for you."

"I hate wine."

"Then have a 7-Up."

"I don't like that either."

"Well, I don't know what to tell you then."

Cage went into the bedroom to dress, and returned to find Larry stretched out in the recliner, staring gloomily at the lighted aquarium.

Cage sat in the easy chair and said, "You got something on your mind, or you just happen to be in the neighborhood?"

Larry said, "I got a lot of things on my mind. For one thing, I owe you an apology, and I don't like having to apologize to anybody. Goes against my natural tendency to feel I'm always on top of things and can't be surprised."

Cage felt the tingling sensation returning. "You talked to the other victims, didn't you? I was right."

"I talked to five of 'em," Larry said. "One family went to Europe for a month. I guess they figured it was a good time, now they don't have any jewelry left to steal."

"And?"

"And, yeah, you were right. They all bought major pieces from Horance Griswald within the last three years. Three in Beverly Hills, one in Bel Air, and one in Truesdale Estates."

Cage said, "And two in Malibu."

Cage fell silent and leaned back in the easy chair. So there it was, he thought, as simple as that. He had no doubt that the family now on vacation in Europe had also purchased some expensive trinket from Horance Griswald. What a scam. Sell them the shit, then steal it back, maybe remount the stones and sell them again. Certainly would cut down on overhead.

And for that, Michael Grady had his head smashed in like a ripe cantaloupe.

There's a point of anger that, once surpassed, brings about an eerie sort of calm. As if the emotional system can't handle any more and has to click off for a while to regroup. Cage had passed that point and felt himself sink deeper into the cushions, totally relaxed.

Larry said, "Good old Paul and his master file. That guy would've been one hell of an FBI agent."

"So now you'll run a make on Griswald?"

"I already did. Called the Department of Motor Vehicles in Sacramento and got his D.O.B. and Social Security number. And guess what? The guy had his name changed legally four years ago. Just before he moved out here from Florida."

Cage nodded, chalking one up for Diane Acres.

"His real name is Harry Grisom, and he's got a sheet. Did twenty-seven months on a five-year bit in Lake Butler. He got caught staging a fake robbery of a jewelry store he owned in Fort Lauderdale."

"How'd you find out his real name?"

"Ex-cons with legal name changes are listed in the computer under both. Or anyone with a criminal record, for that matter."

"Any connection with Bobby Lee Gettis?"

"According to the Florida Department of Corrections, Gettis did his time at Lake Butler too."

Cage said, "There you go. Blackmail. Gettis sees his picture in the paper up there in Walla Walla, only now the guy's name is Horance Griswald and he's connected with the big-money crowd. Gettis comes out with instant dollar signs in his eyes and tells the man to pay up or be exposed."

"That could be it," Larry said.

"Could be, hell," Cage said, "you know it is. He's coming back from Griswald's place with a gun and a briefcase filled with jewels, cash, or both. Only he drives through a Baskin-Robbins window and somebody in the crowd walks away with the gun and briefcase. Diane said that's all he talked about when she went to see him in the hospital. He was all frantic because they'd disappeared. Can you find anything wrong with that scenario? Or do you have something better?"

"No, I don't have anything better. It also puts a different light on how Gettis died. If this Diane Acres told the truth about not bringing him any cocaine, then you have to wonder how he got it."

Silence, both of them watching each other.

Cage said, "You waiting for me?"

Larry said, "Griswald could've easily known he was at Wilshire. There was a big write-up about it in the paper. I saw it. What would you do in his shoes?"

"Not too hard to sneak in there that time of night either."

Larry paused, eyes on the fish tank again, then said, "That would make it homicide, but you'd never prove it."

"*Two* homicides," Cage said. "I don't give a shit about Bobby Lee Gettis, but let's not forget Michael Grady."

"It's gonna be hard proving that one too."

"Sure, if we just turn it over to the cops. They'll just thank us quietly, then go out and ask the guy a bunch of bullshit questions he'll shrug at, and that'll be it."

"It might be enough for a search warrant."

"Larry, the man's not that stupid. Do you really think he's gonna keep anything incriminating lying around? All they'll do is send him running for cover if they come up empty-handed, and nobody'll dig him out."

"I don't like withholding information, Cage."

"What information? All we got here is theory. Larry, we can't blow this. Let the guy think he's in the clear for a while."

Larry looked at him. "And do what?"

"I'll talk to him."

"You'll talk to him? Thought you didn't want to scare him off?"

"I'm not a cop," Cage said, "I'm an ex-con. And we speak the same language." He slid forward to the edge of the chair and rested his elbows on his knees. "Look, I got an idea how we might bring this guy out in the open so he maybe makes a mistake. All I ask is you give me a few days and don't ask a whole lot of questions. If it doesn't work, then I won't leave the situation any worse than we found it. Will you do that for me?"

Larry kept looking at him. "What if I say no?"

"Then I'll do it anyway. But I'd rather have you on my side."

Larry sighed, pushed himself out of the recliner and headed for the door. "Three days," he said. "Then I take it to the police." He paused at the door, hand on the knob, and looked back. "Two conditions. You don't involve the firm, and if you get in trouble, you're on your own. I want your word on that, and this time I don't want any double-talk."

Cage nodded. "You got my word."

"Three days," Larry said, and left.

Cage sat there for several minutes, fine-tuning his plan for meeting Horance Griswald. He had to shake the man up, let him know he was vulnerable without giving him the feeling that all was lost. Force him to react, commit himself. Total exposure.

And then strike.

Grits came sauntering in from the kitchen, licking

his chops and looking around. He dropped to his belly in the middle of the room and regarded Cage through marble eyes that held a hint of accusation.

Cage said, "You miss her too, huh, cat? Well don't look at me with that glassy-eyed fish stare, I don't like it either. She'll be back. But right now we're stuck with each other, so what say we be friends?" Cage patted his thigh. "Come on up here you four-legged ball of fur."

Grits hesitated, then rose to his feet and did a slow stretch. He padded over to the easy chair, leaped gracefully into Cage's lap and settled there, purring.

"So what do you think?" Cage said, and lightly scratched the tiger-striped head. "Does this stuff about marking boundaries with piss have any validity, or what? Guess you never had to try it though, the way Caprita spoils you."

Grits rolled back his ears at the sound of Caprita's name and let out one of his patented meows.

Cage looked at the ceiling and said, "Jesus, listen to me, would you. I'm talking to a fucking cat. And damned if he isn't answering me."

Chapter
—16—

Every time he heard the phone ring or the Soft-Tone door chime when someone entered the shop, Horance Griswald would go tense with dread. The thing with Michael Grady had worn his nerves right to the razor edge, and he was beginning to understand why some criminals breathed a sigh of relief when the cops finally snapped on the handcuffs and said it was over. This kind of heavy shit could make you paranoid for life, drive you to Valiums and Seconal and maybe even the hard stuff.

Not that he had any subconscious desire to be caught. He had carefully gone over every move he'd made since roaring away from the Grady home and nearly running over the man's crippled wife in the process, trying to figure if he'd overlooked anything that could point the finger at him. His equipment was back in the mini-storage warehouse he leased under another name. He'd expressed the goods to Maury Bingham the following morning, and two days later had gotten a return express containing twenty-one thousand, eight hundred dollars. The .380 automatic and license plate were at the bottom of L.A. harbor, and the clothes and shoes he'd worn had been cut to shreds and dropped into a Dumpster. And just in case he'd left any identifiable tire tracks, all four of the nearly brand-new Goodyear radials on the van had been replaced and left in an alley in East L.A., where some Mexican or black would scoop them up in a hurry.

Horance was sitting in the small alcove behind his display case, grading baguettes under a ten-power magnifying glass. He could see only one remote possibility that had the potential to cause trouble— Marilee Grady had described the vehicle leaving the scene in such a hurry without lights as a dark van. But how many dark vans were in Los Angeles and vicinity? And dark what? Black, blue, brown—even purple could show up looking dark at night. That was a lot of vans.

But it was still a small cause for concern, and it bothered him. Maybe he should just get rid of the damn thing. No. That would only create attention. Just wait it out until all the noise died down and Michael Grady was relegated to the back burner with all the others. In the City of Angels, even hotshot movie directors were soon forgotten if you didn't see their names in the credits.

The Soft-Tone chimed and Horance, experiencing another mild jump in his pulse rate, looked to the door. He relaxed when he saw the tall man in the tan workshirt and blue jeans standing there gazing around like he was in the wrong place—which he obviously was.

Horance stood and turned to the counter, saying, "May I help you?"

"This is real nice," Cage said. "Got a great little place here." He bent over, peering into the glass case at the neatly arranged and expensive-looking accessories and nodded appreciatively. "Yes, sir. Bet this stuff cost a pile of money, huh?"

Horance, afraid he was about to be robbed, said, "Those are all synthetic models, sir. You do know what synthetic means, don't you?"

Cage raised up and gave Horance a look that suddenly made him feel very uncomfortable.

"Yeah," Cage said. "I think I know what that means. Artificial. Not genuine. Phony. Fake. Just like you. Am I right?"

"Now wait just a minute—"

"No, you wait just a minute," Cage said, and took a step closer to the counter. "I didn't come in here to play games or listen to any bullshit, I ain't got time for it. I came here to take care of some unfinished business my old partner Bobby Lee Gettis had."

Cage watched the expression of astonishment that crossed the man's face and knew he was right on target. Now to keep the bastard off balance.

"What's wrong, Harry Grisom? You didn't think Bobby Lee was in this all by his lonesome, did you?" He grinned and leaned on the spotless glass counter. "Me and him put this whole thing together right up there in Walla Walla. Only the prick couldn't wait for me like he was supposed to, and had to come down here and go for it himself. Now there's gratitude for you. I even let him have the bottom bunk, and he turns around and tries to fuck me . . . you all right?"

Horance had been standing with his hands clasped in front of him like a statue, unable to take his eyes off Cage. Finally, his voice hardly more than a whisper, he said, "Who are you? What do you people want from me?"

Cage swung his head around in mock innocence.

"What people? There's just you and me. Bobby Lee ain't with us anymore, remember? I'm sure you took care of that little detail too. Not that I give a shit, the way he tried to cut me out." He leaned closer to Horance and winked. "Tell you the truth, you saved me the trouble of doing it myself later."

"I don't know what you're talking about."

Cage held up his hands. "That's okay, that's cool. I told you I don't give a shit about him. What me and you need to discuss right now is what I want. You ready to talk turkey?"

Horance was having a hard time recovering, seeing the guy leering at him from across the counter like he was thoroughly pleased with the situation. What was it with blackmailers anyway that made them take such enjoyment in twisting the screws and watching their victims squirm? Life had become a succession of shocks lately. First Bobby Lee Gettis, then Michael Grady sneaking up on him with his big rifle. Now this. There was a limit to how much pressure a person could take, and Horance figured he'd just about reached his. He didn't even feel like arguing.

He drew in a deep breath and said, "How much?"

Cage said, "Oh, I don't know. I hadn't set an exact figure. See, I'm not greedy, I go with what the traffic can bear."

"The traffic can't bear very much," Horance said. "Your friend took about everything I had. He wasn't content with just blackmail, he had to resort to armed robbery and physical assault."

Cage said, "That's your story. Bobby Lee can't tell his version. For all I know, he never got a dime."

"Never got a dime hell, he beat me with a pistol and walked away with . . . a lot."

"When was this?"

"The same night he smashed his car through a store window and ended up in the hospital."

"And then ended up dead from an O.D. of coke."

"I told you I don't know anything about that."

"Yeah, right."

Horance said, "Look, I have an appointment with a client in twenty minutes. Why don't you give me your name, tell me where you're staying, and I'll give you a call later."

"I got a better idea," Cage said. "I'll come by your place tonight. Eight o'clock. Be there."

"Fine. I imagine you already know the number."

Cage pushed away from the counter, leaving two smudge marks where his forearms had pressed against the glass. He said, "Mister, I know things about you that would make your teeth chatter."

"What's that supposed to mean?"

"You'll find out tonight. And don't be of a mind to do the same thing with me that you did with Bobby Lee. I've got a neat little letter on deposit with a friend that goes straight to the cops if I should happen to disappear or turn up dead. Have a nice day, Mr. Griswald."

Cage gave him a two-finger salute and cool-walked his way to the door and out.

Horance watched him fade from sight into the lobby, then used a jeweler's cloth to wipe the smudges from the countertop. He had collected himself now, and the fear had given way to quiet anger. Who did this asshole think he was coming into his place of business with those sleepy eyes and crooked grin and issuing ultimatums? Yes, this was Bobby Lee Gettis all over again, both cut from the same bolt of cloth.

Well, he'd taken care of Bobby Lee Gettis. He'd even faced up to a man holding a rifle on him and won, his moves as slick and swift as anything the man had ever directed on screen. Only that had been very real. Horance, his mind's eye editing out the panic and blind terror he'd experienced at the moment of truth, could replay the event complete with dramatic sound track and see himself as a man to be reckoned with when the need arose.

He rubbed harder at the glass countertop, even though the smudges were now gone, and thought that perhaps he just might be able to handle the pressure after all.

He would wipe out this new threat just as completely as the stain the man had left behind.

Howie Wallmeyer had Rudy Hicks on his cellular phone while he was weaving his Thunderbird in and out of the San Diego Freeway traffic trying to get to Century City.

Howie said, "Horance Griswald, huh? What the fuck does he want with a security system in the lobby of Century Plaza, for Christ's sake?"

Rudy Hicks, who was talking from a pay phone in the very lobby, said, "I don't know, Howie, but that's where the guy's been. And he's got his work clothes on, like I said, like he's fixing to install something. And Griswald don't have any alarms in his shop."

"Shit, he don't need any, right there in one of the best-guarded hotels in L.A. You sure Cage went there on business?"

"You figure it out," Rudy said, and turned to eye three passing Pan Am flight attendants in form-fitting skirts, grinning at them through his shaggy beard. "What other reason does he have for being here? That dinky outfit doing so good he can afford to come here and order custom jewelry? And he had the guy's attention too, explaining how the thing would work and all. I watched 'em through the window."

Howie said, "Well, maybe Griswald's getting in a big shipment of stones or something."

"That's what I think too, Mr. Wallmeyer. Guy don't want to take any chances."

Howie got hemmed in beside an eighteen-wheeler that wouldn't let him into the fast lane to pass the tour bus he was rear-ending, so he shot past it on the right and nearly broadsided a Toyota entering from the on-ramp.

"That's what you think too, Rudy? Thought you just said you didn't know. Last time you thought something out on your own it made me look like a fool. Letting Twiford con you into admitting I was behind that protest shit."

"I'm right this time, Mr. Wallmeyer, I know it. Don't none of 'em, Cage or any of 'em, go to a place like this wearing work clothes without they're getting ready to install something. You know that, Mr. Wallmeyer."

"Okay, okay, hold on a minute. Where's Cage now?"

"Left about ten minutes ago. Probably going back to the shop for some kinda unit. Wouldn't be a laser though, Banes is the only one puts those in. Whatcha reckon it is?"

"I don't care, Rudy. Whatever he wants, I'll give him the same thing, or the equivalent, and go ten percent under what he's charging. I can play that game too."

"You didn't do that with that old lady on Melrose."

"That place wasn't worth fucking with. I only want the class customers."

Rudy said, "What you figure he'll do when he finds out?"

"I imagine he'll rant and rave and stamp his foot," Howie said, "but that's the breaks. I'm gonna under-bid him on every decent job he goes after even if it costs me money. Now listen, go on home and pick him up again in the morning at the shop. He's not gonna be making any calls today. I don't know how he got by you the first time at Griswald's, unless he sold him before I put you on him."

"Had to, Mr. Wallmeyer. I swear I ain't let him outta my sight, not while he's been on the job."

"Well, maybe I can still queer the deal. It's worth a go. You'd better be right about this, Rudy. I'm risking sure death from these crazy drivers trying to get there."

"It's got to be, Mr. Wallmeyer, got to be."

"Talk to you tomorrow then."

At the sound of the Soft-Tone, Horance Griswald looked up and watched the stocky man in the gray silk suit and apricot shirt enter with open suspicion. Now what the hell did *he* want? He didn't look or act like Bobby Lee Gettis and friend, and his toothy smile and slicked-back hair didn't give him the appearance of a cop, even undercover. But Horance wasn't trusting anyone from here on out, even guys in five-hundred-dollar suits and eighteen-carat gold neck chains.

"Mr. Griswald? Name's Howie Wallmeyer, how you doing?"

Howie stuck a hand across the counter and Horance gave it a limp shake, saying, "What can I do for you, Mr. Wallmeyer? If it's a special design you're inter-ested in, I only show by appointment."

Howie, laughing, said, "No, sir, I couldn't afford your stuff, Mr. Griswald, though I surely wish I could. Works of art, that's what they are, real collector's items. I'm really here to do you a favor. Here's my card."

Horance took the gold-embossed card and frowned at it. "First Alert Security Limited?"

"That's me, yes sir. President and CEO. And if I'm not mistaken, I believe you're interested in a first-rate security system. If you are, I can give you exactly what you need at a price nobody in town can beat."

"What makes you think I'm interested in a security system? The hotel provides all the security I need."

"Well, to be honest, an associate of mine happened to be next door at Gucci's a little earlier and noticed you with one of our competitors. He gave me a call and mentioned it, and I decided to come over personally and acquaint you with our products. We're authorized reps of some of the most respected names in the field."

Horance stood flicking the card with his fingernail while he gave Howie a confused look. "You say he's a competitor? What's he look like?"

Howie thought, Shit, did Rudy fuck up again? "Tall fella, late thirties, sort of dark wavy hair."

"Blue jeans and tan shirt?"

"That's him, I guess. Name's Allen Cage, works for Banes and Twiford." Howie gave what he thought sounded like an apologetic laugh. "We have this little rivalry going where we knock ourselves out trying to attract preferred clients. The main difference between us is I try a lot harder to accommodate the potential client I consider extra special, and you certainly fall into that category. To accomplish that, I'm ready to offer you the identical system he agreed to supply, only manufactured by a nationally recognized firm. And, I'll do it for ten percent less than Banes and Twiford are quoting."

Horance nodded thoughtfully and put the card in his shirt pocket. "Sounds good," he said. "How long has this Allen Cage worked for Banes and Twiford?"

"Six or seven months, something like that." Then Howie threw in what he thought would be the clincher. "Ever since he got out of prison."

Horance raised his eyebrows. "Prison? You mean he works for a private security firm and he's an ex-felon?"

"Well, that's true, Mr. Griswald." Howie sighed, really saddened by the whole affair. "Of course I don't really hold that against him, you understand. People sometimes make mistakes, and I guess he paid his debt to society. I shouldn't have even mentioned it though, I don't want to unfairly prejudice the man. Paul Banes and Larry Twiford are good people, and with a little more experience they're gonna have a decent company there."

Howie looked at his watch. "Jeez, almost eleven. And I'm supposed to be in Burbank by eleven-thirty. Tell you what, Mr. Griswald, you think it over and give me a call if you'd like to see our brochures. I'll bring 'em out myself. I'd sure like to have your business."

Horance said, "I'll do that, Mr. Wallmeyer. Thank you for stopping by, you've been very helpful."

"Well, I try to be," Howie said, and flashed his smile. "That's my job."

Chapter
—17—

Larry kept telling him to keep still, he was causing the tape to pull loose. Cage said if he'd stop pulling the skin so tight like he was trying to close a wound, maybe he wouldn't be flinching as much.

"It's supposed to be tight," Larry said, "otherwise this little sucker could slip right out at a bad time from body perspiration, and wouldn't that be neat."

Larry was talking about the small microphone he was taping to Cage's chest while he sat with his shirt unbuttoned and his legs dangling from Paul's workbench. A thin length of wire protruding from one side of the mike formed a two-inch half–moon curve in the direction of Cage's right nipple.

"You're pulling my hair out, Larry," Cage complained. "Isn't there someplace else you could put this thing where it would be more comfortable?"

"I could, but it's more stable here."

"What's the range? I'd hate to have the man confess and find out you didn't pick it up."

"It's good for at least five hundred feet, and I'll be less than a block away. Just talk normal and don't worry about having to get too close to him. This thing's very sensitive. And try to stay away from interference like the TV or running water."

"Larry, I don't plan on going to the bathroom with him. What's the patch for?"

"So it won't burn your skin. Sometimes these transmitters get a little warm after they've been on awhile. Can't have you hopping around like you've been goosed just when you get to the good part. If you ever do." Larry stepped back. "There, how's that?"

Cage slid off the bench and began buttoning his shirt. "Feels okay. Do we need to test it or anything?"

"Stop worrying, I'll read you loud and clear. I still don't know why I let you talk me into this. The guy's not gonna be dumb enough to come out and admit he pulled a bunch of burglaries."

Cage, tucking his shirttail in, said, "I told you, Larry, I only want him to cop to the Maljean hit. As far as he's concerned, I never heard of the others. If he 'fesses up, then we can definitely make him for doing Michael. He doesn't know we have this profile on him."

"He's not even gonna admit that one," Larry said. "You don't think he's gonna realize you could be wired? Come on."

"I just got out of a joint where I was Bobby Lee Gettis's road dog for three and a half years. I came straight to L.A. to put the squeeze on him. Why would I be wired to learn something I already know? Or where would I even get a wire, for that matter?"

Larry said, "Then remember not to mention anything about a black van. We already know he owns one, and the only time it was spotted was during the Grady hit."

Cage raised his eyebrows. "We do? I didn't know he owned a black van."

"That's what I meant by saying you're too close to this thing to be objective. That's the first question you should've asked yourself. Either you assumed he did or it didn't matter. When you take on this kind of responsibility, my friend, you don't assume *any*thing, and *every*thing matters."

"Marilee didn't say it was a *black* van, she said it was a *dark* van. And whether he owns one or not doesn't make any difference. He could've stolen one just for that job."

Larry waved a hand, dismissing the subject. "Never mind. Just remember our deal. Three days, then I take whatever we got to the police. No compromises."

"I still have two left," Cage said.

"Then you'd better make the most of it. What time did you say you'd be there?"

"Between nine-thirty and ten."

"We'd best get rolling then. I'll stay a couple blocks behind and you can talk to me on the way, just to ease your mind this thing really works."

Larry slipped into his suit coat, hesitated, then said, "You know he's got another choice here, if he feels cornered."

"You mean kill me? I don't think so. I told him not to get any ideas, because after Bobby Lee I put it all on paper and gave it to somebody to take to the police if he doesn't hear from me in twenty-four hours."

"That's awful weak. Everybody says that, but hardly anybody does."

Cage said, "Yeah, but he can't take that chance. Besides, like the man said, if you can't blind them with brilliance, baffle 'em with bullshit."

"What man said that? I never heard that before in my whole life."

"I don't know," Cage said. "Some man must've said it."

The garage door was down and there were no little windows to let him peek inside, so Cage couldn't see if Horance Griswald's black van was inside or not. If Larry said he had one, then that was good enough. He continued on to the front door and rang the bell, easing into the same sleepy-cool attitude he'd affected earlier, hands rammed into the back pockets of his jeans.

Horance Griswald answered the door and gave him a distasteful look. "I see you're right on time," he said, and moved aside.

Cage stood where he was and grinned at him.

Horance said, "What's wrong, you prefer to suck my blood right on my doorstep?"

Cage said, "I hope you don't have any unexpected surprises for me inside, Horance. I wasn't kidding about that letter, and I don't even have a gun." He spread his arms and did a slow turn for emphasis, showing no bulges under the tan workshirt.

Horance said, "Mister, if I wanted to kill you, I wouldn't do it in my own home. I'm the victim here, not you."

"That's very good," Cage said. "You almost sounded like you really believe it."

Horance led Cage into the study and pointed to the same chair Bobby Lee Gettis had occupied, then took a seat behind his desk.

"All right," he said, "let's get down to it. How much is this cowardly blackmail scheme of yours going to cost me?"

"First I think you should know what you're paying for. That way it won't seem like such a bad deal."

"I already know what I'm paying for. Your agreement not to destroy the respectable business I've built up by revealing my past."

"That's not quite all of it. That part would only set you back about—oh, let's say twenty-five thousand. But when you throw in my agreement not to mention the Maljean burglary and a certain necklace you must've wanted pretty bad—well, that's gonna cost you another twenty-five. Make it fifty all together and I'm outta here."

That one got to him, Cage could tell by the way the man sat motionless with his hands gripping the chair arms while he stared at him across the desk.

"Surprised, Horance? Thought you skated on that little move, didn't you?"

Horance took a moment before saying, "Whatever gave you such a preposterous idea as that?"

"Wasn't hard to come up with. I've been real interested in that piece ever since I saw it around that old broad's neck in that newspaper photo Bobby Lee found. You remember that one, don't you? I believe you were the costar."

Horance kept looking at him.

Cage said, "So imagine how disappointed I was to find out somebody beat me to it. With that in my pocket, plus whatever I split with Bobby Lee for keeping your little secret, I'd've been in good shape. But somebody gets the old lady first, then Bobby Lee comes down and puts the arm on you without waiting for me, and suddenly I'm not in such good shape anymore. And I am *mad* about it."

"I sympathize with you, mister . . . whoever you

are. I'm sure it was quite depressing, all that strenuous effort you put forth and not being rewarded."

"Damn straight."

"But how does that make me the thief?"

"By giving it a lot of consideration and putting two and two together," Cage said. "Bobby Lee told me you set up a fake robbery of a jewelry store you owned down in Fort Lauderdale, trying to rip off your insurance company. That didn't work too good, and I think you decided to refine your act. No insurance company's gonna touch you now, not after taking a close look at you. But once a crook always a crook, so now instead of robbing yourself, you steal the shit back *after* you sell it. Same difference, right? Only you got the added luxury of not having to pay all those big premiums. How am I doing?"

Horance said, "Well, you certainly have an active imagination, I'll give you that. I suppose it comes from all that idle time you must have had on your hands up there in Walla Walla."

"Maybe. But you have to admit it's got possibilities the cops wouldn't mind exploring, and who knows what they're liable to dig up."

Horance locked his fingers and rested his head against the chair back, relaxed. "Personally I don't care what you tell the authorities in that regard. The necklace I designed for Frances Maljean was a conversation piece of admiration, a constant advertisement for my work. Having it displayed so prominently at the type of social gatherings she hosted or attended was far more valuable to me than any dollar amount I might receive from stealing it. So don't even try that one, it doesn't compute."

Cage was impressed by the man's ability to bounce

back with such a convincing argument after being caught so off guard. He was a born survivor, able to adjust and ad lib as circumstances demanded, the most dangerous kind of enemy. Larry was probably out there in the car shaking his head right now.

"Since you apparently have no further comment on that hypothesis," Horance said, "I'll consider the matter closed. I believe that brings us back to the original twenty-five thousand you demanded for not giving away my past and ruining the new life I've struggled so desperately to make successful. I made a mistake and I paid for it and was so humiliated by the experience that I changed my name—*legally* changed it."

Cage was puzzled, wondering what the hell the guy was doing giving a sermon.

"However, I don't think I'm going to meet that demand either," Horance said. "That other human leech you referred to, Bobby Lee Gettis, did in fact try to put the arm on me, just like you're doing now. Well, I'm telling you like I told him—no deal. I'm not paying you a dime, and if you want to expose my regrettable past, I can't stop you."

Cage said, "Wait a minute here—"

"No," Horance said, and leaned forward with his arms on the desk. "To echo your words of this morning, *you* wait a minute. Where do people like you get the gall to feed off my old wounds? Even a vulture has the decency to wait for its victim to die before ripping the flesh from its bones. But not you, no. You want to watch me wiggle like a worm on a fish hook. Well not me, mister, I'm not caving in. So go ahead and expose me, I'll take the heat. And if I have to start over again somewhere else, I'll do that too. Now what were you going to say?"

Cage was thoroughly confused as he locked eyes with Horance Griswald and tried to figure out what had made the guy do a complete about-face since morning, when he had been all but quaking in his shoes.

Cage said, "I thought you told me you paid Bobby Lee off. Said he took everything you had and beat you with a pistol."

"I was trying to discourage you, but you're persistent. I refused to give Gettis anything and sent him out of here in a huff. Evidently he was so angry he smashed his car through some store window and landed in the hospital, where it appears he tried to console himself with illegal drugs. Don't expect me to mourn him."

"You're a liar, Griswald."

"Don't you dare call me a liar. The only thing you've been truthful about since barging into my shop this morning was admitting you're an ex-convict—Mr. Allen Cage."

And there was the answer, the end of confusion. Cage wasn't even surprised when Griswald opened the middle desk drawer and removed a compact cassette recorder. He switched it off and placed it upright on the desk.

"Still want to talk about going to the police, Mr. Cage? How do you think they'd take this? A businessman being blackmailed by a security company. Are your employers in on this too, or are you just moonlighting?"

All Cage could think of to say as he sat in the deep cushioned chair with his legs crossed was, "How did you find out?"

"From one of your competitors." Horance took the gold business card from his pocket and looked at it.

"Mister H. L. Wallmeyer, First Alert Security Systems." He put it away again. "He came in shortly after you left this morning. Someone told him you were trying to sell me an alarm system, and he offered me a ten percent discount. Yours must be a very cutthroat business."

"Howie Wallmeyer?"

"That's right. I take it you know him."

"We've met."

Horance smiled. "You'll have to convey my gratitude to him."

"I'll do that," Cage said.

"Now then, would you like to know what I'm going to do with this tape?"

"If I didn't, you'd tell me anyway." Cage felt a warmth spreading across the back of his neck, knowing he'd been outfoxed, and not even wanting to think about what Larry might be doing at that very moment.

"Certainly I'm going to tell you. I'm going to put it in a safe place and leave it for now. But if you or any member of your firm mentions one word about my past to anyone, and that includes the police, I'm going to use this lovely conversation to have you thrown right back in prison. And that's just for openers. I will then file one hell of a lawsuit against Banes and Twiford for accessory to blackmail in an attempt to destroy my business. I promise you if it comes to that I'll end up owning that company. Do you get the picture, Mr. Cage?"

"Banes and Twiford had nothing to do with this," Cage said. "It was my own idea. They don't even know about you."

"That doesn't matter. You're their agent, and whatever information you collected about my background was obviously gained by using their resources. That makes them liable through sheer negligence alone by giving a known ex-felon unrestricted access to their information-gathering apparatus."

"What information-gathering apparatus?"

"Oh, come on," Horance said. "All you people have inside contacts and you know it. I had a friend in your line of work a few years ago who told me all about that stuff. He said by simply using my name alone he could have my home and business phones tapped, learn my checking account number, all my credit card numbers, whether I have a safety deposit box, and every phone number I've called in the last year. And he said he could do it all in one day. That's scary when you think about it. In the hands of such an unscrupulous bastard as you, it could be devastating. The verdict wouldn't even be close."

Cage had an overpowering desire to take the cassette recorder and smash it right into Horance Griswald's smirking face. He managed to suppress that impulse with an effort and decided to settle for just taking the tape. He pushed out of the chair and took two steps toward the desk before Horance went back into the drawer and came out with a snub-nose .38 revolver. Cage stopped and looked at the gun wavering slightly in the jeweler's hand as the man pointed it at him. Cage somehow knew this wasn't the weapon that had killed Michael Grady. Griswald would have gotten rid of that one immediately.

"Touch that, my friend," Horance said, "and I'll shoot you where you stand."

"You don't really want to do that, Griswald. Then you'd have to tell the police everything."

"I don't want to, but I will before I let you take that tape. At the minimum, I'd have the pleasure of sending you to join Bobby Lee Gettis. It's guys like you who give ex-cons a bad name anyway."

"You want to let me hear that one again?"

Horance lowered the gun but kept it pointed at Cage. "Speaking of Gettis, I'm curious about something. How did you know he came out here to squeeze me? How do you even know about him at all?"

"You already said it. I've got access to a good information-gathering apparatus. Better than you realize."

"Oh really?"

"Yeah, really. And you know what? I'm gonna use that apparatus to full advantage and just bet I learn a few other things that'll wipe that silly grin right off your fucking face."

"Like what?"

"Like how many homes have been hit over the last couple of years or so where the owners had bought some of your jewelry. Like even this movie director who got killed last week, if he bought any or not. Like putting the word out on any and everybody known who makes or deals in sequence counters to find out if you're connected to them in any way. You know what they are, don't you? Like turning this city upside down if I have to until I learn where your equipment's buried—which I just know is gonna include a sequence counter. Like I'm gonna be on your back like a tick on a fox every time you make a move, only you'll never see me."

Cage had taken another step forward and had his fingertips pressed against the edge of the desk, causing Horance to raise the gun again, the smile gone.

"In other words, *my friend,* by the time I'm finished I'm gonna have so much shit on you that you're gonna beg me to take your money and throw in that tape as a bonus. Do you get that picture, asshole?"

"Get out of my house," Horance said, "right now! And stay out of my life, I'm warning you."

"I'm leaving. But I'll be back. And then I'm really gonna strip your bones. One thing about vultures, Griswald, they're patient. Sleep well."

Cage turned away, too angry with himself and Horance Griswald to worry about whether the man might change his mind and shoot him in the back.

He left the house and walked slowly to where his Camaro was parked in the middle of the block. He stood on the sidewalk and inhaled the humid night air, trying to calm down.

Larry was parked several car lengths behind, just out of the cone of light cast by the overhead street lamp. Cage sighed and walked back, leaned against the driver's door and looked at Larry sitting inside with his arms folded, contemplating the tape recorder and headset beside him as if they were objects of intense curiosity.

Larry looked up at him and said, "Well, you blinded him with brilliance and baffled him with bullshit, all right. He had you turning around like a dog chasing its tail."

"I'm not in the mood, Larry."

"*You're* not in the mood? I suppose you think I should be overjoyed knowing you just hung us out to dry in there? I swear to God I should've gone in there and shot you myself."

"Howie Wallmeyer gave me up," Cage said. "That spoiled the whole thing."

"I know he gave you up, I heard. And the guy's right. If we went to the police now, it would look like a case of sour grapes, exposing and badmouthing him 'cause he wouldn't knuckle under. He's also right about the fucking lawsuit and you going to jail. That's a real attractive thought right now, you going to jail, but shit, we could all go. And what the hell's wrong with you, putting him on notice about Michael Grady?"

"I had to say something, Larry, the man had answers for everything. I wanted to give him something to worry about."

"You really think he's gonna worry? What can anybody prove? All he has to do is play it straight from here on out and he's home free."

"He doesn't know that for sure," Cage said. "It's eating at him how I got on to Bobby Lee Gettis. I shouldn't know that. So he's got to figure maybe, just maybe, I might luck up and somehow pin Michael on him. Yeah, I believe he'll worry about that. And I believe he might try to do something about it."

"You mean come after you?" Larry shook his head. "It's not his style. Michael Grady was a fluke, he got cornered and acted out of self-preservation. He's not the kind to go looking for violence."

"We'll see," Cage said. "But remember, he thinks I'm free-lancing here and looking for big money. I'm also pissed off and after him with a vengeance. That makes me dangerous, a loose cannon, so he's still gonna be concerned about his self-preservation."

Larry gave him a strange look. "Are you saying you deliberately tried to set yourself up as a target?"

"What else have we got?"

"Jesus. Does getting this guy mean that much to you?"

"It sure does, Larry," he said. "It means an awful

lot." He unbuttoned his shirt. "Here's your mike. I have to do something."

Howie Wallmeyer eased the Thunderbird into its assigned spot in the underground garage and waited for Bob Segar to finish doing "Hollywood Nights," bobbing his head and drumming his fingers against the dash in time to the heavy beat coming from the quadriphonic speakers. Feeling loose and mellow after making a night of it at Club Lingerie with his current flame, a blond hostess at Trumps Restaurant, with jutting tits and an IQ that he figured was about twenty digits higher than her bra size. Still, she could wear out a Posturepedic mattress in about a week and firmly believed the best way to keep a man's interest was by putting her knees behind her ears instead of Chanel. And she'd done just that after Howie drove her home a little after midnight, their bodies still somewhat moist from gyrating on the crowded dance floor, smelling of whisky sours and Tic Tac breath mints, and now Howie was pleasantly pooped.

Bob Segar's Silver Bullet Band brought an end to "Hollywood Nights." Howie said, "Yeah," and went to unbuckle his seat belt when the passenger door opened and Cage got in.

"Might as well leave that on, Howie," Cage said. "We're going for a little ride."

Howie gave him a wide-eyed look. "How the fuck did you get in here? This is supposed to be a security garage."

Cage said, "You're getting careless. Don't they tell you to watch the gate till it's all the way closed? Somebody could walk in right behind you. Not that it wouldn't be easy enough to get through it anyway."

"What do you want? Get the fuck out of my car, it's after two in the morning. I gotta get some sleep."

"I told you we're taking a ride. Now crank this thing up."

Howie started to unbuckle again, saying, "You're crazy. The only place I'm going is to bed."

"Wrong, Howie. Take a look."

Howie looked at the small, chrome-plated pistol in Cage's hand and forgot about the seat belt. "You *are* crazy. You pulling a gun on me? Forcing me to drive somewhere? Man, that's kidnapping."

"Have me arrested. Now start the car."

Howie still hesitated, not liking the idea one bit of driving off in the middle of the night to who knew where with some gun-toting maniac who acted like this was an everyday occurrence.

"You wouldn't shoot me right here," he said. "Too much chance of somebody hearing. What's that anyway, a little .25? Probably wouldn't even stop me."

Cage snaked his left arm along the seat back and got a good grip on the collar of Howie's blue blazer. "You're right, Howie. What I'd do first is pistol-whip the shit out of you while you're strapped in that harness, until I convinced you it would be in your best interest to do what I ask. Unless, of course, you started getting the best of me with all that black-belt training you have, in which case then I'd shoot you seven times. And if that didn't stop you, I'd run all the way home and bolt the door. Now are you gonna start the car or not?"

Howie started the car, backed out, and left the garage.

Cage told him to take La Brea south out toward Englewood and follow his directions.

"Where the hell are we going?" Howie wanted to

know. "Can you at least tell me that?" His eyes darted around desperately, searching for a black and white which he was perfectly willing to ram if necessary in order to attract attention and get the fuck away from this madman. As usual, there wasn't a one in sight, all of the cops probably soaking up free coffee and doughnuts at Winchell's while honest taxpayers were being terrorized on the streets.

Cage sat silent and gazed out the window, the little pistol held loosely in his lap.

Howie said, "Look, is this about that shit with Horance Griswald? It is, isn't it? Okay, so I got a bit overzealous and played dirty pool trying to steal a contract. That's not a felony. But I tell you what, I won't sell the guy anything, how's that? We don't need to get all bent outta shape here. I mean that's no reason to resort to kidnapping and—whatever you plan on doing."

Cage said, "I wasn't selling the man anything. It was personal."

"You weren't? Well shit, what's the problem? I was wasting my time."

"You're the problem, Howie, you always have been. I told you to pretend you never heard of Banes and Twiford, but you couldn't do that, could you? Had to play games. But this isn't a game, Howie. You have no idea what you screwed up."

Howie gnawed at his thumbnail and reflected on that, wondering what the guy was talking about. He said, "Whatever I fucked up, I'll clean up, okay? Just tell me what I can do to make it right."

"It's too late for that. Now just shut up, I don't feel like listening to you anymore."

Howie stopped talking and started looking for police cars again, growing more apprehensive by the minute and knowing the odds of spotting one were getting slimmer every minute. The suburbs had given way to industry and occasional areas of newly excavated lots with half-completed buildings and heavy equipment, everything dark and still now.

After a while Cage said, "There's a narrow dirt road up ahead, on your left. Take it."

Howie became even more alarmed. "That's a landfill back there. What are we gonna do at a landfill?"

"Don't talk, just slow down and make the turn."

The Thunderbird's headlights picked out mounds of dung-colored dirt and clumps of sprouting weeds and wire grass as it bounced over the rough road, Howie cringing as the undercarriage scraped the surface now and then. Cage told him to swing around behind a pyramid of loose gravel and turn off the lights.

"Get out, Howie. This side."

Howie unfastened the seat belt and followed Cage out through the passenger door. The place looked spooky under a crescent moon, the air smelling faintly of garbage and filled with what sounded to him like about a million crickets. Howie shivered and looked at Cage.

"I know you're not gonna kill me," he said. "Are you? You wouldn't do a fool thing like that." He sounded hopeful but not completely certain.

Cage said, "That depends on you. But you definitely need to be taught not to stick your nose in other people's business. Take off your coat and shirt."

Howie took off the dark blue blazer and powder-blue cotton shirt, moving slowly while he tried to figure out what was going on. He dropped them on the ground and stood facing Cage in his white T-shirt and pleated gray slacks. Cage told him to turn around, making sure he wasn't armed, then had him sit down.

Howie said, "Are you gonna let me know what's happening?"

Cage picked up the shirt and went to the rear of the Thunderbird. He said, "You like this car, don't you?"

"Yeah, sure I like it. I got a lot of money tied up—hey, what the fuck are you doing?"

Cage had the gas cap off and was stuffing the shirt into the cylinder. Howie let out a strangled yell and was halfway to his feet when Cage turned the .25 automatic on him.

"Do you like it more than your life? Because I'm very upset with you, Howie, and it's gonna be one or the other. This time you get to choose. Now either keep coming or sit back down."

Howie said, "Jesus H. Christ!" and lowered himself back to a sitting position. "You can't be serious."

"Watch me," Cage said. He took a book of matches from his hip pocket and lit the shirt, making sure it was burning good before moving away. "Maybe you'd better find another place now," he said. "This is gonna be a biggie."

Howie got to his hands and knees and stared in horror at the flaming shirt hanging from his gas tank, then glanced back at Cage, who was moving around behind the gravel pile. He said, "Holy shit," and looked back at his car, estimating his chances for saving it. He decided they weren't very good when he saw the flames licking the neck of the cylinder, and made a mad dash for the gravel pile.

He just did make it. There was a loud *whoomp,* and the night lit up like a giant flashbulb, then diminished to a dull orange glow.

Howie waited a few moments before cautiously

stepping out and surveying what was left of his Thunderbird. The entire rear end and interior were blazing, flames flickering through the shattered windows. While he watched, a rear tire blew, causing him to jump.

"I don't fucking *believe* this!" he said.

"The proud bird with the golden tail," Cage said from behind him.

Howie turned to him, fists clenched at his sides. "You sonofabitch, you're insane! You hear me? Insane!"

"Certified, Howie. Helps me cope with life's disappointments. The bigger the disappointment, the more insane I become. And I'm gonna be hugely disappointed if you do one more thing to irritate me, and that includes filing a complaint. Am I getting through?"

Howie looked back at his burning Thunderbird and shook his head. "I had twenty thousand dollars in that car, *now* look at it."

"That's a lot," Cage said. "Enjoy your hike back to town."

"One thing about it, you're gonna be hiking too."

"I don't think so," Cage said, and pointed to his Camaro parked in the shadow of a low embankment a hundred feet away. "I had the guy runs that little station up the road call me a taxi. But he closes at midnight."

"So you're just gonna leave me out here?"

The other rear tire blew, and Howie jumped again. When he looked back, Cage was walking toward the Camaro.

"Hey, you just gonna leave me here? You fucker. Hey!"

Cage kept walking and didn't look back.

Chapter
—18—

"Seems like every time you call me lately, Horance, you're in some kind a trouble. You've lost your grip on things out there and I'm getting concerned."

"There wouldn't have been this trouble if you hadn't insisted on getting a return in ten days," Horance said. "I told you it was too soon, I didn't have time to set it up properly. Now this man's jeopardizing our entire arrangement, and I'm not going to be able to do any more deals with him snooping around."

Maury Bingham said, "I wish you'd be more careful what you say on the phone. I mentioned that the other day when you called here all in a panic, but it didn't seem to sink in. If this guy works for who you say he does, it wouldn't be any great trick for him to tap you."

"You don't think I know that? I'm in a pay phone in the hotel lobby. And that's another drawback. Christ, I'm afraid to even use my own phones anymore. I don't know how he did it, or how much is only guesswork, but he's got it all together. And he's about to find out about you know who, and that just can't happen, Maury."

"You say he's got all of it together, Horance?"

"Well, maybe not your part. Not yet, anyway."

"Meaning he could?"

"Of course he could, I guess. If he keeps digging. And take my word for it, he's going to do just that unless he's stopped."

Maury Bingham said, "This guy really pushed your button, didn't he? He's turned out to be your worst nightmare."

"And with good cause. I believe he can be a hell of a lot more dangerous than that guy who hit me. Listen to this. I told you about Wallmeyer, right? The guy who came in yesterday and put me on to this Allen Cage? Well, he was all hot to trot on selling me a security alarm, even willing to go ten percent under whatever I was going to pay. After all that's happening recently, I decided maybe putting some kind of system in the house might be a good idea. So this afternoon I call Wallmeyer to check it out, and you know what he told me?"

Maury said, "What?"

"He told me he was sorry, it was all a big mistake. He said he was low on inventory, didn't know when he'd be receiving any new shipments, and in fact he might even be getting out of the business. He couldn't hang up the phone fast enough."

"Is that supposed to tell you something?"

"You're damn right it tells me something. It tells me Wallmeyer had the fear of God put in him since yesterday morning, and we both know who did it. Seriously, Maury, the man has to go. And the sooner the better."

There was a pause on the other end, and Horance took the moment to gaze around the crowded Century Plaza lobby that was mostly filled with prosperous-looking men and women wearing name tags, here to kick off a three-day convention of the American Bar Association. He half expected to see Allen Cage lurking behind a potted tree or someplace, glaring at him with that stony expression, but the man was nowhere in sight. That didn't mean he wasn't around though. Visible or not, Horance was going to assume that he was somewhere close by, watching and waiting. He hated to admit it, but Maury was right. Allen Cage had pushed his button.

Maury, having thought it over, said, "Horance, you've made kind of a mess of things lately. This last deal was bad news, and it's brought a lot of heat. Maybe it'll die down and maybe it won't, but either way we're gonna have to change our way of doing business—which means you're not gonna be sending me any other goods."

That was fine with Horance. He wasn't planning on doing any more work for Maury Bingham anyway, but hadn't told him that because he wanted Maury's help in getting rid of Allen Cage.

"So here's what we'll do," Maury said. "I'll supply you with a few stones as needed to carry you over the hump. Wholesale rates, you pay me after you get yours."

"I'll need quality stuff, Maury."

"You'll get quality stuff. For a while. For old times' sake. But then you're gonna have to find another source. No offense, buddy, but I have to minimize our association."

"What's wrong, afraid I might go down?" Horance didn't care for this feeling of being abandoned. Like suddenly he'd become a liability.

Maury said, "You got to realize it's a possibility."

"How long will you supply me? I want to go strictly

legit, but I don't have the capital now. And no one's going to let me have what I need on credit."

"We'll have to feel our way along on that. But I'll do you right."

Sure you will, Horance thought. In thirty days you won't even know me. He said, "What about this guy, Cage? Will you help me out there? He's my only real threat. If I can lose him, I'll be all right."

Maury, choosing his words carefully, said, "I'm not really in that line of work, Horance."

"You have connections who are."

"Not really. I know people who know people, but nothing direct. And they're expensive. Maybe you'd be better off taking care of it yourself. Shouldn't be too hard, seeing as how you got a little experience now. The guy's nothing but a cheap opportunist."

The phone was getting damp from Horance's clammy palm. Maury Bingham was bailing out on him already. "Then I'm on my own? You can't even give me a name?"

"I'd like to help you, Horance, but . . ." He left the sentence unfinished.

"Thanks a lot, friend. That's fine, I'll take your advice and handle him myself. Didn't mean to trouble you."

"Just be careful," Maury said, ignoring the sarcasm. "But hey, if there's anything else I can do . . ."

Horance hung up and stalked back to his shop. Twenty minutes later, preparing for an appointment, he was still steaming when the phone rang. It was Maury Bingham.

"Just wanted to let you know I've been doing a little thinking, and maybe I got a solution to your problem."

"I don't want to talk on this phone, Maury."

Horance was finding it difficult to maintain a civil tone with the man.

"So what am I saying? All I'm telling you is I might have an answer relevant to our last conversation, and I made a call. I say anything wrong so far?"

"No."

"Then listen. There's a guy in your area I did a couple deals with in the past who might be able to ease your burden. He'll be in touch."

Horance was beginning to take heart again. "Does he understand the situation?"

"And how to resolve it," Maury said. "He'll be sending his emissary around today or tomorrow."

"Emissary?"

"That's what he said, emissary. Colorful language, considering, but he's part of a colorful group."

Horance thought it sounded more incongruous than colorful, but he wasn't going to quibble about semantics. All he cared about was getting Allen Cage off his back. Permanently.

"What kind of fee are we talking about, Maury? As you've already noted, this isn't a major job. I hope your man is reasonable."

"He'll do you right. And what's more, he's dependable. I contracted with him for a few special items a while back, even fronted him a one-third advance, and he filled the order right on time. As of now you no longer have a problem, my friend. Now did I come through or did I come through?"

Horance said, "I'll let you know after he fills my order. But thanks, Maury, I'll accept your judgment."

"That's good, Horance, because if I tell you something, you can count on it. Feel better?"

"Yes," Horance said. "Suddenly I feel a lot better."

* * *

Cage called Caprita to say he'd stop by the next morning after a consultation with a Santa Monica motel owner who'd been burglarized twice in the last month. He missed her, he said, it seemed like she'd been gone forever. She said she missed him too, but that it shouldn't be much longer. She was already screening applicants and had a couple of promising candidates to discuss with Marilee. Another two or three days, she said, four at the most.

"She's starting to come around," Caprita told him. "She hasn't had a drink since day before yesterday, her appetite's picked up, and she's talking to people again. She even ordered a new pair of crutches, the other ones were getting all dented."

"That's good to hear," Cage said. "I'm getting lonely."

"Well, you have Grits to keep you company. You're not abusing him are you? Because if you are, you're in big trouble."

"That's a hell of a thing to say. Have I ever abused your cat? Tell me one time I've ever done that. He's fat and sassy from eating better than I've been lately, and I even cleaned his litter box this morning. Furthermore, the fool cat's lying on your pillow right now, purring so hard I feel like I'm on one of those vibrating beds."

"He's in bed with you?" Caprita was pleased.

"Sure. We've become regular buddies. And anyway, I don't like sleeping alone and figured you'd object to anything female."

"Good thinking. I knew you two would get along if you gave it a chance. You've just been too stubborn and a little jealous."

"Caprita, I'm not jealous of your stupid cat. How insecure do you think I am?"

"More than you like to admit, and my cat isn't stupid."

"You're baiting me again, aren't you? Why do you do that? Here I go out of my way to make friends with your stu—with your cat, and you want to bait me, calling me jealous and insecure."

"I do it to judge how tense you are," Caprita said. "And you're right up there at the top of the scale." Her voice turned serious. "You're obsessed with this man, aren't you?"

"Frustrated, maybe. I wouldn't say obsessed."

"Yes you are. I could see it all over you the other day when you were talking to Marilee. You've turned it into a personal vendetta, and it scares me. I'm afraid what you might do if you decide there's not enough evidence to convict him. I'm even afraid what you might do if there is."

"Why should you be so afraid of what I might do when I don't even know myself? You and Larry both seem to think I'm on some kind of mission here, that I just want to up and blow the guy away or something. All I want is to make sure he doesn't get away with it. What's wrong with that?"

"Larry and I know you, Allen. You have this sense of outrage that blinds you to any other way of looking at things except your own whenever you're hurt or deeply offended."

"That's not true either," he said, then thought of Howie Wallmeyer's charred Thunderbird and added, "not exactly. And what's with all this analyzing me anyway?"

"What I'm leading up to," she said, "is for you to promise me that you won't take the law into your own hands, so to speak. I'll feel much better, and so will Marilee."

"You talked to her about this too?"

"Yes, and she was very concerned. She wants this man punished, but in the right way. She doesn't want any misunderstanding about that. So will you promise?"

Jesus, everybody was wanting his word lately. He said, "Short of the guy pulling a gun on me or anything, I promise not to lift a finger against him. Satisfied?"

"Very. Now I'll let you get some sleep. Love me?"

"Want my promise on that too?"

"Just say it."

"I love you. Except when you're nagging me."

Caprita sighed. "You always have to qualify things, don't you? See you tomorrow. Kiss Grits good night for me."

"Sure I will. Night, babe."

Cage put the phone on the nightstand and leaned back against the headboard, scratching his chest thoughtfully. After a while he looked at Grits curled up on Caprita's pillow and said, "What about it, cat, want me to make any promises to you?"

Grits rolled his ears forward but didn't open his eyes.

Cage reached over to turn out the lamp. "Shit, I'm doing it again. Talking to you."

He turned on his side and went to sleep and dreamed of urinating tigers.

Chapter

—19—

Anton Fowler, at the fresh age of twenty, had a narrow perception of what life was all about. As a boy growing up in Billings, Montana, he'd had the opportunity to observe nature in the raw, and accordingly had formed an unshakable opinion that the planet and all living things on it were governed by one inalienable law: The strong survived, the weak perished, and there was no room for in between. Couple that with superiority in numbers, and Anton was convinced you had an unbeatable combination.

This uncomplicated philosophy was reinforced by young Anton's father, a survivalist and member of a local white supremacist group called the Foragers. Papa Fowler, a bearded and balding giant with a barrel belly, would take little Anton and his older brother Jamel to secret meetings, exposing them to the fine art of bigotry while they were still ripe for learning. In the back room of Silas Feed and Grain, the impressionable youths would listen to dire warnings and tirades from the dozen or so men in attendance. They spoke of white flight and white plight in solemn tones that the boys found confusing, but there was no mistaking the hate in their voices when they

mentioned Jews, wops, niggers, chinks, and spics—
foreign but ominous words to Anton and Jamel. Only
through a united front could the Caucasian race hope
for salvation from this spreading scourge, the men
predicted, for the day was approaching when blood
would flow between the races and only the most
prepared would emerge victorious. And while this
verbal bombardment certainly made an impact on
Jamel, it flat-out scared Anton to death.

Jamel left home first, three months after Papa
Fowler got trampled to death by a wild horse he was
attempting to saddle break in a makeshift corral
behind the barn. Anton had just turned eighteen, five
years younger than Jamel, so he stayed home to tend
the small farm and look after their grieving mother
while big brother went off to Los Angeles, California,
to see what he could get into. There was money to be
made out there, Jamel told him, and others who
thought as they did. Not those wimp Klansmen, who
only wanted to burn crosses and march in parades,
but people who believed in direct action. Jamel had
been corresponding with a guy doing time in Chino
who belonged to the Aryan Brotherhood, and the guy
had promised to sponsor him for membership if he
decided to move to L.A. Now was his chance. "Mama's not gonna last long with the old man gone," he
told Anton. "Stay with her till she goes, then you come
on out and I'll have things set up for you. The A.B. is
the strongest white-power group in the country, and
they don't fuck around. They're our kind of people."

But Anton, in a hurry to broaden his horizons, grew
tired of waiting for Mama to die. Two months before
his twentieth birthday, in the dead of a snowy night,
he stuffed a cardboard box filled with his meager

possessions into the trunk of his primer-spotted Pontiac and split for L.A., never to return.

Only Jamel wasn't around when he got there. He was in Vacaville Prison, doing twelve years for a botched armed robbery of a check-cashing house in Reseda. That's what the tall thin brunette with the multicolored fingernails told him when he showed up at the cramped two-room apartment on Third Street that Jamel had given him as an address. "He got shot in the hip with a shotgun," the girl told Anton without emotion. "That's why he's in Vacaville." Which explained why Anton hadn't heard from Jamel in nearly eight months. "They had to put a pin or bolt or something in it. He walks with this real bad limp now, you know?"

The thin brunette, who said her name was Pam, had looked him up and down and then invited him in. She had offered him some vin rosé, and they ended up lounging on bean bags in front of a thirteen-inch color TV set on a plastic milk crate, drinking from beer mugs and talking about Jamel wasting away up there in Vacaville. With good behavior, she thought maybe he could be out in three years.

Then she'd told him about the Aryan Brotherhood, that mysterious power group he had traveled so far to join. It was her brother that Jamel had been corresponding with in Chino. He was still there, due to come out early the following year. The A.B. had been founded in prison, she said, originally devised as a protective umbrella for white inmates against an overwhelming black majority. The group flourished and grew, spilling into the community as more and more members were released, expanding its power base and sphere of influence from the West Coast to the deep South. Just a bunch of home boys flexing their muscles, she said, united by circumstances beyond their control. They looked after their own and lived by two inviolate vows: to come to the aid of any brother in peril, and to never harm a brother, his family, or a friend. The penalty for violating either was death.

"I want to be a member," Anton had told her, the wine making him loose and mellow. "Jamel said he'd have it set up."

"It's not that simple," Pam said. He had to make an irreversible commitment that would demonstrate the depth of his conviction. Was he ready for that? Yes, Anton said, whatever it took. He just wanted to belong, to be accepted, to be . . . *needed.* The country was going to hell on a sliding board, spiraling downward into a sea of black, brown, and yellow that would eventually dilute the white race into insignificance. Chaos was coming. Government would fall and anarchy would reign across the land. The white ruling class would ultimately see history reversed as *they* became servants and slaves, reduced to second- and third-class citizens in the very country their forefathers had fought and died to build. It would take strength to combat such an onslaught, he said, if not to prevent it, then at least to survive it. And he intended to survive.

Pam had looked at him for about ten seconds before saying, "Do you really believe that?"

"I do," he answered. "And so should you. All the signs are there. Now how do I go about joining up?"

"I'll introduce you around," she said, still reeling from the passion of his words. He was a very interesting guy. A little green maybe, but still interesting. "What's your first name again? Elton?"

"Anton."

"Well, Anton, if you don't have a place to stay yet, you're welcome to park here for a while. You have a lot to learn about the A.B."

"Are you sure Jamel won't mind?" he'd asked.

"I'm sure. Like I said, they look out for their own. And that includes all wants and needs."

Chapter
—20—

Brenda looked up as Cage came in, and said, "Good morning. Larry's in back and wants to see you right away. Better not even make a pit stop for coffee, he's catching a flight to New York in exactly an hour and a half."

"What's he going to New York for?"

"Search me, ask him. All I know is this place sure is getting awfully empty."

Cage went back to the workroom where Larry was sitting on a stool at the drawing table that had blueprints and spec sheets pushed to one side to make room for the reel-to-reel tape recorder.

Cage said, "Olive Oyl tells me you're going to New York. What's up?"

"Sit down and you'll find out," Larry said. He reversed the tape, hit the play button, and Horance Griswald's voice, sounding tense and agitated, came out of the speaker.

Straddling a straight-back chair, Cage said, "You bugged his phone?"

"Not his. The pay phone in the hotel lobby, the one closest to his shop. I didn't think he'd be using his if he made any incriminating calls, not after that crack he made about how easy they could be tapped. It was only a hunch, but it panned out. Listen."

Cage listened, hearing Horance Griswald speaking between brief intervals of silence.

"It's only a one-way conversation," Cage said.

"I had to use the mike. Taped it under the shelf. Pay phones are too much trouble when you're only guessing. Here, listen to this part."

Horance was saying, ". . . I don't know how he did it, or how much is only guesswork, but he's got it all together. And he's about to find out about you know who, and that just can't happen, Maury. Of course, he could, if he keeps digging. And take my word for it, he's going to do just that unless he's stopped."

Larry stopped the tape, ran it fast forward, then hit the play button again.

Horance: "You're damn right it tells me something. It tells me Wallmeyer had the fear of God put in him since yesterday morning, and we both know who did it. Seriously, Maury, the man has to go. And the sooner the better."

Cage raised his eyebrows and whistled. "Sounds like he's really worried, doesn't it?"

"You'd better be worried too," Larry said, and ran the tape forward again.

Horance: "Then I'm on my own? You can't even give me a name? Thanks a lot, friend. That's fine, I'll handle it myself. I wouldn't want to impose on you."

Larry switched the recorder off and looked at Cage. "I underestimated the man. He's coming after you."

"I couldn't be happier," Cage said, though in reality the thought was giving him a few butterflies. "Who's this Maury he's talking to?"

"Maury Bingham. He was originally indicted as a

codefendant when Griswald got popped in Florida. Conspiracy. The indictment charged that Maury Bingham ended up with most of the jewelry Griswald claimed was stolen in his fake robbery, but the charge was dismissed for lack of evidence. At the time Maury was a wholesale distributor working out of Jacksonville. Now he operates a similar business in New York, only bigger."

Cage said, "What is he, a fence?"

"No," Larry said, "he's a legitimate wholesaler of precious stones, only he's got a different twist. He mostly supplies jewelers like Horance Griswald, who reputable dealers won't touch, lets 'em have the stuff on short-term credit at inflated prices. But I think he takes it a step further with Griswald."

"How's that?"

"I think Griswald steals some of the better pieces back after he sells 'em and then sells the stuff *back* to Maury Bingham at a discount. That way they both come out. Griswald gets a nice return on what he originally paid for the shit, and Bingham gets his stones back, which he can resell after popping them from the mountings."

Cage said, "Jesus, that's even better than I thought. So that's where it all goes, huh? To Bingham?"

"Has to be. Griswald knows better than to keep it himself. And this tape makes it pretty clear they have an arrangement—or did anyway."

"So why are you going to New York? You gonna move on this guy Bingham?"

Larry reversed the tape, removed it and placed the reel in a box. "I'm gonna see Vincent Kohleman first, special agent in charge of the Manhattan field office. We go back a ways. He'll come with me when I approach Bingham, but it won't be official. The plan is to make him think I'm there as part of an ongoing investigation into the murder of Michael Grady and that the tape is legally obtained evidence. I'll tell him it would be a good idea if he gave a statement detailing everything he knows about the Grady hit, otherwise he's going down as an accessory. I'll have Vincent sitting there nodding his head but not saying a word after he shows his shield."

"You think he'll really do it?"

"Sign a statement? I believe there's a good chance," Larry said. "He's writing Griswald off, no question about that. I think getting caught up in the murder of a big-name Hollywood director is a little more than he bargained for. Besides, I'll try to make him think he doesn't have much of a choice. I'll tell him when Griswald goes down he's gonna take Maury down with him, unless he cops a deal first."

Larry unzipped a leather flight bag sitting on the floor, put the tape inside, and zipped it closed. "And if he does, Griswald's finished," he said. "Which leaves us with only one more small problem."

Cage said, "What's that?"

"Getting hold of the tape he made when you tried to blind him with brilliance and baffle him with bullshit the other night. It *does* sound like a righteous blackmail attempt, Cage."

"Leave that to me," Cage said. "I'll get it."

"That's what got us in this mess in the first place, leaving it to you. I want you to stay away from him . . ." Larry paused, remembering something. "What did Griswald mean about Howie Wallmeyer having the fear of God put in him? Did you do anything to him?"

Cage spread his hands, a perplexed expression on his face. "I don't know what he meant by that. Maybe Howie had a change of heart."

"Yeah? Well stay away from him and stay away from Griswald, and I mean that."

Cage said, "Fine by me, but you're forgetting something."

"What am I forgetting?"

"Griswald's coming after *me*."

All the way to the airport Cage had to listen to Larry trying to convince him to stay away from his apartment until he got back from New York. Take a motel room, or even stay at his place, Larry suggested, Doris already had the guest room fixed up and wouldn't mind the company. In fact, Larry said, take a couple days off and don't even go to the office, there wasn't anything pressing at the moment that couldn't wait. Cage told him no, he was staying right where he was, no one was running him anywhere. If Griswald was serious about coming after him, then he wanted to be on familiar ground. And he had to take care of Caprita's cat. Larry said to hell with the cat and accused Cage of acting like this was all fun and games. He was playing Griswald too cheap. The man considered him a threat and was obviously ready to take drastic measures to protect himself. But Cage stuck to his guns, saying the whole idea had been to draw Griswald out into the open, and apparently it was working. He said not to worry, he could take care of himself with Horance Griswald. Just go on to New York and do his thing with Maury Bingham and he'd hold the fort here. By the time Cage pulled up in front of the Delta terminal at LAX, Larry was so exasperated that he slammed the car door and stormed into the building without even saying good-bye.

Cage was twenty minutes late for his appointment at the Easy Rest Motel in Santa Monica. The owner was a wizened old man in a baggy blue leisure suit. They sat across the table from each other in the cramped kitchen behind the office while the man chain-smoked Pall Malls and complained about life in general and the motel business in particular, especially the fate of the small independent trying to compete with the big chains that offered everything except Jet Skis for their Olympic-sized swimming pools with the floating bars.

It took Cage about three minutes to realize the old man wasn't the least bit interested in security but was suffering from chronic loneliness after years of riding herd on fourteen stucco units that probably stayed mostly empty. There was just nothing here worth stealing, including the change from the battered Coke machine outside the office door. Cage gave him another ten minutes and two Pall Malls, then quietly said that he had to leave. The old man told him that was okay, he had somebody from National Linen Service coming by shortly anyway, had to replace all those towels people kept walking off with as souvenirs. Cage stood and shook the bony hand that felt cool despite the absence of air-conditioning, and for just a moment he was tempted to follow Larry's suggestion and rent a room for a couple of nights. But he dismissed the thought as quickly as it came, and when Cage drove away he could see the old man through the rearview mirror, standing by the Coke machine in his baggy leisure suit, waiting for the man from National Linen Service.

The meeting left Cage more depressed than he'd been since the day of Michael Grady's funeral, and he hurried out to Malibu to see Caprita.

There was a note with his name on it taped to the door, written in Caprita's familiar backhand scrawl that read: "Didn't know when you'd get here, so went down to the beach to break in Marilee's new crutches & my new swimsuit. Look for the orange & white umbrella—love, C."

He drove down to the beach, parked in the public lot, and walked out to the edge of the sand. He spotted the umbrella off to his left, saw Marilee sitting beneath it in a folding aluminum chair, shading her eyes as she looked out at the water.

Cage picked his way gingerly across the sand and flopped down on the yellow beach towel that was spread next to the chair.

Marilee said, "There you are. We were about to give up on you."

"Had to take Larry Twiford to the airport," he said, pulling off his shoes and brushing the bottoms of his socks. "Then I had an appointment in Santa Monica and was a little late. Where's Caprita?"

Marilee nodded at the ocean. "Out there. Looking absolutely ravishing in a white one-piece I insisted on getting for her."

Cage followed her gaze and saw Caprita splashing around in waist-deep water twenty yards off shore. She dived into an approaching wave, surfaced, and swam straight out to sea with long, graceful strokes.

"She swims like a dolphin," Marilee said. "Those young men playing volleyball over there have been taking turns trying to pick her up. It's a good thing you got here when you did."

"Yeah, those high-cut bathing suits will do it every time."

Cage was glad to see that Marilee was beginning to snap out of the deep funk she'd been in and was starting to regain a semblance of her old self. It would take a while before she made it back all the way, if she ever did, but she was working on it. He studied her profile while she shaded her eyes again to watch Caprita. She wore a bright print sundress that made no attempt to cover her braces, her hair tied back with a white scarf. Grief had deepened the lines around her mouth and forehead, and there was a rigidness in her posture that reflected the conscious effort she was making to pretend that life was normal. He wondered if she had ever once let go completely and cried herself into exhaustion. He doubted it. Marilee wasn't one who would let go of anything completely. Including Michael Grady.

"What do you see?" she asked.

"Excuse me?"

"I said what do you see. I have excellent peripheral vision and you've been staring at me."

Cage said, "I see a lady who from the outside seems to have herself pretty much together. But how are you doing inside? Or should I keep my mouth shut?"

She lowered her hand and looked at him. "I'm learning to live with it. Everyone faces a personal tragedy sooner or later, and we never know for sure how we'll react until it happens. I've accepted the fact that Michael's gone and I'm still here. I have to adapt to that, just like I have to adapt to the degenerative progression of my illness that will probably have me in a wheelchair in another six months. The only thing I would find difficult to accept now is the thought that whoever killed Michael might go unpunished."

Tough lady, Cage thought. "He'll be punished, Marilee. You can count on that."

"But the *right* way," she said firmly, "like I told Caprita. Not by you out of some misguided loyalty you might feel for Michael. I asked you to help find the other one percent that would conclusively establish his guilt. I didn't ask you to mete out any retribution yourself, and I won't have it. The courts will take care of that."

"What if the other one percent's never found, Marilee?" he said. "The system doesn't always work, you know."

"If Horance Griswald is guilty, he'll be convicted and punished. That's the way I want it. Now could we please change the subject?"

Tough, but naive.

He was saved from further comment by the sight of Caprita sloshing out of the water, squeezing her hair and momentarily disrupting the volleyball game again as she trotted across the hot sand to the protective shade of the umbrella. Marilee was right, Cage thought. She looked absolutely ravishing. She dropped to her knees on the towel and began flicking water at his face.

"How long have you been here?" she asked.

"About five minutes. Cut it out, you're getting me all wet."

"Like my new suit? Marilee got extravagant and made me take it. It's a Niko's and cost eighty dollars! Can you imagine?"

"You're spoiling her, Marilee. There won't be any living with her when she gets home."

"It's a small thing," Marilee said, "since she refuses to let me pay her for playing housekeeper and nursemaid."

Caprita said, "It should only be a couple days more. Marilee now has three very qualified ladies to choose from, and they can all start right away. Then I'll come home and see what kind of mess you've created."

Cage, being casual, said, "Why don't you just wait till this business with Horance Griswald gets cleared up? It won't be long now."

Caprita's playfulness vanished. "What's wrong, Allen?"

"Nothing's wrong, but I believe things are gonna come to a head pretty soon, that's all."

Marilee said, "Is there something you're not telling us?"

"Nothing firm. Larry recorded a phone conversation Griswald made to some guy in New York that sounded promising, and he went up there to put some heat on him."

Caprita said, "Larry went to New York? When?"

"This morning."

"What does that have to do with me not coming home?"

"Well, Griswald kind of threatened me a little. I don't think anything will come of it, but I'd rather not take a chance."

Caprita slapped her thighs. "Great. Wonderful. What did he threaten to do, blow up the building?"

Cage said, "Will you just take it easy? He isn't gonna blow up anything. And I wish you'd stop kneeling like that, you've cost those guys on the other side of the net four straight points."

Chapter
—21—

Why anyone would choose to discuss business in a bowling alley was beyond Horance Griswald, even the business of murder. But that's what the man had said. He had gotten the call just before three that afternoon, while he was in the middle of an appointment with a car dealer from Long Beach. No introductions, no hedging, just a flat voice on the other end asking if this was Horance Griswald. Yes, Horance said. The man then asked if he had been expecting someone to contact him about a personal matter he needed to deal with, and Horance said yes again. "Eight o'clock," the voice told him, "Bay Shore Bowl in Santa Monica. Rent some shoes and ask for a lane, somebody'll be by to talk to you." Then the man had hung up without giving Horance a chance to say another word.

At home now, changing into slacks and a cotton vee-neck sweater, Horance was debating the wisdom of his actions. Who were these colorful people Maury Bingham was getting him involved with? Who was this emissary that would meet him at the bowling alley, and how would the guy recognize him? Fifteen hundred dollars seemed cheap for buying murder, unless they had a sale going this week. He would have gladly forked over three times that amount without haggling, to get rid of Allen Cage, and consider it a bargain. Horance was a believer in the adage that you get what you pay for, and fifteen hundred seemed like amateur night to him. Did these guys know what they were doing? So many questions and uncertainties that he couldn't answer or control. Still, it was the best chance he had of freeing himself from what had become an albatross, and he was willing to grasp at any straw that showed possibilities. He wondered if they offered a money-back guarantee.

The Bay Shore Bowl had a good crowd when Horance arrived at ten to eight. It was league night, and the lanes were alive with mixed teams in bright colored shirts sporting legends and logos on the backs. The rumble of bowling balls and crash of tenpins had him thinking that perhaps his contact had made an informed decision in selecting his meeting place. If this deal turned out to be some kind of sting operation with Horance wearing a wire, he wouldn't get much with all that background racket going on.

The man behind the counter observed Horance as he approached. He was young, about twenty-five, with a prematurely receding hairline and a skunk tattooed on his left forearm. Horance asked if a lane was available and said he'd need some shoes, size ten. The man went to a row of cubbyholes and came back with a pair of scuffed red and black bowling shoes. Horance regarded them with distaste as the man slapped them on the counter, wondering if he dared put them on.

"Number thirty-one," the man said, and flipped a switch on his control panel. "I'll need your driver's license. You can pick it up when you bring the shoes back. You'd be surprised how many of these buggers walk right out the door. People think they're Reeboks or something."

Horance said, "I assure you I have no desire to steal your shoes."

"Hey, man, what can I tell you. It's policy." Horance reluctantly handed over his license. The man glanced at it and attached it to a clipboard hanging behind the counter.

"I'll tack on for the shoes when you're finished. Five strikes in a row gets you a free game. Have fun."

Horance followed the lane numbers down to thirty-one. He didn't like giving up his license, letting a total stranger have access to personal information. He would prefer that no one even know he'd been here, just in case anything went wrong and the police tried to link him with his contact. They might keep records of everyone who rented their precious shoes. And what if his contact asked for identification, wanting to be certain he was talking to the right man?

This was a new thought to Horance, and he abruptly turned around, ready to go and ask the man for his license back. Maybe he could offer him a twenty as collateral for his funky bowling shoes. But the man was on the telephone, speaking earnestly and looking in his direction. Horance did a complete three sixty and continued on his way, a light bulb clicking on inside his head. So that's how they were doing it. There would be no chance of mistaken identity with this bunch. Whoever they were, his appreciation of their methods was growing. It was a good sign, he thought. A very good sign.

Horance was in the forth frame, working on a six, ten spare, when he saw the kid come into the pit and slip into the booth behind the scoring table. Horance, pretending like he didn't see him, carefully lined up his shot and let fly. The ball hooked in perfectly and sent the pins scattering. He hadn't bowled in nearly a decade, and it was difficult to keep the satisfaction off his face as he walked back to the booth.

The kid was applauding in slow motion as he slid over and gave Horance room to sit. "Nice shot, guy. You've done this before."

"Not in a lot of years," Horance said. "Who are you?"

"The man you're supposed to say things to," Anton Fowler told him. "Your guardian angel, the answer to your prayers."

Man? The kid didn't even look old enough to shave yet. Horance felt his expectations slipping away. "How do I know that?" he asked.

"Because I'm here, Mr. Griswald. You expecting anybody else?"

"No. You're just so young."

"But I'm enthusiastic, Mr. G, I got dedication going for me. All you have to do is tell me what you want done to who and give me fifteen hundred dollars. You got the money with you?"

"I have it."

"Then we're a third of the way there already. See how easy this is?"

Horance studied the young face that was trying to exude nonchalance but wasn't quite succeeding. Barely out of high school and ready—*anxious*—to kill someone. He was a study in contrasts. With his wholesome boy-next-door appearance and close-cropped haircut, he had country written all over him. Yet there were two fresh tattoos in the shape of teardrops beneath his left eye, the outlines still lightly scabbed. What was the story behind that? Still, the kid seemed confident he could take care of business, and that was the bottom line.

Horance patted his neck with a hand towel, then removed a folded white envelope from his hip pocket and dropped it on the table. "There's your money. I'd appreciate it if you'd take my word it's all there and not count it right now."

Anton nodded and put the envelope into his shirt pocket.

Horance said, "His name is Allen Cage. You'll find all the pertinent information in that envelope. I'd like it to look like an accident, and I'd like it done yesterday. Can you handle that?"

"This guy must've done something pretty bad to you," Anton said.

"That's no concern of yours. I've told you what I want done and to who and that's enough."

Horance rose, went to the ball-return rack and hefted his ball. Anton sucked his teeth and watched him prance to the foul line and sail one straight and true. Horance strolled back to the table like he'd just done his usual, but this time there was no show of applause. He sat down and began unlacing his rented shoes, ready to leave without further ado.

Anton said, "You have a little attitude problem, you know it?"

"It's not a case of attitude, my friend, it's a matter of negotiation—which is over. We have nothing left to discuss, and I'd just as soon not be seen with you any longer than necessary."

"Where I come from we're a sight more sociable."

"That's a strange thing for someone who kills for money to say. I think you're confusing sociable with sociopathic. I don't mean to insult you, and I'm definitely not complaining. But we don't have a great deal in common to chat about. Now how soon can you follow through on your part?"

Anton was beginning to bristle at this holier-than-thou verbal abuse, thinking the jerk had a lot of nerve talking about sociopaths. If it was up to him, he'd give the phony sonofabitch back his money and tell him to do his own dirty work. But he couldn't do that. Not if he wanted to earn his teardrops. Just let it go and get the hell away from the idiot.

"If you gave me enough information," Anton said, "I don't see why it can't happen tomorrow. Assuming he's just a plain, ordinary Joe."

"He is. An ex-con at that, so no big loss."

Man, this guy seemed to have a knack for saying the wrong thing.

Horance said, "How will I know when it's over?"

"I'll send up smoke signals. Read the paper, how do you think?"

"I was just asking. I gave you fifteen bills, I'd like to make sure I got full value."

Anton, figuring he'd had about all he could take, slipped out from the opposite side of the table. He looked down at Horance, now lacing up his street shoes, and said, "Griswald. What kind of name is that? You a Jew?"

"Yes, why?"

"That figures," Anton said, and walked away.

Chapter
—22—

It didn't require any imagination for Anton to connect with Allen Cage. He simply backed his car into a vacant slot outside the man's apartment building at five-thirty the next morning and waited, slouched behind the wheel with his eyes fixed on the blue Camaro parked four spaces down. He'd be coming out sometime between six and eight, according to Griswald's notes. The Jew bastard hadn't pinned it any closer than that, so it might be a while.

Which gave Anton time to do some pondering, because his head was reeling with conflicting thoughts and images that had been plaguing him since he'd moved to the Big City. The first thing Pam had wanted to do was introduce him to Max Radkin, the Brotherhood's second-in-command for the entire West Coast. That had been quite an experience in itself, sitting on a mop bucket in a cluttered garage surrounded by swimming-pool supplies, telling his life story to a guy who was built like Hulk Hogan and wore prescription sunglasses and a ponytail. Max Radkin had an aura of danger that Anton found intimidating, an aura heightened by an overabundance of tattoos on both muscular arms. He also had a tattoo of a spiderweb on the side of his neck and two teardrops underneath his left eye. All very strange. Max Radkin had told him the teardrops were a sign of honor that he'd go into more detail about later. Right then he was more interested in why Anton wanted to be part of the Aryan Brotherhood.

"Because I believe in the superiority and survival of the White Anglo-Saxon Protestant," he'd answered solemnly. Max Radkin had swung his head slowly toward Pam at that, who gave a small shrug and looked away. Max had said that was great, he liked his enthusiasm. His brother Jamel had a similar outlook, and Jamel was "ace boo-coo," whatever that meant. If Anton was anything like him, he would find a warm welcome from the A.B. family. "Provided you're willing to sacrifice and follow orders without question," he'd added. "For the benefit of the cause."

Max Radkin cleaned swimming pools for a living, but the job was mainly a front for casing houses and getting an occasional piece of ass from bored housewives craving adventure. "Maybe I'll take you on as my assistant," he'd said. "But for now just hang loose and let Pam show you around some. I'll probably have something for you to do in a few days. Just be ready and do it right. Then you're in."

Anton had really been impressed with Max Radkin, ponytail and all. He thought that maybe he'd found someone he could look to for guidance and inspiration now that his dad and Jamel were no longer available. He couldn't go running off to Vacaville every time he needed a confidence booster. Besides, it wouldn't look right, make him appear weak and indecisive.

Imitation being the most sincere form of flattery, Anton decided to copy his new idol. He went to a tattoo parlor in downtown L.A. and had two fat teardrops imprinted below his left eye. When he got back to the apartment that afternoon, Pam took one look at him and said, "Oh, my God!" She promptly pulled him down onto a bean bag and set about explaining the significance of the teardrops.

"It's a sign of grief because the wearer has taken a life," she said. "But it's also a sign of honor that demands respect because the life was taken for the benefit of the Brotherhood. Do you understand? No one can wear the teardrops until they've killed somebody under Brotherhood sanction. Max is gonna be really pissed."

And he was. He'd even threatened to tie him up and use sandpaper to take them off, go right down to the bone if necessary. But Pam had pleaded his case, saying he didn't know and shouldn't be held responsible. Which made a lot of sense to Anton. In the end Max had relented, but he couldn't totally ignore the transgression. "It's gotta be made right," he'd said. "I'll have to study on it."

Five days later Max had called him. "Something just came up that might get you off the spot. I'm gonna give you a chance to earn those tears."

And now he was sitting here in the early moments of dawn waiting to kill a man for a smart-mouth Jew in order to be accepted by the Aryan Brotherhood. That was pretty screwy. What the hell was Max doing working for a Jew anyway? And for a measly fifteen hundred bucks at that—a grand of which went to Max. It was something to think about.

Anton took a deep breath and shifted his attention across the driveway to the man's patio gate. He'd probably come out that way. But Anton also had a good view of the side gate leading to the carport in case the guy went out the front. So he had the Camaro covered. The problem now was to figure out the best way to intercept the man.

Anton touched the grip of the army-issue Colt .45 automatic resting between his legs and worked out a simple strategy.

Cage shaved, showered, and dressed, then went into the kitchen for coffee and Raisin Bran. Grits trekked after him and made a beeline for his food dish. He crouched down with his tail curled around his body and waited patiently while Cage took the Tender Vittles box from under the sink and shook it. Empty. He poked through the refrigerator and discovered he was out of milk as well. So much for the Raisin Bran.

"Looks like we're both out of luck, cat," he said, resigned to talking to him by now. "I'll have to do something about this."

The wall clock showed five to seven. There was an A.M./P.M. Mini Mart just up the street. Might as well make a quick run and pick up a few other things while he was thinking about it. Caprita would complain he was wasting money not going to Lucky's only a half mile away, that he was paying twelve to fourteen percent more strictly for saving maybe ten minutes of his extremely valuable time. But Caprita wasn't here. And it felt like she hadn't been here in a very long time.

She was still in his head as he scooped his keys from the counter and went out through the patio, locking the glass door behind him. It was a bright morning outside and the heat was already hinting at things to come. The carport roof protected the Camaro from the direct rays of the sun, but it couldn't do a thing about the heavy air hanging inside. He could feel his shirt sticking to his back even as he started the engine and turned the air-conditioner on full blast. He had learned to tolerate the L.A. heat, which was less oppressive than the summers in his native North Carolina, but he'd never gotten used to the smog. Probably never would, regardless of Caprita's claim to the contrary. He didn't believe that human eyes were designed to absorb the type of atmospheric garbage being spewed out by this city.

He felt something hard and cold pressing against the back of his neck. It was the strangest sensation he'd ever experienced in his life, totally unexpected, and it caused the hairs back there to stiffen as he went completely still. He realized instinctively that Griswald had laid the oldest trap in the ambush manual. And he had daydreamed his way right into it.

A voice from behind said, "Don't try to brush it away, dude, this ain't no fly."

That wasn't Griswald either. So he'd found somebody to take care of his dirty work after all. That was quick. Cage could see the guy in the rearview mirror now, rising up from the floorboard to perch on the edge of the backseat. A young buck with a big gun. And two fresh teardrops tattooed under his left eye. Cage was very aware of what they symbolized. And the knowledge gave him cause for alarm.

Cage said, "Sure you got the right car?"

"I've got the right car," Anton told him. "Got the right man too. Unless you tell me you're not Allen Cage, in which case I'll just take a peek in your wallet and see for myself. Are you?"

"I am." There was no point in denying it. "What now?"

"Now we go for a ride. Just you and me. It's a nice morning for it."

As Yogi Berra would say, it was like déjà vu all over again. Only last time he'd been the one holding the gun while Howie Wallmeyer drove.

Cage said, "How much is Horance Griswald paying you? He's the one who hired you, right?"

"No comment," Anton said. "Now here's the plan. You're gonna cruise out to Pacific Coast Highway, hang a right when you hit Topanga Canyon, and just keep going till I tell you to stop. Like I said, it's a beautiful morning for a drive, so just take your time and be cool."

"Or what, you'll put a bullet through my head?"

"You said it, not me."

"And what happens when we get to Topanga?"

"I know what'll happen right here if you don't move this thing, and now. Use the freeway, I'm in a hurry."

Cage drove, maneuvering through early morning traffic until he reached the Santa Monica Freeway, then staying in the slow lane all the way out to PCH. He didn't speak, and he didn't try any tricks, using the time to study the kid through the rearview mirror. He was still sitting erect on the edge of the seat, the gun out of sight, craning his neck from side to side like a tourist on holiday. If Cage had a gun himself, he could have shot the boy at least twice before the guy even knew what happened. A rank novice who thought it was going to be so easy. Well, it wasn't. Cage was familiar with the route he was taking and knew exactly what he would have to do. And where.

Cage said, "Are you A.B. or just a wanna-be?"

That got the kid's full attention. "What do you know about the A.B.?"

"The teardrops. Only two gangs wear them, the Aryan Brotherhood and the Mexican Mafia. And you don't look Mexican to me. You have to kill somebody to get them. You killed anybody yet, or are you fixing to?"

Anton was having conflicting thoughts again. "The Mexican Mafia? Mexicans wear teardrops too?"

"Sure, they're allies of the A.B." Where had this guy been?

"What kind of organization is this Mexican Mafia?"

"Same as the A.B.," Cage said. "A ragtag prison gang of society rejects who think they're big-time operators. Dopers, pimps, and two-bit hustlers with about as much class as a soup sandwich."

Anton leaned forward, his mouth inches away from Cage's right ear. "You're a liar," he said, his voice strained. "The A.B. represents the betterment of the white race, that's what they stand for. If there were more like them around, maybe we could change things in this country before it's too late. So keep your stupid mouth shut about things you don't know."

"Oh, I know 'em all right," Cage said. "I rubbed elbows with them for seven years in federal prisons from San Diego to Illinois, and the only people whose betterment they represent are their own. Most of 'em would sell their mother for a kilo of coke."

Anton slapped him a stinging blow alongside the head with his free hand. "I told you to keep your fucking mouth shut, and I mean it. Now just drive and cease with the conversation, I'm not in the mood for it."

Anton sat back and began swiveling his head again, intensely interested in the passing scenery. Pretending indifference to the man's bad-mouthing when in fact it bothered him a great deal. Because he was having a hard time defending his argument even to himself.

Working for Jews, having Mexicans for allies. What kind of white power organization was that? Maybe he'd have to make a trip up to Vacaville after all, have a good long talk with Jamel about his new friends. But now he had to do this piece of work for Max Radkin. Except that he was beginning to lose some of his enthusiasm.

They were on Topanga Canyon now, winding their way upward along the steep rim of the canyon wall, and Cage was having thoughts of his own. The kid in back had been silent a long time, but now he was starting to tense up as they neared the top. Cage could see him in the mirror, flicking the safety of the big automatic on and off—*snick-snick . . . snick-snick.* Sounding unnaturally loud inside the closed car. Cage wanted to get him talking again and take his mind off the road.

Cage said, "Mind telling me your name?"

"What?"

"Your name, what is it? I'd like to know who I'm talking to."

"Anton, now shut up."

"Anton, huh? Sounds like a show-business name."

"Yeah, I should've been a rock star."

Snick-snick . . . snick-snick.

"But you decided to join the Aryanettes and become a killer instead, right? That's real bright."

"One more crack," Anton said, "and I'm gonna close that mouth permanently."

"Isn't that what you're gonna do anyway? What's the difference? I might as well have my say, and as far as I'm concerned, you A.B. guys are nothing but a bunch of freaks who ought to be working sideshows. Let everybody line up and look at those silly teardrops and laugh their asses off."

Anton lunged forward and jammed the gun barrel hard into the back of Cage's neck. "You really do have a mouth, you know that? You'll eat those words. This all started out like something that had to be done, nothing personal or pleasurable about it. But now I'm gonna enjoy hearing you cop all kinds of deuces trying to beg your way out of it. I'm gonna remind you of everything you said just now and ask you to tell me what kind of freak I am when you start crawling around and whining . . . hey, where you going? Pull into that turnout over there."

The momentum had slowed as they approached the top of Topanga, but Cage abruptly picked up speed as he crested the top and headed down toward the valley.

"It's too late," Cage said, "I've already passed it."

"Slow this fucking thing down."

Cage had steadily accelerated and was already doing close to fifty, aided by the downhill angle of the road as it wended its way to the valley floor. The oncoming traffic was heavy, an uninterrupted stream of vehicles heading into L.A., but Cage's lane was relatively clear. He hit the gas and began juking the Camaro back and forth, coming dangerously close to the line of traffic on the left and the low guardrail on the right, which was all that separated them from the canyon rim and a sheer drop of hundreds of feet.

"Goddamn it, I said slow this fucking thing down!" Anton was shouting into his ear now, hanging on to the seat back for dear life.

Cage said, "You got two choices, Anton. Pull the trigger and send us into a head-on collision or over the cliff, or drop the gun over the seat. Otherwise I make the choice myself. I'm counting to five. One . . ."

"You crazy sonofabitch, I'll kill you!"

"Go ahead, but you're coming with me . . . two."

Cage juked to the right and barely nicked the guardrail before swerving back to the left. "Three . . ."

"Stop it, goddamn it!"

Cage, doing sixty now, almost sideswiped a gold Lincoln Continental and got an angry blast of horn in response.

"Four . . ."

"No way man, you're not that desperate. Pull over and we'll work it out." Anton's voice had risen an octave, but he was still trying to regain control.

"You want to see desperate?" Cage said. "I'll show you desperate . . . five!"

He swung the wheel hard to the right, straight at the guardrail, and let out a Rambo yell that was echoed by Anton screaming, "Shit, *here*!" He dropped the automatic over the seat, where it bounced once before coming to rest against Cage's leg.

Cage yanked the wheel to the left, slewing the tail end of the Camaro into the guardrail, and began tapping the brake. The rear fender screeched along the metal rail for nearly a hundred feet before Cage, still tapping the brake and fighting the wheel, finally brought the car to a stop three inches away from the guardrail. He looked for the gun, found it on the floorboard near the accelerator, picked it up and twisted around to face the kid in back.

Anton was pressed into the far corner, eyes closed and arms spread wide for support. His face had an ashen tint, and he didn't appear to be breathing. Cage could identify with that. He was feeling a bit queasy himself.

Cage said, "You can come up for air now, we've stopped."

Anton's eyes popped open, but the rest of him remained motionless. He focused on Cage and said,

"That's the craziest thing I ever saw in my life. You're certifiable."

"Where there's no hope there's no fear," Cage said. "Next time you decide to take somebody for a ride, use the front seat. Back there you're helpless, even with a gun. Now give me a name. Who put you up to this?"

Anton pushed himself upright and took a quick gander out the window. Just beyond the guardrail was nothing but empty blue sky. He shivered at how close he'd come to sailing right off the edge of that cliff. Shit, he might still be falling. What the hell, you pull a gun on somebody, they're supposed to do what you say.

"It was Horance Griswald, wasn't it?" Cage said. "How much was I worth?"

Anton said, "I'm not talking, man. I don't see any reason for it. Just take me in and file a complaint, I'll face the heat." He was for sure going to jail anyway, might just as well keep shut. Maybe they'd send him up to Vacaville with Jamel, and he could finally ask him what kind of screwy outfit he'd hooked him up with that worked with Jews and Mexicans.

Cage said, "Anton, I don't know how deep you're in with these A.B. creeps, but you'd better get the hell away from 'em. You don't fit the mold. What I said about them is true, and I speak from experience. They'll run a power game on you, fill your head with a bunch of shit about how they stand up for each other, and use you till you got nothing left to give. Then they'll throw you to the wolves when the wrecking ball hits and pretend they never heard of you. Whoever gave you this contract probably kept half the money, now am I right?"

"Two thirds," Anton said automatically, still looking out at the void.

"I thought so. And you take all the risk. How old are you?"

"Almost twenty-one." Anton was finding it easier to answer now, maybe because of all those thoughts he couldn't seem to shake. This guy was making a lot of sense, while Max Radkin was rapidly shrinking in stature.

"Almost twenty-one," Cage said, and followed Anton's gaze. "You came within about ten feet of not making it. How were you supposed to do it? Was I gonna have an accident? You weren't gonna shoot me, or you would've done it back at the apartment."

Anton gave him a defiant look. "I *was* gonna make you pull into that scenic-view turnout we passed, conk you on the head, and send you and car both over the edge. Somebody said that would be a good spot. Only I damn near ended up going over myself, and I didn't bargain for that. You're right, I'm not cut out for this crap. So regardless of what you do, I'm out of it. I'll do whatever time I get, then I'm going home where people make a little better sense." Anton, having said his piece, looked away again.

Try as he might, Cage couldn't work up a full steam of anger toward the guy. There was something vulnerable about him that lessened culpability, a twisted sense of right and wrong resulting from years of warped mind control that the boy only now seemed to have begun to question. He would have made an ideal terrorist. Give him a cause to believe in, and he would gladly sacrifice his life. But he hadn't quite bought this one, so maybe there was hope for him yet. One thing was sure, he wouldn't find any of that in prison. He would come out a killing machine—if he came out at all.

Cage said, "Anton, you're not gonna do any time for this one. Like you said, I'm crazy. So here's what we're gonna do. I copy down your name and address, file it away, and forget it for now. You go home and start a rock group or something, and if I ever hear of you being in L.A. again, you'd better be a star. Just admit it was Griswald."

Anton turned to him in astonishment, his mouth hung open like he'd just discovered fire. "Okay, it was Griswald. Now tell me you're joking."

"No joke. Take whatever money you have and keep going."

"What's to stop somebody else from coming after you? The man paid good money, he's gonna expect results."

Cage shook his head. "You disappear and the guy who sent you is suddenly going to develop amnesia. Believe me, I know his kind. As for Griswald, I'll get a certain amount of twisted pleasure in calling him up and saying guess what happened to his hit man. Then I'll hang up and let his imagination do the rest. Do we have an understanding?"

Anton said, "Sure, no question. But why the hell are you doing this? Man, I was ready to *kill* you."

"I have my own damn-fool reasons," Cage said. "Let it go at that. In addition, we lose this gun somewhere, and you don't even think about ever holding another one."

Anton ran a finger lightly over the fresh tattoos beneath his eye. "I got to do something about these damn teardrops. See a doctor, a plastic surgeon. My mom will hit the roof."

"Get a big pair of shades," Cage said, turning

around. "They'll fit right in with your new rock-star image. Anton and the Teardrops, how's that sound?"

"Yeah," Anton said, and fantasized for an instant. After today anything was possible. Then he said, "I wonder if you can do me another good turn?"

"Like what?" Cage said.

"Can you drop me off back at your apartment building? I left my car there."

Chapter
—23—

Horance Griswald didn't know the first thing about building a bomb, and he didn't have any idea how to go about getting one. But he did know that in L.A. anything was available for a price, it was just a matter of making the right connections. But that was precisely his problem—he didn't have the connections. And the only person he knew who did, that fucking Maury Bingham, was totally unreliable.

He had just hung up the phone after getting the scariest call he could ever remember. It was that goddamn Allen Cage, his nemesis, the guy who by all rights should be dead by now but wasn't. Calling him up to ask in a cheery voice if he'd heard from his hit man yet. "Guess where he's at now?" the idiot had said. "The same place you're going to be soon. Have a nice day, now." Then the fool had hung up without waiting for a reaction, leaving Horance filled with a sense of absolute disbelief tinged with more than a little outrage at having just given away fifteen hundred bucks.

He knew it had been too good to be true. He wasn't even concerned about what had happened to the kid, because it never entered his mind that Cage might have killed him. He'd been too blasé, too cocky to have just done something that serious and act like he didn't have a care in the world. Horance knew that from firsthand knowledge. And if the kid had said anything to the police—assuming Cage had turned him in—they would have been here by now. No, he was still safe in that regard. But he'd had all the frustration he could deal with over this guy. So now it was time to take matters into his own hands, like he should have done from the start, and be done with it.

Horance stretched out on the couch in the den, rubbing his overnight stubble while he waited for the coffee machine to finish. A bomb would do the trick. Something easy he could rig up that would go bang when he was miles away and scatter Allen Cage over half a city block. The vindictive bastard could be outside right now, eight-thirty in the morning, poking and prying and doing his best to piece together enough information to get him the gas chamber for doing Michael Grady. Horance doubted if he could, but there was always the possibility. As long as the guy was out there. Waiting and watching and dogging his tracks like a goddamn bloodhound.

Horance went upstairs to the bedroom, still struggling with the dilemma as he moved between dresser and closet, laying out a smoke-gray double-breasted wool and silk suit, striped tie, and white cotton shirt with French cuffs. Maybe he should get a copy of that book—what was the name of it? *The Anarchist's Cookbook,* that was the one. He'd heard about it years ago when it first came out. It was supposed to give step by step details on constructing all kinds of bombs, bombs that would blow up whole houses, shit, whole *neighborhoods!* He'd heard about other books that taught the same thing, written by diehard survivalists and guerilla warfare experts with a hard-on for the establishment. Maybe he could put together something simple and effective on his own that would do the job. Then he thought, Hell no, what would likely happen is he'd end up blowing himself sky high in the process. When you started fooling around with explosives, you'd better know what you were doing.

He opened the little mahogany jewelry box on the dresser and took out a pair of gold cuff links, then paused when he saw Howie Wallmeyer's business card lying there where he'd put it the other day. He picked it up, looked at it a moment, then went back into the den and sat down on the couch. Guys like Wallmayer were almost certain to have a few unsavory contacts on the opposite side of the law. Dealing with rough characters now and then was an accepted way of life in the security game, if for no other reason than to keep up with the latest methods of the competition. All Horance wanted was a name. And he knew exactly how to make Wallmeyer give it to him.

Horance went downstairs again and sat on the den couch. He reached for the phone on the end table, pulled it over onto his lap and held it there while he worked out his spiel. Wallmeyer had been reluctant to even talk to him the last time he'd called, and he didn't want the man hanging up on him after half a dozen words. Whatever this Allen Cage had said or done to him must have really gotten his attention.

Horance dialed the number and asked the female who answered for Howie Wallmeyer. When she asked who was calling, he said, "Just tell him it's his favorite customer," then listened to elevator music until Howie came on the line.

"Good morning, Mr. Wallmeyer, this is Horance Griswald. How are you?"

Howie said, "Oh, Jesus—Mr. Griswald, I really don't—"

"I'm not interested in your burglar alarms," Horance said flatly, "not anymore. What I want from you is a name, and I won't take no for an answer."

"What kind of name?"

"Someone who knows the dark side of the city and all its secrets, shall we say. Someone who could arrange for a person to buy just about anything he wanted, legal or not."

Howie, surprised, said, "You into drugs? That what you want?"

"I can buy drugs on practically any street corner in Hollywood," Horance said. "I don't need a middle man with connections for that."

"I can't help you there, Mr. Griswald. I know a couple guys who sell a little dope on the side, nothing heavy you understand, but that's about it. I wouldn't have any idea who to send you to for anything else. Sorry."

Horance, putting more bite in his voice, said, "Now listen to me, Wallmeyer, and listen good. I happen to be a highly respected and reputable businessman who's well regarded in this community."

"I know you are, sir."

"I have a certain amount of influence, and my word carries credibility."

"That's true too, yes sir."

"So how do you think the community is going to react when I spread the word that you're a liar, can't be trusted, and promise things you can't deliver?"

"I wouldn't go so far as to say all that, Mr. Griswald. I kind of ran onto some hard times and—"

"You told me that you would provide the same

system I was getting from Banes and Twiford for ten percent less than they were quoting. Now didn't you tell me that?"

"Well, yeah, but—"

"And I took you at your word," Horance said, "I trusted you enough to cancel my order with them and do business with you people. Then when I call to accept your offer, you start telling me you can't deliver and *may* even get out of the business. Yes, I'd go as far as to say you're everything I just mentioned and more."

Horance could almost feel Wallmeyer sweating through the phone, squirming around in his chair while he tried to think of something to say. Good. It was about time he started making someone else squirm for a change. This mister nice guy shit was over and done with.

Howie, sounding confused, said, "Cage told me he didn't sell you any alarm system, Mr. Griswald."

"Are you calling me a liar?"

"Oh, no sir."

"Then give me a name, Mr. Wallmeyer. Or your prophecy about maybe getting out of the business is definitely going to be fulfilled."

After a brief silence Howie said, "Well, could be I know a guy who could help you out. I'll have him call you."

"No, you won't," Horance said. "You'll have him meet me. At the Stage Deli on Santa Monica Boulevard, one o'clock. I'll have a table in the outside patio. All he has to do is ask for me when he comes in. You know where it is?"

"Yeah, Century City."

"Right. Now what's his name?"

"Rudy Hicks," Howie said. "He's dumber than a sled dog, but he's a real mixer."

Rudy Hicks was thinking this sure was a strange place to be talking about bombs, sitting out in the patio of a chintzy restaurant surrounded by what he liked to refer to as the Smart Set, people who looked like they posed for magazine ads, whether sporty casual or business conservative. Rudy, in his two-year-old corduroys and button-down yellow-and-white striped shirt, thought he was dressed like a scarecrow by comparison, but nobody seemed to mind. Maybe they thought he was an artist or middle-aged hippie, with his full black beard and shock of wavy hair that never stayed in place.

But the man sitting across the table from him, Horance Griswald, didn't seem phased at all by the conversation; he was acting like it was the most natural and legal thing in the world to be calmly discussing bombs and destruction while he ate his cheese blitzes and kreplach soup. He had a green cloth napkin tucked under his chin that he would occasionally use to dab at his lips, nodding once in a while to a passing waitress who would smile and greet him by name.

Horance said, "Anyway, Mr. Hicks, our mutual friend tells me you might be able to help me out with this little matter. He speaks highly of you as a man who knows how to get things done."

That would be the day, Rudy thought. Howie Wallmeyer treated him like a lackey, taking advantage of his limited employment opportunities due to a bum ticker, to use him for gofer work. And then calling him an idiot because he sometimes misinterpreted things and fucked up. The man took him for granted, tossing a fifty or hundred spot at him now and then like he was throwing a dog a bone, expecting him to be grateful for small favors. Still, it was the only thing Rudy had going outside the two-hundred and forty dollars a month partial disability he had to live on, and he couldn't afford to blow it. Maybe he could make a little decent money out of this deal, if he played it right. This big-time jeweler man was flush.

Rudy said, "I don't know, Mr. Griswald, something like that's hard to come by." He stuffed a pastrami sandwich wedge into his mouth and chewed thoughtfully. "We're talking heavy duty here, and a federal offense to boot. I just don't know."

"I have confidence in you, Rudy," Horance said. "May I call you Rudy?"

"Sure, that's okay."

"Well, consider this, Rudy. You get me what I want and I'll give you twenty-five hundred dollars. Cash. How does that sound?"

Rudy swallowed the sandwich wedge and washed it down with a long pull from his bottle of Miller Lite, trying to cover his elation. Shit, he didn't need to milk this guy, the man was ready now. He sure did want a bomb bad.

Rudy said, "Let me ask you, how big does this potato have to be? I mean what have you got in mind for it?"

"Big enough to blow a good size stump to pieces," Horance said mildly. "I've got this pesky thing in my backyard I've been meaning to get rid of for quite some time now. It's getting to be a real headache."

Rudy grinned. This guy must have thought he was a bigger idiot than Howie Wallmeyer did. He said, "Pesky stump, huh? Yeah, those buggers can be real stubborn. Take a good blast to lift that thing outta there. What you'd have to do is dig a hole down underneath it, get in real close to the tap root, then shave your charge—"

"Rudy," Horance said gently. "Can you get me what I want or not?"

"You want it on a timer, fuse, or manually activated?" Rudy asked quickly.

"That's better." Horance dabbed at his mouth with the napkin and thought about it. "Manually activated, I think. What I'd like to be able to do is stand some distance away and maybe set it off by pulling a string. Something like that. Any problems there?"

"Man, you're gonna need a long string."

"I've got a long string."

Rudy Hicks scratched his beard and gazed off at the next table, seeing two women in sharp tennis outfits laughing over raised glasses of ice tea. Rudy was fifty-four and hadn't been getting any since his triple bypass a year ago, afraid the exertion might be too much for the damaged heart tissue the doctors told him about. He was too embarrassed to ask if a good fuck might possibly do him in, but the way his heart lurched at the sight of those bronzed legs glistening in the sunlight, he was pretty sure it would. A few months earlier he tried going down on a clean-looking hooker from Plano, Texas, but she'd jumped out of bed within thirty seconds complaining that his beard was giving her razor burn. He'd told her about his heart then, explaining that what he needed was a gentle come, and she'd said, "You idiot, there ain't no such thing as a gentle come," and stormed out.

Even hookers were calling him an idiot, and Rudy was beginning to develop a complex. But this jeweler was going to give him a chance to show just how smart he really was and help perk up his sagging self-esteem. If he wanted a bomb, he'd give him a fucking bomb. He'd make it himself. He knew how to do it, thanks to a talkative ex-cop turned wino who lived two doors down from him and loved to come over and tell war stories. Yeah. He'd pocket the twenty-five hundred, purse his lips and go duh duh duh all the way to the bank. All he needed was four or five lengths of inch-and-a-half galvanized pipe, some wire, powder from about ten boxes of double-ought shotgun shells. Better make it fifteen, the man wanted a big one.

"How about it, Rudy?" Horance said. He pushed his plate away and pulled the napkin from his collar. "Can you handle it?"

"Sorry, Mr. Griswald, I was just thinking who I could go to. And I know just the guy. Makes these things himself, does a hell of a job. He's a little expensive, but I'll take care of him out of the twenty-five you give me."

"Excellent. When can I have it?"

Rudy cocked his head and looked up at the sky, figuring how long it would take him to round up what he needed. Not long. Two hours should do it. Another two and half or three to put the thing together. He said, "Tell you what, I'll give you my address. You come by tonight about seven and I'll have it for you."

"For sure?"

"For sure. But I'll need a couple hundred right now, you know, expense money, 'cause I might have to get the guy some materials. You can knock it off the total."

Horance removed his wallet from his inside coat pocket, took out two hundred-dollar bills, and handed them to Rudy.

"Thank you, Mr. Griswald. We're on our way."

"This is going to work, isn't it, Rudy? Because I would be very upset if it didn't."

"Is it gonna work?" Rudy scooted his chair closer to the table and hunched over his plate, a man ready to share secrets. "Let me tell you how good it's gonna work. You're gonna have four or five pieces of steel pipe taped together and packed with gunpowder, each one equal to a stick of dynamite, maybe stronger. They're gonna be capped airtight with electrical leads coming outta the ends and joined together on one side of a clothespin, one of these wooden kind that snaps shut with a little spring? Wrapped around the other side of this clothespin you're gonna have another electrical lead connected to a nine-volt battery. Separatin' these two leads is a small square of stiff plastic, about the size and thickness of half a credit card, and that's what your string's gonna be tied to." Rudy scissored his first two fingers and placed a paper coaster between them. He closed them again and gave Horance a knowing grin. "Now guess what happens when that piece of plastic is pulled out."

Horance leaned back to avoid the man's hard breath and said, "That's obvious. The circuit is completed and the charge explodes. Not bad."

Rudy jerked the coaster from between his fingers for emphasis, wadded it between his big hands and dropped it on his plate next to the lone wedge of pastrami sandwich. "You called it. And the beautiful thing about it is the other end of that string can be attached to anything." He picked up his Miller Lite, turned sideways in his chair, crossed his legs and winked. "Know what I mean?"

"Your demonstration was most graphic," Horance

said. "Simple, but ingenious. You'll have this all set up for me when I pick it up tonight?"

"All you'll have to do is connect the lead to the battery and pull the string, Mr. Griswald. But just remember what I told you, make sure you got a loooong string."

"And what exactly is going to happen to my pesky stump when I pull the string, Rudy?"

Rudy spread his hands, put a quizzical look on his face and said, "Hey, *what* stump?"

While Horance Griswald and Rudy Hicks were at the Stage Deli discussing how to blow up stumps, Cage was preparing to commit a B & E on the jeweler's house in Brentwood. He wasn't being very sneaky about it either, just pulled his Camaro into the driveway and stopped in front of the closed garage door, grateful for the tall hedges that shielded him from the eyes of curious neighbors. On the seat beside him was Paul's frequency finder, a battery-powered unit half the size of a shoe box, which Paul had designed for calibrating the operating frequencies in his remote-door locks. It was capable of sending out a radio signal across a wide bandwave spectrum.

Today Cage was using it as a super Genie garage-door opener. He set the selector dial at the lower end, pressed the transmit button, and slowly began rotating the dial clockwise. In less than a minute he heard the garage door hum and watched it lift open, a yawning mouth that showed a black van parked against the left wall.

Cage eased the Camaro in close to the van, cut the motor and got out. The control buttons for the garage door were on the wall next to what he assumed was the kitchen entrance, just below the light switch. He turned on the light, closed the garage door, then went over to the van for a closer look.

It was last year's model, a customized Econoline with bubble side windows of silver-tinted glass. It was midnight black, clean and sleek, and Cage felt his skin crawl standing next to it in the closed garage that smelled of paint thinner, oil, and exhaust fumes—as if it were a devil machine that came alive only at night to go out in search of prey. Just like its master.

He made a slow circle of the van, looking it over, vaguely aware of another scent hanging in the still air. Rubber. New rubber.

He looked at the tires, then squatted down to examine them one by one, running his hand lightly over the treads. All brand-new Goodyear radials, the two on the rear still showing white chalk marks bearing their identification numbers. Why would the man need four spanking new tires on a van that was only a year old? The answer came to him immediately. Griswald had been afraid he might have left imprints in the soft earth at the top of the hill above Michael Grady's house. Marilee had said the van had been coming from that direction when it almost ran her over. The guy was definitely covering all the bases.

Cage didn't waste time checking the inside, knowing he wouldn't find anything of interest there. He moved to the entry door, took one look at the token knob lock, and realized he wouldn't need the set of picks he'd brought along. His credit card would get him through that in about five seconds. For a sophisticated thief who should know better, Horance Griswald certainly hadn't devoted a lot of effort to personal security.

But that is the nature of predators, his private dinosaur said, while he slipped the card into the crack between the doorframe and latch. They refuse to accept the possibility that they might become prey themselves . . . until it's too late.

It wasn't a kitchen that he entered, but a utility room with a piggyback washer/dryer and an ironing board that folded out of the wall. The kitchen was beyond, large and airy, with a chopping-block table in the middle of the floor and a windowed door on the opposite side that led to the backyard. Cage went to it and looked out, seeing a blond cocker spaniel dozing in the shade of a birdbath, chin lying on its paws. He hoped the dog wouldn't wake up and sense that a stranger was inside and start barking its head off.

Cage turned away and made for the study, deciding that was the most logical spot to begin his search for a cassette tape.

An hour later he was right back where he started, sitting behind the desk in the high banker's chair, swiveling from side to side and trying to think if he might have missed anything. He'd gone through the entire house, from bottom to top and back again, methodically checking every place he felt could reasonably hide a cassette, with no luck. He had even gone through Horance Griswald's considerable collection of tapes on the off chance he might have copied the cassette onto one of those. But all he heard were show tunes and cabaret music and a nice assortment of Susan Ackeman folk-rock songs that he would have really enjoyed under different circumstances.

He had found the little empty recorder next to the loaded .38 in the middle drawer, had set it on the desk and was gazing at it as he swiveled, like he was expecting it to tell him things. The cassette was somewhere in the house, Cage was convinced of that. Griswald might have it with him, but that was unlikely. The man had a stash right here, a clever little cubbyhole that had held whatever Bobby Lee Gettis had had in that briefcase he lost. But damned if Cage could find it, and the fact that he couldn't was putting him in a foul mood and making him wonder—not for the first time—if he wasn't in the wrong line of work.

He picked up a silver Parker fountain pen and began tapping it irritably against the edge of the desk. He would start all over again, this time beginning with the van. He'd feel like a fool if the cassette turned up in the glove box, or if that workbench along the back wall of the garage had some hideaway compartment that was chock full of goodies, including an alleged sequence counter that he had never before in his life actually set eyes upon but would dearly love to see in action.

He dropped the pen, and when he scooted the chair back and leaned down to pick it up, something caught his eye through the clear plastic carpet protector. It was a slight separation in the cream-colored carpet underneath. He pushed the chair aside, slid the tough square of plastic out of the way, and knelt down to investigate. He could see it plainly now, a small slit in the plush piling that had widened from the constant weight being placed on it. He tugged at the nap and a section of the carpeting lifted and folded back to show the face plate of Horance Griswald's circular floor safe.

Cage thought, Jesus, I've been sitting right on top of it the whole time. Well, in this game you had to be a little lucky once in a while. That's where his cassette would be, maybe a few other interesting items as well. But he was no safecracker, and this thing was set in about eighteen inches of concrete.

He lowered the carpet, put the plastic protector and chair back in their original positions, and said, "No problem." He'd be back tomorrow. He might not have a fancy sequence counter, but he certainly knew another surefire way of getting to what was in that cylinder.

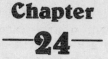
With each whiskey sour that Howie Wallmeyer downed, his anger increased. And he had downed seven of them in the two hours he'd been perched at the Grand Avenue Bar in the Biltmore Hotel, so he was steaming, his brain moving toward alcoholic vapor lock as he sat stoop-shouldered over his glass, snapping pieces from his swizzle stick. Jorge, his favorite bartender, would come ambling along from time to time, wipe the broken pieces into an ashtray, and give him a new swizzle stick. Normally Jorge would stand there and shoot the breeze with him awhile, tell him about his ex-wife's latest attempt to get money from him. She was in Kingston, Jamaica, and kept bugging him to help care for the three-year-old son she swore was his, but he knew better. He would point to his brown eyes, a wide grin on his almond face, and ask Howie if those eyes looked blue to him. But not tonight. Tonight he left Howie to contemplate his own demons and took up a station opposite two businessmen and a skinny redhead at the end of the bar. Howie saw him polishing ashtrays, flashing his pearly grin and pointing at his eyes.

The demon that Howie Wallmeyer was contemplating was Allen Cage, the fucker who had kidnapped him, blown up his car, and left him to hitch a ride to the city limits with a sixty-year old fag who kept telling him what a lovely chest he had. Wanted to know if that was the latest fashion with the in crowd these days, wearing blazers without any other upper body covering. Once the old guy had even reached over and tried to tweak his nipple, and Howie, already in an evil frame of mind, had tried to break his wrist. That's when he'd gotten out and called a cab from a nearby all-night diner, finally getting home somewhere around four-thirty in the goddamn morning.

Allen Cage, Howie thought, and snapped another half inch off his swizzle stick. He should have called the cops, had the bastard prosecuted and sent back to the joint. But the guy had gone completely off his rocker lately, assaulting him in an elevator, kidnapping him with a gun he wasn't even supposed to have as an ex-felon. Blowing up his fucking car, that was maniac work there. No telling what the crazy sonofabitch would do next. And bad as Howie hated to admit it, even to himself, Allen Cage had made a believer of him. He was terrified of the man. So he had called the police and his insurance agent, reported the Thunderbird stolen, and was now hailing taxis until he decided whether to buy or lease his next set of wheels.

But it was a blow to his manhood, made him feel like he was wimping out, and every time he had a few drinks, the anger would rise from deep inside him like heated mercury and flood his head with thoughts of revenge. The alcohol would fuel his courage right up to the point where he was ready to do something drastic, but he always seemed to stop one drink short of direct action.

Until tonight, he thought, and snapped another

inch off the swizzle stick. Tonight he was going to have that extra drink that would provide the added boost necessary to propel him clear across town and right through Allen Cage's front door, where he would haul the crazy motherfucker out of bed by the scuff of his neck and proceed to beat the living dogshit out of him. That's exactly what he would do, or his name wasn't Howard Lenwood Wallmeyer.

He tossed back the last of his whisky sour and held up a finger to Jorge, who was now giving him a concerned look as he rang up a tab for the trio at the end of the bar. He placed the tab in a wooden tray next to the register and made his way down to Howie, his professional grin back in place.

Howie said, "Jorge, do this again, make it a double."

Jorge leaned an elbow on the bar and said, "Mr. Howie, you drinkin' a lot tonight, mon. Maybe you let me order you a nice hot liter of espresso. I will even make it myself, just like we drink in Jamaica. It will warm the stomach like the hands of a good woman. What do you say?"

"I say I want another fuckin' drink, a double. Gives me all the warmth I need."

Jorge put on his concerned look again and struggled for diplomacy, aware of the management's policy against serving drunks who might cause the hotel a big liability suit if the guy then went out and played demolition derby on the freeway. But Mr. Howie was a regular customer and a big tipper who would be very offended if he was refused service.

He tried once more. "Mr. Howie, you should not be driving like this. Is almost time to close anyway. You come back tomorrow night and I give you two free ones. What do you say, mon?"

Howie looked up at him through bleary eyes. "Jorge, I'm not drivin'. I haven't *been* drivin' for a couple days now. I've been walkin', I've been catchin' cabs, I've been ridin' with old fags hung up on nipples, but I haven't been *drivin'* any fuckin' place. Now you gonna give me a drink or a lecture?"

Jorge could see his fat tip staggering out the door right now. He stood there undecided, not wanting to risk his cushy job.

Howie said, "Don't worry, if it'll make you feel any better, I'm havin' somebody pick me up after this one. Satisfied?"

Jorge thought he could live with that. "You got a deal, Mr. Howie. I fix you one good one. You need a phone?"

"Yeah. And bring me some peanuts, the kind don't have any salt on 'em. I don't need to be gettin' thirsty after I leave here."

Jorge, grinning again now that his tip was assured, brought Howie his double whiskey sour, a bowl of unsalted Planter's peanuts, and half a dozen swizzle sticks for the mon to break up. He placed the Princess phone with the long cord next to Howie's elbow and picked up the bar tab.

"There you go, Mr. Howie, you all set now," Jorge told him, and winked. "But I only charge you for a single. You have enough swizzle sticks?"

Howie waved him away, fumbling with the phone. He had to organize his thoughts before he could remember Rudy Hicks's number, but he was pretty sure he dialed it right. Rudy answered after the fifth ring, saying hello in a groggy voice.

Howie said, "Rudy, you in bed?"

Another pause, then Rudy said, "It's ten after one, Mr. Wallmeyer, sure I'm in bed."

"Well, get your ass up and get over here to the Biltmore, I need you to take me somewhere."

"Now?"

"Yes, now, soon's you can get here. I'm in the Grand Avenue Bar."

"Mr. Wallmeyer, I'm not feeling so hot. My heart's been acting up a little, and I need my rest."

"Rudy, there's nothin' wrong with your fuckin' heart, you're runnin' that shit in the ground. Your heart's in better shape than mine is, and you know it. You could probably run a marathon, only you're too lazy."

"That's not true either, honest. The doctor just told me last week, as a matter of fact, said I needed a good eight hours sleep every night, square business."

"What, does your heart stop pumpin' when you're asleep? cut the crap and get over here, Rudy. And hurry up, I'm on my last drink."

Rudy made a grumbling sound and said, "Well where do you want to go, Mr. Wallmeyer?"

"I'll let you know when you get here." Howie was about to hang up when he put the phone back to his ear and said, "Hey, did you meet Griswald today?"

"I saw him."

"What'd he want?"

"A bomb."

"A *what?*"

"For real, Mr. Wallmeyer, the guy wanted a bomb. Said he had a pesky stump in his yard he wanted to get rid of. Like I just rolled off a turnip truck or something. Who'd figure him for that type, huh?"

Howie said, "So did you get him one?"

"Hell, I made him one," Rudy said.

"You *made* him one? Where'd you learn to do somethin' like that?"

Rudy, sounding cockier than Howie could remember, said, "I can do a lot of things, Mr. Wallmeyer. You'd be surprised."

"I'm beginnin' to appreciate that, Rudy. Guess I've been underestimatin' you."

"Yes sir, you sure have."

"I'll keep that in mind," Howie said. "Meanwhile, how about gettin' your butt over here and pick me up. I might find out just how responsible you really are before the night's out."

Howie hung up, tossed a handful of peanuts into his mouth and chased them down with his whiskey sour. Holy shit, he thought, a fucking bomb? What the hell did a Century City jeweler want with a *bomb?*

He'd have to think about that later. Right now he had more pressing matters on his mind.

It was a simple matter to plot methods for vengeance and visualize manly scenarios for physical confrontation while hunched over a glass in an alcoholic haze in the Grand Avenue Bar. It was something else again to be in the breezeway lobby of the small apartment building on Camden Avenue at three in the morning when it was time to put those plans into action. The effects of his whiskey sours were beginning to diminish, and so was Howie's courage.

Now he was standing under the yellow dome light surveying the short row of mailboxes recessed into the stucco wall. Looking at number six, to be specific, the one that had Cage/Arciaga embossed across the metal door. He was making excuses to himself while Rudy Hicks waited by the wrought-iron gate leading to the courtyard and fenced swimming pool, the whole area dead silent at this hour.

It wouldn't work, Howie thought. By the time he

busted through the guy's door—if he could bust through it—Cage would be waiting for him with that little .25 automatic he wasn't supposed to have. Ditto with smashing a window. He'd also wake up the entire building, and the cops would be there in two minutes, pulling him off the sonofabitch even if he could get to him without being shot. So it looked like Allen Cage was going to get out of a good ass-whipping, the lucky prick.

But Howie had to do *some*thing after telling Rudy on the way over here that he was going to settle an old score with the guy that was long overdue. The question was, *what?*

Rudy came over and stood next to him, scratching his beard and trying not to show how nervous he was, wondering what Howie was going to do now that they were here. The drunken fool just kept staring at the man's mailbox, his mind off somewhere in the twilight zone. Rudy wanted it to be over and done with, whatever it was, so he could get back home and to bed. He was also worried about the twenty-three hundred dollars Griswald had counted out for him when he had collected his ready-to-go bomb. The money was buried in a box of Tide under the kitchen sink, so it should be safe. But you never knew what might happen. The building could catch on fire. Or a water pipe could break and give a whole different meaning to the term money laundering.

Rudy, speaking quietly, said, "I got a suggestion, Mr. Wallmeyer, if you really want to get this dude good."

"What's that, Rudy?" Howie didn't sound too enthused.

"Put shit in his mailbox. I gotta go anyway. I'll find a paper bag, do my business, we'll pop the lock and dump that sucker right in there. Can you picture the look on his face when—"

"Rudy, will you just shut up? Only you could come up with an idea that stupid."

Howie started to move away, then suddenly turned back to Rudy. "Cage drives a Camaro, doesn't he? Older model?"

"Yeah, dark blue. 'Seventy-eight or 'seventy-nine. Why?"

"Come on," Howie said, and led the way around the side of the building, walking with purpose now, Rudy tagging along behind like an obedient puppy unsure of its master's intent.

Howie was checking the cars lined up under the darkened carport, finally spotted the Camaro, and stopped, waiting for Rudy to catch up.

Howie, whispering, said, "Find me a rag or some newspaper. There's a Dumpster at the end of the driveway there." He squatted down behind the Camaro and removed the gas cap.

Rudy said, "Wait a minute, what are you gonna do?"

"I'm gonna blow his car up," Howie said. "Now hurry up and find me something."

Rudy thought, sweet Jesus, the man was drunker than he figured. He said, "Mr. Wallmeyer, this is crazy," and looked around at the dark row of windows along the length of the building, expecting to see lights wink on any second. He felt his heart flutter and slapped his pants pockets, knowing he hadn't brought his nitro pills. "I mean we can't just blow up the man's car. We'll have the whole neighborhood down here in thirty seconds."

Howie was still hunkered down behind the Camaro, pushing on the bumper and listening to the gasoline sloshing around in the tank. As best he could tell, it was nearly full.

He said, "Rudy, we'll be out of here and gone before it goes up, if you'll just get me something a couple feet long. Now will you *move?*"

No way, he wasn't about to get involved with this shit, Rudy told himself. He'd made twenty-three hundred and change today, and didn't feel like giving it all to a lawyer to defend him on an arson charge. Howie was taking this grudge business too far. Rudy eased over and bent down to look through the driver's window, the moonlight showing him what appeared to be a nifty Hurst four-in-the-floor and genuine leather upholstery. Pretty nice-looking stereo too, from what he could see.

Rudy said, "Mr. Wallmeyer, why don't we just steal it?" He could live with that. "I know a guy would give us a couple thousand for it with no questions asked. Be simple as pie, we just roll it to the end of the driveway and hotwire it. By the time he gets up, it'll be sittin' in a garage in Silver Lake. See? It ain't even locked."

Rudy opened the door and the earth shook.

The pipe bomb that had been rigged to the Camaro's inside door handle also ignited the fuel tank, and the two almost simultaneous blasts sent shock waves through the calm night that shattered the rear window of four apartments and created panic among most of the tenants who had been jarred from a sound sleep, many of them believing that an airplane had crashed into the building.

It sent Cage leaping out of bed and Grits scrambling beneath it, Cage instinctively reaching for the .25 automatic that was taped to the back of the nightstand. He decided against it and hurried to the broken window, detouring around the shards of glass on the carpet. There was no need to turn on the light, because the darkness outside had been transformed into a flickering orange sunset that illuminated the bedroom with its glow.

His Camaro was a flaming pyre, the heat so intense he could feel it from the window. The door on the driver's side had been blown completely off and was lying next to Jack Brian's Buick, formerly white but now scorched and dented on one side. It looked like there was a body underneath it. The carport roof buckled outward, and small patches of burning gasoline were scattered everywhere. There were shouts, and someone screamed.

Cage put on his pants, jammed his feet into a pair of shower thongs and ran through the living room and out the patio door. He unlatched the gate and stepped into the driveway, seeing other tenants in nightclothes rushing outside to find out what was happening, but keeping a safe distance from the inferno as they watched, horrified. Someone was still screaming, and Cage saw that it was Kristina Urton. She was standing outside her patio gate in a yellow robe, staring at a burning object near the side of the building. It was another body. A man, judging from its shape. The explosion had blown him clear across the driveway and slammed him against the wall, drenched with burning gasoline and now charred beyond recognition. The stench of burning flesh was almost overpowering.

There was nothing to be done for that one.

Cage dashed across the driveway and knelt beside the body lying half under the Camaro's door, the heat prickling his exposed back. The man's face had been shredded like raw hamburger from the disintegrating glass that had hit him like a sandblaster, but the familiar beard, burned back to a frizzled stubble, was identification enough for Cage. It was Rudy Hicks, Howie Wallmeyer's faithful puppet. And that meant the body still burning over by the wall had to be Howie.

What the hell was going on here?

There was nothing to be done for Rudy either, so Cage sprinted back to the patio and connected his garden hose to the outside faucet, snaking it through the gate to direct a stream of water onto the burning body of what had been Howie Wallmeyer. Jack Brian had brought his hose out too and was dousing the Camaro and carport roof, which was also starting to burn. The wail of sirens could be heard now, faintly, but drawing closer.

Cage finally thrust the garden hose into a pair of unknown hands and walked slowly to the mound of smoldering, blackened flesh, breathing through his mouth. He looked down at it in revulsion, but with a gradual awareness of what had happened. Someone had planted a bomb in his car; that was obvious from the way the driver's door had been ripped off its hinges. There was also the unmistakable odor of cordite in the air, mingling with the smell of gasoline and burnt flesh. Howie Wallmeyer and Rudy Hicks had been unscrupulous pains in the ass, but they weren't murderers. Howie had decided to retaliate for the destroyed Thunderbird by either stealing or destroying his Camaro, but his timing had been lousy. Because, Cage concluded, someone else had already decided to destroy him.

And he knew of only one person who would want to do that.

Cage looked up as the first fire engine turned into the driveway. Once again, he thought, he had really underestimated Horance Griswald. Except for a quirk of fate, that would have been him lying under the Camaro's door with his face looking like it had been stuck in a Waring blender. Or it could have been Caprita. Cage had a fleeting vision of her opening that door, before he was able to force the image from his mind.

Well, he wouldn't underestimate Griswald anymore. It was time to quit playing games and get serious with the man.

Chapter
—25—

Horance Griswald could not believe what he was seeing on the six A.M. newscast. He hadn't expected to see anything at all until after eight, figuring Allen Cage wouldn't be leaving his apartment any earlier, but had turned on Channel 2 just in case.

And there it was, the lead story of the day. The camera focused first on the scorched remains of the blue Camaro being examined by half a dozen police and fire officials, then cut away to show two covered bodies being wheeled to a waiting ambulance while the male voice-over was saying that the victims had now been identified as Howard Wallmeyer, owner of a local security agency, and Rudolpho Hicks, an unemployed electrician and handyman. Police were theorizing that the pair had been in the process of planting what was described as a "crude but effective" homemade bomb in the vehicle when it had detonated prematurely, killing both instantly.

The camera was panning the area now, showing the Camaro's door lying next to a badly wounded Buick, the buckled carport roof, broken and scarred apartment windows, and a wristwatch belonging to one of the victims that the announcer was saying had been found sixty feet away, pinpointing the time of the explosion at 3:07 A.M.

Two hours after Horance had painstakingly installed the thing, carefully following the instructions Rudy Hicks had provided for bringing about his own death.

Talk about weird. What the hell were they doing there?

But Horance, down on one knee in front of the TV, was experiencing a strange sense of power looking at the carnage he had created. He was awed by it. He could look at the results of his handiwork with a curious sort of detachment, like a running back studying the game film of his ninety-yard touchdown run, and think, *Did I do that? Wow!* Until two weeks ago he had never committed a violent act in his life, had never even been in a fistfight as a kid. Now he had killed four people.

And he was starting to enjoy it.

The camera was on Allen Cage now, shirtless and smudged, being interviewed by a breathless woman reporter who was asking if he knew why anyone would want to kill him. Cage, running a nervous hand across his face, said no, unless it had something to do with his work. It was easy to make enemies in the security business, he said, and you never knew who they were. The woman asked if he expected any further attempts on his life, and Horance leaned closer to the screen, observing the man's worried frown as he answered that he certainly hoped not, this was as close to death as he wanted to come. She wanted to know what he was going to do now. He told her that he had a vacation coming and this might be a great time to take it. "This whole thing's been a little unnerving, to say the least," he said, and smiled weakly at the camera.

Horance patted the screen where Cage's tousled hair was and said, "Smart man. Not so cocky now, are you?"

He switched the TV off, went into the bathroom and turned on the shower. Then he peeled off his robe and stood in his jockey shorts in front of the large mirror, checking every inch of his reflection before finally locking eyes with his image. He was seeing a new facet of Horance Griswald, and was pleased with the discovery. People kept coming at him, taking him for a patsy, and he had bested every one. Even missing his intended target would work to his advantage in this instance. Allen Cage had come face to face with the grim reaper and had been frightened out of his wits. He knew full well who had been responsible for the bomb, Horance was positive of that. No one else had cause or nerve enough to do it. But to remove all doubt, he would call the man later in the day, if he hadn't already left on vacation, and drop a few hints. Close call, huh, Mr. Cage? What a shame! You must have really gotten someone upset. Perhaps you should be more careful in the future, because you never know, it could happen again. Open a door sometime and . . .

Yes, he would know. And the fear would always be with him. In the meantime the only person who could connect him with the bomb had been eliminated by it. All nice and tidy, no dangling ends. Even Maury Bingham couldn't have worked it better. He didn't need that two-faced bastard after all, and he didn't need his so-called underworld "professionals" who charged a small fortune for work such as this. He didn't need anybody.

Horance slipped out of his shorts and stepped into the shower, feeling better than he had in years.

It was nearly eleven when Cage pulled into Horance Griswald's driveway in the battered El Camino he'd borrowed from Chopper, his friendly parking lot attendant. The bombing incident had occurred too late to make the morning papers, and neither Chopper nor Olive Oyl had watched the TV news, so he'd been spared from having to go through all the gory details. Apparently Caprita hadn't heard anything yet either, or she would have burned up the road getting to him. Right now he didn't need any distractions. He'd wondered if Griswald was going in to his shop today, all things considered, but his answering machine had been on at least since nine-thirty, and the house appeared to be empty. He'd know for sure in a minute.

Cage went through the procedure with Paul's frequency finder and the garage door swung upward. Nothing in there but the van, though it looked like it was parked a little more to the right than he remembered. The devil machine had been busy last night.

Inside the garage he used his credit card on the entry door and made a careful search of the house, making certain that Horance Griswald wasn't lurking around waiting for him. In his hand was the little .25, ready for use. He wasn't taking anything for granted where this man was concerned. Not anymore.

When he was satisfied the place was empty except for the little cocker spaniel in the backyard, Cage returned to the garage and lowered the tailgate on the El Camino. He hefted the heavy duty jackhammer he'd rented from Pacific Industrial Supply Company and carried it into the study, propping it against the desk. He went back and connected the two forty-foot extension hoses, joined one end to the twenty-horsepower air compressor in the bed of the El Camino, then played out the hose through the kitchen, den, and into the study, where he coupled the other end to the jackhammer. He went out to the El Camino again, put on a pair of work gloves, and fired up the gasoline-powered compressor. He was going to make some noise, but he didn't think it would matter even if someone happened to be home next door and overheard. The human mind, he had once read, automatically conjures up preprogrammed images in association with certain readily identifiable sounds. Air compressors and jackhammers form visions of construction or excavation; they do not signal a burglary in progress.

Back in the study, Cage shoved the banker's chair and plastic protector out of the way, pulled back the flap of carpeting and took an appraising look at the safe. He thought the concrete foundation it was anchored in probably extended outward six or eight inches beneath the floor, forming a square around the cylinder approximately two feet in diameter by eighteen inches deep. Much too heavy to carry. The thing to do, he decided, was break through the concrete around the barrel of the safe, keeping as close to the cylinder as possible, until it was loose enough to lift out by the handle across the face plate.

He spat on his gloves, rubbed them together, carefully positioned the jackhammer and squeezed the trigger.

It kicked and bucked like a rodeo bronc and gave out a racket like a tommy gun, but the steel bit sent chunks and fragments of concrete flying in all directions, stinging his face and forcing him to squinch his eyes into narrow slits. He'd forgotten to bring goggles.

He worked steadily for several minutes, making good headway, then paused to wipe away the beads of perspiration that were starting to trickle from his forehead. In the sudden silence he could hear the little dog yipping and scratching like crazy outside the kitchen door, wanting to get in and find out what all the ruckus was about. Cage got a fresh grip on the handles and attacked the concrete once more.

It took twenty minutes to clear a space around the cylinder all the way to the bottom. He set the jackhammer aside, wrapped his hands around the steel body of the safe and wiggled it back and forth, breaking it loose from the last patches of concrete, then took hold of the handle and hauled it out of the hole and onto the carpet.

He leaned against the desk for a minute, getting his wind back and listening to the cocker spaniel still yapping away. Then he picked up the safe, lugged it out to the El Camino, and returned to the study.

The place was littered with concrete, and a fine chalklike residue covered the mirror surface of the desk. Cage stood near the gaping hole in the floor and surveyed the room, letting his eyes sweep over the expensive furnishings, lingering on the grandfather clock standing proudly between two colorful abstract paintings that Cage imagined would impress an art critic.

He was suddenly struck with an urge, and he grinned at the thought. Well, why the hell not? Give the man something to really think about.

Cage lifted the heavy jackhammer, cradled it in the crook of his left arm, squeezed the trigger, and made a slow circle around the desk, punching holes in the polished wood until it resembled Swiss cheese. He moved to the grandfather clock and hit the trigger again, smashing the delicate glass panels and clock face and sending pulleys, flywheels, and gears bouncing off the wall and across the carpet. He got the two abstract paintings and several others for good measure, moving slowly along the wall, firing as he went. He turned a maple bookcase into kindling, split a French end table in half, and pulverized a Tiffany lamp in the process. He went into the den, gunning the jackhammer like a motorcycle, and exploded the twenty-five-inch screen on the Magnavox TV and punctured silver dollar-sized holes in the stereo speakers; he reduced the coffee table and two end tables to rubble, pounded the stuffing out of the leather sofa, and machine-gunned a gilt-framed oval mirror off the wall.

Still revving the jackhammer, he moved into the dining room and wreaked havoc on a Thomasville hutch, along with about two thousand dollars worth of accessories, and was zeroing in on a dainty-looking china cabinet when he ran out of hose.

Just when it was getting good to him.

Reluctantly he trudged back through the demolished den and into the kitchen, pausing long enough to slake his thirst with a can of soda he found in the refrigerator. Then he went into the garage and was about to put away the gear when he hesitated again, eyeing the black van sitting there like a huge silent beetle.

The devil machine.

Once more the jackhammer stuttered to life, and Cage, walking backward with the tool nestled in his arm and his finger tight on the trigger, did a slow turn around the van, causing it to shudder under the impact of the steel bit that gouged, smashed and pummeled everything in its path. It ripped jagged holes in the smooth metal, tore away sections of polished chrome, shattered the bubble side windows, windshield, and headlights. By the time Cage completed the circle, the once gleaming van looked as if it had been caught in a crossfire.

Cage disconnected the hoses, loaded everything into the bed of the El Camino, and shut off the air compressor. His arms and shoulder muscles ached, and his body still tingled from the vibrations of the air tool. He felt great. Physically drained, but mentally rejuvenated, the rage and frustration that had been building over the past week at last vented. Not completely spent, but certainly more manageable. Enough so that he could now do what remained to be done in a relatively calm manner.

Which reminded him that he'd almost overlooked one important thing. He opened the big toolbox behind the cab, rummaged around until he found a small rat-tail file, and went back into the house. This would only take a few minutes.

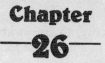

Cage didn't feel like crossing busy Santa Monica Boulevard in broad daylight toting a fifty-pound floor safe with bits of concrete still clinging to the cylinder. And he didn't feel like answering Chopper's obvious question of, "Hey, man, where the hell did you get the safe?" when he returned the borrowed El Camino to the parking lot. So he pulled into the alley behind the office, double-parked next to the delivery entrance, got out and rang the bell. Brenda Alworth was waiting for him by the time he hauled the safe out through the passenger door.

"What in the world is that?" she asked as he brushed past her.

"A safe, what's it look like?"

She followed him into the workshop. "A safe? What are you doing with a safe?"

"I stole it," Cage said, and hefted it onto Paul's work bench. "Do me a favor will you, Olive Oyl? Don't ask any more questions right now, I've got to get this thing opened."

"You expect me not to ask any questions after just telling me you stole a safe? I thought we were in business to prevent that sort of thing."

"Only for clients," Cage said, moving to a corner of

the room where Paul kept his acetylene rig. He wheeled the tanks over to the workbench, wrestled the safe into the jaws of a large vise mounted on one end, and clamped it firm.

Brenda watched, wide-eyed with wonder, then threw up her hands and turned to leave.

"I don't want to hear any more," she said. "That way maybe I won't be called to testify against you in court." She stopped and looked back at him. "Paul called this morning. He wanted to know why Larry went to New York, and I told him I had no idea. Then he asked where you were, and I told him I didn't know that either. The only thing I do know for sure is that people are acting awfully weird around here. And now you come in with a stolen safe."

"Was he upset?"

"He wasn't upset, he was pissed off. He seems to think you two are up to something with Horance Griswald. Are you?"

"I thought you didn't want to hear any more."

Brenda folded her arms across her small breasts and said, "Suit yourself. But you're going to have to tell him, and I mean soon. He's leaving the convention early, coming in tomorrow morning at eight-twenty. He wants you to meet him at the airport, and I wouldn't want to be in your shoes if you aren't there."

She turned on her heel and went into the office.

Perfect, Cage thought. Now he was going to have Paul to deal with on top of everything else. And when Paul learned what had been going on at home while he was playing with his remote lock in Denver, Paul's usually understanding nature was going to take an indefinite leave of absence. And this time Larry would catch it too.

But maybe it would be over by then, and there

would be no need for lame excuses. The truth, as they say, would be self-evident.

Cage put on gloves and goggles, lit the burning rod and adjusted the mixture. With the safe's bottom tilted upward at a forty-five-degree angle, he began cutting a thin line around the cylinder, pausing frequently to let the smoke and sparks clear to check his progress. He had considered using the cutting rig instead of the jackhammer to begin with, but had decided not to risk setting off the smoke detectors he had seen throughout the man's house. Besides, the jackhammer had been more satisfying.

When he had nearly completed the circle, Cage set the cutting rig aside and knocked off the two-inch-wide bottom section with a ball-peen hammer. It fell to the wooden bench with a thud, wobbled around, then came to rest with the jagged edge still smoking.

Now then, let's see what we have here.

He reached a gloved hand into the cylinder, careful not to let his bare forearm touch the hot metal, and pulled out a banded roll of hundred-dollar bills. Two more rolls followed, and then the familiar cassette in a plastic case.

Here's your hole card, Griswald. Now there's nothing left to hide behind.

He peeled off the goggles and gloves and took the money and cassette into the office, sat down at his desk and spread the items out in front of him. He stared at them, thoughtful, then stripped the rubber bands from the tightly rolled bills and began counting.

Brenda, flipping through an open file-cabinet drawer, turned to watch him with a neutral expression. "Well, I see you made a good score anyway. What's on the tape, your confession?"

"Something like that," Cage said.

"Would I be warm in guessing that used to belong to Horance Griswald?" she asked. Then rolled her eyes and said, "I can't help it, I have to know."

"Nothing Horance Griswald has ever belonged to him," Cage said. "Including his name."

"So that *is* where you got the safe. This is going to get very interesting when Paul finds out."

"I suppose so," he said, rolling the bills back together and snapping the rubber bands in place. "But if Paul wants a piece of me, he's gonna have to wait his turn. Griswald just lost seventeen thousand, four hundred dollars, by my count, and that makes him first in line."

"Does he know you have it?"

"Not yet, but he will. And that reminds me, do you happen to have his business number somewhere?"

"No, but I can look it up. This I really do want to hear."

Brenda went to her desk and was removing the thick L.A. directory from the bottom drawer when the phone rang. She answered, listened, then said just a minute and put the caller on hold.

"You're not going to need the number," she said, giving Cage an amused look. "That's old what's-his-face himself, and he wants to talk to you. Mind if I eavesdrop?"

"Help yourself," Cage said, and picked up the extension.

The voice on the phone said, "Mr. Cage? Horance Griswald. How are you?"

Very cordial and professional. The man obviously hadn't been home yet.

Cage said, "I've been better. But then I guess I could be worse."

"Yes, so I hear. I was watching the news this

morning. Terrible thing, just terrible." The voice filled
with concern now. "You were fortunate not to be
killed. Honestly, I don't know what this city's coming
to. No one is safe anywhere these days. Are they?"

"That's for sure, Mr. Griswald. Too many predators
running around, it's gotten to be a real jungle."

Brenda was giving him a questioning look, the
phone pressed to her ear with one hand covering the
mouthpiece. Cage touched a finger to his lips and
shook his head, listening.

Horance said, "Predators. That's an interesting
term. Why do you suppose Howard Wallmeyer and
Rudy Hicks would want to prey on you?"

"They didn't. They just happened to be in the
wrong place at the wrong time."

"Really? Then who would do such a thing? Someone would have to be very angry with you to resort to
putting a bomb in your car."

Brenda's mouth dropped at this, and she gave Cage
a hard stare.

"And if it wasn't the two individuals just mentioned," Horance said, "then that means someone
could try again. That is, if you continued to give that
person good cause. And then again it could be as you
said. I imagine it is rather easy to make enemies in
your line of work. Especially if you were to use your
position to, say, launch a personal vendetta. You
haven't done anything like that, have you?"

Cage, tired of the man's smug tone, decided to bring
the charade to an end.

"Cut the shit, Griswald, you know as well as I do
who planted that fucking bomb. You did."

"Excuse me?"

"You heard what I said. Now you call me up trying
to act like Charles Bronson and expect to find me

shivering like a dog passing peach seeds. What kind of movies have you been watching?"

"I don't know what you're talking about."

Griswald's voice was guarded now, less certain. Cage bored in on him, forceful, but able to keep his temper on low burn, thanks to his recent jackhammer therapy.

Cage said, "Did you really believe I'd ignore this and not get back? You're a lightweight, Griswald, fly-swatter material, and if you're all I ever have to worry about in life, I can rest easy."

In the silence that followed, Cage visualized the man struggling to absorb the assault on his ego.

Horance said, "You've always had an exaggerated sense of your own abilities, haven't you, Mr. Cage?"

"No. I just have a diminished sense of yours. And I've got news for you. Because of that little stunt you pulled, my price just shot straight through the ceiling. See, I've done some more investigating, used some of those resources you spoke about, and I now have enough to nail you to the wall. I'm gonna own you for the rest of your life, Griswald, or else the state of California will. And since I was positive you'd want to cooperate, I've taken the liberty of collecting the first installment."

"Now what the hell are you talking about?"

"Have you been home lately, Griswald? Since you left for work this morning?"

Another silence, this one unbroken by the voice on the other end of the line.

Cage said, "Got you thinking, haven't I? And I do believe you're on the right track." He laughed, putting into it all the contempt he felt for the man. "Go home, Griswald. Take two aspirin and I'll see you tonight. We'll talk. And if you don't think I have enough to keep you in my pocket forever and a day, then I'll give back your seventeen thousand, four hundred dollars. But I'll hang on to the cassette, if you don't mind."

Cage hung up and tilted back in his chair, satisfied, as Brenda replaced the phone and swung around to face him.

"Allen, what's going on here? He put a bomb in your car? When?"

"Last night. Sometime between ten-thirty and three, near as I can figure it. Then Howie Wallmeyer and Rudy Hicks came sneaking around, up to no good, and set it off. They're both dead. The police think they were responsible for the bomb, but I know better."

"My God," Brenda whispered. "I haven't heard a word. Does Caprita know?"

"I don't think so, not yet." He gave her a sharp look. "And don't you go calling her. I'm going out there in a little while, I'll tell her myself."

"And then you're going out to see Horance Griswald, right? Why, to give him another shot at you? Do you have a death wish?"

"We've become a personal challenge to each other, Olive Oyl. For him it's a matter of self-preservation, doing away with the only real danger he faces. He sees me as a predator too, out to feather my own nest at his expense, and he's not worried about me bringing in the police. I've tried to blackmail him, burglarized his home, and stole his money. Those aren't exactly actions a law-abiding citizen interested in the true administration of justice would take."

"You're telling me," Brenda said, nodding.

"So tonight I'll go out there, baffle him with some more bullshit, and force him to make a move. He won't have any choice."

"He's also going to be furious."

"You don't know the half of it," Cage said. "I'm counting on that too."

"I was right. You have a death wish."

Cage brushed the cassette into his top drawer and swiveled around to gaze out the window at the Santa Monica Boulevard traffic.

"I won't be exactly unprepared, Olive Oyl. I'll have a surprise or two. And one big advantage."

"Such as?"

"He thinks I want his money. He doesn't know what I really want is him."

Cage turned back to the desk, flicked the rubber bands from the three rolls of bills and flattened them out. He searched through the drawers until he found a manila envelope, stuffed the bills inside and licked the flap.

He said, "Do you mind if I tell Chopper you'll give him a ride home this evening? I'm gonna be needing the El Camino for a while."

"No problem," she said, watching him with concern. "And bad as I want to know, I'm not going to ask what you have in mind for Horance Griswald. Because if you told me, I'm more than likely to do something silly, like call the police. So I'm just going to assume you know what you're doing and ask you to be careful."

"Thanks, Olive Oyl. It's nice to see somebody has a little confidence in me."

"Yes, and it'll be valid until midnight."

"What?"

"If you haven't called me at home by midnight saying you're okay, or if Caprita hasn't called me—then I am calling the police. Agreed?"

Cage got up and made for the back door. "I knew it was too good to be true," he said.

Caprita felt something shrinking inside her as she sat at the kitchen table with Marilee and listened to Cage describe the bombing, his voice deadpan and his words precise, as if relating an event he had merely witnessed but had no part in. He sat there, turned sideways in the padded straight chair, and played with the salt shaker while he explained in an oh-so-casual tone that he never would have gotten into the Camaro without closely checking the interior anyway, now that he was on the alert for Griswald, so it wouldn't have worked. It was just a shame, he said, that somebody had to get killed because of the man's stupidity and desperation, even if it was Howie Wallmeyer and Rudy Hicks, who for some unknown reason seemed to have been attempting to steal his car.

And the constricting of Caprita's stomach tightened yet another notch, causing a wave of nausea to rise in her throat which threatened to send her running to the bathroom, because she knew damn good and well that he would have gotten into that car without a thought to making sure it hadn't been tampered with. The very notion that he would even try to convince her otherwise, to run such a weak story on her, showed just how close she had come to losing him. The certainty of it brought an ashen pallor to her face and a tremor to her hands that could only be controlled by placing them under her thighs.

And through it all she was unable to utter one word—all she could do was sit on her hands and stare at him in frozen silence while he did his best to assure her that there was never any chance of him being ripped apart by that bomb.

None whatsoever.

Marilee wasn't buying it either. She sat quietly gazing down at the cover of a magazine, harboring her own images of what surely would have occurred if Rudy Hicks had not opened the door of that Camaro. Death was becoming a contagious disease, she thought, striking all around her, indiscriminate and unpredictable. And in her fervent desire that Michael's murderer not escape punishment, she had actively encouraged Allen Cage to make sure that justice was done—and nearly caused Caprita to suffer an identical loss. And if that had happened, Marilee knew she would never have been able to forgive herself. At the same time, she also realized that it had gone much too far to ever talk Allen into backing away now.

So Cage told his story in a mission-control voice to two women who received his words with separate yet similar emotions—one ready to throw up her lunch, while the other was ready to throw in the towel.

Cage ran out of words and looked at them in turn, waiting for someone to speak. When no one did, he pushed the manila envelope across the table to Marilee.

"This is rightfully yours," he said. "There's seventeen thousand, four hundred dollars in there, what Griswald had left from selling off your jewelry. Bobby Lee Gettis tapped him out, which is why he had to make a quick move." He made an awkward gesture with his hand. "It's something anyway."

Marilee pushed the envelope back. "I don't want it, Allen. Thank you though, it was awfully thoughtful.

310

My things were fully insured and so was Michael. Keep it, you've earned it."

Caprita, tracking the back and forth movements of the envelope, frowned and said, "How did you manage to get seventeen thousand, four hundred dollars from Horance Griswald?"

Marilee said, "That should be rather obvious, Caprita. He stole it. Didn't you, Allen?"

"Well . . . yeah."

Caprita said, "You stole it? When?"

"I was in his house this morning, looking for something else. I ran across this."

"You were in his house stealing his money after he killed two people last night while trying to kill you?"

Caprita was incredulous. She was also angry, more so than he could ever recall seeing her, and he was beginning to feel uncomfortable. It seemed like everyone was getting upset with him lately instead of Horance Griswald.

"It was not his money, Caprita," he said defensively. "And I told you, I was looking for something else. The guy had a tape I needed to get back, the one he made when I—"

"Oh, *damn* your obstinance!" Caprita said, her voice breaking. She jumped up and stormed out of the kitchen, leaving Cage staring helplessly at Marilee.

"What did I say?"

Marilee gave him a tolerant smile. "It's nothing you said, Allen. She's terrified, that's all, and she's expressing it through anger. How can you see so much and not see that? How would you feel if you knew someone was trying to kill her?"

"That's simple," he said without hesitation, "I'd try to kill him first."

"Yes, and I suppose that's a typical male reaction. Women, on the other hand, at least most women, are not so physically aggressive. Nature has blessed or maybe cursed us with certain limitations in that area, and it can be very frustrating. We feel the same distress as men when our loved ones are in danger, only we don't have the luxury of being able to purge it through direct physical confrontation. Unless it involves our children, and then we will die. So remember that next time you hear some uninformed man joke about how emotional women are. For most of us, it's the only form of expression we have."

Cage said, "I don't see you expressing a whole lot of emotion, Marilee. You threw a glass one night and that's been about it."

"You haven't seen me in my bedroom at night. The down in my pillow is still wet. It's getting better—or perhaps I'm getting used to it. But I have my moments, Allen. I have my moments. And while we're on the subject, I think it's time we turned all this over to the authorities. So I'm asking you not to do anything more on my behalf. Give them whatever information you have and then take Caprita to the mountains for a few days. Michael bought a lovely cabin at Lake Arrowhead last year, and you'll love it there. I've already selected a new housekeeper, she can start any day."

"Thanks for the offer," he said. "I'll let you know in the morning."

"Why in the morning?"

"Because by then Larry should know if Griswald's partner in New York is willing to roll on him or not."

"And in the meantime you'll leave him alone?"

"I'll tell you the same thing I told Caprita. I won't

make any move against him unless it's in self-defense."

Marilee nodded, gathered up her shiny new crutches and struggled to her feet. "Caprita said you could be very noncommittal. Now I know what she means. Go find her, she needs you now. I'm going upstairs and take a nap."

Cage found her on the sun deck, standing at the railing, hugging herself as she looked off at the ocean and the tiny jet skiers and wind surfers skipping across the waves. He came up behind her and stopped, hands in his pockets, seeing her grip tighten on her slender shoulders. She was wearing the tube top and shorts again, looking both appealing and vulnerable. He wanted to say something reassuring that would put the spring back in her posture and restore the bouncing enthusiasm that was all part of what made her so special to him. But when he spoke, all that came out was, "Are you all right?"

She tossed her head. "Oh, I'm fine. Never been better."

"This is almost over, babe."

"It was almost over last night, that's for sure. Or it would have been this morning. And please don't give me any more of that it-wouldn't-have-worked nonsense, because I know different. What do you take me for?"

"Okay, so it might have. But it didn't, I'm still here, and by this time tomorrow Griswald will more than likely be cooling his heels in the L.A. County Jail. So you don't have to worry anymore."

"Maybe," she said, "and maybe not. But that still doesn't alter the fact that you had no business getting this deeply involved to begin with. I knew something like this was going to happen right from the first. I felt it. And I'm even a little resentful at Marilee for allowing it. But then she didn't know how unorthodox and bulldoggish you can be."

"We wouldn't even know it was Griswald if I hadn't gotten involved," Cage said. "At least we've accomplished that much."

"Yes, and nearly got yourself killed while you were at it."

He reached out to turn her to him, but she pulled away and moved farther down the rail, stiff and unyielding.

Cage said, "Caprita, what did you expect me to do? You know how I feel about this thing. Would it have made you feel better if I'd just shrugged and said hey, that's life? That's not me, and you know it."

"Getting involved is one thing," she said. "Running around acting like the Equalizer is another."

The *Equalizer?* "Now what's that supposed to mean? And what happened to this deal we made a few days ago where you agreed to stop criticizing me?"

Caprita spun around and said, "Oh no you don't, Allen Cage. You've gone way beyond that. It's fine for you to give me lectures about driving to work alone after dark. But you expect me to bite my tongue when I find out some man's trying to murder you. That's about as warped a statement as I've ever heard. And I'll tell you something else too, my nerves have had it. So like it or not, I'm coming home tonight. I happen to love you, damn it, and if you want to consider this as criticism, then call me a meddlesome bitch. But I will not stand idly by and watch you turn yourself into a martyr. Not if I can help it."

She brushed past him and stormed into the house,

leaving him standing in her wake with a different perspective. He hadn't really considered how all this might be affecting her. Why put her through it anymore? Maybe she and Marilee were right. He'd done his part, drawn Horance Griswald out into the open and put him on display like one of his synthetic jewelry designs. The man was finished, it was just a matter of time. Larry would terrorize Maury Bingham into signing a statement to save his own skin; and shortly after that some stern-faced homicide detective would show up on Griswald's doorstep with a first-degree-murder warrant. Case closed. Cage felt that he could even live with the bombing of his Camaro, which was designed to take his life. It wasn't like he had let it go unanswered. He'd retaliated by taking seventeen thousand, four hundred dollars from the man and taking a jackhammer to his ritzy Brentwood home. He asked his private dinosaur if that was a reasonable quid pro quo.

Sounds like a fair exchange.

Caprita was in the kitchen unloading the dishwasher, not being very quiet about it as she separated the silverware and dropped the pieces into individual drawer compartments. Cage came in, watched her for a moment, then sat down at the table.

"Tell you what," he said. "I've got Chopper's El Camino outside. I'll take it back, clean up a few details I've been neglecting at the office, and you can pick me up about five-thirty or six. How's that sound?"

Caprita looked at him over her shoulder. "You mean it?"

"Yeah. If you're sure Marilee can get by without you."

"She can. She's already hired a new housekeeper, who can start tomorrow if she wants. Why the change of heart all of a sudden?"

"Because bad as I hate to admit it, you're right. It's not my place to be playing cop, especially when Griswald's about to be nailed anyway. It's that prison mentality coming out, and I didn't even recognize it. Feeling like I had to settle the score myself. See what I mean about adjustment? For a while it's easy to lose your awareness."

Caprita began stacking plates in the cupboard, more gentle now. "If that's an apology, then I accept. I just don't want us fighting over this anymore."

Cage was about to tell her that it wasn't an apology, only an explanation, but just then the phone rang.

Caprita answered. "Oh, hi, Brenda. I'm fine, just trying to get this dishwasher emptied. Yes, he's here. I'll talk to you tomorrow, okay?" She stretched the wall phone over to Cage. "It's Brenda," she said, and went back to the dishwasher.

"What can I do for you, Olive Oyl?" Cage said.

"Well, for openers you can stop being so abrupt. Is my timing bad or something?"

"These are tense times, Brenda. They'll pass."

"If you say so. Anyway, I just got a call from Larry, and he'll be back tomorrow too. So we'll be one big happy family again."

"And he wants me to meet him at the airport, right?"

"Exactly, eleven-oh-five A.M."

"And Paul wants me to meet him at eight-twenty. What am I, a shuttle? I don't even have a car, did you tell Larry that?"

"No, because that would have led to a lot of questions I didn't think you'd want me to answer.

316

Don't worry, you can take my car. Oh, and he gave me a message for you."

"I hope it's good news," he said.

"It doesn't sound like it. He said Maury Bingham was a no go. He refused to discuss anything without his attorney present. He said he'd tell you more about it tomorrow, but for now it's back to square one. End of message."

And that, thought Cage, was the end of Larry's con game. No lawyer of Maury Bingham's would be talking deals with anyone except the U.S. Attorney's Office, and they wouldn't even know what he was talking about. Without Maury Bingham, Horance Griswald was virtually untouchable.

Legally.

Cage said, "Thanks Olive Oyl, you just made my day. See you in the morning."

"Come early," she said. "Remember your shuttle schedule. And don't forget what I said about midnight. If I don't get a call by then, I'm going to assume you turned into a pumpkin and notify the police. I mean that, Allen."

"I understood you the first time, Brenda," he said, clearly irritated. "Good-bye."

Caprita had been following the exchange with interest. She took the phone from him, hung it up, and observed his stony expression. "Something wrong?"

"Larry's coming back from New York tomorrow. And Paul's coming back from Denver. That's two trips I have to make to LAX. I love my job."

"Then we're still on for this evening, right?"

"Nothing's changed there. I'll see you between five-thirty and six. Try Marilee with the money again, see if you can get her to take it. If she won't, bring it with you, I'll damn sure keep it."

"I'm not so sure I like that, Allen. It isn't your money."

"I know, it's Marilee's. What she does with it is her business, she can give it to charity if she wants. But just remember that I need a new car."

He stood, ready to leave. Caprita put her arms around him and squeezed, then leaned back and searched his face, looking for signs of deception. It wasn't like him to give in this easy.

"Are you going to cause me any more problems?" she asked.

"No," he said. "After today I'm out of it."

"Then go get your work done. And try to stay out of trouble until I get there."

Cage went out to the El Camino, got in, and folded his arms over the steering wheel while he pondered the latest turn of events. For a short while there he'd been willing to let it go, get away from this vindicator role he'd fallen into and allow due process to take its course. He wanted this entire mess over and done with and Caprita back home where she belonged, with him and her cat and her medicinal herbs, but without the storm cloud that was Horance Griswald hanging over their heads, about to erupt without warning. He wanted Caprita back at Wilshire Memorial, preferably on day shift, and he wanted things to return to normal at Banes and Twiford. He wanted Marilee to heal, pick up the pieces and get on with her life and stop drowning her pillow in tears at night.

I don't want this man to walk, Marilee had told him.

Well, he was going to walk, if he wasn't given one more good push. He was going to skate clean away with at least three kills to his credit, probably four, feeling invincible and more dangerous than ever.

Unless Cage finished it himself.

And he didn't have much time. He had Paul and Larry coming in tomorrow morning, and after six o'clock this evening Caprita was going to be covering him like a blanket. So tonight was out.

But he was free right now. Go back to the apartment, collect the .25 automatic he'd dropped off on the way over here, then scoot on out to Brentwood and catch the man by surprise. He was there this very minute, Cage would bet on it. Standing over the hole where his safe had been, roaring like an aggrieved tiger, enraged that his spray had been ignored.

He would attack.

And this time, Cage thought, he would be ready.

Chapter
—27—

Horance Griswald wasn't standing over the hole in the floor where his safe had been, and he wasn't roaring. He was in his banker's chair, fingers steepled beneath his chin, calmly rocking to and fro while his mind drifted in a sea of demons who were systematically dismembering a screaming Allen Cage.

Every so often he would look down at the gaping mouth in the carpet, a jagged-edged chasm surrounded by broken concrete, and the man's face would materialize there as well. Only it would be grinning up at him, mocking him, taunting him . . . defying him. Horance would have to concentrate during those moments, remind himself it wasn't real, then tear his eyes away and direct his attention somewhere else.

Only everywhere he looked there was ruin. That was real all right. The room looked like a cyclone had come through it. The same with the den and most of the dining room. The beautiful furnishings he had selected with such care, the cherrywood wall paneling, his expensive Vega seascape, his van—all totally destroyed. Even now, three hours after charging through the front door and being halted dead in his tracks at the sight that greeted him, he was still stunned. How could anyone commit such a vicious act, unleash such wanton fury against objects so lovely? He felt defiled, like a victim of rape.

And he wanted vengeance.

He pulled out the middle drawer, removed the .38 and opened the cylinder. The six brass cartridges nestled in their firing chamber reassured him, brought back that sense of power he'd experienced when watching the devastation his explosion had created on the morning news. He snapped the cylinder shut with a flick of his wrist and took careful aim at the wing chair across the desk, squeezing one eye tightly closed while he lined up the sight with an imaginary Allen Cage, sitting there in that arrogant slouch—then remembered you were supposed to keep both eyes open, make the weapon an extension of a pointing finger. He tried again, getting the feel of it, concentrating on the body area. A head shot would be too quick. He wanted to put six right in the chest, a close grouping that would hopefully avoid the heart, and see him jerk with every hit. Horance wanted to talk to him while he died, point out where the cheeky bastard had gone wrong. Maybe kick him a couple of times while he was fading and ask him if he could feel it. Then take the body out and bury it someplace where it would never be found.

Horance put the revolver back in the drawer and went upstairs to the master bathroom. He felt the urge to void, spurred by the laxative of anticipation, and he allowed his mind to swim with the demons again while he emptied his bowels. Cage was coming here tonight—actually coming here. Now there was nerve for you. Or lack of respect. Calling him a lightweight, fly-swatter material. Saying he had enough on him now to keep him in his pocket the rest of his life. Horance wondered briefly what it was the man thought he'd discovered to inspire all this confidence. Then he dismissed the thought—it didn't matter. Allen Cage was coming here tonight, that was what mattered. And Horance was going to eliminate the only threat left to him and enjoy every second of it.

He finished, washed his hands with care, and went back downstairs, wincing as he moved through the wrecked den and into the study, feeling stressed once more at the sight of his prized possessions lying broken and scattered like rubble.

"How you doing, Griswald?"

Horance stood motionless in the middle of the floor and glared at Cage, who was casually spinning the hour hand on the ruined grandfather clock that had cost him thirty-two hundred dollars. He wasn't even surprised to see him. After all the bizarre happenings of late, Horance was beyond surprise. Now he was quietly incensed.

"You sonofabitch," he said, "how did you get in here?"

"Right through the front door," Cage said. "Not only didn't you lock it, you didn't even close it all the way. Not a good idea, Griswald. Not a good idea at all."

"Would it have made any difference?"

"Not in the slightest."

Horance shook off the temptation to rush over and strangle him, to put an end to that infuriating attitude. He'd stick to his game plan.

"You did a real good job in here," Horance said. "What did you use?"

"Jackhammer."

"A jackhammer?" That did surprise him. "All that noise and nobody even came over here to check it out?"

Cage said, "Kind of makes you wonder, doesn't it?"

He turned away from the clock and strolled over to take a seat in the wing chair. Slouching, just as Horance knew the bastard would do. Tugging at his pants creases and acting like he owned the place. Probably thought he was going to.

"Get over where I can watch you, Griswald. I like to look at people when I'm talking to them."

Gladly.

Horance moved around behind the desk, eased into the banker's chair and locked eyes with Cage. He said, "Where's my safe and my money? I don't care about the tape."

"Right now," Cage told him, "I'd say that was the least of your troubles. I'm keeping the money for a new car, and you won't be having enough to need a safe for in the near future. I said I was gonna own you and I am."

"You haven't got a damn thing on me."

"I know Michael Grady had you make a pretty expensive necklace and matching earrings for his wife. Fits the same pattern as all the others."

"So?"

"Oh, that's not all," Cage said. "I was saving the best for last. While I was here remodeling this morning, I noticed you put all new rubber on that van. Actually, I noticed it yesterday first, but today I came back with another thought in mind. I said, Now why would he do a thing like that? Could it be he thought the cops might match the treads with the ones he left in that little power-plant turnout just up the hill from Grady's house? That's the most logical place to park, and that's the direction you were coming from when you almost ran over the man's wife."

Horance hiked the chair a little closer to the desk,

pretending he was trying to get away from the hole in the floor. He said, "Think whatever you want."

"I can do more than think," Cage said, "I can prove you were there."

"Really? How?"

"You might've gotten rid of the tires, but you forgot about that bare spot of ground just as you turn into the driveway out there. Know what I'm talking about? Right there by the reflector. Looks like you cut it short a few times, and I'll bet anything at least one of those imprints match the tread marks found up at that power plant. What do you want to bet?"

Horance looked at him without speaking.

"Didn't think of that, did you?" Cage said. "And they're real plain too. Looks like they were made when the ground was wet, maybe after it rained, and the sun baked 'em into a perfect cast. I took some good thirty-five-millimeter pictures, nice close-ups. And guess what, Griswald? We don't come to terms here and now, I pick up the phone and call the cops. And I'll wait for 'em till they get here."

Horance opened the drawer and came out with the .38 in one continuous motion. He thumbed back the hammer and centered the sight on Cage's chest, his face twisted with rage, squeezing the walnut grip with such strength that the weapon trembled in his hand.

"By God, I've had enough of you," he said through clenched teeth.

Cage said, "Put the gun down, Griswald, you're not gonna shoot me. Remember what I told you about a letter. Everything's laid out in detail. Anything happens to me, you're gone."

"I'll take that chance," Horance said. "Personally, I don't believe a word of it. And it still wouldn't prove anything if you did. So if you thought you could walk in here and be protected by some mythical letter, you made a mistake. A fatal one. Allen Cage, are you ready to die?"

It was Cage's turn to be silent. Staring back into Griswald's eyes that had a somewhat dazed look in them. At that moment he realized the man had gone a little mad.

Horance said, "Let me know how this feels," and pulled the trigger.

The click sounded abnormally loud in the quiet room.

Horance frowned over the gun sight, thumbed back the hammer and tried again.

Click.

Cage hadn't moved, just kept staring into the man's eyes, which were now beginning to show signs of panic as he pulled the trigger several more times in quick succession.

"I believe this is where you're supposed to get so frustrated you throw the gun at me," Cage said. "I knew there was something else I forgot to tell you. It just flat slipped my mind. Before I left here yesterday I filed down the firing pin. I might use bad judgment from time to time, but I'm not suicidal."

Horance slowly lowered the .38 and placed it on the desk. He looked away, moistening his lips. "I'll need time to get you more money." His voice was raspy, like something was caught in his throat. "But I want those pictures."

"That's another thing," Cage said. "I never took any pictures. I never even saw any tire marks. I just wanted to force you to make a move, but I see you were gonna do that anyway. See, I don't want your money, Griswald. I never did. All I ever wanted was to find out who caved in Michael Grady's head, 'cause I really liked the guy. At first I wanted you myself, for personal reasons. Then I thought maybe I'd be satisfied just getting enough evidence to help convict you." Cage rubbed his eyes and let out a tired breath. "Hell, I don't know what I wanted. But this is the third time you've tried to kill me, and now I know what I have to do."

Horance said, "What's that?"

"Isn't it obvious? Nobody's ever gonna make you for doing Michael Grady or anybody else. And you're too dangerous to be running around loose. A menace to society, as they say. You're certainly a menace to me."

Cage shifted his weight, reached into his hip pocket and brought out the .25 automatic. He jacked a cartridge into the chamber and let his hand rest on the arm of the chair, holding the pistol in a casual way that suggested familiarity.

Horance tried to swallow but couldn't. "You can't be serious."

"Oh, but I am," Cage said. "Very serious. You've lost all perspective, Griswald, and you've gone slightly insane. I don't mean in the legal sense, I mean in the lust for power and self-gratification department. I've seen it enough in federal prisons to recognize it. A con gets transferred from another prison after stabbing his sleeping cellmate forty times and immediately starts rooster-strutting across the yard. Don't fuck with me, he's saying, I am somebody. I have power. It's on the other side too. Some inoffensive guy who's been in the background all his life comes in and gets a job as a guard. After three days training at Glynco, Georgia, he's a regular Hitler, stalking the tiers with his jaw thrust out and issuing all kinds of orders, half of them not even making sense. Look at me now, he's saying. I have authority. The trouble is, those guys have to keep proving it to themselves, 'cause they don't know how to handle it, and they get bolder all the time. It's a new feeling, this power and authority trip, and they love it. So the con keeps looking for victims to stab, and the guard keeps issuing senseless orders. And nobody in the general population is safe from either of them. And that's why I have to kill you, Griswald. Because as long as you're alive, I'll never be safe. And I don't intend to spend the rest of my life looking over my shoulder."

Horance opened his mouth to say something then abruptly closed it, recognizing the futility of further speech. His eyes darted around the room, wide and desperate, searching for a place to go, a way out.

The door bell chimed.

Horance jumped as if hearing a gunshot, and for a split second that's exactly what he thought it was. Then a ray of hope lit up his face as he looked at Cage.

"I'd better answer that," he said. "I'm expecting company, and they'll know I'm home."

"Just stay where you are," Cage said. "They'll go away."

The door bell chimed again, longer this time, someone really leaning on it.

Horance said, "I could go answer it anyway, and you wouldn't shoot. They'd hear you and go call the police."

"If you're positive of that, Griswald, then go right ahead."

Horance sat where he was and waited.

They heard footsteps in the foyer and Cage grimaced, remembering that he hadn't thought to lock the door after closing it. He got to his feet and moved quickly around the desk to stand behind Horance, the .25 hidden from view by the banker's chair.

"Allen? Allen, where are you?"

Cage closed his eyes and breathed deeply. Caprita. What the hell was she doing here?

"Allen, I know you're here, damn it, I saw the El Camino out on the street!"

The voice was impatient, demanding. And getting closer, footsteps muffled now by the thick carpeting. Cage heard her say, "Oh, my God," apparently in reference to the debris she was wading through as she picked her way across the den.

And then she was there, still in her shorts and tank top, only Cage was finding her anything but appealing at that particular moment. She halted just inside the doorway and gawked at them, not immediately grasping what was going on.

Cage said, "Caprita, I don't know why you're here, but I want you to turn around and leave. Griswald and I are discussing private business."

"I'm here," she said, "because Brenda broke down and decided to tell me what you had planned tonight. And when she said that you still hadn't shown up at the office, Marilee had a hunch you'd be here. What do you think you're doing?"

"He came here to kill me," Horance said, sensing a potential ally. "He has a gun at my back right now. And if you have any influence with him, miss, I'd be grateful if you would use it to save my life."

Caprita said, "Is that true?" and moved farther into the room, trying to get a better angle.

Cage stepped out from behind the chair and positioned himself at the end of the desk, stopping Caprita from coming close enough to Griswald to let him take her as a shield. She focused on the gun and flushed with anger.

"Have you lost your mind?" she said. "Put that away this instant."

"Get out of here, Caprita," Cage said. "This is between me and him."

"I will not get out of here! You've taken this quite far enough."

"Thank you, miss," Horance said. "This entire episode has gotten—"

"Oh, shut the fuck up!" Caprita said, wheeling on him, hands clenched at her sides. She turned back to Cage, struggling for calm. "Now you listen to me, and so help me God, Allen, I mean it. I will not live with a murderer. If you use that gun, we're through. Now please, don't test me."

"Don't say that, Caprita."

All heads turned to the doorway to see Marilee leaning on her crutches. She looked exhausted from the effort of push-pulling her way through the house, but there was a commanding strength in her voice. Cage, not for the first time, found it astonishing how she could dominate a room just by her physical presence.

"Those are almost the identical words I spoke to Michael the night he went rushing back to the house," she said. "And they were the last words I ever said to him. I'll always wonder if he died not knowing that I really didn't mean them."

Caprita went to her and guided her over to the wing chair, saying, "I asked you to stay in the car. Nobody ever listens to me."

Marilee smiled as she settled into the leather cushion and gathered her crutches into her lap. "Of course we do, dear. We just sometimes disobey you."

She finally turned her attention to Horance, who hadn't been able to take his eyes off her since she first appeared in the doorway.

"So Mr. Griswald," she said. "At last we meet. I've heard a great deal about you."

"And most of it completely untrue," Horance said, and shot a look at Cage. "Your friend here has the unshakable conviction that I was responsible for your husband's death. My condolences, but I assure you I had nothing to do with it. He was ready to shoot me when you came in."

"Yes, well Allen can be a bit impetuous at times." She looked at Cage. "You can get rid of the gun, Allen. Please."

Cage reluctantly put the .25 back in his hip pocket, but with the grip exposed so he could get to it in a hurry if needed.

Horance let out a breath and ran a hand through his hair. "Thank you, Mrs. Grady. I don't know what's gotten into this man, but—just look, he completely destroyed half my house."

"I would've destroyed the rest of it," Cage said, "if I hadn't run out of hose."

Horance gave him a withering look, then adjusted his expression and said to Marilee, "I'm sincerely sorry about your husband, Mrs. Grady. I know what a tragic loss it must be. He was a fine man."

"You're correct on both counts," Marilee said. "His loss is tragic, and he was indeed a fine man. One of the finest. Did you know my husband, Mr. Griswald?"

"Only as a customer. But he left a tremendous impression on me."

"Yes, Michael did have that ability. A pity you didn't know him better. He was the kindest, most gentle man I've ever met. And he possessed a quality that seems to be fast disappearing in this day and age. A sense of honesty and fair play. I'm convinced those admirable traits are what caused his death."

Horance said, "How's that?"

"Because he would have given whoever was in our house that night a chance to surrender. He had every right under the law to use deadly force, but he wouldn't have done so unless it was absolutely necessary. He would not have killed in cold blood. The person he encountered had no such scruples. Would you agree, Mr. Griswald?"

"Absolutely. I believe your friend, Mr. Cage, used the word predator. Meaning, I suppose, one who has an insatiable lust to victimize. A term that seems to describe him rather adequately, I might add."

Cage returned the glare Horance gave him without speaking, restraining himself from pulling out the .25 again and shooting him anyway.

Marilee said, "You're wrong about that, Mr. Griswald. Predators also strike without warning, and Allen would never do that. He simply thought you were the person who killed my husband and was trying to find enough evidence to substantiate it. Admittedly he got a little overzealous."

Horance said, "A little? He came here to kill me. That's about as overzealous as you can get. And I did not kill your husband, Mrs. Grady. I liked your husband, he was a good and talented man. *Angel Wars* is one of the best pictures I ever saw, and he deserved the award he received."

Cage and Caprita exchanged looks. Caprita turned away, a disgusted expression on her face.

"You saw *Angel Wars?*" Marilee asked.

"I sure did—twice. And I loved it."

"Who was your favorite character?"

Horance rocked back and gazed at the ceiling, considering. "I would have to say that archangel of death—"

"Soul death," Marilee said, correcting him. "His name was Lel."

"Right. Soul death. That was a nice touch, the way the music would swell while the camera moved in tight on his face, preparing himself mentally for battle. It gave me goose bumps when he looked straight into the lens, I can tell you that, those eyes almost filling the whole screen. The guy was a good actor, but it was the directing that made it so memorable. Everyone in the audience could feel the passion in those eyes, believe they were seeing right into their soul. It was beautiful. And then, just as the music reached its peak, the eyes would suddenly spring wide and he would say—"

"Itchy-gay," Marilee whispered.

The explosion was deafening in the confined space of the room, causing Caprita to scream and spin around with her hands pressed to her ears, while Cage, caught totally off guard, yanked the .25 from his hip pocket and dropped to one knee, the pistol aimed at Horance Griswald's chair.

At the back of his chair.

It was several seconds before Cage rose and moved cautiously around the desk, pistol extended. With his free hand he slowly swiveled the chair around to the front.

Horance Griswald came into view, slumped to one side with his head practically resting on his shoulder —what was left of his head. The right side, from the bridge of his nose to just above the temple, was a bloody indentation, and it didn't require taking any vital signs to tell that the man was dead.

Cage, still confused as to what had happened, said, "Jesus," and swiveled Horance back toward the wall. He looked at the women—Caprita standing like a statue with her face set in horror, Marilee staring calmly at the back of the banker's chair with a distant dreaminess in her eyes.

Holding a crutch with tendrils of smoke drifting lazily out of the end.

Cage put the .25 in his pocket and went to her, gently removed the crutch from her hands. She didn't resist or even react. It was surprisingly heavy, the barrel warm to the touch, and Cage saw that it was made from steel instead of aluminum. He examined it closely, fascinated by the contraption, and found the minute break just below the hand grip where the barrel was screwed into place. Above the grip and cut into the frame was a narrow slot about two inches long, from which a fake wing nut protruded. He slid the wing nut back and felt a spring lock into place inside the frame.

"How do you fire it?" he asked her.

"By pushing the set screw under the hand grip," she said tonelessly. "Don't worry, it only holds one twenty-gauge shotgun shell."

"Unbelievable," he said. "So this was the reason for the new crutches. How did you get hold of something like this?"

Marilee took a few moments before answering, absently rubbing her right forearm where the kick from the exploding shell had pitted steel against flesh.

"A good friend of Michael's is a prop man at Universal," she said, her gaze still fixed to the back of the banker's chair. "He designed that for a film Michael was going to make about a crippled Viet Nam veteran who was plotting to kill the President. But the project was canceled two days before shooting was to start, and the crutches went back to the prop department. I knew about them because Michael brought them home one day and joked that maybe he should give them to me for protection."

Caprita, coming out of her shock, said, "So that's who brought them over. And like a dummy I believed you when you said he was from Valley Medical Supply."

"No reason why you shouldn't have, dear," Marilee said. "You would have had to be clairvoyant to know the truth."

Caprita had moved forward and was directly behind Marilee now, looking down at her head in blind fury. "You disgust me," she said. "All this talk about justice and wanting him punished the right way."

"I didn't want Allen robbing me of my pleasure," Marilee said.

"Pleasure! Is that what you call it, Marilee? Pleasure? Was it enjoyable, did it make you *feel* good to commit murder?"

"Yes," Marilee said softly. "It did. It felt wonderful."

Cage looked at Caprita, saw her fighting back the tears, and wanted to hold her. But at that moment he knew that she wouldn't let him. So he kept his silence and fiddled with the crutch and let her get it out.

"Then I feel sorry for you," Caprita said. "Because you're no better than he was. In fact you're worse. You used Allen to set him up for the kill, let him be your stalking horse to flush out the game, and goddamn near got him killed. And I can never, ever, forgive you for that."

"I didn't know Allen would take it as far as he did," Marilee said. "I never expected him to get into any personal confrontations with Horance Griswald." For the first time she turned her head and looked at Cage. "I'm sorry, Allen. I would never have deliberately endangered you. I would like for you to call the police now."

Caprita said, "You bet he'll call the police. Because if he won't, I will."

And with that she whirled around and left the room.

Cage watched her go, then said to Marilee, "I might be able to clean this up. No need for anybody to go to jail over that animal."

"I don't want it cleaned up," Marilee said. "And no one is going to jail. Take my word for it, when all is said and done, no twelve-member jury in this state will convict me of anything. My attorney will plead temporary insanity to give them a legal excuse to acquit me, and they'll jump on it. Now be a dear and make the call. And if you don't mind, I'd like to be alone until they get here."

Dismissing him just like that.

"All right," he said, "if that's the way you want it." He placed the crutch on her lap and patted her shoulder. "You just might pull it off at that. But as a backup I suggest you knock that .38 on the desk off on the floor and throw in self-defense. The firing pin has been filed down, but they aren't likely to check that."

"Thank you, I may do that."

"No need for thanks, I'm looking out for me too. You can say he accused you of having him burglarized, and the police will probably think you did whether you admit it or not. Maybe you can get away with murder, Marilee. But there's no way in hell they'd let me get away with burglary. Good luck to you."

He went into the den and found Caprita on the broken and battered couch, leaning against the cushion back with her eyes closed. He watched her a few moments, then walked to the end table that was split in two pieces and picked up the cordless phone lying on the floor.

Without opening her eyes Caprita said, "You know what she's doing, don't you? The reason for this whole sick charade?"

"It's called getting even," Cage said. "I wouldn't read any more into it than that."

"Oh, but there is more. Marilee's making the movie Michael never made. And she's the tragic heroine. Ready to martyr herself for the sake of her murdered husband. Only in this particular movie, she was the director as well as the star, and she orchestrated it beautifully. Even to the point of leading Griswald into the finale with her prompting about who his favorite character was in *Angel Wars*. And he fell right into it—even provided the music and camera angle, for God's sake. She must have been ecstatic." She laughed, a short sound without mirth. "And mark my words, now a movie will be made, only based on fact instead of fiction. Her lasting tribute to Michael Grady, both forever immortalized on cellulose."

"I won't say you're wrong," Cage said. "But I won't say you're right either. What I think we should do is give her the benefit of the doubt and let it go at that."

"You do, huh?"

"Yeah. No need to complicate it with suspicions you can't prove."

"Speaking of suspicions, you never had any about her at all, did you? I thought you were the pessimist here. You're the one who skips past the smile and canned pleasantries to search for hidden motives. Well, you missed this time."

"I didn't say I was infallible," Cage said defensively.

"And with good reason." Caprita looked at him then, conducting her own search for elusive answers. "Let me ask you something. If we hadn't arrived when we did . . . would you have used that gun?"

Cage took his time, concentrating on the phone he was holding. "I don't know," he said. "At first I thought I could, and I wanted to, I really wanted to. But I never would've known for sure until it was time to pull the trigger with Griswald looking me in the eyes, waiting for it and perhaps wondering himself if I could actually send that little piece of lead slamming into his brain and end his life forever. Just like that. Now I'm the only one left to wonder. Except maybe for you. And that's the only answer I can give either of us."

Caprita closed her eyes again, and Cage dialed 911.

"Allen?"

"Uh-huh."

"I'm going to give you the benefit of the doubt too," she said.

Postscript

On March 3rd, 1990, the following article appeared in the *Los Angeles Times:*

BAG LADY CLAIMS "POT OF GOLD" TURNED IN SIX MONTHS AGO

By Steve Milligan
Staff Writer

Hollywood—Bernice Wilkens, 67, described as a "professional" street person familiar to most uniformed patrol officers covering the Hollywood beat, today became the city's wealthiest bag lady.

Last September, police at the Hollywood Division substation were stunned when the elderly woman shuffled into the station house and plunked down a briefcase containing more than $400,000 in cash.

Sgt. Boyle Addison was filling out an arrest report behind the booking desk when Wilkens approached him.

"She said, 'Here, take this dad-gum thing, it's driving me crazy,' then just slammed it on the counter," he said, shaking his head in amazement. "I opened it real slow, not knowing what to expect, and when I peeked inside I fell over."

According to Sergeant Addison, the final tally
—consisting of banded rolls of fifty- and
hundred-dollar bills—came to $419,850.

"She said she found it next to the curb up on
west Wilshire," Sergeant Addison said. "She just
sat on it for about two weeks, not knowing what
to do with it. Unbelievable!"

A check by police officials revealed no reports
of such a large amount of cash being lost or stolen
in the recent past.

"We would know about any theft or robbery of
that magnitude anywhere in the state," said Lt.
Jerome La Corta, LAPD spokesman from Parker
Center. "We assume it's drug money, but have
not been able to prove it."

Under California law, if no one can show
proper ownership within six months, and if authorities cannot prove that the money was related
to criminal activity, the entire amount—less
state and federal taxes—goes to the finder.

Outside the Hollywood substation, wearing
olive-green work pants, torn sneakers, a faded
brown cardigan, and a fruit salad hat that partially obscured her lined and weathered face,
Wilkens was asked the obvious question—why
would a person of the streets voluntarily surrender over $400,000 in apparently untraceable
cash?

"Lord, I don't know what to do with that kind
of money," she replied, leaning on the Big Star
shopping cart that held her meager worldly possessions gleaned from trash bins and collection
boxes. "And besides, it wasn't mine."

Asked if she hadn't been frightened carting so
much money around the streets of Los Angeles

for two weeks without any protection, her gray eyes glinted.

"Who says I don't have no protection?" she snapped. "Anybody fooling with me is gonna get a rude awakening! And that's all I got to say about that."

Asked what she plans to do now that the money has reverted to her, Wilkens says that she will give some to her married son in Alhambra, "but not enough to spoil him," and donate the rest to a shelter for the homeless. She, however, will continue to live the life that she has grown accustomed to and learned to love—trudging the streets behind the Big Star shopping cart and "not being beholden to nobody."

But there is one thing that Wilkens admits she will do for herself. "Get me a set of new teeth," she said, flashing a gummy smile. "Some of those kind they put in that don't come out."

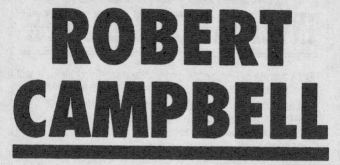